D0032312

Praise for *In The Clearing*

"Tracy displays ingenuity and bravery as she strives to figure out who killed Kimi."

—*Publishers Weekly*

"Dugoni's third 'Tracy Crosswhite' novel (after *Her Final Breath*) continues his series's standard of excellence with superb plotting and skillful balancing of the two story lines."

—*Library Journal*, starred review

"Dugoni has become one of the best crime novelists in the business, and his latest featuring Seattle homicide detective Tracy Crosswhite will only draw more accolades."

—*Romantic Times*, Top Pick

"Robert Dugoni tops himself in the darkly brilliant and mesmerizing *In the Clearing*, an ironically apt title for a tale in which nothing at all is clear."

—*Providence Journal*

Praise for *Her Final Breath*

"A stunningly suspenseful exercise in terror that hits every note at the perfect pitch."

—*Providence Journal*

"Absorbing . . . Dugoni expertly ratchets up the suspense as Crosswhite becomes a target herself."

—*Seattle Times*

CALGARY PUBLIC LIBRARY

FEB   2017

"Dugoni does a masterful job with this entertaining novel, as he has done in all his prior works. If you are not already reading his books, you should be!"

—Bookreporter

"Takes the stock items and reinvents them with crafty plotting and high energy . . . The revelations come in a wild finale."

—Booklist

"Another stellar story featuring homicide detective Tracy Crosswhite . . . Crosswhite is a sympathetic, well-drawn protagonist, and her next adventure can't come fast enough."

—Library Journal, starred review

Praise for *My Sister's Grave*

"One of the best books I'll read this year."

—Lisa Gardner, bestselling author of *Touch & Go*

"Dugoni does a superior job of positioning [the plot elements] for maximum impact, especially in a climactic scene set in an abandoned mine during a blizzard."

—Publishers Weekly

"Yes, a conspiracy is revealed, but it's an unexpected one, as moving as it is startling . . . The ending is violent, suspenseful, even touching. A nice surprise for thriller fans."

—Booklist

"Combines the best of a police procedural with a legal thriller, and the end result is outstanding . . . Dugoni continues to deliver emotional and gut-wrenching, character-driven suspense stories that will resonate with any fan of the thriller genre."

—*Library Journal*, starred review

"Well written, and its classic premise is sure to absorb legal-thriller fans . . . The characters are richly detailed and true to life, and the ending is sure to please fans."

—*Kirkus Reviews*

"*My Sister's Grave* is a chilling portrait shaded in neo-noir, as if someone had taken a knife to a Norman Rockwell painting by casting small-town America as the place where bad guys blend into the landscape, establishing Dugoni as a force to be reckoned with outside the courtroom as well as in."

—*Providence Journal*

"What starts out as a sturdy police procedural morphs into a gripping legal thriller . . . Dugoni is a superb storyteller, and his courtroom drama shines . . . This 'Grave' is one to get lost in."

—*Boston Globe*

THE TRAPPED GIRL

ALSO BY ROBERT DUGONI

Damage Control

The Tracy Crosswhite Series

My Sister's Grave
Her Final Breath
In the Clearing
The Academy (a short story)
Third Watch (a short story)

The David Sloane Series

The Jury Master
Wrongful Death
Bodily Harm
Murder One
The Conviction

Nonfiction with Joseph Hilldorfer

The Cyanide Canary

THE

TRAPPED

GIRL

ROBERT
DUGONI

This is a work of fiction. Names, characters, organizations, places, events, and incidents are either products of the author's imagination or are used fictitiously.

Text copyright © 2017 by Robert Dugoni
All rights reserved.

No part of this book may be reproduced, or stored in a retrieval system, or transmitted in any form or by any means, electronic, mechanical, photocopying, recording, or otherwise, without express written permission of the publisher.

Published by Thomas & Mercer, Seattle

www.apub.com

Amazon, the Amazon logo, and Thomas & Mercer are trademarks of Amazon.com, Inc., or its affiliates.

ISBN-13: 9781503940406
ISBN-10: 1503940403

Cover design by David Drummond

Printed in the United States of America

First edition

To Dr. Joe Doucette.
Words can't describe how grateful I am for your time,
expertise, and guidance. See you at ninety.

Even a dog knows the difference between being stumbled over and being kicked.

Justice Oliver Wendell Holmes, Jr.

CHAPTER 1

Seattle, Washington
Saturday, June 24, 2017

Kurt Schill dragged his fourteen-foot aluminum boat across the beach logs he'd set to minimize the scraping of the hull against the rocks. He wanted to protect his recent investment, but he really wanted to avoid a confrontation with the residents living in the condominiums and apartments bordering the narrow access to Puget Sound. At four thirty in the morning, they would not take kindly to having their peace disrupted. If they bitched to the police about Schill launching his boat from what was strictly a walking path, he would have little to say in his defense. The posted signs were frequent and explicit.

Schill entered the water to steady the boat and felt the chill of the forty-six-degree Puget Sound through his rubber boots. He gave the boat a shove and leapt in, banging his knee hard, the boat rocking and rolling until he'd adjusted his weight on the center seat. The V-shaped hull felt more stable than his fiberglass boat, which was difficult to maneuver when the water got rough. He'd have to wait until he got a bit farther away, though, before he fired up the six-horsepower Honda engine and got the real feel.

He slid the wooden oars into the rowlocks and rowed from shore, silent but for the splash of the blades and the click of the oarlock with each stroke. The aluminum hull glided across the pitch-black waters. One more thing he was digging about the new rig. He'd saved his money and bought it off a guy on craigslist for two grand—boat and trailer. It was more than the $1,500 he'd budgeted—his father had helped him out, though he'd have to pay back that money. He figured he could save by avoiding boat launch fees at the local marinas and by hauling in more crab. Fish and Game put a limit of five Dungeness per person, but Schill wasn't about to throw any keepers back, not with his restaurant contacts paying cash under the table.

He rowed in the direction of Blake Island, a black hump rising out of the water, though dwarfed by the shadowy presence of the significantly larger islands behind it—Bremerton and Vashon. To the north, the lights of the eastbound Bremerton ferry inching toward Seattle made it look like an illuminated water bug. Perspiration trickled down his chest and back beneath his waders and life vest, and Schill was thankful for the light breeze blowing cool on his neck.

Several hundred yards offshore, he shipped the oars and moved to the rear of the boat. He hooked the kill-switch to his life vest, squeezed the ball on the fuel line three times to pump gas to the engine, adjusted the choke, and pulled the rip cord. The engine cranked, sputtered, and died. He made sure the gear was in neutral and the throttle on the tiller twisted to the turtle, and pulled again. The engine chugged and sputtered. Then it kicked to life.

Legally, only the Native American tribes could crab this early in the season, and the fine if you got caught was steep, but Schill had found a sweet honey hole at the end of last year's run, and he was eager to find out if it was still producing. To avoid detection, he set his pots after sundown and retrieved them before sunrise. Still, there were risks. Running without a light increased his chance of being hit by another boat or hitting a log floating on the water. Either would ruin your day, big time.

Schill turned the tiller hard to the right, and the bow swung sharply. In no time, the hull was cutting across the surface, leaving a V-shaped wake. *Sweet!*

As he neared his honey hole, he eased back on the throttle, slowing, and searched the shoreline for the split tree, his landmark. Spotting it, he flipped the engine into neutral and scanned the surface of the water for a conical-shaped shadow, his red-and-white buoy. He felt anxious when he didn't see it; tribal members took gear that infringed on their fishing rights.

Retrieving the flashlight from beneath his seat, he skimmed the light across the surface. On the third pass, he spotted his buoy, bobbing up and down in the waves. Relieved, he motored to it, grabbed the ring, and took up the slack in the rope until he felt the weight of the crab pot. He looped the rope onto the block wheel at the end of the davit pole—another perk he didn't have on his smaller, fiberglass boat—and continued pulling in line, coiling it at his feet.

"Crab time," he said.

He'd become pretty good at estimating his haul from the weight of the pot. It wasn't foolproof; he'd brought up heavy pots only to find them filled with sunflower stars, flounder, and rockfish. This pot felt heavier than any he'd ever pulled up, and his shoulders soon burned. He had to tie off the rope to give his arms a break.

"Damn," he said, feeling that familiar flutter of anticipation in his stomach.

He braced the soles of his rubber boots against the side of the hull, untied the rope, and immediately felt the weight of the cage. The boat listed, starboard side, the davit pole tipping down toward the water. Schill estimated he'd pulled in sixty feet of line, which still left about twenty feet to go. Something didn't seem right though; the rope was not perpendicular to the water, but angled at forty-five degrees, which usually indicated a snag.

Whatever it was, it was coming up first, his basket somewhere beneath it. That worried him. If he'd snagged a big bed of seaweed, or a lost boat anchor, and had to cut it free, he could end up cutting his rope and losing his pot. Good-bye, profit margins.

He gave another pull, the muscles of his thighs, arms, and shoulders now all burning. Sweat trickled down his forehead into his eyes and he shook it away. Finally, a crab pot broke the water's surface. Though hard to see, it appeared rectangular. His pot was an octagon. Either his line had become entangled with the line of a pot set close by, or he'd snagged a rogue pot.

He tied off the rope and carefully slid across the bench seat. The davit pole lowered another six inches. Reaching carefully for the rope, afraid he might tip the boat over, he grabbed it and dragged the pot close enough to reach the cage, holding it close. With his free hand, he retrieved the flashlight and directed the beam over the contents.

The pot looked full, but with what?

He saw seaweed and starfish, but also a few crabs scurrying about, feeding.

Then he saw the hand.

CHAPTER 2

Tracy Crosswhite parked her Ford F-150 facing north on Beach Drive SW, pulled her blonde hair into a ponytail, and quickly wrapped it in a hair tie. She didn't wear a ponytail often anymore. At forty-three, she didn't want to come off as one of those women still trying to look a perky twenty-three, but at this hour of the morning, she didn't feel perky and didn't much care what she looked like. She hadn't showered, and she hadn't bothered to put on any makeup.

She opened the notepad app on her cell phone and scrolled to just below her first entry. She'd dictated the time she'd received the call from Billy Williams, her detective sergeant at the Seattle Police Department's Violent Crimes Section. She hit the microphone button and said, "Time: 5:45 a.m. Parked on Beach Drive SW near Cormorant Cove."

Williams had called roughly twenty minutes earlier. Dispatch had received a 911 call about a body in Puget Sound, and the skull of death hung from Tracy's cubicle—literally a fake skull the detectives hung on the cubicle of the homicide team on call, in this case, Tracy and her partner, Kinsington Rowe.

Williams had said he was still gathering facts, but someone had reported finding the body near Cormorant Cove, which was just a few miles from Tracy's rented home in West Seattle's Admiral District. She'd beat everyone to the scene except the responding officers. Their patrol cars sat parked across the street facing the opposite direction.

Tracy stepped down from the truck's cab. A slice of the fading moon in a pale-blue sky grinned at her. The temperature, already pleasant, meant another day of unpleasant heat. With six days above ninety degrees, this June was shaping up to be the hottest on record.

Tracy dictated another note. "Weather is clear, no appreciable wind." She checked the weather app on her phone and said, "Fifty-three degrees in West Seattle."

A Saturday morning, the beaches and elevated sidewalk would soon be teeming with dog walkers, joggers, and families out for a stroll. Encountering a dead body on the beach would put a real damper on the start to their weekend.

She grabbed her SPD ball cap, threaded her ponytail through the gap for adjusting the size, and tugged the bill low on her forehead. Next came the 50-SPF sunscreen, which she rubbed on her arms, neck, chest, and face. She'd had a scare two months earlier when her doctor noticed a discoloration near her collarbone during a routine exam. A subsequent trip to the dermatologist revealed skin damage, but no cancer. The joys of getting older—crow's-feet, belly fat, and applying sunscreen before going outside.

She jaywalked to the three black-and-whites—two sedans and an SUV—parked in front of the Harbor West apartment complex. Built on pilings and piers pounded deep into the mud, the complex extended out over the Sound and gave new meaning to the term "living on the water." No thanks. One sizable earthquake could snap one of those wood beams. Then again, her home was perched on a two-hundred-foot hillside. When you chose view over practicalities, you picked your poison, though this view was spectacular. Vashon and Bainbridge Islands, and the much smaller Blake Island, created the picturesque backdrop that warranted the exorbitant rents and condominium prices along Beach Drive SW.

Three uniformed officers on a footpath watched Tracy's approach from behind black-and-yellow crime scene tape. Tracy didn't bother showing them her shield. Even without the branding on her windbreaker and ball cap, after more than twenty years, she knew she'd acquired a cop's self-assured gait and demeanor.

"Tracy," a female officer said.

She also remained Seattle's only female homicide detective, and she'd recently received her second Medal of Valor for a high-profile investigation and capture of a serial killer known as "the Cowboy." Frankly, she could have done without the attention. She and her partner, Kins, had heard the whispers around Police Headquarters about how they always seemed to be the team on call when the department got a "whodunit." The insinuation that their captain, Johnny Nolasco, was feeding them cases was more than absurd. Tracy and Nolasco got along worse than those women on the *Housewives of Wherever* television shows.

"Katie," Tracy said.

Katie Pryor worked out of the Southwest Precinct. She was one of many officers Tracy had trained to shoot to pass her qualifying exam.

"How are you?" Pryor asked.

"I could use more sleep," Tracy said. Instinctively, she was already considering the area as a whole. She noted beach logs leading to the water, and a young man standing beside a beached aluminum fishing boat. A taut rope extended eight to ten feet off the back of the boat, then plunged into the blue-gray water. Tracy questioned why a beached boat would need an anchor.

"I take it that's the guy who reported finding the body?"

Pryor looked over her shoulder. "His name's Kurt Schill."

Tracy shifted her gaze up and down the rocky beach, which was strewn with bleached-white logs. "So where is it?"

Pryor said, "I'll walk you in."

Tracy scribbled her name on the sign-in sheet and ducked beneath the tape. Pryor handed the clipboard to one of the two remaining officers.

Tracy noticed people starting to linger on the beach and turned to the other officers. "Move everyone off the beach and onto the elevated sidewalk. Tell them the beach is going to be closed most of the day. And find out if anybody saw anything or knows anything." She surveyed Beach Drive, spotting a blue truck with a boat trailer. "After you move them, write down the license plate numbers of every car parked along Beach Drive to Sixty-First Avenue and back down Spokane Street." She knew the three streets intersected, creating a scalene triangle with Beach Drive SW making up the longest side. It was not unheard of for a killer, if they were dealing with a murder, to come back to the crime scene and watch the investigation unfold.

They moved toward the water. After the cumulative days of hot weather, the beach held a distinct briny smell. A uniformed officer, bent over, hammered a stick into the sand, presumably to tie the other end of the crime scene tape he'd strung to create a U-shaped perimeter.

"We got the call from dispatch at five thirty-two," Pryor said, her boots sinking into the rocks and making a sound like rattling change. "When we arrived, he was waiting for us by his boat."

"What did you say his name was?"

"Kurt Schill. He's a high school student here in West Seattle."

Tracy stopped walking to consider the logs positioned parallel to the water. "Did he do this?"

"Not sure," Pryor said.

"Looks like a makeshift boat ramp." She took a couple pictures with her cell.

"He said he was crabbing and his pot snagged something as he pulled it up," Pryor said.

"A body?" Tracy asked, thinking that would be a first.

"Another crab pot."

"I thought he found a body?"

"He's pretty sure he did," Pryor said. "Inside the pot."

Tracy looked from Pryor to the boat and beyond it to the taut line. Not an anchor. She'd come to the site predisposed to find a body on the shore, perhaps a drowning or boating accident, what they referred to in the section as a "grounder" or easy play. If the body was inside a crab pot, that changed everything, in a big freaking way.

"Have you seen it?"

"The body?" Pryor shook her head. "Water's too deep. And I'm not sure I want to. The kid said he thought he saw a hand sticking out from under crab and starfish. Creepy stuff. He towed it back here."

"A hand or the whole body?" Tracy asked.

"He said he saw a hand. Based on his description of the weight of the pot, though, likely the whole body."

Tracy reconsidered the young man. She could only imagine the horror of seeing a decomposing body fed on by marine life.

She followed Pryor to the water's edge. Waves lapped gently over the rocks. The officer establishing the perimeter stood and wiped perspiration from his forehead.

"Thanks for setting the perimeter," Tracy said. "But we're going to need it to be a lot bigger, all the way down to those logs and up to the boardwalk. I'm going to ask for a screen to block the view from the seawall, and I'll need you to set it up when it gets here. You haven't moved or touched anything?"

"Nothing but a few rocks to drive the stakes," Pryor's partner said.

"What about Harbor Patrol? Anybody call them to send out divers?" Tracy asked.

"Not yet," Pryor said. "We figured it best to leave everything as is until somebody came up with a plan."

Tracy spoke to the second officer. "Call it in. Tell them we're going to need them to set a perimeter offshore to keep boats away until we find out what we're dealing with." She turned to Pryor. "What was the guy in the boat's demeanor when you got here?"

"Pretty shaken up. Confused. Frightened."

"What did he have to say?"

Pryor looked to her notes. "He said he went out early this morning to retrieve his pot down near Lincoln Park. He said he'd set it in about eighty feet of water, and when he pulled it up, it felt way too heavy. When it broke the surface he realized it wasn't his pot."

"It's not?" Tracy asked.

"No. Apparently, he snagged it. Said when he brought it closer he used a flashlight and saw what he thinks is a human hand. Scared the crap out of him. He dropped the cage, and the weight of it nearly pulled his boat over. He managed to tow it back until it grounded, beached the boat. He called 911 on his cell."

"What else do we know about him?"

"He just finished his sophomore year at West Seattle High and lives over on Forty-Third Street. His parents are on their way."

"What's a teenage boy doing up this early?"

Pryor smiled. "I know, right? He *said* he sets his pots early so he's not competing with the bigger boats."

Tracy picked up on Pryor's intonation. "You don't believe him?"

Pryor said, "The thing is, it's not crabbing season yet, not for anyone but the tribes."

"You know that?"

"Dale and I crab a little. We do it mostly to take the girls out on the boat. The tribes can crab pretty much whenever they want. For everybody else, the season doesn't open for another week—July second, I believe."

"So why's he out here?"

"He said he didn't know. Personally, I think he's playing dumb."

"Why?"

Pryor nodded to the aluminum boat. "That's a pretty good rig right there. Guy with that kind of rig would more than likely know the rules;

the fines can be steep. I think he was sneaking out early to get a jump on the season and poach a few crabs from the tribes. Some local restaurants pay good money. Not a bad way for an enterprising high school kid to make some cash."

"Except it's illegal."

"Yeah, there's that," Pryor said.

"Introduce me," Tracy said. "Then I'd appreciate it if you could take some pictures for me with your cell. Everything and anything."

They approached Kurt Schill together. Tracy allowed Pryor to make the introduction. Then Pryor walked off to take pictures. Schill extended his hand and gave a surprisingly strong handshake. He didn't look like he was old enough to shave yet. Acne pocked his forehead.

"Are you doing all right?" Tracy asked.

Schill nodded. "Yeah."

"You want to sit down?" She motioned to one of the beach logs.

"No. I'm okay."

"I understand you've been talking to Officer Pryor about what happened this morning; would you mind if I asked you a few questions?"

"No." Schill closed his eyes and shook his head. "Sorry. I mean sure."

"Okay, just take it slow," Tracy said. "When did you set your crab pot?"

Schill's brow furrowed. "Um. I guess it was . . . I'm not exactly sure."

"Mr. Schill." Tracy waited until Schill made eye contact. "I'm not Fish and Game, okay? I don't care about any of that. I just need you to be honest and tell me exactly what you did so I can find out whether you saw anything."

"Whether I saw anything?"

"Let's back up. Start with when you set your pot."

"Last night. Around ten thirty."

"Okay, so I'm assuming it was dark."

Schill nodded. "Pretty dark, yeah."

In June, in Seattle, the sun didn't set until after nine o'clock, and twilight could linger another forty-five minutes.

"Did you see anyone else out on the water? Any other boats?"

"Maybe one or two."

"Crabbing?"

"No. Just . . . out there. I think one might have been trolling."

"Fishing?"

"For salmon."

"In the same area where you set your pot?" Tracy asked.

"No. I just saw them, you know."

"Nothing unusual then?"

"Unusual? Like what?"

"Was there anything that caught your attention, gave you pause, made you look twice. Anything at all?"

"Oh. No. Nothing really."

"What time did you return this morning?"

"Around four."

"Why set the pots so late and retrieve them so early?" Tracy asked, though she suspected she knew the answer.

Schill frowned. "To get the pot before anyone saw me."

"You do this often?"

Another sheepish grimace. "A couple times this week."

"And again, did you see any other boats or anything that gave you pause or second thoughts?"

Schill took a moment before answering. Then he shook his head. "Not really, no."

"Can you take me to the spot where you pulled up the pot?"

"Now?" Schill asked, sounding alarmed.

"No, in a little while. We're going to have some divers come out, and I'd like you to take us back to where you found the pot."

"Okay," Schill said, sounding reluctant.

"Is that a problem?" Tracy asked.

"I have an SAT prep class this morning."

"I think you're going to miss it today," Tracy said.

"Oh."

"Your parents are on their way?"

"My dad's coming."

"Okay, you just hold tight for a bit," Tracy said. She started to walk to where Pryor was taking pictures.

Schill called out. "Detective?"

Tracy turned back. "Yes?"

"I don't think she's been down there too long."

Tracy stepped back toward him. "You think it's a woman?"

"Well, I mean, I don't know for certain, but the hand . . . the fingernails—they still had polish on them."

She considered the information. "Okay. Anything else?"

"No."

Katie Pryor called Tracy's name and pointed to the road.

A KRIX Channel 8 news van with a satellite dish protruding from the roof had parked on the street, and the Violent Crimes Section's favorite muckraker, Maria Vanpelt, was stepping out the passenger door. Vanpelt had been a rising star in the local news media, a good-looking blonde who seemed to have a nose for the sensational, but she'd got her hand slapped for mishandling coverage of the Cowboy. Tracy had not seen her for several months, and absence had not made the heart grow fonder. At the Violent Crimes Section, the detectives referred to Vanpelt as "Manpelt" and speculated that one of the men she clung to was none other than their captain, Johnny Nolasco.

Tracy called Billy Williams on her cell. She told him to have CSI bring a tent in addition to the screen. They'd set the tent up at the water's edge to serve as a command center and provide further privacy. She suspected news helicopters would not be far behind the vans. She could seek a no-fly zone, but if the news stations thought the story worthy, they'd just pay the fine. As Tracy listened to Williams, she turned back to the water. Her eyes followed the rope off the back of the boat.

Definitely not a grounder.

—

The circus had come to the beach and so had the crowds. People stood elbow to elbow along the metal railing, news reporters and cameramen among them. Add several police vehicles, two blue-and-white Harbor Patrol boats sweeping the Sound to keep sail- and powerboats at bay, a gaggle of uniformed and plain-clothed officers, and a tent, and the allure was too much to resist. Even the tourists were ignoring two of the region's most iconic views—the booming image of Mount Rainier dominating the southern horizon, and the gleaming white stucco walls and red tile roofs of the Alki Point Lighthouse to the north, with Elliott Bay and the Seattle skyline serving as a spectacular backdrop.

Divers had managed to retrieve the tangled mess behind Kurt Schill's boat, which had grounded in less than ten feet of water. Schill's pot, perhaps two feet in diameter, would be accompanying his boat and his car to the police impound where CSI would process it for fingerprints and DNA. The larger pot remained inside the tent, and its contents had indeed been gruesome.

The body inside the pot was that of a woman. Naked, her bloated skin had turned the color and consistency of abalone meat: pale gray, rubbery, and traversed by a road map of purple lines. It showed evidence where marine life had fed. In sharp contrast to that gruesome image were the bright-blue fingernails. They looked like the painted nails on the hand of a porcelain doll, nicked and scratched after years of use.

The debate continued inside the tent on how to transport the body to the ME's office on Jefferson Street in downtown Seattle. Although Tracy controlled the crime scene as the ranking detective, her authority did not extend to the body. That was the ME's domain, and King County Medical Examiner Stuart Funk could be righteous about it. Funk had opted not to remove the body from the pot to avoid the potential of disturbing evidence. Problem was, no one was certain whether the pot would fit in the back of the ME's blue van, and everyone wanted to avoid having to flip it on its side with the crowd watching. Funk sent someone in search of a tape measure.

Tracy waited outside the tent with Kins, Billy Williams, and Vic Fazzio and Delmo Castigliano, the other two members of the Violent Crimes Section's A Team and the next team up for a homicide. Dressed in slacks, sport coats, and loafers, Faz and Del looked like New Jersey hit men unsuccessfully trying to blend in on Cocoa Beach. The King County prosecutor had also sent Rick Cerrabone, a senior prosecutor from its Most Dangerous Offender Project—MDOP. Tracy had worked several homicides with Cerrabone, though there was little for him to do at what was a highly untraditional crime scene. Evidence would likely be limited. Salt water would have destroyed fingerprints and DNA on the cage, and since the pot had been submerged in eighty feet of water, there was no sense scouring the beach for other evidence.

"No way to even know where a boat would have put in," Tracy explained to the others. "There are several ramps along this side of the beach, and you have the Don Armeni ramp around the point. Assuming they even used a ramp. Schill didn't."

"They could have put in anywhere from the San Juan Islands to Olympia," Faz said, the words sounding as if they were scraping his throat and thick with his New Jersey accent. He alternately wiped his brow and the back of his neck with a handkerchief.

"I don't think so," Tracy said. "They would have dumped the body in deeper water, farther out from shore. I suspect it's here because it was convenient, the killer knows the area, or he didn't have to travel far."

"Any idea when she was dumped?" Del said.

"Funk's initial impression is a couple of days at most; there's very little swelling of the hands and the outer layer of skin remains intact."

"Still going to be like looking for a needle in a haystack," Faz said.

"Maybe," Del said, "but I'd take those odds over the odds the kid randomly hooked on to the pot."

"You don't think he did?" Tracy said.

"Just saying it's a hell of a coincidence," Del said.

"Bet he won't be eating crab anytime soon," Faz said.

Tracy looked to ensure that no patrol officers stood close by. With new rules in place, officers were required to wear body cameras. That meant everyone had to be more careful about what they said, and with their facial expressions. Detectives laughing at a crime scene easily could be misconstrued. The general public didn't understand that gallows humor was often a defense mechanism detectives employed to do their job without throwing up. Cell phones had made the scrutiny of police conduct worse. Now everyone was an amateur videographer.

Williams pointed to the two buildings closest to the beach access. "Let's canvass the buildings and the local marinas. Maybe somebody saw something."

"Be easier if we could get a decent picture of the victim first," Faz said. "See if anyone recognizes her."

"Are we jumping the gun?" Kins asked. "Maybe we get lucky and her prints are in the system. She could be a hooker or a junkie."

"Doubt the killer would have bothered to go to this extreme to dispose of the body if she was a hooker or a junkie," Tracy said.

"Well, if she *isn't* a hooker or a junkie then someone should have reported her as missing," Kins said.

"This is the way the gumbas do it back in my hometown," Faz said. "One tap to the back of the head and you sleep with the fishes."

"You might be right," Kins said. He looked to Williams. "I'm just saying we could save a step."

Williams shook his head. "Let's ask now, when everything is fresh. Besides, if she was shot, it means there's another crime scene somewhere."

"Which might be as easy to find as determining where the boat put in," Kins said.

Funk exited the tent. For a change, he did not resemble an absent-minded professor. A recent haircut had tamed his silver hair, which often looked as though Funk didn't own a comb, and the sunglasses he'd donned were far more fashionable than the silver-framed spectacles too large for his narrow head.

"We can fit the cage in the van. I'll take it back to the office," he said, "but I won't get to it today."

"Any tattoos or piercings?" Tracy asked.

"Not that I can initially see," Funk said.

"What about track marks?" Kins asked.

Funk shook his head. "Again, don't know yet."

"How long you estimate she's been down there, Doc?" Faz asked.

"Two to three days," Funk said. "No more."

"I want to keep the crab pot intact as much as possible," Tracy said. "Maybe something on it will provide a clue where it came from."

"I'll do my best," Funk said.

"Call us when you get to her," Tracy said.

As Funk departed, Williams turned to Del and Faz. "Get started canvassing the buildings." Tracy and Kins would go with Harbor Patrol to where Schill had found the pot. "Let's meet back downtown later this afternoon."

As Tracy and Kins walked toward the waiting boat, Kins said, "You got sunscreen?" Tracy handed him the tube. He squirted the cream into his palm and applied it to the back of his neck. "I could think of worse ways to spend a Saturday afternoon."

"Bet Jane Doe can't," Tracy said.

—

Tracy and Kins spent the remainder of the afternoon getting baked by the sun. The temperature hit ninety degrees, but it felt hotter on the water, with no hint of a breeze. When Schill took them to his "honey hole," several problems quickly became apparent. With the strong current and a rope longer than eighty feet, Schill could not be precise about where he'd snagged the commercial pot, or even where, exactly, his pot had come to rest on the Sound's bottom. That increased the search area significantly. The water was also dark and murky at that depth, limiting visibility to no more than a couple feet. The divers had scoured as large an area as they deemed reasonable, but failed to find a gun or anything that appeared to relate to the woman in the trap. It didn't come as a surprise. The killer had clearly intended that the body would never be found.

After getting off the water, Tracy wanted to drive home and jump in a cold shower, but that would have to wait. She and Kins returned to Police Headquarters downtown and met in a conference room with Faz, Del, and Billy Williams. Faz reported that their initial canvass of the condominium and apartment buildings, as well as the marinas, had failed to produce anything significant.

"Would be better if we had a photograph," he said again.

Tracy had called Funk when she got off the boat. His office had extricated Jane Doe from the pot, but he said it was unlikely they'd get a usable photograph from the autopsy. A sketch artist might be able to fill in the significant blanks where the marine life had fed on the flesh, but at present the only thing that would come from Faz and Del showing Jane Doe's autopsy picture to tenants in the buildings or boat owners at the marinas would be a lot of vomit.

CHAPTER 3

After a long weekend, Tracy met Kins on Monday morning at the Medical Examiner's Building at Ninth and Jefferson Street, just across from the Harborview Medical Center. The fourteen-story building, all tinted glass and natural lighting, was nothing like the cement tomb where the ME once worked. While the rest of the building had been dressed up, not a lot could be done to make over the processing room where Funk and his team examined and cut open victims' bodies. Cold and sterile, the room contained stainless steel tables and sinks, with drains and traps illuminated beneath bright lights.

Jane Doe's body lay naked on the table closest to the door. A body block beneath her back forced her chest to stick out and her arms to slump away, making it easier for Funk to do his work. Ordinarily, there would have been a body bag, but given the nature of the crime and crime scene, that was not the case.

At the moment, Jane Doe was less a human being and more a piece of evidence, something to be dissected and processed. The impersonal nature of autopsies remained a stark and harsh reality Tracy had yet to fully accept, even after nine years working violent crimes. It stemmed from the knowledge that her sister's bones, recovered from a grave in the mountains above her hometown twenty years after Sarah had disappeared, had once been pieced together on a similar table—like a fossil find from an archaeological dig. Tracy had vowed to never forget that the body on the table had once been a living, breathing human being.

She sat on a rolling stool out of Funk's way. Kins stood beside her, the two of them watching and listening as Funk dictated each step with practiced precision and documented his findings with extensive photographs. Funk had weighed and measured Jane Doe—she was five foot six, though it was difficult to be precise because the body had been manipulated to fit inside the crab pot, and weighed approximately 135 pounds. He took vaginal and rectal swabs to check for semen. He examined the skin for petechiae—pinpoint, round blood spots indicating asphyxia—though the cause of death was readily apparent. Jane Doe had been shot in the back of the head. The killer had likely used a 9mm handgun—not that the gun mattered at this point. Without the bullet, which had passed through the skull, they would not be able to confirm the particular gun, if they ever found it.

Funk's exterior examination revealed no jewelry, though the earlobes had been pierced, further confirming Tracy's suspicion the killer had stripped the body. Funk found no tattoos or other distinguishing marks, nor did he find track marks or other signs the woman had been a junkie. He'd taken fingerprints to run through the AFIS database, but unless the woman had been convicted of a crime, served in the military, or had been employed in a job requiring workers to be fingerprinted, the system would not provide an identity. He'd also taken blood and saliva samples for DNA analysis, but similarly, unless the woman's DNA was in the CODIS database, there would be no hit.

Funk was preparing to x-ray the body.

"You okay?" Kins asked.

Tracy looked up at him from her rolling stool. "Huh?"

"You've got that look in your eye . . . And you're quiet. Too quiet."
After eight years working together, they had become adept at reading

the other's moods. "Don't make it any more personal than it is, Tracy. This shit is hard enough."

"I don't try to make it personal, Kins."

"I know you don't try," he said, fully aware of what had happened to her sister, as well as Tracy's compulsion when it came to killers of young women.

"But sometimes you can't change the facts."

"No, but you can change how you react to them," he said.

"Maybe," she said, not wanting to sound defensive. "I was just wondering who raises the kind of person who would shoot someone in the back of the head and stuff her body in a crab pot like a piece of bait?"

Kins sighed. They'd had similar conversations. "Think about it from the parents' perspective. As horrible as it would be to hear this has happened to your child, I also can't imagine being told I'd raised a child capable of doing something like this."

"Seems like it's getting worse, doesn't it?" Tracy said. "People have no respect for other people's boundaries. They think nothing of breaking into someone's car or home. Did you read the stories last December of people stealing Christmas presents from porches and taking lawn decorations?"

"I saw that."

"Who raises these people to think that's okay?"

"I don't know," Kins said. "When the economy isn't good, people get desperate."

"That's a load of crap," she said. "There are a lot of really poor people out there who would never think to do those kinds of things." She looked to the body on the table.

They watched Funk work. "What did you think of Schill?" Kins said.

"I think Faz and Del are right; I don't think he'll be poaching crabs again anytime soon."

"I meant about what Del said—about the odds of Schill hooking on the pot."

Tracy heard doubt, or at least skepticism, in Kins's tone. "I don't think the kid's capable of something like this."

"I'm just saying we don't rule him out yet."

"Okay, we don't rule him out, but why would he bring the pot in and call 911 if he was somehow involved?"

Kins shrugged. "He might have gotten cold feet. Maybe he kills her but spooks and can't go through with it, so he comes up with a different story. 'I hooked on the pot.'"

"He seemed genuinely shook up."

"Doesn't mean he didn't kill her."

"No, it doesn't."

"I say we have Del and Faz ask around, find out if any cats have gone missing in the kid's neighborhood or if he trolls the Internet for those morbid sites about murder."

"I don't know," she said.

"It's happened before," Kins said.

"What?"

"Someone finding a body in a crab pot. Two years ago a fisherman found a skull in a crab pot out on the coast near Westport."

"That was the guy's pot," Tracy said, recalling the story.

"Never did find out how the skull got in there though. And then they found that body in the pot down in Pierce County, near Anderson Island."

"They didn't find it. The boyfriend confessed and led them to it."

"Exactly," Kins said.

"Detectives?" Funk stepped back from the table and lowered his mask. He'd donned full surgical gear, including protective eyeglasses.

Tracy and Kins raised their surgical masks to cover their mouths and noses, though it did little to block the smell.

Funk moved to the computer on the nearby table. It showed images of a series of X-rays of the woman's body. Using the mouse, Funk clicked his way through the images until finding the ones he wanted. "There. You see?" He pointed to the woman's face. "She had implants on her chin and her cheekbones. She's also had her nose altered."

"Plastic surgery?" Tracy said.

"Not the kind you're thinking of," Funk corrected. "This is facial structure alteration."

"Someone trying to change their appearance," Tracy said.

"And recent. I'd say within the month, two months tops. And her hair has been recently dyed a darker color." Funk turned back to the body. "Her natural color is light brown."

Tracy and Kins both knew from a prior investigation that implants included a serial number. Plastic surgeons were obligated to record the serial numbers in their patients' charts and provide that information to the manufacturer in case of a problem with the implant.

"Looks like we can cancel the sketch artist," Kins said. "We just found Jane Doe."

―

Kins and Tracy returned to Police Headquarters. Kins traced the serial numbers to Silitone, a Florida manufacturer. A Silitone worker bee took the information and called back within the hour. The implants had been shipped to a Dr. Yee Wu in Renton, Washington, a city located at the southern tip of Lake Washington, about a twenty-minute ride from downtown.

Kins called Dr. Wu's clinic. The staff member gave him the standard admonitions about HIPAA laws and patient privacy. She stopped talking when Kins said he was a homicide detective investigating a potential homicide. HIPAA laws continued after a patient's death, but Kins and

Tracy weren't interested in Jane Doe's private medical history—at least not yet. They just wanted to know who she was.

They took a drive to Renton. Judging from the outside of the one-story stucco building, Tracy would have been nervous to get her nails done by Dr. Wu, let alone allow him to operate on her face. But according to Wu's website, he'd studied at the University of Hong Kong, did his residency in plastic surgery at UCLA, and was board certified by the American Society of Plastic Surgeons.

"Testimonials tout him as the greatest sculptor since Michelangelo," Tracy said.

"And of course we know if it's on the Internet it must be true," Kins said, pulling into a parking space.

They exited the car to the sound of a jet engine taking off from nearby Boeing Field, and made their way to the glass doors. The interior had a distinctly Asian feel, from the décor to the half a dozen patients seated in the lobby. A petite Asian woman in blue hospital scrubs identified herself as Dr. Wu's physician assistant and said the doctor would be with them shortly.

"Heard that before," Kins said as they retreated to seats in the waiting area. "Can you imagine if these guys had to keep a bus driver's schedule? It would be mass chaos."

Tracy handed him a Chinese magazine from the coffee table. "At least you won't have to read a six-month-old copy of *Time*."

The physician's assistant reappeared in ten minutes. Rather than barking out their names, she discreetly indicated Dr. Wu would see them.

Kins put down the magazine. "And I was just getting to a good part."

Dr. Wu stood behind his desk as Tracy and Kins entered his cramped office. Small in stature, perhaps five foot three, with large silver-framed glasses, Wu wore a white doctor's smock over a blue shirt and a maroon knit tie, the end of which he tucked into the waistband of his pants.

"Thank you for seeing us," Tracy said.

Wu's hands were as soft and small as a young boy's. After introductions, he sat and opened a file already on his desk. "The implant numbers you provided my PA correspond to a patient, Lynn Cora Hoff," he said in a thick Chinese accent.

Jane Doe had a name. Simple as that.

"What can you tell us about her?" Tracy said.

If Wu was worried about HIPAA, he didn't express it. He used the ball of his thumb to shove his glasses onto the bridge of his nose. "Ms. Hoff is twenty-four years old, five foot seven, one hundred and thirty-two pounds. Caucasian. She had her nose shaved, a chin implant, and two cheekbone implants."

"When was this done?" Tracy asked.

"June third."

"Recently," Kins said.

"Yes," Wu said.

"Had you worked with Ms. Hoff before?" Tracy asked.

"No."

"Did she say why she wanted the surgery?" Tracy asked.

Wu looked up as if he didn't understand the question. The glasses had already slid down the bridge of his nose. "Why?"

"Why she was having reconstructive surgery?" Tracy said.

"Many women have reconstructive surgery," Wu said, as if changing your face was an everyday occurrence. He again used his thumb to push the glasses onto his nose.

"I understand," Tracy said. "But this seems more invasive than routine plastic surgery."

"Women"—Wu looked to Kins—"and men, have surgery for many reasons."

"So she didn't say why?" Kins said.

"She did not."

"Did she provide her medical background?" Tracy asked.

Wu undid brass prongs at the top of the file and removed the contents. He handed Tracy a multipage document that she shared with Kins. The first page was a patient registration form filled out in pen. Kins copied Lynn Hoff's date of birth and Social Security number, as well as an address, which appeared to be an apartment in Renton. Hoff provided only a cell phone number. She did not provide an emergency contact or anyone with whom her medical information could be shared.

The second page was a patient health questionnaire. Hoff had checked "No" to every question, noted no prior medical history or surgeries, and no current medications. As for her family history, she'd circled "No" to the questions of whether her mother or father were living and did not list any brothers or sisters.

Tracy set down the forms. "Do you have before and after photographs?" she asked.

Wu sat back in his chair. "No."

Tracy glanced at Kins before reengaging Wu. "You don't have any photographs?" she said, not trying to hide her disbelief.

"No," Wu said again, his voice almost inaudible.

"Dr. Wu, wouldn't it be normal procedure to have before and after photographs of a patient undergoing surgery such as this?"

"Yes," he said. "It is normal procedure."

"Then why don't you have any photographs?"

"Following her surgery, Ms. Hoff requested all photographs."

"She asked for the pictures you'd taken of her?"

"Yes."

"And you gave those to her."

"She signed a waiver," Wu said. He leaned forward, fumbled in the file, and handed Tracy a two-page document. It was a simple release of liability. Lynn Hoff acknowledged receiving all photographs in Dr. Wu's possession. In exchange, she had agreed to waive her right to bring any claim against Dr. Wu for any reason or circumstance.

"Did you have a lawyer draw this up for you?" Kins asked.

"Yes," Wu said.

"So this is unusual," Kins said.

"Yes," Wu said.

"Did Ms. Hoff say why she wanted possession of the photographs?" Tracy asked.

Wu shook his head. "She did not."

Tracy suspected Wu had speculated why Lynn Hoff wanted her photographs, and probably came to the same conclusions she was now formulating—that he had, maybe unwittingly, operated on a fugitive from justice or someone running from enemies.

"Did Ms. Hoff return for follow-up treatment?" Tracy asked.

"No," Wu said.

"And again, was that unusual?"

"Yes."

"Did she schedule any follow-up appointments?"

"A visit was scheduled, but she did not keep that appointment."

"Did your staff call to find out why not?"

"The number provided was no longer in service," Wu said.

"Where was the surgery performed?" Tracy asked.

"Here," Wu said. "We have accredited surgical suites. It helps keep the costs affordable."

"How much does something like this cost?" Kins asked.

Wu consulted his file. "Six thousand three hundred and twelve dollars."

Tracy had noticed a sign on the counter indicating Wu accepted Visa and MasterCard. "How did she pay? I'm assuming insurance doesn't cover it."

"No insurance," Wu said. "Not for elective surgery. Ms. Hoff paid cash." Wu handed Tracy a receipt.

Kins looked to Tracy and she knew he was thinking it further evidence that Lynn Hoff was a prostitute. She made a mental note to have Del and Faz call local Renton banks to determine if Lynn Hoff had any accounts.

"How did Ms. Hoff get home after surgery?" Tracy asked. "I assume she couldn't drive."

"A note in the file indicates she used a car service."

"What about care at home after the surgery?" Kins said. "Would someone have to look after her?"

Wu shrugged his shoulders. "I do not know."

"You didn't ask her?" Tracy said, deciding to push him.

"No."

"Didn't all of this strike you as odd, Dr. Wu?"

"Yes," he said.

"But you didn't report it to anyone?"

"Report what? To who?" Wu looked at her with the flat expression of someone who had already consulted a lawyer and knew he had done nothing wrong. "My obligation is to my patient."

"True," Kins said, "but your patient ended up at the bottom of Puget Sound, and our obligation is to find out who put her there, and why."

CHAPTER 4

I'm getting married.

Those might be the last words I thought I'd ever say out loud—but I am. I'm standing inside the lobby of the Multnomah County Courthouse in downtown Portland wearing—get this—a white dress. The shock is not that the dress is white—every girl wears white, regardless of, you know. The shock is that I'm wearing a dress. I didn't even own a dress before I bought this one. I've never worn anything but pants to work, usually blue jeans. It is Portland, after all, which, translated, means, "casual." People come to work in spandex. That's not a joke. One of the insurance adjusters in our office rides his bike to work and likes to parade around in his tight shorts showing off his package, of which he must be very proud since he does it so frequently. He comes into my cubicle asking me some inane question to get a rise out of me. Yeah, that's going to do it. If I could wash my eyes with disinfectant, I would.

But I'm digressing.

So cue the music . . . "I'm going to the altar and I'm . . ."

Except, I'm not going to the altar—or to a church for that matter. I'm going before a justice of the peace at 3:00 p.m. on a Thursday afternoon.

I wanted to wait for the weekend, but getting married on a weekday saves thirty-five dollars, and Graham—that's his name, Graham Strickland— said there's no reason to spend the extra money for the same service.

No, it's not exactly the wedding every young girl dreams about— walking down a long aisle draped on my father's arm with the veil trailing behind me—but that dream sailed nine years ago. I was thirteen when a drunk driver crossed the center divider, went airborne, and landed on top of our car, killing both my parents. Something about being in the backseat saved me, the doctors said, like it was a good thing to be trapped alive in a car for two hours with your dead parents. Can you say years of counseling?

I went from Santa Monica, where my father had been a doctor, to live with an aunt and uncle in San Bernardino, which is where my mother grew up, but where I didn't know a soul. I should clarify that I only lived with my uncle Dale for about nine months. That's when I told my counselor that my uncle liked to climb in bed with me at night. My counselor told the police, and they called Child Protective Services, and a whole shit storm hit. Can you say more counseling?

In addition to not having a father to walk me down the aisle, I can't fill my cubicle, let alone a reception hall, with friends and family. I also don't think we could find anyone to give even a thirty-second toast about Graham and me. We've known each other less than four months.

Besides, I'm not a big cake fan anyway. I know. I know. Who doesn't like cake?

Me.

We are, however, going on a honeymoon—of sorts. We're going to climb Mount Rainier. I know what you're thinking because I was thinking the same thing. Hiking at 14,000 feet and getting frostbite. Great . . . Don't get me wrong. I love the outdoors. I spent much of my summers hiking in the Sierra Nevada Mountains. The outdoors is one of the reasons I moved to Portland. That, and it rains all the time here, which means I don't have to come up with an excuse to stay inside and read, which is my absolute, number one passion. In fact, it's what I would have preferred to have been doing the night I met Graham.

We met at a party—not so much a party as a business function sponsored by the insurance company I work for. Don't ask me why a lowly assistant needed to be there. I mean, if the company's incredible and wide array of insurance policies (sarcasm) or free booze and free hors d'oeuvres (definitely not sarcasm) didn't entice new clients, I failed to see how my presence would. My boss, however, who has taken it upon herself to be my surrogate mother, said my attendance was "nonnegotiable."

Brenda Berg walked into my cubicle the afternoon of the function and asked why I hadn't RSVP'd.

"Because I'm not going?" I said, though my voice rose so it sounded more like a question.

"Excuse me?"

"I'm not going," I said more definitively, though not with any real conviction.

"Why not?"

I shrugged and resumed typing on my keyboard—rude, I know. "I don't like parties. Most are boring."

"More boring than going home and sticking your nose in a book?"

"Definitely," I answered, though I'm certain she meant the question to be rhetorical.

"What, are you rereading Fifty Shades of Grey over and over again?"

"No," I said, though again it was without force and I'm pretty certain I blushed. Truth was, curiosity got the better of me and I did read it. I ordered it online and had it sent to my post box, then smuggled it home in a plain brown bag like a fifth of vodka. Sure the writing was juvenile, but it's like they say, "You don't buy Playboy for the articles." Not that I've ever bought a Playboy. I'm definitely not a lesbian.

"Then tell me what is so interesting at home that you can't go to a party for a couple of hours?" Brenda asked, undeterred.

"It's just not my thing," I said. "I'm not good at mingling."

"I'll help you."

"I don't have anything to wear."

"I can help with that also."

I was quickly running out of excuses and racking my brain. The dog I don't have ate my invitation. I'm actually Michael Jackson disguised as a woman, and I got too close to a pyrotechnic prop filming a Pepsi commercial and my hair caught on fire.

"You're smart," Brenda said. I know she meant it as a compliment, but it sounded kind of sad. "You pick up things faster than most of the people we hire who went to college and took our six-week training program. I've never seen anyone pick things up that fast, and you know more about computers than our IT guy."

Did I mention I have a lot of free time on my hands?

"You just need to show a little initiative and you could have my job someday."

Hooray! At least I'd have a window to throw myself out of when the boredom becomes unbearable.

"So you're going tonight, and that's final," she said, sounding a lot like my mother used to. "You'll never meet anyone going home and reading."

"Fine," I said. Why? I don't know why. I have this aggravating need to be agreeable. I'm pretty sure there's a medical term for it. Spinus Missingus—Of or relating to the lack of a spine.

"Good," Brenda said, eyeballing me with distrust. "I'm going to call if I don't see you."

"I'll be there," I said.

"I'll be looking for you," she said. Then she smiled. "It'll be fun. Trust me."

I think Custer uttered those final words to his troops just before leading them into the Battle of Little Bighorn, but I was good as my word. I did *attend. And I'll be shit struck if I didn't actually meet someone. Graham Strickland.*

The gathering was in the ballroom of a luxury hotel called The Nines in downtown Portland. Since my loft was in the Pearl District, at least I didn't have far to walk. I searched a table set up outside the room with name tags arranged in alphabetical order. Of course, I didn't see my name, probably because I hadn't RSVP'd. After the woman at the table asked me about a billion questions to confirm I wasn't some freak looking to crash boring insurance parties, she grinned and said in a perky voice, "Well, I'll just make you a name tag."

I cringed. That meant instead of the preprinted name tags with the company logo and typewritten name everyone else was wearing, I'd be wearing a handwritten piece of paper slapped onto my sweater. "Why don't you just brand my forehead with a big L for 'Loser,'" I said.

I wish. I'd said that to myself.

I walked into the ballroom with my loser name tag looking like I had a big scarlet A on my forehead. The room was packed, which I also found really pathetic. Didn't these people have anything better to do?

I didn't see Brenda, not right away, and I didn't really know anyone else, except in passing in the hallways, so I sort of just meandered until I found myself near the buffet. Eating would at least give the appearance I was doing something. To my surprise, it wasn't a bad spread. Swedish meatballs, chicken skewers, fruit and cheese plates, bread rolls, and a man cutting small pieces of prime rib. I mainly subsist on tuna fish and peanut butter and jelly, so this was a major score.

I was making my way through the food line when someone said, "You were last minute too, huh?"

It was the guy behind me, though I wasn't sure he was speaking to me. Then he smiled and made it pretty clear he had been. Love at first sight? Not on your life. First impression? I thought Graham looked like something out of that television show, Mad Men, *with his hair gelled and parted low* on the side of his head, his suit a size too small, his tie too narrow, and his day-old growth too forced. Trying way too hard, pal.

"Your name tag," he said, pointing. "You must have RSVP'd late also."

That's when I noticed his name tag had also been hand printed. Duh. "Oh, yeah," I said.

"Me too," he said, like that somehow made us brothers in arms.

I looked around for a moment. I didn't know who this guy was or who was standing within hearing distance, but I threw caution to the wind. "My boss said if I didn't attend, she'd fire me. I think she was kidding, but I wasn't sure. So . . ."

He chuckled at that, and it actually looked and sounded genuine. "Mine said I needed to cultivate business opportunities if I want to be considered partnership material."

He spoke the words with an affected, authoritative tone.

"You're a lawyer," I said.

"I work at Begley, Smalls, Begley, and Timmins." He leaned closer and lowered his voice. "That's BSBT, or Bullshit Big Time."

I laughed. "You said 'Begley' twice."

"Father and son. Old fart and heir apparent." He rolled his eyes. "If he wasn't the founding partner's son, he'd be serving food in a soup kitchen. Guy has the imagination of one of those drones who sits in cubicles punching numbers all day."

That would be me! I shouted inside my head. Can you introduce me?

"I think my firm and your company do some business together," he said.

"So you're a lawyer," I said, stalling, while I mentally calculated his age—four years of college and three years of law school—Graham was, at a minimum, twenty-five. Turns out he was twenty-eight, six years older than me. "Sounds like you don't like it much." I suddenly realized I was holding up the buffet line, grabbed a couple cubes of cheese, and slid down the table.

"I don't mind the practice of law," Graham said, lowering his voice. "I just really don't like the corporate environment. I'm an entrepreneur. I like to build things from the ground up."

"Start-ups?" I asked.

"Exactly. Get the prime rib," he said. "It might make coming here worthwhile."

"I'm a vegetarian," I said. Only I wasn't and I had no idea why I said I was.

He stuck out his free hand. "I'm a carnivore. Nice to meet you." He pointed to his handwritten name tag. "Strickland," he said in a British accent. "Graham Strickland."

My first thought wasn't James Bond. It was crackers—Graham Crackers. You know, the kind you use to make s'mores. My second thought was pretentious. My third thought, however, was talking to anyone beat standing alone looking like a big loser, and that thought won the day.

"You want to sit?" Graham said, motioning to one of the round tables.

"Sure," I said—per my earlier rationalization.

We made our way through the crowd to one of the white-linen-draped tables and banquet chairs. Graham set down his plate and asked, "You want a glass of wine or a beer?"

"I don't drink," I said.

"Don't drink, don't smoke. What do you do?" he sang. When I didn't respond he said, "Adam Ant. 'Goody Two Shoes.' It's a song."

"Oh," I said. Then, for no particular reason, I added, "Wine. I'll have a glass of wine."

That's how the evening went, with me saying things I'd never said before, especially after I'd had a second glass of wine. Like when Graham said, "Do you want to get out of here?" And I said, "Sure." Or later when we went to a bar and he said, "Do you want a drink?" and I said, "Sure," again. And when he drove me home in his Porsche and parked and said, "Are you going to invite me up for coffee?" and I said, "Do you drink coffee?" and Graham said, "No," and I said, "Okay."

And just like that, I slept with him. The very first night! I know, pretty sleazy, right? Maybe it was the wine and the cocktails, or maybe it was *reading* Fifty Shades of Grey. *Honestly, I thought I'd never hear from the guy again, but then he sent me an e-mail asking me to go out. I debated it for a day. I did not show it to Brenda. I did, however, show it to my friend Devin Chambers. Devin started at the company about the same time I did, though she worked for another adjuster. I told her about my night with Graham, and she was like, "What? No fucking way? You slept with him? Holy shit!"*

Did I mention that Devin swears like a sailor with Tourette's? Anyway, she thought I should go out with Graham again, so I did.

So I guess I have Devin to thank for me standing in the marbled entry of the Multnomah County Courthouse, waiting for Graham. I have to admit I am a bit nervous. I mean, we've only been dating a few months. I haven't even met his family. He says I should thank him. His father is some CEO in New York, which Graham says is why he lives in Portland, as far away as possible without leaving the lower forty-eight states. His mother, he says, mostly stays in their Manhattan apartment, drinking. So, in a sense, Graham doesn't have any family either, and in that we have a common bond. We're orphans, and if that isn't a reason to get married, then I don't know what is (sarcasm, again).

I felt awkward just standing there in a white dress. I was sure everyone walking past was giving me pitying looks, certain I was about to be stood up. Truth was, I had the same thought. Sad, I know, but I never had figured out why Graham wanted to marry me—my counselor said I have a self-esteem issue. Really? And I would have thought every girl who watched her parents die and was molested by her uncle would be brimming with confidence!

Graham, however, seems to think we have a lot in common, but that's because I pretty much say yes to everything he wants to do. I guess I'm afraid that if I said no, well, it would be like my boss saying if I didn't go to the party she'd fire me. I really wasn't certain what might happen.

"Hey." I turned at the sound of his voice, relieved to see him hurrying across the rotunda's terrazzo tile floor, slightly out of breath when he reached me. "Sorry I'm late. Something came up at work."

"I thought you took the afternoon off," I said.

"I'd hoped to, but something came up. Small fire. Nothing big. So you ready to do this thing?"

Do this thing?

"Sure," I said, though I was pretty sure I smelled the faint odor of alcohol on his breath when he leaned forward to kiss me.

CHAPTER 5

Tracy called Faz after leaving Dr. Wu's office. She provided him the name Lynn Cora Hoff, her date of birth and Social Security number, and asked that Faz run her through the National and Washington State Crime Information Centers as well as the Department of Licensing. She and Kins drove to the address Lynn Hoff had provided Dr. Wu, a motel in an industrial area of the city. Tracy noted from a billboard that you could rent a room for $22 a night or $120 a week. According to the woman working in the office, Lynn Hoff had rented the room for the month, paying cash.

"Was it unusual for a guest to stay that long?"

"It doesn't happen that often, but it happens—you know, people in between leases or relocating from out of state, stuff like that," the woman said.

The rental agreement consisted of boilerplate language. It asked Hoff to write down the make and model of her car and license plate number. Hoff had drawn lines through those spaces.

"What kind of tenant was she?" Tracy asked.

"No problems with her." The woman led them from the office to the back of the building. She was dressed for the weather in shorts, a tank top, and flip-flops. Tracy envied her. The heat coming off the asphalt permeated through the soles of her shoes. It now seemed all but a certainty Seattle would break the June record for the number of days eclipsing ninety degrees. All across the state, record highs were being set, with fires raging out of control in eastern Washington. For the first time in her life, Tracy heard people using the word "drought"—which seemed incomprehensible coming out of the mouths of Seattleites.

"You ever see any men coming and going from her apartment?" Kins asked.

"I didn't," the woman said, glancing over at him as she started up an exterior staircase to the second floor. "We really don't get prostitutes. Mostly we get the Mexicans who work in the factories around here. They stay until they can get their papers and a paycheck. Then they move into an apartment. So what happened to her? Is she dead?"

"We're just starting our investigation," Tracy said.

The manager stopped on the second-floor landing. "Is she the woman they found in that crab trap? It's been all over the news."

It had been, generating local and national publicity. "We can't provide any details about our cases," Kins said.

"So she *was* the woman in the pot?" the manager said as if they were all sharing a secret.

"You said you have some residents who stay for as long as a month?" Tracy said.

"She was the woman in that trap," the manager said to herself, sounding as if Lynn Hoff had been Princess Diana, and the room would become a tourist attraction. She continued down the landing to the northwest corner and the apartment door farthest from the parking lot and the manager's office.

"Did Lynn Hoff say why she needed the room?" Kins asked.

"She said she was relocating from somewhere." The woman scrunched her face in thought. "New Jersey, I think. I remember 'cause she said something about waiting for a vacancy in an apartment building she liked, and she didn't want to enter into another lease."

"Did she say what she did for a living?"

"No," the woman said.

"You have any other conversations with her?" Tracy asked.

"Not really. Honestly, I got the impression she didn't want to be bothered."

"Why do you say that?" Tracy asked.

"She wasn't unfriendly but . . . mostly she kept to herself. And when I did see her go out, she wore those big sunglasses and ball caps. So, was she hiding from someone?"

Tracy and Kins didn't answer.

"She was hiding from someone," the manager said.

She stopped outside a red door with a gold "8D." Kins set his go bag on the landing—a black-and-yellow tool bag he'd bought at some big-box store because he liked all the pouches and pockets. Typical guy. He removed two pairs of latex gloves and handed a pair to Tracy. If they stepped in and saw blood spatter on the wall or a large stain on the carpet, they'd step out and wait for the CSI unit to process the room.

"Anyone been in here since her?" Tracy asked.

"No. It's still rented to her."

The manager used the master key to open the door, then stepped aside.

"We'll need you to wait outside," Tracy said. The woman stepped back.

Tracy had more than her fair share of experience with motel rooms recently. The Cowboy had killed his victims in cheap motel rooms along the Aurora strip. They could be difficult to process. The latent-fingerprint examiners could find enough prints to start a small village, especially if Lynn Hoff had been a prostitute. When Tracy crossed the threshold she paused, surprised to find the interior so neat and clean. Perhaps too clean.

"Shot to the back of the head would be messy," Kins whispered to Tracy, reading her thoughts and keeping his voice low. He moved farther in, looking about. "I doubt she was killed here, but I guess we'll find out."

An inventory of the refrigerator included a Styrofoam box containing a half-eaten spring roll and leftover pad Thai, but no indication of the restaurant. Tracy also found a half-full pint of 1 percent milk, which, from the smell of it, had soured, a loaf of wheat bread showing the first signs of mold, and a block of cheddar cheese. A half-finished bottle of chardonnay was in the door tray.

In the bedroom closet, Tracy found a couple of blouses, a jacket, shorts, blue jeans, a pair of tennis shoes, ankle boots, and flip-flops. She moved to the bathroom. On the counter she noted a makeup kit, but with just the bare essentials. The shower was clean, with a small bottle of shampoo and conditioner.

"Sparse," Kins said, sticking his head into the bathroom.

"Definitely," Tracy said.

She went back into the kitchen, opening up the cabinet under the sink and pulling out the garbage pail. It had not been emptied. She rummaged through it and found a wadded-up piece of paper—a withdrawal slip from a bank, Emerald Credit Union. The address was also Renton, Washington. "Might have found her bank," Tracy said.

Kins walked over and took a look, then considered the rest of the apartment. "No wallet. No cell phone. No laptop."

"Lynn Hoff did not want someone to find her," Tracy said.

"But someone did," Kins said.

Faz and Del rotated their chairs from their desks as Tracy and Kins entered the bull pen. The desks were positioned in the four corners, a worktable in the center. Tracy couldn't help but compare them to Rex and Sherlock, Dan's 140-pound Rhodesians, who reacted just as quickly every time Tracy walked in the door. The last time she'd seen the dogs had been early that morning. Dan, a lawyer, had left before her, flying to Los Angeles to argue in court against a motion to set aside a verdict in his client's favor. Rex hadn't even bothered to raise his head from his dog bed as Tracy departed the apartment. Only Sherlock had been chivalrous enough to walk Tracy to the door. For that gesture, he'd gotten to enjoy a synthetic dog bone.

"NCIC and WCIC came up negative for Lynn Hoff," Faz said.

"Seriously?" Kins said, disbelieving. He'd been even more certain that Hoff had been a prostitute after learning she'd been paying cash for her reconstructive surgery and rent at the motel.

"Not even a parking ticket," Del said.

"What about the Department of Licensing?" Tracy asked.

"More interesting," Del said. He swiveled his chair and retrieved an 8½ x 11 sheet of paper from his desk, handing it to Tracy. "Meet Lynn Hoff. I've asked for a copy of the actual photograph."

Plain looking, Lynn Hoff, if that was her name—Tracy now had doubts—had straight brown hair parted on the side that extended past her shoulders. She wore heavy black-framed glasses. The license indicated she was five foot six and 135 pounds with brown eyes, which corresponded with Funk's autopsy findings.

"The DOL issued the license March 2016 but has no prior licenses issued in that name," Del said.

"She's twenty-three," Tracy said, looking at Kins. "Might not be her real name."

Tracy and Kins had come to that conclusion on the drive back from the motel, after they'd turned jurisdiction of the room over to the CSI sergeant.

"Likely an alias," Faz said. He swiveled his chair to follow Tracy as she crossed the bull pen to her cubicle and deposited her purse in her locker. "I ran a LexisNexis search on her and came up with bubkes.

No past employers, no former addresses. I also ran her name through Social Security. The number appears legit but no employment. She's a ghost," Faz said.

"A ghost on the run," Kins said. "She had reconstructive surgery on her face and afterward insisted on getting back all the photographs. She didn't provide any personal information or family history, and she paid cash for a motel room. It also looks like someone cleaned it. No cell phone. No wallet. No computer or laptops."

Tracy handed Faz a copy of the receipt from the bank she'd found in the garbage. "Found this in the trash, though. Can you log it in and run it down for me?"

"No problem," Faz said.

The yellow light on Tracy's phone blinked, indicating she had a voice mail message—or several dozen. One or two were likely from her favorite muckraker, Maria Vanpelt. Bennett Lee, SPD's public information officer, had also likely called, in part because Vanpelt had called him. Lee would be seeking a statement for the media. It was unlikely Nolasco had left a message. He liked to be an ass in person.

"How does someone exist today without debit or credit cards?" Del said, facing the interior of the A Team's shared workspace.

"Prepaid credit cards and burner cell phones," Faz said. "You use them and throw them away."

Faz had spent four years working with the fraud unit before homicide. Though he and Del went out of their way to keep things in the section loose, they were far more than just comic relief. Promoted to homicide the same year, twenty-one years ago, they had worked as partners for seventeen and had solved every homicide put before them. Yeah, they played two Italian gumbas, but Faz also had college degrees in accounting and finance, and Del had graduated from the University of Wisconsin with a degree in political science. Over lunch one afternoon, Faz had told Tracy he'd been headed to grad school to get his master's in tax, but needed to make some money to pay down his student loans. An uncle secured a summer internship for him at the Elizabeth Police Department in New Jersey, and Faz found his calling—much to his mother's disappointment.

"But you said you didn't find any prepaid credit cards or cell phone," Del said to Tracy and Kins.

"Didn't even find a wallet," Kins said. "She paid cash for the surgery and a month's rent. Close to seven grand."

"Where's she getting that kind of money?" Del asked.

"Don't know yet."

"Someone could have whacked her and cleaned up the motel room," Faz said. "They certainly didn't intend for her body to ever be found."

"Whacked her?" Del said to Kins while jabbing a thumb toward Faz. "He thinks he's Michael Corleone."

Tracy turned to Kins. "What about running her photograph through facial recognition software, see if we find a license under a different name?"

"How're you going to get the DOL to authorize that?" Kins said.

After a $1.6 million investment, SPD had the facial recognition software and staff trained to use it, but the Seattle City Council had only approved its use to go through jail-booking mug shots. The DOL had the most comprehensive database of photographs of Washington residents, but the powers that be would not allow SPD to use that database to hunt down criminals because an ACLU lawyer had argued it could invade John Q. Citizen's personal privacy rights. Yeah, better to let the criminal kill John Q. Citizen than learn how tall he was, or how overweight. And God forbid they determine the identity of a dead person so they could advise their next of kin.

"Maybe they'll make an exception," Tracy said. "She's dead."

"A government bureaucrat willing to think outside the box for the greater cause," Del said. "Good luck with that! While you're waiting for them to say no, I'll do things the old-fashioned way and take a look through the missing persons database."

"Let's at least take the photo back to the condominiums and show it around the marinas," Tracy said.

"We can do that," Faz said.

"CSI is processing the motel room, so there could be another list of names to go through when we get the report from Latents," Tracy said, growing more frustrated. "Screw this. I'm going to ask Nolasco to push the DOL on the facial recognition. The woman is dead. Whose privacy are we invading?"

"Can I get an amen?" Faz said, shaking his hands in the air.

Del obliged him without looking up.

"You want me to come with?" Kins asked.

Tracy only briefly considered his offer. If Nolasco was going to turn her down, it wouldn't matter if Kins was with her or not. Kins's offer had more to do with chivalry, like Sherlock walking her to the door in the morning. Tracy and Nolasco's volatile history dated to the police academy, when she'd stood up for a female recruit during a pat-down demonstration. Nolasco had ended up with a broken nose and singing soprano from a well-placed elbow and knee. More recently, Tracy had inadvertently exposed Nolasco and his former homicide partner, Floyd Hattie, for their somewhat questionable investigation techniques when she discovered one of their cold cases in her search for other possible victims of the Cowboy. That had sparked a full-blown investigation by the Office of Professional Accountability. Hattie, long retired, fell on his sword, and Nolasco, snake that he was, had managed to slither away with only a written reprimand.

"No," she said. "If he's going to turn me down, it won't matter whether you're there to see him do it or not."

"Maybe we get lucky and somebody recognizes her," Kins said. "She had to come from somewhere, right?"

"Unless she hatched," Faz said.

Tracy left the bull pen and walked the hallway between the inner offices and the outer glass walls that provided glimpses of Elliott Bay between the high-rise buildings. A haze hovered over Seattle and a thin red line extended across the horizon. Smog. It seemed as unfathomable as a drought in the Emerald City, but there it hung, where it couldn't be ignored. She stepped into Nolasco's office with a short rap on his open door.

The captain sat at his desk, talking on the phone. He didn't wave her in. He didn't even acknowledge her. He just kept her standing in the doorway, like smog on his horizon. Nolasco said something about having the best outfield with both Mike Trout and Bryce Harper, and she deduced that he was discussing his fantasy baseball team. Fantasy football, March Madness, fantasy baseball—Nolasco played them all. Divorced twice, how else was he going to spend his time? God forbid he should let the murder of a young woman interrupt his make-believe life.

While waiting, Tracy checked her messages on her cell phone. Dan had texted to let her know he'd arrived at LAX and would be home by six. Tracy had never had anyone check in with her just to check in, and it felt comforting to know that Dan cared enough to do so. In the two years since they'd reconnected, Dan—a childhood friend—had never made her feel like an afterthought. She was always on his radar. She had typed a partial response that she would be late getting home when she heard Nolasco say, "Gotta go." He hung up his phone and said, "What is it?" presumably to Tracy. She didn't immediately acknowledge him. Instead, she finished texting Dan.

"Hey, I got things to do," Nolasco said.

Tracy lowered her phone and stepped into the office. "Need to talk to you about the woman in the crab pot."

Nolasco's brow furrowed. "We got an ID?"

"We do and we don't."

"What does that mean?"

"We have a name, Lynn Hoff, but we think it's an alias. We think she's a ghost. We're not finding anything on her in any of the systems. Kins and I took a drive out to her last known address—a motel in Kent. She was either getting ready to run or already on the run. We think someone cleaned up the place. No wallet. No cell. No computer."

"So she was into something illegal."

"Don't know."

Nolasco scowled. "How else would you explain it?"

"I can't yet," she said.

He leaned back from his desk. "Sometimes things are as they appear, and it appears she was either a hooker, a druggie, or had pissed off the wrong people."

"Initial autopsy examination doesn't indicate druggie, and why would someone go to the effort to stuff a hooker or druggie in a crab pot and dump her in Puget Sound?"

"Don't get all crusader on me, Crosswhite. We get Jane Does all the time."

"Not in crab pots."

"Like I said, sounds like she pissed off the wrong people. She doesn't come up in missing persons or nobody comes to identify her, the city will cremate her and six months from now she'll get a decent burial out at Olivet. We have more pressing matters."

Like fantasy baseball? Tracy wanted to say but refrained. "Fingerprints didn't come up in the system," she said, further evidence Lynn Hoff wasn't a hooker or a druggie.

"Run her through missing persons. I'm betting she shows up."

"Del's doing it now. She also had surgery to alter her appearance."

"A lot of women do. It's called vanity."

"Men too," Tracy said. Rumor had it Nolasco's two-week vacation to Maui had actually been a trip to a plastic surgeon. He had the wide-eyed look of the perpetually surprised. "This wasn't cosmetic. This was reconstruction. She was changing her appearance."

"How do you know that?"

"Funk found implants. That's how we got a name. Her doctor said she provided little in the way of personal information and no family history, but she insisted that she get back all the before and after photographs. Del ran her through DOL and came up with a photograph, but no prior licenses, which seems odd given she's twenty-three. I want to use the facial recognition software on DOL's database and see if we can find any other matches. I need you to make it happen."

Nolasco shook his head. "DOL won't do it."

"I know that's the party line, but I'm hoping you can convince them. The woman is dead. It's not like we're invading her privacy."

"ACLU says we can't use it unless we suspect criminal activity."

"We do suspect criminal activity. Someone killed her and stuffed her in a crab pot."

"Let's wait and see what Del finds before we go running off spending the budget."

"Del's not going to find her in missing persons. She wasn't missing. She was hiding."

"From who?"

"Whoever killed her."

"Send the photo to vice. Have them show it around downtown and see if anyone on the street recognizes her. Sometimes good police work is about pounding the pavement, not just the keyboards."

Tracy bit her tongue. "Thank you, Captain." She turned for the door, got an idea, and turned back. "By the way, I heard Trout has a bad hamstring that could bother him most of the year."

Nolasco looked up, initially puzzled by her comment and clearly not expecting it. Then his perpetually wide eyes widened further. "What would you know about it?"

"Me? Nothing. But Dan knows a guy on the Angels' medical staff."

As Tracy departed, Nolasco picked up his desk phone. She hoped Mike Trout hit three home runs that night.

———

Tracy took Nolasco's advice and gave Billy Williams a copy of Lynn Hoff's photograph to give to the sergeant in vice. She asked that patrol officers show it around the city's well-known prostitution areas. She didn't do it because she thought it was a good idea, or because she thought it would yield results. She did it so she could tell Nolasco she'd done as he'd suggested, and he'd been wrong. Lynn Hoff might have been doing something illegal, but Tracy was convinced Hoff wasn't a hooker or a druggie, and she wasn't homeless, not if she was spending that much money to change her appearance and paying rent up front.

She'd been on the run.

Tracy left the office at just after nine, which was well past when her shift ordinarily ended, but early for the first forty-eight hours working a murder. It would take Del time to go through missing persons. Funk wouldn't have the toxicology report for a couple weeks, and DNA analysis would take almost as long. They didn't find Hoff's fingerprints in AFIS, and Tracy doubted her DNA would be in CODIS.

She drove home. The sight of Dan's Suburban parked in front of the gated courtyard brought a smile to her face, the way the sight of his bike lying on its side in her parents' front yard used to make her smile when she was twelve. She hadn't been in love with him then, far from it, but Dan had always been fun to have around.

They'd reconnected in Cedar Grove, when hunters discovered Sarah's remains in a shallow grave and Tracy went home to lay her only sister to rest, and to pursue her killer. Dan attended the funeral service. They'd been dating since, though they saw each other more now that he had moved from the North Cascades to a five-acre farm in Redmond. So far, the extra time together had not diminished her romantic feelings for him—or his for her. She'd thought of marriage, though neither had broached that topic. Each had been married and divorced, and neither appeared in a rush to make things official. Dan had recently hit several large jury verdicts, including the recent verdict against the Los Angeles company, and he was not in a hurry to get back into any prolonged litigation. Instead, he'd used his free time to remodel the house on the farm—work he enjoyed and did well. He'd remodeled his parents' entire home in Cedar Grove. Dan would work on the remodel during the day, then drive out to West Seattle to cook her dinner and spend the night. He was the better cook, and as crazy as it sounded for a woman who carried a Glock .40 and could shoot faster and more accurately than any officer on the force, Tracy slept better with Dan and the two dogs in the house.

Rex and Sherlock greeted Tracy as she came through the side door from the garage into the kitchen, though it was without their usual enthusiasm and seemed more obligatory. They quickly retreated out the sliding glass door to the deck, and plopped down on their sides, their tongues hanging from their mouths, panting, and otherwise looking miserable. Thank God they were shorthaired.

Shirtless, Dan stood on the deck wearing cargo shorts and flip-flops and looked anything but miserable. He kept himself in good shape running and lifting weights several times a week and getting out for hikes in the mountains on the weekends. In the winter, he still skied like he was eighteen. His stomach remained flat and his chest well developed, with just the right amount of chest hair. At the moment, he wasn't wearing his round wire-rimmed glasses that, along with his curly hair, made him look like a college professor.

"What did you do to them?" Tracy asked, nodding to the dogs as she stepped out the sliding glass door.

"Just a walk," Dan said. "You know they're big babies in the heat." He opened the grill and quickly became enveloped in a cloud of smoke.

"Do I need to bring out the fire extinguisher?" Tracy said, closing the sliding glass door so the smoke didn't fill the house.

Dan fanned a burst of flames and flipped a piece of chicken with tongs before quickly closing the hood and stepping back. "If you know any way to barbecue chicken without starting a three-alarm blaze I'm all ears." They kissed and Dan gestured to a table between two deck chairs. "I poured you a glass of wine."

"Thanks. I'm going to change first. You look a lot more comfortable than I feel."

Dan threw back his head and spread his arms. Though dusk, it remained warm and he had always loved the heat. Even as kids growing up in Cedar Grove, Tracy remembered his unbridled joy on hot summer days. "The hotter the better," he used to say, then he'd rattle off all the things they would do—like riding their bikes into the hills and jumping from the rope swing into the river.

"The weather stays like this, you may never go back to work," Tracy said.

"I wish. I have yet another trip down to Los Angeles to deal with my favorite opposing counsel."

"You didn't get it resolved today?"

"We got that resolved. The judge called their motion frivolous, gave me my attorney's fees, and told them to get the case finished. I'm flying down to put the judgment on the record and start the appeal clock."

"Can't you do it over the phone or by e-mail?"

"I don't trust them. I want it on the record in open court."

"When do you have to go?"

"Friday."

"If I didn't have this new case I'd go with you; we could have spent the weekend at the beach."

"That sounds a lot better than dealing with those jackasses. Resolve your case and we'll do it."

"Turning out to be easier said than done. Let me change and I'll tell you about it."

Tracy went inside and exchanged her work clothes for shorts and a tank top. Back on the deck, she said, "Much better." Dan sat in one of the two lounge chairs sipping a Corona. With the sun fading fast, the deck on the east side of the home provided relief from the heat, though the thermometer on the wall indicated it remained seventy-two.

"I assume this has to do with the woman in the crab pot?"

Tracy sat in the empty chair and sipped her wine. "We've had a hell of a time trying to identify her."

Dan grimaced. "That bad?"

"The body's in decent condition. We think she's a ghost."

"A ghost?"

"Someone deliberately living off the radar." Tracy explained how they'd tracked down the name Lynn Hoff, but also the seeming dead end they'd reached. "Nolasco wants us to wrap it up, declare her indigent, and let the city cremate her."

Looking suddenly alarmed, Dan stood and said, "Speaking of cremation." He quickly grabbed the tongs. When he opened the barbecue only a small puff of smoke emerged. "They're alive." He plucked each piece of chicken off the grill and set them on a nearby plate. For all the flames, the chicken looked golden brown and crisp. Tracy had no idea how Dan did it. He turned the knobs off, killing the flames, then shut off the nozzle supplying the propane.

Tracy went inside to get place settings and Dan retrieved a salad and dressing from the fridge. They went back onto the deck, sat, and dished out food. Below, on Elliott Bay, tiny white triangles tacked back and forth in the ripples of waves. The sky, devoid of a single cloud, provided no indication the heat wave would end anytime soon.

As they ate, Dan said, "So tell me why you think this woman is a ghost."

Tracy explained what they'd found at Dr. Wu's and the motel room, and through the DOL, and the basis for her conclusion that Lynn Hoff was not a druggie, a prostitute, or homeless. "If she's not a druggie or a prostitute, why wouldn't someone have reported her as missing?"

"Maybe it's like you said—she wasn't really missing if she didn't want to be found," Dan said. "So maybe nobody suspects she's missing."

"But if she's hiding from someone, that means she has some identity, right? Nobody can just walk away from everyone and everything unnoticed. She had to have some family, friends, work colleagues. Nobody can fall off the radar that easily, can they?"

"They can for a while—depending on what they tell everyone . . . or if they die," he said, chewing on a drumstick.

"That's not a bad thought."

"What?"

"We've been focusing on whether she had a prior criminal record, but that might not be the right focus. Whoever Jane Doe is, she might have been using a false identity because she knows Lynn Hoff is not going to show up in any database. She could be dead."

Tracy's cell phone rang. She recognized her desk number. When on call, or working a fresh homicide, she had her calls at the office forwarded to her cell. "I have to take this," she said. Dan picked up his wineglass and sat back. Tracy excused herself from the table and walked to the deck railing. "This is Detective Crosswhite."

"Detective Crosswhite, this is Glenn Hicks. I'm a district ranger with Mount Rainier National Park."

"What can I do for you?" Tracy asked. She turned and looked south, where the mountain loomed ever large.

"Well, to be honest, I'm not exactly sure." Hicks gave a long sigh through the phone. Then he said, "But I think you might have found one of my corpses."

CHAPTER 6

*M*arriage is bliss.

*That's what people say, anyway. I found it not all that differ-
ent from being single, except for little things, like I had to clear space in the
closet for Graham's clothes, and there was twice as much laundry and twice
as many dirty dishes. I hadn't anticipated we'd live in my loft, which isn't
much bigger than a studio apartment, but Graham said it was less expensive
than his apartment and we'd save money, plus we'd be living in the Pearl
District and could walk to all the cool restaurants and stores.*

*Not that we ever do walk to all the cool restaurants and stores. It's been
six weeks since the big day—I did summit Mount Rainier, by the way,
though Graham didn't make it. He had to turn back at Disappointment
Cleaver with altitude sickness. I thought he'd be happy I'd made it, but he
was more upset with the guides, who he said didn't prepare him well enough
for the ascent.*

*Anyway, Graham has been working late—a lot. He has a big public
offering for one of BSBT's signature clients and says that if he pulls it off,
there's no way he can't be made a firm partner. It's okay with me he's working
so much. Like I said, I was used to living alone and it's been an adjust-
ment having someone else in the loft. I've never been much of a talker, but*

Graham likes to talk when he gets home, sometimes anyway. He has a lot of big ideas about companies he wants to someday start, though he says he hasn't found "that magic fit" just yet.

Graham working late gives me more time to spend reading, though he keeps encouraging me to go back to the gym. That twenty pounds I lost training for and climbing Rainier? I found it. I should say, it found me. I certainly wasn't looking for it. I think it's genetics. I can remember my father saying to my mother that no matter how much he ate, or how far or how often he jogged, he could never get below 190 pounds.

Not that I'm 190 pounds!

Good God.

Still, I'm 135, which isn't exactly lean and mean.

The sex has been less frequent than I expected. Graham says he's tired after the long days, but I'm wondering if it has to do with those pounds. Before we got married, Graham used to say, "I like my women with a little meat on their bones." Now he'll say things like, "You should go to the gym when I'm working late, or go out for a walk. You don't have to be cooped up in here all night."

I like cooped up. I like my books. And I don't mind the pounds. My wardrobe is built for it!

I was cooped up on a Wednesday night, reading The Nightingale, *a book that had transported me back to 1940s Paris, when Nazis goose-stepped down the Avenue des Champs-Élysées. I heard someone at the door. My loft is on the third floor of a converted warehouse. It's the only loft on the floor and while you can access it by stairs or take an elevator, you have to punch in a four-digit security code to get in the front door and to get the elevator to ascend. My front door is also keyless. I think the landlord got tired of getting calls in the middle of the night from tenants who'd locked themselves out. I use the same four-digit code for the elevator and my door—the day and month of my birthday. Real sneaky, I know.*

Anyway, we don't get solicitors, so the sound of someone at the door that early in the evening surprised me. I glanced up at the clock on the wall near the windows that provided a partial view of the Willamette River and Broadway Bridge. Six thirty. I wasn't expecting Graham that early. Lately, he had not been getting home until after ten.

"Hey," he said, stepping in and giving me a quick glance before shutting the door and setting down his backpack.

"Hey," I said, sensing something wrong. Graham's moods could be hard to predict. When he was happy, he was a ball of fast-talking energy. He'd go on and on whether or not I participated in the conversation. Then he'd catch himself and say, "I'm sorry. I haven't given you a chance to say anything." But before I could say anything, he'd start talking again. Those were the good nights. The not-so-good nights were when Graham came home sullen, bordering on angry. The first few times I'd asked if he was all right, but I'd stopped after he'd said, "I don't want to talk about it, okay? I talk all day. Just give me some peace and quiet."

Tonight he stood at the door, eyes seemingly searching the ceiling rafters. He looked disheveled, which was not like him. I'd had to give him more space in the closet for his clothes, which was fine since I didn't have much in the wardrobe department. Remember—cubicle worker. Portland. Graham needed suits, and shirts and ties for work, which he only bought from Nordstrom. He had a personal shopper who knew his tastes, and Graham liked the way they tailored his clothes. He looked like he'd stepped out of the pages of GQ. I usually looked like I'd rolled out of bed, thrown on the first thing I selected, and headed out the door without even bothering to put on mascara, which was exactly what I did most mornings.

Tonight, Graham's tie was loose and the top button of his shirt undone. He looked sweaty, like he'd run home.

"I have to get out of that place," he said.

"What place?"

"BSBT." He tossed his car keys on the counter that divided the living area from the kitchenette. A staircase led to the loft where I kept my bed and where the bathroom was located.

"I thought you were liking it better," I said. "I thought the public offering was going well."

"You would think that." The comment stung. Graham sighed and I noticed his eyes were glassy, like he'd been crying—or drinking. "I'm drowning there. Can't you tell?" He paced near the front door, talking without expecting a response. "It's death by a thousand paper cuts and I'm bleeding all over my body. There's no creativity. None. Everyone is so robotic in their thinking and actions. No one thinks outside the box. No one. And if you do, you get slapped back in line with the rest of the drones." He shook his head, still pacing. "I can't do it anymore. Fuck it. I won't do it anymore."

"What would you do?"

He stopped pacing, nodding his head the way he did when something was exciting him. Just like that his mood changed. The shadow of darkness lifted. He became animated. His eyes darted all over the room. He approached the couch and dropped to his knees. "I've thought about this a lot the last six months." I smelled alcohol. "I told you that I was looking for that magic fit. You remember? Well, I think I've found it. I've been doing some research."

"About what?" I managed to get in.

"Marijuana," Graham said, eyes wide, his face beaming.

"What?" I had no idea what he was talking about.

He got to his feet, rubbing his palms together. "Oregon is legalizing marijuana. It's going to be a total cash cow. I talked to some people in Seattle who said the people who get in on the ground floor are going to be making money hand over fist."

I earmarked the page in my book and set it on the seat cushion beside me. I'd recently read about this in the newspaper. "I read an article that said that with all the medical marijuana dispensaries, it's going to be more difficult for independent stores here, and not like Seattle."

"Those are just the naysayers," Graham said, sitting so close that I had to tuck my legs up under me. "Those are the drones, the people without any *imagination. Trust me, I've been looking into this and the money is there for the making."*

"When have you been looking into it?"

"What?"

"When have you been looking into it? You've been working so late, and every weekend."

His eyes went wide again, only this time it looked more like someone walking in on a surprise. "Are you listening to me? I'm telling you we have a chance to do something for ourselves, and you're more interested in interrogating me."

"I'm not interrogating you. I just asked—"

"Well then, at least show me a little bit of enthusiasm." He moved toward the window but turned back to where I was sitting. "Is that too much to ask? You're my wife. You're supposed to support me."

I didn't know what to say to that so I didn't say anything. In truth, neither of us really supported the other. Graham thought it best we keep our finances separate—separate credit cards, separate bank accounts, separate debit cards, separate phone bills, though occasionally he would ask to borrow my credit card when the law firm's paycheck hadn't cleared, or when we went out, because he didn't like the way his wallet fit in the back pocket of his pants.

"I want to leave BSBT and open up a marijuana dispensary," he said matter-of-factly.

"You want to leave now? But you've been working so hard and you said you were so close to being made a partner."

He came back to his place on the couch. "That's my point. I'm working hard . . . for them." He reached out and took my hand. "This is a chance for me to work hard for myself . . . for us," he added quickly. "We could do it together."

"What do you mean?"

He squeezed my hand so hard it hurt. "I mean we could open the business together, the two of us. You could get out of that cubicle."

But I liked my cubicle. "I like my job."

"It's a dead end. Do you want to die in that place? Cubicles and offices are coffins. It's where the truly gifted go to die."

He was leaning forward again, enough to make me pull back from the alcohol odor. "I don't know," I said. "The article I read said that getting licenses to open a dispensary is expensive, not to mention all the start-up costs and the overhead. And we don't have any experience growing . . . well, anything."

"I've been reading up on it too," he said, getting up suddenly and hurrying to the front door to retrieve his leather satchel. He made his way back to the couch, sat, pulled out a manila file about three inches thick, and moved the magazines on the coffee table to spread out its contents.

"We don't have to grow. We buy our product from distributors."

I was amazed at the level of detail Graham had gone to. It looked like he'd put together a complete pro forma statement, including start-up and operating costs.

"I want to call it Genesis," he said, "like the first book of the Bible, because this would just be the beginning."

"The beginning of what?"

"A corporation," he said. "We can use the money from the dispensary to invest in other start-ups and businesses. I spoke to the bank and between our two salaries we should have no problem qualifying for a loan—"

"When did you speak to the bank?"

He waved off my question. "See, look. We have excellent credit scores."

"We don't have any collateral."

"I told them I was going to be made a partner and my salary was going to increase."

"But you're not going to be working there."

"They don't know that, and I can stay until we get the loan."

"But that's . . ."

"It isn't a lie," he emphasized. "I was going to be made a partner. I'm just choosing not to accept it."

"*They told you that you made partner?*"

"*No, but that's just a formality.*"

"*I don't think we can list your salary if you won't have one.*"

"*It's just to get the loan.*" He grabbed my hands as if he wanted to take me out on the dance floor and twirl me. "*Come on. Start being more optimistic and not so doom and gloom. This should be an exciting time in our lives. What better time to go for something like this than now, before we have kids?*"

We'd never discussed kids. I pulled back my hands and looked more closely at Graham's numbers. He hovered over me as I did, occasionally pointing and explaining the numbers to me. What I'd initially thought to be a detailed statement seemed to be a lot more speculative upon closer inspection.

"*Do you think maybe you've underestimated the start-up costs? I've read with start-up businesses you should assume that you won't make a profit for at least the first six months, sometimes as long as eighteen months. And you don't have any salaries here for either of us. How will we pay our bills?*"

Graham groaned, stepped in front of me, gathered his materials, and closed the file. "*Excuse me for trying to do something to improve our situation. In case you're forgetting, I'm the one who went to college, and I'm the one with the advanced degree, and I'm the one who's been working the past three years in corporate law.*" He shook his head and turned his back to me. "*You know what, forget it. Just forget I ever mentioned it.*"

He tossed his file on the coffee table, walked back to the front door, and grabbed his car keys off the counter.

"*Where are you going?*" I asked.

"*Out,*" he said.

The door slammed shut. Minutes later, the Porsche roared as it exited the underground garage and accelerated down the street. I looked out the window at the glow of the streetlamp and the tops of the trees planted in the sidewalk. The moon had settled over the bridge, light reflecting off the river. After a moment, I reconsidered the file on the table, opened it, and studied the numbers again.

CHAPTER 7

Having lived her entire life in the Pacific Northwest, Tracy was familiar with both the statistical facts and the mystique of Mount Rainier. At more than 14,000 feet, Rainier wasn't just a mountain, it was a volcano of head-swiveling immensity that dominated the region. Visible for hundreds of miles in every direction, it was so immense and tall it created its own weather patterns. Even when the mountain could not be seen, when the Pacific Northwest gray hung like a thick curtain over the region, you could sense the mountain's presence. Seattleites said things like, "The mountain is out," as if Rainier were a living, breathing thing.

As beautiful as Rainier was, its allure could frequently be deadly. Thousands attempted to reach its summit each year, though more than half failed. Some died. Of those who had perished, some had never been found, their bodies buried under avalanches of ice, snow, and rock, or frozen at the bottom of hundred-foot-deep crevasses.

For someone looking to fake her own death, Mount Rainier was the perfect killer.

Just short of an hour and a half after leaving Seattle, Kins drove beneath the peaked pediment designating the northeast entrance to Mount Rainier National Park. He followed the road to an American flag hanging from a pole outside a log cabin no bigger than a schoolhouse set amid tall pines.

When Tracy stepped from the car and stretched the tightness from her body, she smelled the familiar scent of wintergreen, which made her fondly recall growing up in the North Cascades, but also the odor of ash and soot. A rust-colored haze from fires raging unabated in eastern Washington choked the air.

She and Kins entered the White River Ranger Station. A ranger greeted them in khaki shorts, a matching short-sleeved shirt, and boots. "You must be the two detectives from Seattle." He extended a hand. "I'm Glenn Hicks. We've had our share of weirdness, but this takes the cake."

"Ditto," Kins said.

Hicks stood an inch or so shorter than Tracy, perhaps five foot nine, but with a wiry build, meaty forearms, and prominent calves. His hairline had receded, which was ironic because hair seemed to cover every other visible part of his body. A five o'clock shadow and tufted eyebrows that sloped in toward the bridge of his nose gave him a perpetually disappointed look.

"Come on back," Hicks said, inviting them behind a wood counter to an office not much bigger than a child's bedroom. A wooden desk reminded Tracy of the teachers' desks at Cedar Grove Middle School. On it rested a lone manila file.

"When was this cabin built?" Tracy asked.

"The station?" Hicks said. "1929. They built them to last back then, though without many amenities." He stepped behind the desk. "You have the picture?" he asked, clearly interested in getting to the bottom of the mystery.

Tracy opened her leather saddlebag and pulled out the picture of Lynn Hoff's driver's license. This was not a photocopy but a five-by-eight glossy Faz had obtained from DOL. She handed it across the desk. Hicks put on a pair of cheaters, held up the picture to consider it, then methodically opened the file on his desk, pulled out a second photograph, and held the two side by side, eyes shifting back and forth between them. His head did that slow shake of someone who couldn't believe he'd had one pulled over on him.

"That's her," he said, jaw taut. "I don't know who Lynn Hoff is, but that right there is Andrea Strickland."

He handed both photographs to Tracy and Kins. They compared the two. Though in the DOL's photograph Strickland wore thick-framed glasses, it was not difficult to tell it was the same person.

"I have others," Hicks said, opening a manila envelope and taking out color photographs. "Her husband provided them just about four weeks ago, when we thought she'd gone missing on the mountain."

In one, Andrea Strickland stood on a rock, dressed in shorts and a tank top, a long-sleeve shirt tied around her waist, the immense summit of Mount Rainier rising up behind her.

"What can you tell us about that?" Tracy said.

"I can tell you she apparently caused us a lot of unnecessary aggravation and put the lives of my rangers at risk," Hicks said, sounding like a jilted lover. "Someone who does this has to be incredibly selfish."

Well, she's dead, so she paid the ultimate price, Tracy wanted to say, but refrained. She and Kins were content to let Hicks vent. He had the right. Andrea Strickland *had* pulled one over on Hicks and his men. She'd pulled one over on everyone, except the person who'd eventually found and killed her.

Hicks swiveled his chair, which squeaked and creaked, and pointed to a tattered US Geological topo map on the wall. The area looked to be of the entire park, pocked with prominent red Xs, some circled. "The Xs mark the locations where each person still missing on the mountain was last seen. The ones circled are the bodies we've eventually located and recovered. Sometimes it's a few days. Sometimes it can be months and years. Sometimes they're never found. With the warm weather the past few years, the glaciers are receding at an unprecedented rate. We're finding bodies of climbers gone missing for decades, and let me tell you, it never becomes routine. You're haunted by the ones you can't find, always second-guessing yourself, wondering if maybe they were just a few yards from where you were probing the snow, or lying in a crevasse just beneath your boots."

Hicks opened the desk drawer, took out a permanent marker, and drew a circle around one of the Xs. He capped the pen and looked back at them. "Andrea Strickland. I don't need names. I can plot where each climber was last seen in my sleep." Hicks's finger moved to the specific areas as he said them, "Near Success Cleaver, a crevasse on the Cowlitz Glacier, in the Carbon River area." He tapped the pen on the X he had just circled. "Liberty Ridge. You know why we work so hard to get the bodies back?"

Tracy did. She'd spent twenty years looking for Sarah, though she'd known with near certainty they would find only her remains. "Closure for the families," she said.

"Closure for the families." Hicks nodded. "Not everyone buys our bullshit that the mountain is a beautiful final resting place for their loved ones. I don't blame them. But it's also closure for us. May 30, 2014, we lost six in one incident. We found three of the bodies last summer. Some years, like last year, we get lucky and don't lose any. It's a tough mountain and it can turn mean in a hurry. One minute the sun is out and the next it's a whiteout and the wind is blowing eighty miles an hour. You can never predict what it might do on any given day, and that means you can never relax. That radio can go off at any moment."

"What can you tell us about Andrea Strickland?" Tracy asked.

Hicks realized he'd been venting. "Sorry. I guess I'm a little emotional about this."

"No worries," Kins said. "I'd say you have the right."

Hicks took a moment to gather his composure. "Andrea Strickland and her husband, Graham, took out a wilderness permit to climb

Liberty Ridge on May 13, 2017. Liberty Ridge is no picnic. It's one of the least climbed paths to the summit."

"How many paths are there?" Kins asked.

"Fifty, at least."

"And this one is not frequently climbed because it's difficult or dangerous?" Tracy asked.

"Both. It's not technically challenging. There are one or two spots where you have to rope up and belay someone, but you're not climbing ice cliffs."

"What makes it so difficult?" Tracy said.

"The north face of the mountain—Willis Wall. It can be like a bowling alley, especially the last few years with the warmer weather. As the glacier melts and the snow destabilizes, rocks and boulders tumble down the slope."

"So not many people on that route," Kins said.

"No," Hicks said, "which might be why they chose it."

"What do you mean?" Tracy asked.

"I checked the permits taken out that weekend, hoping someone might have seen her. No one else took out a permit to climb that route that weekend. They went early in the season for Liberty Ridge, which is limited to a six-week-to-two-month window of opportunity, weather permitting. I remember questioning the husband about why they'd chosen to climb that route so soon in the season."

"What did he say?" Tracy asked.

"He said they wanted the challenge, that they'd done Disappointment Cleaver and the Emmons Glacier. Those are the two most popular routes. Turns out, only she made the summit on Disappointment Cleaver. He crapped out. Altitude sickness. They didn't climb Emmons Glacier. He lied. I found that out after the fact."

"Why would he lie?"

"To get the Liberty Ridge permit. Make it look like they had experience. He talked a big game, I remember that."

"So they weren't that experienced?" Tracy said.

"Experience is a broad spectrum. They'd climbed before, but I wouldn't call either 'experienced' and I told them so."

"I take it they didn't have a guide?" Kins asked.

"No." Hicks leaned back. "Twenty-five percent of the fatalities on the mountain each year occur on that route. Guides don't like it."

"So what did happen?" Kins asked.

Hicks chuckled but there was no joy in it. "Well, now I'm not so sure."

"What did the husband say happened?" Tracy asked.

"The husband came down all flustered and exhausted. He said they'd climbed up to Thumb Rock. Hang on." Hicks opened desk drawers and pulled out a map, unfolding it and turning it to face Tracy and Kins. He leaned over the desk, pencil in hand. "Okay, like I said, they took out a wilderness permit May thirteenth here at the Wilderness Information Center. The Liberty Ridge climb can take anywhere from three to five days. Most do it in three. I know people who have done it in two. The husband said they left the White River Campground and spent the first night at the Glacier Basin Camp." Hicks scribbled a few pencil lines to indicate the area. "The next day they hiked here, to the Wedge. The route to the left takes you to Camp Schurman over the Emmons Glacier. To the right is the Liberty Ridge route. They crossed Saint Elmo Pass, descended onto the Winthrop Glacier, and made their way to Curtis Ridge and set up camp the second night. He said they awoke at midnight, roped up, and made their way up to Thumb Rock." Hicks circled the two words on the map.

"They hiked at night?" Kins said.

"You go when it's cold out to minimize the chances of getting hit by loose rock and because the snow is firmer and easier to climb. That's about a four-to-five-hour hike from about 8,800 feet to just under 11,000 feet. They set up camp at Thumb Rock the third night."

"And they were alone?" Tracy asked. "No other climbers up there."

"No," Hicks said. "But this is where the husband's story started to break down, or at least I thought it did." Hicks stretched his back as if it hurt him. "He says they had a light dinner, drank tea, and went inside their tent at around eight to rest. They planned to get up at one and head for the summit. He said he heard Andrea get up but he didn't check the time. She told him she was going out to pee and he says he went back to sleep." Hicks made a face like he wasn't buying it. "He claims he slept through his alarm, that when he woke it was morning and his wife wasn't in the tent. When he went outside looking for her, she was nowhere to be found. He made it here to the ranger station at just after five that afternoon and reported her missing."

"Why didn't he call? Why did he wait until he got back down?" Kins asked.

"Cell reception is spotty at best on the mountain."

"What was his demeanor?" Tracy asked.

"Measured," Hicks said without hesitation.

"So not panicked or distraught?" Tracy said.

Hicks shook his head. "If anything, I'd say he looked and sounded more confused than distraught. He said he didn't know why his wife might have wandered off or what could have happened. Then he started hypothesizing, saying that maybe she'd gone out to go to the bathroom and became disoriented, lost her way, and fell off the side of the mountain. Here's what I don't understand. She doesn't come back and he doesn't go looking for her immediately? People are anxious the night before a climb. They don't sleep well, if at all. This guy says he slept through his alarm? I was dead certain he pushed her over the edge."

"Did you find any sign of her?" Tracy asked.

"We did," Hicks said with just the hint of a smile. "The search involved about twenty people, climbing rangers, and Nordic Ski Patrol Search and Rescue. I had members of the Tacoma, Everett, and Seattle mountain rescue units conducting the ground search, and the US Army Reserve 214th Aviation Battalion from Lewis-McChord conducting the air search. Like I said, a lot of resources and a lot of money. We arrived at Thumb Rock late the following afternoon. The air search spotted what appeared to be a debris field here, at the base of the Willis Wall."

Hicks made a mark on the map.

"A debris field of what?" Kins asked.

"Crampons, a pack, water bottle, a few articles of clothing."

"The husband identified them?"

"He did."

"But no body?"

"No body."

"How far a fall is that?" Tracy asked.

"Couple thousand feet."

"Seems if there was debris there'd be a body," Kins said.

"Not necessarily. I can tell you what we were thinking at the time. There's a bergschrund at the base of the wall." Hicks continued to use the pencil on the topo map.

"A bergschrund?" Tracy asked.

"It's a German term. It means a large crevasse where the glacier ice separates from the headwall."

"And the presumption was she fell into that crevasse, never to be found," Kins said.

Hicks nodded. "No way to get her body out of there. The Willis Wall cleaves constantly. My climbing rangers won't go there and I don't blame them."

"So the perfect place for someone to stage their own death," Tracy said.

"Apparently, but that's not what I was thinking at the time."

"You thought it was the perfect place for the husband to kill his wife," Kins said.

"No reason for her to put on her crampons and other gear just to go to the bathroom."

"Makes sense," Tracy said.

Hicks sat and leaned back. "I was convinced he shoved her over the side—right up until I came in late yesterday and saw that flier on my computer you sent out. I don't forget those missing on the mountain," he said. "They're permanently imprinted on my mind."

"So what do you think happened now?" Kins asked.

"Now? Now, I don't know what to think. But I'll tell you this. She didn't make it off that mountain on her own. No way. Somebody had to have helped her. Hell, the husband could have been in on it for the insurance money. The Pierce County detective said they took out a policy and there were problems in the marriage," Hicks said.

Tracy had made contact with the Pierce County Sheriff's Office that morning. They had an appointment to speak to the investigating detective from the Major Crimes Division later that day.

"I spoke to the detective this morning. He said the husband was a person of interest," Tracy said.

"Maybe." Hicks picked up Andrea Strickland's picture. "Thing is, I don't know now if this exonerates him or implicates him." Hicks looked up at the red X he'd circled. "But I guess that's not my job anymore. My job is done; looks like yours is just getting started."

CHAPTER 8

I'd had more than my share of doubts about Genesis, but Graham had been so optimistic, so sure of its success, that I had finally relented, despite my reservations. I don't want to say Graham wore me down, or that I caved to his repeated attempts at persuading me, but it had become so unbearable at home I knew we couldn't go on the way we had been. Graham would come home and slowly begin with the numbers, then tell me he'd spoken to another dispensary in Washington and about how much money we would make. When I tried to question his numbers, he would dismiss me or accuse me of not supporting him. Then he would either leave pissed off and not come back until late, or sulk the rest of the evening and not say two words. He needed my income to get the loan.

When I finally said yes, his eyes widened like a man who'd just been told he was cancer free, and he gave me a bear hug and a kiss.

"You're not going to regret this," he said, holding me by the shoulders. "This will be the best money we've ever invested." Then he hugged me again.

"I hope you're right," I said, trying to smile through my apprehension.

"I can feel this, Andrea." He paced the apartment. "I can feel this is going to be my big chance."

We'd lit a strawberry-scented candle and made love that night on the couch, the way we had when first married, like it mattered. Like I mattered.

Thereafter, our lovemaking sessions continued almost nightly, until we went to visit the banker about our business loan. We had to disclose our assets and debts. The only debt I knew of was the lease on Graham's Porsche. We had no real savings, despite Graham saying we'd save money because he'd moved into my loft. I was uncomfortable with him lying about becoming a partner at BSBT, and already nervous when we sat down on the opposite side of the desk from the banker—a tall, officious-looking man with a head of silver hair who asked a lot of questions and filled out forms.

After about forty-five minutes, he looked rather grave and said to Graham, "You have quite a bit of credit card debt."

I was not aware of that.

"I had a sick parent and I'm the primary caregiver," he said. "But that's over now."

I was surprised at the ease with which Graham lied.

"Well, do you have a way to pay that down?" the banker asked.

"I'm going to have a substantial increase in income when I make partner," Graham said.

"When will that be?"

"I believe it's first of the year," Graham said.

"Perhaps you could provide a letter from the law firm confirming that?"

"Certainly," Graham said.

Maybe it was my nerves, but I suddenly felt compelled to mention my parents' trust, though its terms would not allow me to use it as collateral.

Graham went white as a sheet. I swear I could hear the thud of his jaw hitting the desk. He leaned forward, though there was no way the banker could not overhear our conversation.

"You have a trust?" he said.

I glanced at the banker. He sat with the uncomfortable smile of a man who'd walked in on an argument and was trying to find an inconspicuous way to exit. He made an excuse about having to find some other form, and left his desk.

"What are you talking about?" Graham asked.

"When my parents died, their estate was left for me in trust. I gained limited access to it when I turned twenty-one."

Graham stared at me with a look of disbelief, then glanced over his shoulder to be sure the banker was out of earshot. He leaned even closer, his jaw taut and his voice hushed. "Jesus H. Christ, Andrea. When did you plan on telling me about this?"

"I didn't think it was relevant," I said.

"Not relevant?" He cleared his throat and sat back, lips pursed. "What are we doing here?" He asked the question in that patronizing voice I hated, like I was a child. "We're borrowing money that we're going to be paying interest on because I thought we needed it."

"We do need it."

"Maybe not," he said. "How much is the trust?"

"It's not important, Graham."

He scoffed. "Not important? I'm your husband. What other secrets have you been keeping from me?"

"What? I'm not keeping . . . No, that's not what I mean."

"What do you mean? Because it sure sounds like you've been keeping a very big secret from me."

"I mean it's not relevant because we can't use the trust. We can't use the money."

"You mean you won't use it."

"No, I mean we can't."

His cheeks flushed red and his blue eyes became more a shade of gray. "Why the hell not?"

"Because of the way my parents had the trust set up. It's designated as my separate property and has restrictions on how it can be used. It can't be invested in a business. It's just for my well-being."

"Your parents are dead," he said, emphasizing each word.

"I'm aware of that, Graham, but the terms of the trust still remain in place. When I turned twenty-one I had full say in the use of the interest, but there are restrictions on the principal until I turn thirty-five. My parents set it up that way so I would always be taken care of."

In truth, I knew my parents well enough to know they'd set it up that way so no one could ever take advantage of me, marry me believing they would get half the money, or take it from me in a divorce.

"So it's yours and yours alone?" Graham said.

"Technically, yes."

"What does that mean, 'technically'?"

"It means, what do you think I've been using to help make ends meet each month when we didn't have enough money to pay the rent or the lease on the Porsche and the other expenses? I've been using the interest money I get from the trust."

"Oh, so you're saying, what? I'm some kind of sponge?"

"No, I'm not saying that." I wanted to scream.

"How much is the trust?"

I didn't want to answer.

His jaw clenched. *"How much, Andrea?"*

"The principal is half a million dollars."

Graham scoffed and laughed at once. It sounded almost like a man choking. *"Are you kidding me? You're sitting on half a million dollars? What the hell are we doing here?"*

"I told you, I can't use it—"

"Andrea, I'm a lawyer. Every contract can be broken and a trust is basically a contract."

"Not this one," I said. *"My trustee said my parents had it put together so that it can't be broken."*

He shook his head and rolled his eyes. *"Why don't you let me worry about that? Can you get the money?"*

"It can't be done, Graham."

"Can you get it?"

"I can get it, but I can't use it for this type of stuff. So I say we end the lease on the Porsche, apply that money to your credit card debt, and get our loan as we'd intended."

Graham bit his lower lip and rolled his eyes. "You want me to give up my Porsche? I'm a lawyer, Andrea. I have to maintain a certain image."

"But you won't be a lawyer anymore."

Thankfully, the banker cleared his throat when he came back to his desk. "Are we set to move forward?" he asked.

Graham still looked angry but he smiled as if nothing was wrong. "Of course," he said. "Let's get this ball rolling."

Graham remained upset for the next two days. He traded in his Porsche and we applied the lease payment to his credit card bill. I also chipped in another $2,000. "I intend to pay you back," he said. I wasn't holding my breath. Nor did I really care. I'd never cared about money. I'd gotten by with virtually nothing my entire life, and now it seemed money just created problems.

The third day, Graham came home with a bouquet of flowers and an apology. I almost wished he hadn't. Just when I thought I'd figured out his mood for the week, it would swing again.

"I'm sorry I've been such a jerk," he said, handing me the fragrant bouquet. "It's just that you really caught me out of the blue at the bank and I felt like I'd been put in an embarrassing situation, you know? I mean, here I was getting ready to take out a bank loan, and I'm supposed to be a lawyer, and I didn't even know my wife had this massive trust."

"I should have told you," I said, though it was more to appease him. "It's just, like I said, I didn't think it would make any difference since we can't use it."

"Then why did you bring it up?"

"I was nervous. I didn't want you to lie on a bank application and say you were going to be made a partner of the firm."

He smiled, but it was patronizing. "Andrea, you're such a Goody Two-shoes. Nobody is going to check on that, but it's cute that you were looking out for me. And I get it. We can't use the trust for the business, but hey, it's nice to know that we have it, right? I mean, it's like we have a net under the trapeze."

"What do you mean?" I asked, suddenly leery of where he was taking the conversation.

"I mean we can use it if things get a little tight getting the business up and running, or to do things like travel—or buy a boat, you know, fun things as a couple. Wouldn't it be great to have a boat? I mean we can use it like that, can't we?"

"I suppose," I said, wary. "The interest anyway."

He leaned closer. "Do you forgive me?"

"Sure," I said. What else was I to do?

"You know what I want to do?" He moved quickly, the way he did when he had a thought that excited him. I was praying he wasn't about to say, "Have sex."

"I want to go out to dinner and celebrate our new business. Someplace special."

With Graham I was learning that "special" meant "expensive," and I already knew whose credit card we'd be using.

Over the next two months the bank approved the loan, and Graham searched for space to rent and researched inventory. He'd been energized, upbeat, and excited like the Graham I'd met and married. He couldn't get enough of me either. We had sex all over the loft, and in creative ways. I'd tried to be optimistic that the business would succeed, but my doubt grew when Graham told me he'd found a small shop right there in the Pearl District, which was one of the highest-rent districts in Portland—and that was saying something. I'd read an article that said, since 2015, Portland's residential and commercial rents had shot through the roof. All the newspapers lamented how Portland was losing its identity as longtime residents and small businesses were forced farther and farther out of the city core. The rent on my loft had skyrocketed from $900 a month to $1,250 in just three years, and the space Graham chose to open Genesis was $23 a square foot.

I tried to persuade him to open the dispensary in a more industrial area where the rent was $11 a square foot, where we would have plenty of parking, and where we would be farther away from the medical dispensaries, but Graham dismissed it.

"It's the first rule of real estate," he said. "Location, location, location. We're going to be in a prime location within walking distance of all the businesses and law firms, and that's where the money is. Those are the people we are going to cater to. Besides, think of the money we'll save by not having to drive."

Between the bank loan payment, the rents on the loft and the building space, and Graham's lease on his Porsche—which he renewed once we got the loan—we were going to have to clear close to $6,000 a month just to break even. That didn't include our regular expenses or the cost of the business permit to sell marijuana, and Graham had pretty much blown through the loan on our portion of the tenant improvements and other start-up costs. He kept opting for upgrades like Brazilian hardwood floors and high-end glass cabinets with recessed lighting to display the different kinds of pot, as if it were jewelry.

"I want this place to shout 'class' when people come in," he said. "I don't want to be catering to some lowlife losers."

I didn't care who we catered to so long as those lowlife losers had real American dollars, but if I expressed any reservation or tried to get him to opt for a cheaper alternative, he'd just smile and say, "Relax, we have the trust income we can pull from if we're a little short this month."

Beyond all of that, I was worried because I'd been reading that city officials were contemplating allowing Portland's medical marijuana dispensaries to sell to recreational users. It would be a huge windfall for the dispensaries. They wouldn't have the same start-up costs and could drive down the price, not to mention increase competition. When I brought it up with Graham, however, he dismissed it. "Those places are pits. That is not our clientele. And our reputation is already spreading."

And it seemed it was—to some extent anyway. They ran an article in the Portland Tribune—the free weekly paper—and it included a picture of Graham standing beneath the store entrance and green neon Genesis sign. Graham had framed the article and the photograph and hung both on a wall in the store.

And for those first few months, Graham came home happy and our lovemaking sessions remained frequent and fierce, and I thought that maybe, just maybe, everything was going to be all right.

CHAPTER 9

Tracy scanned the significant number of web hits for Andrea Strickland on her iPad as Kins drove down the mountain. With a portion of Mount Rainier located in Pierce County, the Pierce County Sheriff's Department had asserted jurisdiction over the disappearance of Andrea Strickland. The case had generated a lot of publicity. The DA had been careful not to call Graham Strickland a suspect—but, of course, he was. He was the prime suspect. The infamous murder of a pregnant Laci Peterson in Modesto, California, had beaten that point home. The sad truth was that more people died at the hands of people they knew, and loved, than from some random killer.

Stan Fields, the detective from Pierce County's Major Crimes Division, told Tracy over the phone he'd be "happy to speak with her." She sensed that Fields, like Ranger Glenn Hicks, didn't appreciate having the wool pulled over his eyes by Andrea Strickland, or by both her and her husband.

And Andrea Strickland had fooled them. She'd fooled everybody, at least for six weeks. Everybody but the person who'd eventually killed her.

Fields's ego likely wouldn't let him admit he'd been fooled. No detective *liked* to admit that, which was why, during what should have been a short telephone conversation to set up their meeting, Fields had felt compelled to add that he'd *suspected* things were "not as they'd seemed."

When Tracy sensed the content of the Internet articles becoming redundant, she closed her iPad and wedged it in the space between her seat and the center console. She grabbed her plastic water bottle and took a sip, but the water had become lukewarm. Even in the air-conditioned car, she felt sticky from the heat.

"She was the perfect candidate to disappear," she said, returning her water bottle to its designated holder. "Parents deceased. No siblings. No one to miss her."

"Except, of course, the husband," Kins said. He shifted in his seat, also looking uncomfortable, and no doubt wishing he could exchange his blue jeans for a pair of shorts like Ranger Hicks wore. Blue jeans were standard attire for Kins when not in court, and it seemed an odd choice. Four years of college football and a year in the NFL had left him with overdeveloped calves and thighs even a decade after he'd retired. "I'm assuming no kids?"

"Thankfully not," Tracy said.

"Work colleagues?"

"She and her husband owned a marijuana dispensary in downtown Portland. It was just the two of them."

Oregon had followed Washington and Colorado in legalizing marijuana, which had come as little surprise to anyone who knew the state's politics. The populace was generally considered even more liberal than western Washington, which was saying a lot.

"Like I said, she wasn't going to be missed." Kins glanced in the rearview mirror, put on a blinker, and exited the highway. "What did they do before selling dope?"

"He's an attorney. She worked at an insurance company in downtown Portland."

That caused Kins to glance over at her. "Insurance?"

"I've got it on the list of questions to ask him about."

"So neither of them was stupid."

"Definitely not stupid," Tracy agreed. She adjusted the vents on the dash so the cool air hit her neck and chest, and she fanned her shirt.

They drove through Tacoma's mostly deserted surface streets, residents seeking refuge in air-conditioned offices and retail establishments.

"How far did Pierce County get in their investigation of the husband?" Kins asked.

"According to the detective, and the articles I've found, the DA named him as a person of interest but not a suspect," Tracy said.

"So he was *the* suspect," Kins said.

"Clearly."

"But not charged?"

"Without the body they probably didn't think they had sufficient evidence," Tracy said. "Only two people know what happened on that mountain, and one was presumed dead. So everything's circumstantial."

"Hopefully, this guy Fields can shed some light on it."

Stan Fields had suggested they meet at a restaurant on Pacific Avenue called Viola. The last time Tracy had visited Tacoma, a decade earlier, Pacific Avenue had been a haven for prostitutes and drug dealers, the buildings graffiti-tagged with gang symbols and the streets littered with trash. Downtown Tacoma had been undergoing a massive renovation by community activists and business leaders tired of the city being known as the blue-collar stepchild to Seattle—more for a blend of industrial stink referred to as "the aroma of Tacoma." Pacific Avenue was clearly a part of that renovation. The two- and three-story stucco and brick industrial buildings had been renovated and freshly painted. Storefront advertising revealed professional businesses, retail stores, boutique shops, and restaurants.

Kins found a parking spot at a meter half a block from the restaurant. As they approached, Tracy noticed a man standing outside the restaurant, smoking in a patch of shade. He made eye contact, nodded, and blew out smoke. "You Crosswhite?" he said.

Stan Fields looked like a holdover from the seventies, with slate-gray hair pulled back in a short ponytail. A bushy mustache drooped below the corners of his mouth as if weighted by the heat. Fields wore a dark-blue polo shirt that bore the department's emblem—the words "Pierce County Sheriff" stitched in gold over snow-covered Mount Rainier.

Tracy introduced herself and Kins. "I got a table inside," Fields said. He raised the cigarette to his lips for the final extended drag of a chain-smoker about to go cold turkey for at least half an hour, then blew a stream of smoke into the sky and flicked the burning cigarette into the gutter.

Viola had glass doors pulled back on runners to allow for outdoor seating, though today no one sat at the sun-drenched wrought-iron tables and chairs. The open doors allowed the heat, sticky as syrup, to seep inside, and the overhead ceiling paddles looked sluggish in their effort to offer relief. Tracy removed her sunglasses. It took a moment for her eyes to adjust to the darkened interior. Fields led them to a booth near the kitchen, the brick walls adorned with colorful Impressionist paintings.

Tracy and Kins slid across the booth from Fields onto a leather bench seat. Sweat trickled down Tracy's back from the short walk and caused her shirt to stick to her skin.

Fields nodded to two glasses on their side of the table. "I ordered you water—figured you'd be thirsty after the drive."

Tracy and Kins thanked him. Each took long drinks. What Tracy wanted was to run the cool glass over her forehead and down her neck but decided it would be unprofessional.

"I moved here to *escape* the heat," Fields said, sounding perturbed. Most Northwest transplants complained about the rain and overcast gray skies. It rang odd to hear someone complain about the heat—though Seattleites were quick to blame their changing weather patterns on global warming, or what Faz unapologetically called "global whining."

"Where're you from?" Tracy asked.

Rich smells of garlic and butter and sage wafted from the kitchen.

"Phoenix," Fields said, "but I moved around a lot as a kid; my dad was in the army."

"The hottest summer I ever spent was a winter in Phoenix," Kins said.

"Tell me about it." Fields had a habit of twitching his mouth, which made his mustache move like the whiskers of a mouse, likely a tic. "I started out running the borders down there with INS, then moved to narcotics, mostly undercover. Spent more time than I cared to in the desert tracking drug runners."

Fields had the weathered face of someone whom the sun had baked for a few years. With the ponytail and gravelly voice of a smoker, he fit the part of an undercover narcotics agent, and Tracy was picking up the cocky demeanor those officers needed to be convincing.

"Tough gig," Kins said. "Wears you out after a few years."

"Yeah, you do it?" Fields asked.

"Two years," Kins said.

Kins had grown out his hair and a wispy goatee, and someone in narcotics had christened him "Sparrow" after the Johnny Depp character in the *Pirates of the Caribbean* movies. The nickname stuck. Unlike Fields, however, Kins had been eager to cut his hair and shave when he left narcotics.

"When did you move to Tacoma?" Kins asked, running a finger along the condensation on the outside of his glass. Tracy sensed he was giving them all a chance to settle in, while also getting a feel for Fields. Fields was likely doing the same.

"Just about a year ago. I lost my wife and needed a change of scenery. I was tired of the heat and the sun. I was looking for rain and fog. Seattle wasn't hiring detectives but Tacoma was."

"Sorry about your wife," Tracy said.

Fields gave a curt nod. "She was undercover too, got too close. Someone ratted her out. They shot her and left her in the desert."

The news gave Tracy a different perspective of Fields, who at first impression didn't evoke much sympathy. Losing a spouse was horrific under any circumstances, but losing a spouse in the line of duty, and in that manner, could eat at a person. No wonder Fields had left Arizona.

"Did they get the people who did it?" Kins asked.

Fields gave them a sidelong glance, intended to convey they'd done more than arrest the killers. "Yeah. We got 'em."

The waitress appeared and Fields shifted his gaze, grinning at the tall young woman like she was on the appetizer menu. "You got the company card?" he asked Tracy, meaning the ability to expense the meal.

"Yeah," Kins said.

"Then I'll take a sixteen-ounce pale ale and your linguini and clams," Fields said without considering a menu. "Tell the chef I like enough garlic so my cat won't love me for a week." He gave the waitress a wink. The young woman responded with an uncomfortable smile and quickly looked to Tracy and Kins's side of the table.

"Diet Coke," Kins said. "And a bucket of water I can throw over my head."

The waitress smiled.

Tracy said she was good with the glass of water.

Fields gave the waitress's backside a lingering once-over when she turned and walked off, which was not only disrespectful but ridiculous. He was old enough to be the young woman's father, but in Tracy's experience that didn't stop some men from thinking they had a chance.

Fields reengaged Tracy. If he was self-conscious Tracy had busted him, he didn't show it. In fact, she got the impression he enjoyed getting caught. Pathetic.

"Nothing to eat?" Fields said. "Best perk of the job."

"We stopped for a late lunch," Tracy said, feeling nauseated.

Fields draped an arm over the back of the booth. "So, Andrea Strickland is dead . . . again."

"Apparently so," Tracy said.

The mustache twitched. "I'd have bet my badge the husband gave her a little shove off the mountain. I was sure he killed her."

"Maybe he still did," Kins said.

"Maybe," Fields said.

"Can you fill us in on your investigation?" Kins asked.

The waitress set Fields's beer and Kins's Diet Coke on coasters. Fields took more than a sip and wiped foam from his mustache with the paper napkin. "His story didn't add up." He set down his beer and sat back, again draping one arm over the back of the booth. "It stunk. Wife gets up to take a pee and he doesn't get up with her? Or wonder where she is? You talk to people who climb that mountain and they'll tell you they don't sleep well, if at all, the night before they summit. They lay down when it's still light out and the adrenaline and anxiety are pumping, but this guy says he slept so soundly he didn't even know she was gone? Come on. So my radar was already pinging before I ever met the guy." He looked at Tracy and his eyes took a quick dive to her cleavage. "And my radar is rarely wrong."

"What'd you find?" Tracy asked, her skin now crawling for reasons that had nothing to do with the heat.

"Turns out the wife took out an insurance policy naming him the beneficiary shortly before they climbed. Quarter of a million bucks. That was the first red flag."

"Did he take out a policy naming her?" Kins asked.

"Nope," Fields said. "He said she had some kind of trust fund from her parents and, according to him, he and the wife figured if anything happened to him she'd be fine. That was his story, anyway. Me? I'm thinking that he's thinking: *Why pay a second premium?*"

"We understand they'd climbed before," Tracy said.

"Once, and didn't take out policies," Fields said, finishing her thought. "And the wife worked for an insurance company before they opened the marijuana shop."

"So she knew the ins and outs of the business?" Tracy asked.

"She was a flunky, but according to her boss, she was smart, picked up things quick."

"You consider they could have been in on something together?" Kins asked.

"I was working under the strong premise he killed her, but yeah, I was open to that possibility."

"Did the husband recover the insurance proceeds?"

"Not yet, not with the investigation active, but he wasted no time filing for the benefits after he got off the mountain. I made a call. His claim is still under investigation. Looks like it will be a while."

Tracy looked to Kins. "If the husband and wife had been working together—the delay might not have been something they'd anticipated."

"Or the husband could have made the wife think they were in it together, then killed her. Since she was already technically dead, and no one was going to find her body in a crab pot, no one would be any wiser," Kins said.

"Maybe," Tracy said. "But if that was the case, why wouldn't he just push her off the mountain? Why wait to kill her?"

"The husband's one of those guys that's just easy to not like—you know the type?" Fields said over the sound of banging pans and voices coming from the kitchen.

Tracy did. She was sitting across from one of them. "Anything else set off your radar?" she asked.

"Yeah. Their new business venture wasn't doing well. In fact, it had tanked," Fields said. "No surprise there. Husband set it up in a high-rent district in downtown Portland thinking they'd be a more upscale establishment and capture all the business-crowd potheads. Here's a fun fact: turns out Portland has more medical marijuana dispensaries than almost any other city in the country. What a surprise, huh? Well, shortly after the law went into effect legalizing marijuana, a city ordinance allowed the dispensaries to sell retail. Two were close to the Stricklands' store. Portland also has a robust black market—meaning the non-business crowd had a readily available and cheaper source."

"How bad was it?" Tracy asked.

"I got the sense talking with the wife's boss that Andrea Strickland had been more than reticent about the business, but the husband had talked her into it. She had a large trust—"

"How large?" Tracy asked.

Fields smiled. "The principal was half a million dollars."

"No shit," Kins said.

"No shit. But the terms prohibited her from using it to start a business," Fields said.

Kins whistled.

"Tell me about it," Fields said. "So they borrowed $250,000 from the bank, and signed personal guarantees on both the lease and on the loan. Also turns out the husband lied on the loan application."

"Lied how?" Tracy asked.

"Said he was being made a partner of his firm, with a substantial increase in salary—even presented a letter from the managing partner. Turns out he forged the letter. The firm had already told him to hit the bricks."

The waitress arrived with Fields's linguini. He lowered his arm and asked for grated cheese. Tracy watched him eye the woman's breasts as she worked the hunk of Parmesan over the grater. The long hair and mustache weren't the only things Fields had kept from his undercover days; some of the sleaze had also rubbed off on him. Any sympathy she'd felt for him for having lost his wife had quickly waned.

"Thank you, darling," Fields said when the young woman finished. As the waitress departed, probably to take a scalding shower in disinfectant, Fields looked to Kins and Tracy. "You sure you don't want anything? It's good food. I come here at least once a week."

The waitresses must have been thrilled about that.

"We're good," Kins said.

Fields twirled his fork in the pasta and brought a ball to his mouth. He wouldn't have to worry about his cat. From the smell drifting across the table, the garlic was strong enough to kill a grizzly.

"What more can you tell us about the husband?" Tracy asked.

Fields wiped his mustache on his napkin and sipped his beer. "Like I said, a big shot. Drove a Porsche and wore those suits that look like they're a size too small. Smarter than everybody too, always looking for the next big deal just around the corner, and believed it was just a matter of time before one of them paid off. Big bullshitter. I think he convinced the wife this was their ticket. They pretty much liquidated all their community assets and put it into the store. He'd also maxed out their credit cards and the creditors were calling. And like I said, the bank found out about the forged letter from the law firm, and he was looking at criminal prosecution and maybe a little jail time if he couldn't pay back the money."

"So you thought he was after the wife's trust?" Kins said.

"I did," Fields said in between another bite of his pasta. "Seems that money disappeared from Andrea's personal account."

"Disappeared where?" Tracy asked.

"Don't know. The husband swears he had nothing to do with it and has no idea where it went."

"What about the trustee?"

"Same thing. No idea."

"You think the husband and wife could have been trying to hide it from the creditors?"

"Yep. You said she had a Washington license under a different name?"

"Lynn Hoff," Tracy said.

"Then I'm betting that's where you'll find the money."

Tracy recalled the receipt for the Emerald Credit Union she'd found in the garbage can at the motel room.

Fields sat back with a shit-eating grin. "Then there was the little issue of the girlfriend."

"I figured that was coming," Kins said.

"There's always a girlfriend. Am I right?" Fields used a hunk of bread to wipe up sauce from his plate.

"You talk to her?" Kins asked.

Fields shook his head. "Haven't determined who she is yet. Andrea told her boss she *thought* her husband was cheating on her, but she didn't say with who."

"Any evidence that was the case?" Tracy asked.

"I was still running it down, but apparently it wasn't the first time. He'd been banging a little hottie from his law firm before they got married and I guess didn't think a wedding band should inhibit that activity."

"You talk to her?" Tracy asked.

"Ain't my first rodeo, Detective." He popped a piece of bread into his mouth.

Tracy really didn't like this guy.

"She says she broke it off when she found out he'd gotten married. Apparently, he'd kept that little trinket from her for a couple months."

"Sounds like a dirtbag," Kins said.

"Yeah." Fields nodded. "The wife also told her boss she was going to consult a divorce lawyer."

"Did she?" Tracy asked.

"No evidence she did."

"I think I'm seeing her motivation for disappearing," Kins said.

"Divorce doesn't get her out of the debt with the personal guarantees out there," Fields said. "And because Oregon is a community-property state, Andrea was jointly liable for all the debts."

"She was worried she'd lose her trust," Tracy said.

"He declares bankruptcy, no big deal," Fields said. "He's got nothing but debt. Her? She's sitting on a big pile of money the creditors would love to go after."

"Why'd they take out a loan in the first place?" Kins asked.

"Like I said"—Fields took another bite of the linguini—"she wouldn't let him use the trust money."

Kins looked at Tracy.

"Yeah," Fields said, reading the look. "The guy's got motivation up the ass to kill her."

"In which case, he would have just shoved her off the mountain," Tracy said, thinking there had to be something more to it.

"It was the perfect setup," Fields said, shrugging. "People die on that mountain every year. I think that's why it was just the two of them—no guide. Husband claims wife's death was a tragic accident. Who was going to be any wiser?"

"But he's a lawyer," Tracy said, still not completely convinced. "He had to have at least realized that the bankruptcy, the insurance policy, and the bad marriage, not to mention the girlfriend, would be pretty solid circumstantial evidence it was no accident."

"He claimed he didn't know about the insurance policy," Fields said. "Or about any girlfriend."

"He says it was her idea to take out the policy?" Tracy asked.

"And to climb the mountain," Fields said. "Like I said, I was sure he killed her. Now? Well, she's unhappy too, right?" Fields said. "So maybe she sees this trip up the mountain as the perfect opportunity to fake her own death, get out of a bad marriage, and stick the husband with the bills and headaches."

"And maybe get even for the girlfriend while she's at it," Kins said.

"Hell hath no fury like a woman scorned," Fields said, wiping the corners of his mustache with the napkin.

"Maybe," Tracy said. "Or maybe she suspected the husband didn't intend for her to make it off the mountain and beat him at his own game."

"Why would she go if she knew he was going to try and kill her?" Kins said.

"She has to go if she wants to fake her death to get out of the marriage and the debt," Tracy said.

Kins shook his head. "She could have just run."

"Running doesn't mean she's dead," Tracy said. "This way, she hides the trust money, plants some seeds—like the insurance policy—and tells her boss the husband is cheating on her and she wants a divorce. When he goes to sleep, she walks off knowing everyone will blame the husband." She looked to Fields. "The ranger says she had to have help getting off the mountain."

"Yeah, I know, but I don't know who that would have been. Her parents are deceased and the only relative is an aunt in San Bernardino who hasn't been in contact with her since Andrea left for Portland. Number's in the file. There's the husband—"

"Who we can rule out," Kins said.

"—her boss, and one friend," Fields said.

"Who's the friend?" Tracy asked.

"Devin Chambers. They worked at the insurance company together."

"You talk to her?" Tracy asked.

Fields gave her that look again. "Like I said, not my first rodeo. I checked her out. She said Andrea confided in her that the husband had admitted to the girlfriend and that he'd physically abused her."

"She said he physically abused Andrea?" Tracy asked.

"That's what she said, but before you get too excited that it was Chambers who helped Strickland, I can tell you that the weekend of the climb, Devin Chambers was at the coast. She produced a credit card receipt for the hotel and restaurants."

"Were you able to verify those?"

Fields scoffed again and Tracy was starting to tire of it. "Like what, that she walked into the restaurant, ordered a meal to go, drove six hours to Mount Rainier, helped the wife disappear, and drove back? I had the receipts saying she was there."

Kins jumped in. "Okay, so regardless of who helped her, now what? He figures out she played him, goes after the money, and kills her? Since she's already dead, nobody will miss her, so long as they don't find the body—which explains the crab pot."

"He'd still be my primary suspect," Fields said. "And I'd work him hard, but you got a body now, so I guess it's gonna become your rodeo."

"Does he have a lawyer?" Kins asked.

Fields nodded. "A good one in Portland."

"How long were they married?" Tracy asked.

"Right around a year. They got married within weeks of meeting. So now you're wondering if he chose her on purpose, someone with money and without any relatives. Am I right?"

"So you suspected it?" Tracy said.

"Absolutely I suspected it, but I didn't find anything in his past to indicate that was the case—first marriage for both of them. Plus, I don't think she's the innocent little girl she portrayed herself to be. These kinds of people tend to find one another, know what I mean?"

"So no other suspects?" Tracy asked.

Fields finished the last of his beer. "No need. It was like after the OJ trial when the press asked Gil Garcetti if they were going to pursue the real killer, and Garcetti said, 'The killer just walked out the door.' I was convinced that was the case here. Still am."

"Any indication he owned a boat or fished?" Tracy asked.

"Not that I'm aware of. He didn't strike me as that type."

"What type?" Kins asked.

"Someone who'd bait his own hook."

"But you think he's capable of killing?"

Fields slid the empty plate away from the edge of the table. "I have no doubt he had the intent. Maybe now you can prove the act to go with that intent."

CHAPTER 10

*G*enesis made a profit our first month in business and Graham's mood was sky high, but that just made the fall that much farther and the landing that much harder. Business steadily declined as the novelty of legalized marijuana wore off. Then the laws changed, as the article I had read suggested, allowing medical dispensaries to sell retail. That was the kiss of death, that and Graham had insisted on a Pearl District address and tenant improvements that would have made King Louis XIV blush. Turns out our "high-end" clientele really didn't care about things like Brazilian floors or display-case lighting. They cared about price.

I wanted to say I told you so, but I suspected—no, by this time I knew—where that would lead.

The minute the business started to tank, so did our relationship. Graham's mood swings had become more frequent and more dramatic, sometimes violent. He seemed to always be on edge, stressed out, and it didn't take much to set him off. We were deep in debt and I didn't know how we were going to pay the rent on the dispensary or the loft. Even using the interest payments I received from the trust, we were going to be significantly short.

The sex had become nonexistent, but now we didn't even talk. Graham had been bringing home edibles—marijuana in dried fruit, cookies, even things like gummy bears. He said it helped him to relax and fall asleep. It definitely did that. Most nights he passed out on the couch, which was a blessing, because if he'd also been drinking, which was not infrequent, he quickly became incoherent—or belligerent. Half the time his speech was so slurred, I couldn't even understand what he was saying. And the one time we'd tried to make love, he hadn't been able to get a hard-on, and that had just made him angry and spiteful.

"I'm tired, Andrea," he'd said, quickly getting out of bed. "I'm under a lot of stress at work. What did you think was going to happen?"

"I was hoping it would help you relax," I'd said.

"You want to help me relax? Talk to your trustee and see about using the funds to help us pay some of these bills. I'm killing myself at the store. The hours are killing me." Then he'd stormed out of our bedroom and slept on the couch.

I was walking home from the dispensary with a massive headache, the kind that makes you squint because the light hurts your eyes. My stomach churned as though I'd been standing on the deck of a boat in high seas trying to read a book. My lunch was in a knotted plastic bag, and my inability to eat it, again, had left me feeling weak. I had an appointment later in the week to see the doctor for what I was sure was an ulcer.

As I stepped from the elevator onto our landing, I just wanted to change into my sweats, curl up on the couch with my latest novel, and lose myself in some fictional world.

I punched in the four-digit code to our keyless door lock. The lights were off, but the pale-blue light of a streetlamp filtered through the blinds. I noticed this because I never lowered the blinds. The window looked toward the Willamette River, and the view was the best part of my now-pricey loft that I doubted we'd continue to be able to afford.

Graham sat on the couch with his back to the door, so still it was like looking at the back of the head of a mannequin in a department-store display. His suit coat, the black-and-white checked pattern he'd recently bought, hung haphazardly over the back of the sofa, as if tossed, which was not like him. He was meticulous when it came to his clothes.

"Graham?" I said, my voice questioning.

His head moved, but it was more of a flinch, which was a relief because the thought had crossed my mind that he had died seated on that couch.

"Graham?" I said again, stepping farther in.

"Well, it's over," he said, voice hoarse and soft.

I set my keys on the kitchen counter and stepped to the side of the couch with the window at my back. I was looking at him in profile. His hair was untamed, as if he'd been tugging on it. Beside him, on the couch, his tie lay balled up. He had his shirtsleeves rolled up his forearms in tight bunches. On the table was a bottle of Jack Daniel's and a glass. Thankfully, the bottle looked relatively full, but beside it was an open mason jar from the dispensary filled with dried apricots laced with THC, the chemical in marijuana that causes the high.

"What happened? Did you talk to the bank?"

He'd had an appointment that afternoon to speak with the bank about extending the loan payments, or securing an additional loan. Judging from his demeanor, the meeting had not gone well.

He nodded slowly, almost imperceptibly, his lips pursed. Then he stood so suddenly I flinched. He grabbed the bottle and came around the couch, leaning down into my personal space. The alcohol and smell of the apricots was strong, almost enough to make me puke. My stomach lurched but I looked away and sucked in air.

"I did." He grinned and stepped past me to the window. He put his fingers between the blades of the blinds, pulling them down so that they crinkled, and peered out like a man in hiding.

"What are you doing?" I asked.

"What does it look like I'm doing?" he said. "I'm eating the inventory."
He turned and smiled at me, again without any humor.

"How many have you had?" I asked, looking at the mason jar. I had learned that the potency level in the edibles was much higher than smoking a joint, but the real problem was that the level of THC was difficult to measure. People made the mistake of eating one edible, feeling nothing, and eating another, not realizing the effect from the first edible had yet to kick in. When it did, it could be debilitating.

"I don't know," Graham said, running his hand down the blades as if over harp strings. "And I don't really give a shit."

"Do you think you should be drinking?"

He glanced at me out of the corner of his eye. "What would you have me do, Andrea, read a book? Live in a fantasy world?"

"Is it that bad?"

He approached. His grin had now become more sinister, the kind you carved into a jack-o'- lantern to scare trick-or-treaters on Halloween. When he leaned forward, I took a step back.

"Yes, it's that bad," he said, voice soft and deliberate. "What did you think the bank was going to say?" He dropped his voice an octave. "'We're not only willing to forego your loan, here's another one. Have a nice day.'" Graham paused as if he'd just remembered something. "Oh, yeah, he also questioned why I had no law-firm income. He said the bank was going to start an inquiry with my former law firm. So, in addition to being bankrupt and losing everything, I may also be going to jail for fraud. How does that grab you?"

He stepped away to our tiny kitchen and set the bottle on the counter.

"We can start over," I said, trying to find something to hold on to.

He laughed. "You would say that. You're such a dreamer."

"We can. We can hire an attorney and work out a payment plan on the loan. The bank won't prosecute you; they just want their money. You can practice law and I can get my job back and we'll pay off the loan."

Graham spun on his heels and raised the bottle. "And live on what?"

"We can move—someplace cheaper, and get rid of the lease on the Porsche and cut other expenses." I was just thinking quickly and out loud.

"No." He shook his head. "No way am I going back to practicing law. That is a death sentence. Is that what you want for me?"

"It doesn't have to be forever," I said. "Just until we get back on our feet."

"Really? Really?" He walked back to me. "You want us to get back on our feet?"

"I'm willing to try," I said, and I was willing.

"No, you're willing to sentence me to an office for the rest of my life, but you're not willing to lend me the money to pay our bills so I can make this work. Put your money where your mouth is, Andrea."

I was so tired of this debate. I tried to remain calm. "We've talked about this, Graham. Even if I could, it's not going to solve our problems. What do we do next month and the month after that?"

"All I need is another month to turn this thing around," he said.

"You said that last month," I said before I could stop myself.

He glared at me. "I didn't know you were keeping score."

I took a breath. "Look, this wasn't your fault. The timing was wrong and the location was too expensive."

"Oh," he said, voice rising. "So this is all my fault. Is that what you're saying?"

"I said it wasn't your fault."

"I heard what you said and I know what you mean. You think it's my fault. Well, I don't, Andrea. I did my homework and I did my research. I had the vision. I put in the time and the sweat equity. What I needed was more capital. What I needed was support. For better or for worse, Andrea. Do you remember those words, 'for better or for worse'?"

He had no idea how many times I'd heard those words every day in my head, like the beating of tribal drums just before an attack. He moved quickly to the front door, to where I saw he had set his leather satchel. He carried it back to the couch, going through it, and pulled out papers, letting the satchel drop onto the couch. He thrust the papers at me.

"I prepared loan documents, Andrea. You want to help. Put your money where your mouth is. You can loan the business the money."

"What would be the collateral?"

"Are you kidding me?" he shouted. "Are we really going to go there?"

I was confused and worried. I put the papers down, trying to think. "I can't loan the business the money, Graham."

"No. You won't loan me the money!" He closed the distance between us and shoved the papers into my chest hard enough to make me step backward. "Well, guess what, Andrea? In addition to that little letter from the law firm that I forged, I also forged your name on the personal guarantees to the bank and on the lease."

I felt as though I'd been kicked in the stomach. "You did what?"

He gave me a sardonic smile. "How does that grab you? So, you can either give me the money so I can get this to work, or you can just sign it over to the bank."

"You bastard."

He laughed. "Doesn't feel so good when your ass is on the line, does it?"

"I'm not giving you the money," I said, now defiant. "Let the bank come after it. My parents' attorney says the trust can't be broken."

Graham closed the distance, backing me up until I was at the kitchen counter. I had nowhere to go. "I'm through playing around, Andrea. I need that money. I am not going to jail."

"I'm leaving." I tried to step around him to the front door but he blocked my escape.

"I need that money, Andrea!"

"No." I bumped him out of the way and started toward the door.

He grabbed my wrist hard and spun me. I shot out my foot, kicking him hard in the shin. He winced and moaned but did not release his grip. He shook me, bending my wrist. "I need that Goddamn money!"

"No!" I yelled. "You're hurting me."

And then he slapped me, hard, across the face.

The blow knocked me to the ground.

It happened so fast I wasn't really even sure he'd hit me, but then my face stung and burst into flames.

The room fell silent, the air so still I could hear the clock on the stove ticking. I had my head down, my hand pressed to my cheek, which was warm to the touch. Above me, I heard the faint sound of Graham breathing. I sat there, my gaze on the floor, hair covering my face, tasting the metallic tinge of my own blood. Then, slowly, I looked up at him. I looked up at the man I'd married.

His hand remained balled in a fist.

CHAPTER 11

Late on a weekday afternoon, Faz and Del stepped through the doors of the Department of Licensing on Spring Street in downtown Seattle. A mass of bored humanity sat in uncomfortable-looking plastic chairs, which was just what Faz had expected to find. An automated female voice identified the next customer and directed the person to the proper window, everyone moving like robots.

"It's like something out of an apocalyptic movie in which machines have taken over and humans are drones," Faz said. "I think I watched this on TV last night."

"How many you think are here for the air-conditioning?" Del said.

"What do you want to bet the library's a madhouse too?" Faz said.

Seattle had spent millions on a one-of-a-kind glass-and-steel eleven-story library in downtown, but a public building is open to the public—all the public. The library had become a safe haven for the homeless, the mentally disturbed, and those seeking to use one of the facility's four hundred public computers to search the Internet for porn and do unspeakable things right there in the public domain. Those numbers swelled in the winter when the temperature dropped near or below freezing, and again in the summer when Seattle baked.

"If you build it, they will cum," Del said, laughing.

"Wouldn't touch those computers with your hands," Faz said.

Television and computer screens indicated the numbers the clerks in the booths were serving, but the numbers everyone intently watched were on the digital clock: 4:18.

"The office closes at four thirty," Del said.

"Good thing we ain't waiting," Faz said.

"You wanna bet?" Del asked.

"Early dinner?" Faz said.

"Loser buys sandwiches at Salumi," Del said.

"I like that bet. I win either way. I can also pick up some pasta for Vera and be twice blessed."

"Happy wife, happy Faz," Del said.

At the counter, Faz showed his badge and ID to a woman behind the partition. She didn't look impressed.

"We have an appointment with Henrik . . ."

When he fumbled over the last name the woman said, "Engvaldson."

"That's it," Faz said. "Tongue twister."

She didn't smile, pointing to the chairs, then picking up the phone. "Take a seat." Del smiled as they turned for the white plastic chairs. "I can taste the grilled lamb sandwich already, and you know what is going to make it especially good?"

"It's free," Faz said.

"Bingo," Del said.

Del wasn't cheap; he'd bought his share of meals. He just liked a good bet. He couldn't watch a game or a fight without placing a bet of some kind. It was never much, just a couple bucks, and Faz admitted it did make things more interesting.

Faz hoped Engvaldson could provide a little detail on what Andrea Strickland had used to obtain a driver's license in Lynn Hoff's name. At this point, any information would be welcome.

They didn't wait long. A very tall man in khakis and a light-blue button-down greeted them in the lobby. "Detectives," he said, extending a hand as if it were on the end of a crane. "I'm Henrik Engvaldson. Which of you did I speak with on the phone?"

"That would be me," Faz said, feeling small, and that was saying something. Faz stood six foot four and, as of that morning, he weighed 268 pounds, butt naked. Del was an inch taller and ten to fifteen pounds heavier, though he would never admit it. The gut, however, didn't lie.

They followed Engvaldson to a door at the back of the room. He had to duck to pass under the header, which confirmed he was taller than six foot eight. Faz gave Del a look as they continued down a narrow hallway.

"What nationality is 'Engvaldson'?" Faz said.

"Apparently, it's Swedish," Engvaldson said. "I grew up thinking I was Norwegian until my wife did that Ancestry.com thing. Big mistake. Turns out my ancestors are from Sweden."

"Like that commercial," Faz said.

"Exactly."

"Me? I don't want to know about any of that," Del said. "I'm liable to find out things I don't want to know."

"Like maybe you aren't human?" Faz said.

Engvaldson led them into an office typical for a government employee, small and utilitarian, but serviceable. When he sat, he looked too tall for his desk. He opened a file and handed Faz an eight-by-ten copy of a photograph of Lynn Hoff's—aka Andrea Strickland's—driver's license. "She preapplied for her license—"

"Preapplied?" Del asked. "What does that mean?"

"Filled out her application online, then came in to finish it. It saves time."

"Good to know," Del said.

"What did she use for ID?" Faz asked.

"Certified birth certificate," Engvaldson said, reviewing the file.

"So a legitimate person then," Faz said.

"Maybe. Maybe not. Our clerks have access to the forms used by each state, but unfortunately detecting a forgery is not so simple. The feds have been working on a standardized document, but back in 1992 each state used its own form."

"So what, she could have forged the certificate and faked the name?" Del asked.

"She could have," Engvaldson said.

"This your busiest office?" Faz asked.

"It is," Engvaldson said, clearly knowing where Faz was going with the question. "And with the federal government requiring everyone to now have an enhanced driver's license, we're busier than ever lately."

Which is likely why Strickland chose to come here, Faz thought; the busier the clerk, the less time she had to spend on something like this, especially if the certificate looked like it passed muster.

"She provide a Social Security number?" Faz asked.

Engvaldson handed Faz another document.

Faz compared the number with the number he had obtained from the Social Security Administration for Lynn Cora Hoff. It matched. "So it's an active number," Faz said, sounding surprised.

"What does 'active' mean, that she's alive?" Del asked.

"Not necessarily," Faz said. "Back in the old days, before computers, the con would go to the cemetery and find a tombstone of a child who'd died but would have been about the same age as the con. He takes that kid's name and date of birth and gets a Social Security number. With computers, the SSA now links its data to the database of deaths."

"Right, so we'd know if she's dead," Del said. "So how did she get a living person's number?"

Faz said, "Drive to Chinatown with a couple thousand dollars in your pocket and you can get just about anything you want. It could also be that the person, Lynn Cora Hoff, was indigent, had no criminal record, and had no relatives or anyone to identify her body. If that was the case, her death would have never been reported to SSA. She just ceased to exist."

"I'm surmising that takes a lot of research by somebody," Del said.

"Yes, it does," Faz agreed. "Which is why I'm surprised it's active."

"So this isn't like when my son spent twenty bucks to get a fake ID so he could buy beer," Del said.

"No, it's not," Engvaldson said. "It's much more elaborate."

"At least we know how she did it." Faz stood and extended a hand. "Thanks for your help."

"No problem." Engvaldson unfolded from his chair like the stalk in the children's fairy tale.

"How do you fly?" Del said, looking up.

Engvaldson thrust out his arms in a Superman pose. "Usually like this." He laughed. "I get that question quite a bit. I ask for the bulkhead or the emergency row. The airlines have to accommodate me."

"Yeah? Do they have to accommodate fat guys like us?" Del asked.

"That, I don't know. I'll let you out."

The main room had cleared out. Engvaldson unlocked the glass door and pulled it open. They thanked him again for his time and walked to the elevator.

"So if she gets a driver's license, can we assume she intended to live in the state?" Del asked.

"Maybe. Could be why she was also getting her looks changed, but not necessarily," Faz said. "She might have obtained the Social Security number so she could *get* the driver's license to make it easier to *get* a passport and take off. And you need a license to open a bank account. Think about it. What was she going to do with her trust? If you're going overseas you're not going to be flying with a bunch of cash in your suitcase, and she couldn't use her real name. She would have needed a license to get the money into an account in the name Lynn Hoff, or some shell corporation. Then she begins to wire it out of the country.

From there, you move it a couple more times to places that provide confidentiality. Eventually, it disappears."

"She must have been pretty desperate," Del said.

"It's called pseudocide," Faz said. "The person fakes their death, usually to collect insurance money or escape creditors, then resurfaces as somebody else." Faz looked at his watch. "Banks will be closed."

"Yes, but Salumi is open and I'm hungry," Del said.

—

When Tracy and Kins arrived back at Police Headquarters they had a surprise waiting on their desks—sandwiches wrapped in white butcher paper. The sticky note said it all.

Don't say I never gave you nothing.

"Isn't that like a triple negative?" Kins said.

"I love him anyway." Tracy ripped open the wrapping. "I'm starving and I'm betting these are from Salumi."

"If you're starving, why didn't you order something to eat at the restaurant?"

"I lost my appetite when Fields started talking."

Kins's forehead furrowed. "I didn't think he was that bad."

"You wouldn't."

"Sounds like something my wife says when I'm in trouble and don't know why. What'd he do?"

"You mean besides undressing the waitress with his eyes every time she came to the table? How much cheese can you put on linguini and clams?"

"Really?" Kins said.

"You didn't notice?"

"I noticed the waitress."

She rolled her eyes. "Pig."

"Actually, mine's lamb," Kins said, holding up half his sandwich. "Did you get the pork shoulder?"

"Idiot."

Kins laughed while rummaging in his desk drawer for a couple bucks. "I'm going to grab a soda. You want one?"

"I'm good," she said.

Tracy took a bite of her sandwich. Faz *had* bought her the pork shoulder. Not that she was going to tell Kins.

"Crosswhite."

Tracy cringed at the sound of Nolasco's nasal whine. She set down the sandwich.

"Where's Kins?" Nolasco said, entering their cubicle.

"Getting a soda," she said, finishing her bite.

"What the hell is going on with the woman in the trap?" Nolasco said. "The media is calling, saying she's the same woman presumed dead on Mount Rainier last month. Is it true?"

"Appears to be," Tracy said, upset that the media had the information, which meant it was likely the husband had it as well.

"Did you tell them?"

She scoffed. "Of course not. Why would I tell them?"

"Well, somebody did."

"Well, it wasn't me, and it wasn't Kins. I can tell you that."

"Wasn't me what?" Kins reentered the bull pen with a Diet Coke.

"The media knows about Andrea Strickland," Tracy said.

"How?"

"It aired all over the six o'clock news," Nolasco said.

"Manpelt?" Kins said.

"Among others," Nolasco said. "Phones are ringing off the hook, the brass is calling, and I don't know shit."

"We learned about it last night and took a drive out to Rainier and Tacoma," Kins said. "Just getting back now."

Nolasco looked at Tracy, disbelieving. "You have no idea how the media found out?"

Ordinarily, Nolasco would have been Tracy's first choice as the leak. The department was a sieve, the brass often giving up information to cull favors with the media. She couldn't tell if Nolasco was being sincere or just looking to redirect blame. "None," she said. "We were hoping to talk to the husband before the story broke."

"You can forget about that. He was prominently featured."

"What did he have to say?" Tracy said.

"Exactly what you'd expect him to say. He was both profoundly shocked and saddened and had no idea what would have compelled his wife to fake her own death or who would have wanted to kill her."

"Sounds scripted and well rehearsed," Tracy said.

"Of course it was," Kins said.

Nolasco eyed Tracy. "You didn't say anything, to anyone?"

Tracy suspected Nolasco was setting her up. "Why would I?"

"That's a good question. Here's another one—why would a woman in Renton who manages a motel tell a reporter that the victim lived at the motel for almost a month and that two homicide detectives had been there asking questions?"

"That's true," Kins said. "We were there and we did ask questions, but we didn't say anything about the victim."

Nolasco looked between the two of them. "I want a written statement before you leave tonight that I can take to the brass. They want Lee to put something out," he said, referring to Bennett Lee, the department's public information officer.

"We don't have any DNA. It's premature," Tracy said.

"Not when motel owners have figured it out, it isn't," Nolasco said.

"Fine, Lee can tell them she wasn't a prostitute, a druggie, or homeless," Tracy said.

Nolasco glared at her. "Anything useful?"

Kins stepped in. "We spoke to the ranger on Mount Rainier and got a copy of his report and we talked to the Pierce County detective. We'll put something together but couch everything to be part of an ongoing investigation."

"I want to be kept fully apprised going forward," Nolasco said, directing his comment and lingering glare at Tracy. "Is that understood?"

"Absolutely," Tracy said.

Nolasco walked from the cubicle, but stopped and came back to Tracy. "And you can tell your boyfriend's friend who works for the Angels he doesn't know shit. Trout hit a home run and drove in four runs the other night."

Tracy struggled not to break into a grin. "Wow. Really?"

"Yeah, really."

Nolasco left. Kins stared at her.

"Mike Trout? The baseball player?"

She shrugged and smiled. "Heard he had a bad hamstring."

"You don't even like baseball."

"I also don't like it when Nolasco ignores me."

Kins shook his head. "You just can't help sticking your hands in the lion's cage, can you?"

"It worked, didn't it? Piss him off enough and he usually leaves."

They ate their Salumi sandwiches while discussing what to put in the statement to the brass and media that would sound like they were providing information but not actually doing so.

"Let's watch the news," Kins suggested. They taped the broadcasts. "We can find out what's already been reported and just regurgitate it." He crumpled his butcher paper into a ball, and spun and shot it at the Nerf basketball hoop hanging off the back of Del's cubicle. It went through the net and landed in the garbage can.

"That's it," Kins said. "I'm buying a lottery ticket on the drive home. Are we still taking the drive to Portland tomorrow?"

She nodded. "The husband's always a suspect."

CHAPTER 12

*A*t just after 11:00 p.m. Sunday night, the Porsche's engine purred outside. I set down my book and went to the window, creating a separation in the blinds to peer down at the street. Graham had left the loft after hitting me, and he had not been back for two days. I watched him drive the Porsche into the garage. He was not going to be happy. I'd decided to park my car in my parking space beneath my building.

Minutes later, the Porsche reappeared and parked on the street beneath a streetlamp. When Graham got out, the first thing I noticed was he was not wearing the same clothes he'd left in. He wore skinny jeans, topsiders, and a brown suede jacket. I was fairly certain he had not come home to change, though I had left the loft Saturday afternoon for my doctor's appointment. No doubt he'd put the clothes on his credit card, though it had to be close to maxed out.

I watched him walk around to the passenger side and open the door. He bent and reached inside, retrieving something, likely a peace offering. His routine had become predictable—except he'd never hit me before. He'd crossed a line, and I wasn't willing to give him the opportunity to cross it again.

I went back to the couch, grabbed my novel, and curled up in the corner with a blanket over my legs. I'd made myself a cup of mint tea, which the doctor said might help my nausea. When the door opened, I turned the page in my novel and continued reading.

"Hey," he said, keys hitting the entry table with a dull thud.

I glanced at him but said nothing. As I'd predicted, he'd come bearing gifts—a stuffed bear holding a book, The Girl on the Train. *Next would come the apology.*

I went back to reading my novel.

I heard him approach the back of the couch but I didn't turn to look. "I am so, so very sorry," he said, "and ashamed for what I did." He sounded sincere, but then, Graham always sounded sincere. I'd come to learn that was one of his skills. "Can you at least look at me?"

It was so pathetic. He looked like a little boy who'd dropped his ice cream cone on the sidewalk. I set my novel in my lap, but kept it fanned open to the page I'd been reading.

Graham came around the end of the couch to sit, but hesitated when I didn't immediately move to accommodate him. I made him wait a moment before sliding back my legs.

He sat facing me. "I would never, ever hit a woman," he said.

"Except you did," I said, nearly dumbstruck by the idiocy of his statement. "You hit me."

He shook his head. "I know, and I'm so sorry."

"You said that," I said.

"It's just . . . everything came crashing down on me the other night, Andrea. You just can't believe the weight I felt at that moment, like an anvil had fallen on my chest. I couldn't breathe. It felt like I was suffocating. There is a very real possibility I could go to prison."

I didn't respond. I also wasn't sympathetic. This was also his MO. Excuses for his behavior so he wouldn't have to accept what he'd done.

"Look, I don't even know who that person was," he continued.

I do, I thought. It's the man I married.

"It scared me," he said.

Scared him?

"That's why I left. I had to leave because I just couldn't face what I'd done."

I didn't bother to ask him where he'd gone or where he'd spent the night. I didn't really care anymore. I'd thought maybe he'd run to the associate at his old law firm, the one he'd admitted to sleeping with after we'd married, but I'd done some additional fact gathering and learned she too had since married, which meant Graham had no place to go. In other words, he needed me. More to the point, he needed my loft and he needed my trust funds. I suspected that was the real reason he'd come back. He was going to be prosecuted for fraud if he didn't find a way to make things right.

"I'm going to do better," he said, reaching out and taking my hand. "I'm really going to work to do better. I'll even go to counseling . . . if you want. I want to make this work, Andrea. I really want to make this work."

Translated, that meant, I really don't want to go to jail or work as a lawyer, but I really want to continue to drive my Porsche, screw around on the side, and live off your trust until I come up with the next great business idea. Where else was he going to get such a sweet deal?

"I don't know what I want," I said. I did know, but I couldn't articulate it, not to Graham. At the moment I was as stuck as he was, though I'd had all weekend to consider my situation and was figuring a few things out on my own.

"I know. I know," he said, rushing his words as if to silence me before I could ask him to leave. His eyes were wide and animated. "And I don't blame you. What I did was inexcusable. It was unforgivable. But I'm asking you to give me a second chance. Look, I've been thinking about this. You're right—we can start over. I can get a job practicing law. I realize now my mistake with Genesis."

"What was that?"

"I was out of my field of expertise," he said, as if he had come up with that all on his own. "I didn't know what I was doing. Good idea but poor execution. I have a much better plan this time."

I was almost afraid to ask. "Which is what?"

"Opening my own law firm," he said. I thought for sure he was going to add, "Ta-da!" Thankfully, he refrained.

I realized Graham was delusional, and based on my Internet research, likely manic-depressive. I didn't bring up the fact that he could be going to jail, that we were facing bankruptcy, and that those two things would pretty much make it impossible to get a bank loan to pay the start-up costs of running his own law practice. In fact, there was a very real possibility he could lose his law license entirely. Graham wasn't stupid; he knew that. He was begging because he was going to try to hit me up for the start-up funds from the trust, which, if my attorney couldn't keep the bank lawyers from getting their hands on it, wouldn't even exist. This, I realized, would be a never-ending cycle that I could no longer allow to continue.

"You don't even have to go back to the insurance company," he said. "Unless you want to. I'll support us."

I refrained from laughing. "Our problem isn't money," I said. "It never was."

"I know. I know. We need to get back to who we were before all of this."

And there was my opening.

"I have something in mind," I said, trying to sound hesitant.

"What?" He looked and acted eager to listen.

"What do you think about climbing Rainier again?" I asked.

"What?" he asked, sitting back, clearly perplexed.

Rainier had been more than just a blow to Graham's ego. It had been a blow to his psyche. He'd failed to summit, and I had. He could blame it on an overcautious guide all he wanted, but we both knew he couldn't physically do it. I had done it, and, to be honest, it had not been that hard. Maybe all those years growing up hiking in the mountains in Southern California had acclimated me.

"It would give us something to focus on, something not work related. It would help get our relationship back on track. I really believe that's what we need, to get back to being the two people we were when we met, before all this stress changed us," I said, even sounding sincere.

"You want to climb Rainier?" he asked, voice soft and doubtful.

"Remember the last trip? Remember how much fun it was and how it brought us together? We need to find hobbies that we can do together." Unlike sleeping with your associate, I wanted to say, but didn't.

"Well," he said. "I don't know."

"I think you could probably do it this time," I said, tweaking his ego. "You could train harder because you won't be working so much."

"I could have made it last time," he said, and I could hear the indignation mounting. "It was the guide."

"Well, this is your chance to prove he was wrong," I said.

"The guides are always going to be overcautious," he said.

"We don't have to worry about that," I said. "I was talking to someone who's done the Liberty Ridge route and you don't need a guide."

"Liberty Ridge?"

"You do it early in the season when it's cold and the snow isn't melting. In fact, she said it's not technical, just a grind, but if you take your time, it's no big deal." I could see he was still hesitant so I added, "You wouldn't have to worry about some guide overreacting."

His ego took the bait. "I could have summited last time. The guide was just overly cautious."

"Well," I said, "this time there won't be anyone to make you turn back."

"No guide?" He became thoughtful. "What if something happened?"

I waved it off. "Nothing is going to happen. The odds are, like, less than five percent." I again sensed his reticence and added, "I also know I could afford to lose a few pounds. Bikini season is coming up."

Graham smiled, but I could see the doubt in it. "Yeah. I mean, maybe we could at least train, you know, and see where we're at."

"We can begin tomorrow morning," I said, figuring the sooner I made him commit, the less likely he could back out.

He picked up the book he'd brought and held it up so I could read the cover. "The woman at Powell's said it was really good. She said you'd really like it."

I'd already read it, and at the time I had liked it. But now I had a different view. The book was about a pathetic woman recently divorced, still pining away for her former husband. She was an alcoholic, willing to do just about anything to get back a guy who really wasn't worth getting back, no matter how much he humiliated her.

I could no longer be that woman.

CHAPTER 13

Tracy knew Kins hated traffic, and with the explosion in Seattle's population over the last decade, and resulting traffic nightmares, it had become his pet peeve. He voiced his objection frequently to her, and the focus of his blame was usually the DOT, which he said stood for "Dunces of Traffic." Then he'd recite the evidence to support his diatribes—projects like bike lanes and free-bike programs had failed miserably, and designated toll-commute lanes had only made traffic worse. Tracy listened, though she considered complaining a waste of time and energy. It was like Stan Fields voicing his displeasure about the weather and Dan yelling at the television when a referee or umpire made a bad call. She figured it was a man thing and she humored them to keep the peace.

Kins's pet peeve, however, meant they had been in the car since the crack of dawn. Tracy had protested the early hour, pointing out that the heavy commute along the I-5 corridor was in the opposite direction, north, into Seattle. That had not been Kins's concern. "I don't want to hit Portland morning traffic," he'd said.

They hadn't entirely avoided Portland's traffic, but as they crossed the rust-colored Broadway Bridge spanning the Willamette River, Kins wore a smug expression that begged for a compliment.

"Go ahead," Tracy said.

"What's that?" Kins said, playing dumb, though not convincingly.

"Go ahead. Say 'I told you so.' We avoided the morning commute."

"Did I say that?" Kins said.

Tracy rolled her eyes. "Yeah, right."

"We made good time," he said. "I will say that. Not my best, but . . ."

"So sue me because I made you stop for a bladder break."

"Did I say anything?" Kins said, his smile widening. "I don't think I said anything."

"Yeah, you didn't have to. You're smiling like you had sex this morning."

Kins laughed. Then he said, "So you think this guy will talk to us?"

"He'd better if I'm up this early," Tracy said.

She'd called Graham Strickland the prior afternoon when they'd learned they weren't going to surprise him, not with Maria Vanpelt "breaking the story," as she so often liked to proclaim. Strickland had directed Tracy to speak to his attorney, Phil Montgomery. She'd debated just showing up at Strickland's residence. She didn't need to go through his lawyer, but three hours was a long way to drive for nothing. So she'd played nice and called Montgomery, who'd agreed to make Strickland available.

Montgomery's law office was located in a renovated brick building not far from Union Station. They found parking on the street. A cherry-red Porsche sat parked in a loading zone in front of the building entrance. The personalized license plate said "Genesis." The car said "Ego."

"Hang on." Kins took out his cell phone and snapped several photographs of the car. "This would have been hard to miss if he showed up around that Renton motel."

Inside the building lobby, Tracy noted software, investment, law, and design firms on the building directory. They took an elevator to the second floor and found the suite for the Montgomery Group. The reception area was what Tracy would call modern, with uncomfortable-looking furniture, low tables, and distinct prints hanging on brick walls. She informed the receptionist they had an appointment with Phil Montgomery. After a phone call, the young man escorted them to the conference room in the northwest corner of the building. Montgomery greeted them in the hallway. Tracy estimated him to be midsixties, with silver-gray hair and sturdy-frame glasses. Dressed in slacks and a black sweater, he looked more like an accountant than a criminal defense lawyer.

"Is my client a suspect?" Montgomery asked.

Most Americans were familiar with their Miranda rights; they'd heard the words recited so often on the plethora of police and detective shows populating television, they could recite their Miranda rights from memory. What most didn't know was their right to an attorney was guaranteed by the Fifth Amendment, but only during a criminal interrogation, and only if the person was taken into police custody—the right was intended to prevent coercion and intimidation. Even fewer knew the Sixth Amendment embodied a second constitutional right to counsel when a prosecutor commenced a criminal prosecution by filing a complaint, or the suspect was indicted by a grand jury. The fallacy most Americans harbored was that they could simply shout, "I want a lawyer!" when confronted by a police officer, and the officer couldn't talk to them. Not so. In fact, in the absence of a criminal charge, and so long as they didn't take Strickland into custody, Tracy and Kins could talk to him until the cows came home. For now, however, Tracy was content to humor Montgomery.

"Not at this time," Tracy said. "We'd just like to ask him a few questions about his late wife."

"As we discussed on the phone, I'll allow him to speak to you, but you can't record the conversation, and I won't allow him to answer questions regarding the prior investigation. I think we can all agree that ship has sailed and not without considerable disruption to Mr. Strickland's life."

"We weren't on that ship," Kins said.

"Be that as it may," Montgomery said.

"Your conditions are fine," Tracy said, not interested in pissing on the furniture to establish dominance, though she wasn't convinced the ship had sailed. If Strickland had formulated the intent to push his wife off a mountain, who was to say he didn't shoot her and drop her in Puget Sound as crab bait? But she'd let others make that argument. Right now, she just wanted to talk to Strickland and determine what he knew and what she was dealing with.

They followed Montgomery into the conference room. Graham Strickland waited near two arched windows that afforded a view of maple trees and the brick buildings across the street. Strickland's appearance looked affected. He was thin and no more than five foot seven. He wore his hair short on the sides and long on top, a day-old growth of beard, and a silver suit that, as Stan Fields had described, looked a size too small, the pants short enough to reveal cream-colored socks.

They sat on opposite sides of a cherrywood table.

"We're sorry about your wife," Tracy said.

Strickland appeared caught off guard by the sympathy. "Thank you." His voice was soft and an octave higher than Tracy anticipated.

On the drive, she and Kins had agreed that she would take the lead. She had a softer approach and they suspected from Stan Fields's description of Graham Strickland that he'd be more inclined to answer questions from a woman. "How did you find out?" she asked.

"A reporter called. It was . . . quite disturbing."

"Maria Vanpelt?" Tracy asked.

"Yes, that was the name."

"What did she tell you?"

Strickland leaned away from the table, though he kept one hand connected, middle finger lightly tapping the surface. "She asked if I knew that my wife was the woman whose body was found in a crab pot in Puget Sound."

"What did you say in response?"

Strickland broke eye contact and looked away. Ordinarily, Tracy would have attributed Strickland's reaction to being emotionally upset, but his movements seemed rehearsed. He reengaged Tracy and said, "I didn't say anything at first. I was confused. I thought the reporter had to be mistaken. I said, 'You're mistaken. My wife died on Mount Rainier six weeks ago.' I told her I thought it was a sick joke and I didn't appreciate it."

"Did she convince you otherwise?"

"I hung up and got on the Internet. I saw the picture of Andrea, the driver's license photo."

"How did that make you feel?"

Strickland's brow furrowed. Again, he hadn't expected the question and was thinking through his response, like an actor still learning his lines and making acting choices.

"Sad. Confused. Angry. It was a surreal experience. This entire episode has been a surreal experience."

"I take it you had no communication of any kind with your wife since her disappearance?"

"Of course not." Strickland bristled. "I believed she was dead."

"And you were not aware she had obtained a new identity and was living in Seattle as Lynn Hoff?"

"No, I was not. It was a huge surprise."

"Did your wife ever express any desire to change her identity?"

"Not to me."

"Do you have any idea where she got the identity 'Lynn Hoff'?"

"None."

"You'd never heard that name?"

"No."

"When you were married you were in considerable debt." Strickland did not respond. An attorney, he was waiting for a question. "Did you and Andrea ever discuss, maybe in passing, changing identities and starting fresh?"

Strickland glanced at Montgomery, but the attorney did not voice any objection.

"No. I believe in paying my debts."

It sounded rehearsed and likely had been.

"Yet you filed for bankruptcy, didn't you?" Kins said.

"What's the relevance of that question, Detective?" Montgomery said.

"I'm interested in whether any of his creditors might have been upset they were stiffed," Kins said, doing his best to tweak Strickland, and in the process hopefully making him more willing to answer Tracy's questions.

Montgomery nodded to Strickland.

"Yes, I filed for bankruptcy. I had little choice after Andrea disappeared and the Pierce County Sheriff named me a person of interest. It completely disrupted my life and my business. I had no way to make a living."

"Did any of your creditors threaten you in any way?" Tracy asked.

"I let the attorneys handle all of that."

"So you're not aware that any of them would have been angry enough to go after you or your wife?"

"Go after?"

"For the money owed."

"No."

"The bank advised you that they were going to sue you for fraud, did it not?"

"I was aware of that threat, yes. Again, I left that to the attorneys."

"So you were under considerable financial distress."

"Yes. It was a difficult time."

"Did you borrow any money from any individual who would have been unhappy about not being repaid?"

Strickland shook his head, looking and sounding bored. "No."

"You were convinced your wife was dead?" Tracy asked.

"Yes, I was convinced, and I told the rangers and the Pierce County Sheriff I was convinced. I was the only one there. She left the tent and never came back. What else was I to think?"

"How come you didn't get up with her that night?" Kins asked.

"No," Montgomery said, head shaking. "We are not going there, Detective. Mr. Strickland has answered all of those questions before and they are now irrelevant. I suggest you speak to the Pierce County Sheriff's Office if you have any questions regarding their investigation."

"I was just following up on what he said," Kins said.

"Do you know anyone who would have wished your wife . . . Andrea, harm?" Tracy asked.

"No one, but . . ."

Strickland paused, and again Tracy had the distinct impression he'd done so on purpose, the actor engaging in a dramatic moment. "But what?" she asked.

"Well, it doesn't appear I knew my wife all that well, does it?"

"Were you having marital issues?"

"Again, Detectives, that investigation is over," Montgomery said. "Unless you consider him a suspect in his wife's death, in which case we won't be answering questions."

"It's okay, Phil," Strickland said. Even before he continued speaking, Tracy knew what Graham Strickland was going to say. "I have nothing to hide, Detectives. I told the Pierce County detective that Andrea and I were having difficulties stemming from my infidelity early in the marriage."

"What do you mean by difficulties?" Tracy asked.

"I don't understand the question."

"You said you were having 'difficulties.' Did you ever strike her?" Tracy asked.

"Never," Strickland said. "I would never strike a woman. We were just trying to get through a difficult time."

"Whose idea was it to climb Mount Rainier?"

"Andrea's."

"Not yours?"

"No. I really hadn't had the time to even think of such things. We'd been so immersed in trying to make a go of the business that we had lost touch with each other. The stress was tremendous. We'd hoped that climbing, something we enjoyed doing together, would help us both remember why we'd fallen in love in the first place."

"And was her taking out an insurance policy benefiting you also her idea?" Kins said.

Strickland shifted his gaze and gave Kins a smug smile. "Actually, it was, Detective."

"And you had no idea your wife was planning on leaving you?" Kins said in a tone intended to get a rise out of Strickland.

"None. I've thought about it, obviously. I've thought about it a lot."

Tracy wondered how that was even possible, given that Strickland had only learned the evening before that his wife had walked off the mountain. "And what did you conclude?" Tracy asked.

"Clearly, Andrea had to have planned this. At the very least she had to have a separate set of crampons and clothing to get off the mountain."

"So she clearly didn't think the climb was going to repair your marriage," Kins said, ever the annoying fly.

Montgomery sat up, now poised to respond each time Kins asked a question, which Tracy knew was the reason Kins kept doing it. He was diverting Montgomery's attention, and his displeasure, so the attorney would be less inclined to object to Tracy's questions. "He's not going to speculate about what Andrea thought or believed."

"Seems self-evident now," Kins said, shrugging and sitting back.

"Did your wife have any relatives?" Tracy asked.

Strickland shook his head. "No. Her parents were deceased."

"How about friends who would have assisted her?"

"I'm not sure anyone did," Strickland said.

"She had to get from Mount Rainier to Seattle some way," Tracy said.

"Yes, but she could have rented a car and hidden it somewhere."

"Did the Pierce County detectives indicate they'd found evidence she'd done so?"

"No," Strickland said, "but she could have used her false identity." Again, he looked pleased with his reasoning. Fields was accurate: Strickland believed he was smarter than everybody.

Tracy thought Strickland's speculation of a rental car unlikely, but she made a mental note to find out. "Assuming she didn't, can you think of anyone who would have assisted your wife?"

"Andrea was an introvert," Strickland said. "I was the more outgoing one."

"She didn't have *any* friends?" Kins said.

"It wasn't that. It was just that mostly her friends were my friends . . . our friends."

"So no close girlfriend who may have helped her?" Tracy pressed, wondering why Strickland was being evasive about Devin Chambers.

"Not that I can think of . . . I mean, for someone to do that . . . It's a pretty terrible thing to do to someone."

"Do you mean to Andrea or to you?" Kins asked.

"To me," he said. "They would have had to really hate me to let me go through something like this. I could have spent the rest of my life in jail."

"What about someone named Devin Chambers?" Tracy said.

"Andrea and Devin worked together," Strickland said, seemingly unflustered.

"Were they close?"

"I don't know. I think it was more of a work relationship."

"Did you speak to Devin Chambers after your wife's disappearance?"

"Why would I have done that?"

"Did you speak to her when you learned your wife had walked off the mountain?"

"No."

"Did you speak to anyone when you received the news?"

"Just Phil."

"Your wife had a trust, did she not?"

"Yes," Strickland said.

"It was in excess of half a million dollars?"

"That's correct."

"Did you obtain that money after your wife disappeared on the mountain?"

"No, and I have no idea what happened to it."

"It's gone?" Tracy asked.

"Apparently."

"And you don't know where it is?"

"I don't."

"You said you and Andrea loved the outdoors?" Tracy asked.

"We did," Strickland said, though he definitely didn't strike Tracy as the outdoor type.

"What did you do besides climbing?"

"We hiked quite a bit. Skied in the winter."

"Water-skied?"

"On occasion."

"Can you drive a boat?" Kins asked.

Strickland shrugged, meeting Kins's gaze, and in that brief moment letting Kins know he knew exactly where Kins was going, and he had already beaten him there. "Just about anyone can drive a boat," he said.

After another thirty minutes, Tracy looked to Kins, who gave her a slight shrug. They weren't going to get much more out of Strickland.

He was slick, as Fields had warned, and he had Montgomery running interference for him. She thanked both Strickland and Montgomery and handed them a card. "If you think of anything that might be helpful, you can reach me at that number."

As they left the building, stepping from air-conditioning into a quickly warming day, Tracy said, "You knew he didn't own a boat."

"I just wanted to know if he knew how to drive one," Kins said.

CHAPTER 14

*A*fter leaving the DOL, I practiced the name, saying it out loud and in sentences like, "Hi, I'm Lynn Hoff." I drove to Renton, which was on the way back to Portland. I'd found a bank online the previous night called Emerald Credit Union. I stopped in a gas station restroom and applied mascara, eyeliner, and lipstick. I also brushed out my hair and removed my wedding band.

Inside the bank, I approached the counter and told the woman I was hoping to open a new bank account. She directed me to four desks at the back divided by cubicle walls. Two of the desks were empty. A woman who looked to be in her midthirties sat at the third desk. At the fourth sat a guy who looked about my age, with wisps of hair above his upper lip. The nameplate said "Branch Manager." I quickly approached.

"Hi," I said, smiling brightly. "I'm hoping you could help me open an account."

He looked up from his computer and smiled. His eyes ran down my body. I knew I looked as good as I ever had, with the weight loss and the workouts in preparation for climbing Mount Rainier. "I'd be happy to," he said.

"I just recently relocated," I said, sitting and moving close so that I could lean an arm on the edge of his desk. "So I have a temporary driver's license."

"That's fine," he said, still smiling. His gaze dropped for just a brief second to the V in my blouse before reengaging my eyes. "What brings you to Washington?"

"Work," I said. "My company transferred me here to open an office." I reached out and shook his hand. "Lynn Hoff." I liked how the name just rolled off my tongue.

"Kevin Gonzalez," he said. "I'm the branch manager. What kind of work do you do?"

"It's an outdoor apparel company, a start-up."

"What's it called?" he asked. "Maybe I've heard of it."

"Running Free," I said, having thought of the name the night before.

"Great name." He opened his desk drawers and removed paperwork. "How much will you be depositing with us today?"

"In that account?" I paused. "Just a few hundred dollars. My company will be wiring me additional funds once I provide them with the routing and account numbers, and I'll be making frequent online deposits, probably daily."

"We can certainly do that," Kevin said. "I noticed you said, 'that account.' Will you be opening another account?"

"I want to also open a personal account," I said. "It's quite a bit of money, a settlement from a lawsuit. I was in an accident several years ago. Now that I'm moving here, I want to transfer the funds."

"We can certainly accommodate you with that as well," he said. "I hope you weren't hurt too badly?"

"I was in the hospital and rehab for a while," I said.

"Well," he said, blushing. "You rehabbed nicely, if I can say so, Lynn."

I leaned closer to the desk, allowing my shirt to open just a peek lower. "That is so sweet of you, Kevin," I said.

CHAPTER 15

Thursday morning, with a subpoena for Lynn Hoff's bank records tucked into his file, Faz pulled open the car door and slid into the passenger seat, bumping shoulders with Del as the two of them struggled to pull seat belts across their bodies.

Someone had once commented that Faz and Del in the front seat of the Ford looked like two grizzlies squished in a circus clown car. Faz just laughed. He and Del knew they were the comic relief around the Violent Crimes Section and they embraced that role. They provided a diversion from an often stressful and disheartening profession. After nearly twenty years, Faz knew from experience that detectives witnessed the worst that humanity had to offer, the carnage the sick and depraved left behind. They did not have the luxury the rest of the population had to cover their eyes or look away. They had to rummage through that carnage in the most minute detail and, when they had finished, when they had put the murderer in jail, they got to do it all over again. There would always be another murder, as sure as taxes and dying, as Faz's mother liked to say. People had been killing one another since Cain killed his brother Abel. Since they had been the world's first two births—according to the Old Testament anyway—and since only Cain had survived, Faz figured the capacity to kill was part of every human being's DNA.

When his kids were young, Faz had often struggled with what to tell them he did for a living, about how he spent his day. He'd done his best to shield his sons from the worst of his work, but he couldn't shield himself. His job was to look closely, to try to get into the minds of criminals. He'd hunted serial killers, killers who had dismembered bodies, jealous husbands, and the gangbangers who'd shoot someone over a dime bag of dope. Then he'd driven home, where he was expected to help with the homework, and get the boys ready for dinner. Some nights, he'd driven home and sat in the car, a block from the house, just trying to make sense of it. Some people asked why he and Del made jokes. They asked how they could laugh about such things. Faz didn't know. He just knew he would have gone crazy a long time ago if he hadn't found a reason to smile, maybe even a moment of laughter amid the horror. Some days that was the only thing that made him feel human.

Del pulled into a strip mall that included a teriyaki restaurant, a fitness studio, a UPS store, and the Emerald Credit Union.

"Bank to go," Del said. "You can eat lunch, work it off, and make a deposit or withdrawal."

"One-stop shopping," Faz said.

Del maneuvered the car into a spot reserved for bank customers and partially shaded by the building overhang. Since they were ten minutes early for their appointment, Del kept the engine running, blasting the air-conditioning.

"So why'd she bother to open a corporation?" Del asked. "Why go to that trouble?"

The prior afternoon, Faz had run down the account on the receipt Tracy found in the motel-room trash. Conversations with the bank manager revealed both a personal account for Lynn Hoff and a business account for a company called Running Free. Faz had looked up Running Free, Inc., on the Secretary of State's web page, uncertain he'd find anything. Turned out Running Free existed—a subchapter S corporation formed in Delaware in March 2017, two months before the Stricklands' final excursion up Rainier. The timing further confirmed that Andrea Strickland had planned her disappearance, and she'd been meticulous about it.

"It's one more layer between her and anybody looking for her," Faz said. "You can do all the paperwork online so you can remain anonymous."

"I take it she chose Delaware because they do a lot of business?" Del asked.

"More companies incorporate there than any other place in the world," Faz said. "You come up with a business name, decide on the type of entity you want to form, pick and designate a registered agent in the state of Delaware from a list, pay the fee, and wah-lah, you get your certificate of incorporation."

"So a safety-in-numbers sort of thing?"

"Maybe, although now computers make it easier to track, which I suspect is why she didn't designate herself an officer or shareholder."

"You think the officers are fake?"

"No doubt. If you need to sign a lease or open a bank account, you say you've been relocated and the company is paying your living expenses. That way, the lease agreements and bills for utilities, which enterprising persons such as us use to track people down, aren't in your name. Another layer of deception. And the name of a company also gives the landlord the warm and fuzzies that they're guaranteed payment, especially if the bank is local."

Del looked out the window at the glass-door entrance to Emerald Credit Union. "Might be local, but I've never heard of this place. I take it that was also intentional?"

"Easier to make a personal connection with the branch manager and teller at a small bank."

"But I thought the whole point was *not* to draw attention to yourself."

"You want to avoid the wrong kind of attention, like going through an airport security checkpoint, or customs, with a bag full of cash."

"So she dumps it in a bank account," Del said.

"Not all at once. The banking laws are designed to prevent people from hiding large amounts of cash. Anything over ten grand and the bank has to fill out paperwork and report it to the feds."

"So she makes sure to make deposits under $10K," Del said.

"And the feds countered that strategy with the Bank Secrecy Act, which requires a bank to file a report if it *suspects* a person is making multiple cash deposits to avoid the reporting requirement."

"So you're saying she goes into the local bank and makes nice so they're less inclined to report her."

"I'm betting she had a ready-made story to dump that much cash into one account without triggering the reporting requirement."

"So then what? She slowly withdraws the money in that account and deposits it into the business account?"

"Bingo. At the same time, she withdraws money from the business account, as if paying business expenses or whatever, but what she's really doing is transferring it to a different account in a different bank, in a different name. Layer by layer, it disappears."

"How the hell does a woman with a high school education figure this out?" Del said, shaking his head.

"You kidding? You can buy books that tell you how to do it step-by-step."

"Too much trouble," Del said.

"Yeah, you got to know how to read."

"Only books I read are on the Civil War," Del said. Faz knew Del had a collection that would make a librarian blush. "If they had that category on *Jeopardy*, I'd be on a beach in Greece."

"Greece is bankrupt."

"Exactly. I'd be like a tycoon over there." Del killed the engine and checked his watch. "Let's you and me go figure this out."

Inside the bank, they walked past the three bank teller stations to a cluster of four desks. Del stopped at the obligatory table with Styrofoam cups and complimentary coffee and snacks. He snagged a couple of miniature chocolate chip cookies, popping one into his mouth.

A female bank employee was waiting on a customer at one of the four desks. The other three desks were empty. On one of those empty desks sat a nameplate holder with a plastic removable sign. "Branch Manager."

"Why is it removable?" Del said.

"Maybe it's the guy's name," Faz said. Del gave him a look. "Hey, it would save money on business cards."

Faz noticed a gangly young man standing behind the teller stations glance in their direction. "I'll bet that's Branch right there," he said.

The young man took paperwork from a teller and walked to the far end of the bull pen, emerging from a rear door and proceeding to the branch manager's desk.

"Detectives?" the young man said, inadvertently drawing the attention of the person seated at the adjacent desk. He lowered his voice, though he would have needed to use sign language to keep the others from hearing—the desks were that close. "I'm Kevin Gonzalez, the branch manager."

Gonzalez looked to be mid- to late twenties but with one of those prepubescent faces still fighting acne, and a wispy mustache that made him look sixteen.

Faz introduced them both. They all took seats.

"You have the subpoena?" Gonzalez tried to be all business, then added in an almost apologetic tone, "I called the home office and they said you would have a subpoena."

"Where's the home office?" Faz asked, hoping a routine question would help Gonzalez relax. The manager was doing his best to look professional, but he couldn't completely hide the nervous shake in his hands or his voice.

"Centralia," Gonzalez said, referencing a small town about an hour and a half south of Seattle.

"How long has this branch been open?"

"About five years, I believe."

"And how long have you been the branch manager?"

"Nine months."

"Congratulations."

Gonzalez paused, as if uncertain what to say. Then he smiled. "Thank you."

"Did you work here before becoming the branch manager?" Faz asked.

"I was a teller for two years. Can I offer you some coffee?"

"We're good," Faz said.

"Makes me sweat in weather like this," Del added. "And I don't need any help in that department."

Faz handed Gonzalez the subpoena. He doubted the young man had ever seen a subpoena before, but Gonzalez took the time to make it appear he knew what he was doing. "We're concerned about the privacy of our customers," Gonzalez said.

"Don't be," Del said. "This customer is dead."

"Oh." Gonzalez looked and sounded both surprised and saddened.

"Did you know Lynn Hoff?" Faz asked.

"Yes," Gonzalez said. He appeared frozen for a moment. He shook free. "Wow. Sorry. I opened her accounts."

"The personal account and the business account?" Faz said.

"Yes."

"Tell me about the personal account."

"She deposited a large settlement from a car accident, more than $500,000."

"Do you remember the day she came in?" Faz asked.

"It was March twelfth."

"No, I mean do you remember that day?" Faz noted Gonzalez was not wearing a wedding ring and guessed the young man had recalled an attractive young woman like Andrea Strickland.

"Oh, uh, yes. Sort of."

"Tell us what you remember," Del said, taking out a small spiral notebook and pen.

Gonzalez's gaze flicked to the pad and pen, then back to Faz. "Just that she wanted to open the two accounts. She said she'd been relocated by her business."

"Did she say what type of business?" Faz asked.

"It was an outdoor apparel company, I believe."

"Did she say where she'd moved from?"

"Somewhere in Southern California, I believe. I remember because she joked about the company having more clients since it rains so much here."

"What else do you recall?" Faz asked.

Gonzalez glanced away as if trying to remember. "She said she'd just divorced and was tired of the guys in Southern California. She said the whole scene was too superficial for her. She said she was staying with a girlfriend until she found her own place."

And Faz was certain that nugget of well-placed information had piqued Gonzalez's interest, just as Andrea Strickland, aka Lynn Hoff, had intended it to. High school education maybe, but she was smart and she knew how to play the game.

"You helped her open the accounts?" Faz said.

"I did."

"How much did she deposit in the business account on her initial visit?"

Gonzalez didn't even look at the printed sheets of paper on his desk. "It was just a couple hundred dollars."

"Did she make deposits to that account?"

"Almost daily."

Faz noticed Del glance at him. He loved being right.

"May I?" Faz asked.

Gonzalez handed him the sheets of paper. Del leaned over Faz's shoulder. As Faz had suspected, Strickland had made a steady stream of deposits and withdrawals intended not to draw attention—$1,775, $1,350, $2,260. Over the ensuing month and a half, these small deposits and withdrawals to the business account had increased. The amount of money that had moved through the account had added up to $128,775.42. The Emerald Credit Union was clearly not the only bank account Andrea Strickland had opened. The question was, where had she transferred the rest of the money, and in whose name? Faz was betting the money had gone overseas, to a country that did not report on the identity of its customers.

The number that caught his eye, however, was in the far column on the last line, the one indicating Lynn Hoff's balance in both accounts: $0.00.

"She closed the accounts," Faz said, looking up at Gonzalez. "Did she close the accounts?"

"Apparently."

"You didn't close it for her?"

"She didn't come in."

To open an account a customer had to personally go into a bank and provide proper identification. That was not necessary to transfer the money and close the account, which could be done electronically—if the person had the account number and password.

Faz looked at Del. "She closed the account June twenty-sixth," he said, not bothering to elaborate. Del knew it was the Monday after Kurt Schill had pulled Andrea Strickland's body from the depths of Puget Sound.

CHAPTER 16

I got my job back at the insurance company working for Brenda, and that first week back she invited me to lunch to "catch up." I think she was worried about me and, as my surrogate mom, felt it her duty to make sure I was okay. I wasn't, of course. I now fully understood the man I had married—manipulative, abusive, probably manic-depressive. I knew he would continue to try to take advantage of me so long as he thought he could gain access to my trust funds. At present, he was on his best behavior, but only because he had to be. He had nowhere to go. His job search was not going well. BSBT, not surprisingly, would not provide him with a recommendation. When prospective employers called, BSBT's human resources director "declined to comment," which was a law firm's way of saying the ex-employee was incompetent or dishonest, without getting sued, and every employer knew it. Graham continued to spin it, saying he didn't want to work for someone else, that the real money "was in working for himself." I ignored his comments. Most recently, Graham was talking to a law school roommate who had opened his own firm in a house and was looking for some attorneys to attend depositions and appear in court.

Brenda chose a restaurant called the Port House—a chic brewery that was so Portland with plank floors, a tall wood-beam ceiling, and brick walls.

She had an appointment out of the office and suggested we meet at 1:15 p.m., after much of the lunch crowd had thinned. I removed my sunglasses as I entered but didn't immediately see her. The hostess led me to a table on the sidewalk patio where I could people-watch while waiting. I pulled up my latest novel on my phone to read. A man's voice interrupted me.

"Excuse me?"

I figured it was a panhandler about to hit me up for change. To my surprise, the man standing on the other side of the small wrought-iron fence wore a suit.

"I'm sorry to bother you," he said, smiling. "I don't normally do this, but if you're not waiting for someone, I wonder if I could buy you a beer?"

I was stunned and unsure of what to say. I'd never had anyone pick me up, and I wasn't even sure that was the guy's intent. I know you can't judge a book by its cover, but he seemed so earnest, even a bit sheepish in his approach, like he really never had done this before. Some people give off a vibe, you know?

"I'm sorry," I said. I truly was. "I'm having lunch with my friend. But, thank you for asking."

He nodded as if he understood my situation, though I'm certain he couldn't have. Maybe it was my vibe. Maybe my vibe was sadness and desperation.

"No worries," he said, taking a step back from the fence. "I just saw you sitting alone and thought . . ."

The hostess appeared at the table, escorting Brenda.

"Well," the man said, nodding to us both. "Sorry to interrupt. Have a nice lunch."

Brenda gave me an inquisitive, arched eyebrow. "Friend of yours?"

"No," I said, watching the man walk away. A part of me wanted to chase after him, tell him I'd love to have lunch, and then we'd talk and I'd realize he was my soul mate. But I knew that was just an age-old fairy tale that had been done a billion different ways in books and movies.

"He just wanted to buy me a beer," I said.

She smiled. "I don't blame him. You look great. You've lost weight and you look really toned."

I could again fit into what I referred to as my "skinny wardrobe." I felt comfortable.

Brenda was casually dressed—casual for her, anyway. She wore slacks, a colorful blouse, and a brown jacket she quickly ditched over the back of her chair. For someone who'd just had her first child, she was in phenomenal shape, but then she was obsessed with working out. I knew Brenda was a member of the local YMCA and, when the weather got nice, she ran. Apparently, she and her husband participated in CrossFit competitions.

The waiter arrived. "I'll have a Mac & Jack's," Brenda said.

He looked to me.

It was lunch and Brenda was my boss. "I'll have iced tea."

"Nonsense," she said. "She'll have what I'm having."

After the waiter departed, Brenda said, "The doctor says beer helps produce milk when you're breast-feeding. Who am I to argue? So what have you been doing to look so terrific?"

"I've been working out," I said, sensing the opening. "Graham wants to climb Rainier. He thinks we need a hobby, that it will help our relationship."

"Are things going better?"

When I asked Brenda for my job back I'd told her we had to file for bankruptcy and that the stress had impacted our marriage. "We're working at it," I said. "Actually, that reminds me. I need to get an insurance policy."

"An insurance policy?"

"Life insurance," I said. "Graham thinks it would be wise, given the climb is coming up. Could you help?"

"Sure," she said. "So, co-policies?"

"No. Just a policy for me."

Her eyes narrowed. "Just for you?"

"Well, we can't really afford the premiums on two policies, and Graham says that if anything were to happen to him, I'd have my parents' trust, so I'd be okay."

"So he just wants a policy on you—with him as the beneficiary?"

"Right."

She seemed to give that some thought. The waiter appeared with our beers. Brenda raised her glass and I met hers across the table. "Cheers," she said. "It's good to have you back."

Brenda ordered a Caesar salad. The thought of anchovies, even just the smell, almost made me lean over the railing and vomit. "I'll have a house salad with oil and vinegar on the side."

"Well, I'm glad things are going better," Brenda said as the waiter departed.

I diverted my gaze.

"Andrea? Things are going better, right?"

"A little," I said. Then I just blurted out, "Actually, I think he might be cheating on me again."

The saddest part might have been Brenda's reaction. She did not look surprised. She set down her glass and reached out a hand to me, her multiple bracelets clattering against the tabletop.

"How long has it been going on?"

"Well, the first time was before we were married."

"What?"

"It was an associate in his law firm. He'd been seeing her before he met me and said it had been difficult to break off because he didn't want to hurt her. I'm an idiot, right?"

In hindsight, I knew I had ignored all the signs—the late nights, Graham coming home smelling of alcohol, the lack of interest in me except when it suited him. I had been an idiot, but I was no longer going to be an idiot. I had to have a different plan now, and telling Brenda was part of it.

"No," she said, looking at me as if I were a broken little bird. "Don't blame yourself for this. Have you confronted him about it?"

I shook my head. "He'll deny it and turn it around, say I don't trust him."

"How did you find out?"

"I wasn't snooping," I said. "I wouldn't do that."

"Of course not."

I sat back from the table. "It's just that, the business was doing so poorly and Graham handled all the business financials. I decided to pay closer attention to the credit card statements. I didn't know where the money was going, or how we were going to pay our bills each month. The expenses were way beyond what the business was generating."

"Did you find something on the credit card statements?"

I nodded and took a sip of beer. "Graham was making trips to Seattle, and to Vancouver and Victoria, and charging the hotel rooms to the company credit cards. There were also restaurant charges, and a few bars."

"Could they have been business trips?" Brenda said, though not with any real conviction.

"That's what Graham said."

"So you did confront him."

"No, that's what he told me when he said he had to leave town for a few days—that they were business trips."

"But they weren't?"

"I called the distributors and dispensaries in Seattle he said he was meeting. They'd never met Graham in person. They had no idea what I was talking about, and pot hadn't been legalized in Canada when he made those trips."

Brenda sighed. "Do you know who it is?"

"No," I said, taking another sip. "And then there's the stress that Graham could be going to jail."

Brenda set down her glass. "What?"

"Graham lied on the loan application to the bank. He said he was being made a partner at a higher salary. They asked for a letter to confirm it and he typed it up on the firm letterhead and forged one of the partners' names."

"And the bank found out?"

I nodded.

They were never going to make Graham a partner. In fact, they'd given him sixty days to find another job. I saw the severance letter. It was right around the time he came home all excited about opening Genesis. He said he wanted to leave the firm because it was stifling his creativity and he needed to be in business for himself. More bullshit.

"He said they offered him a partnership, but he was tired of working for someone else and wanted to work for himself. None of it was true."

"I'm so sorry for you, Andrea." Brenda sat back and gave me that look of pity I saw for so many years when my aunt would tell others that my parents were dead. "I know it's early, but do you know what you're going to do?"

"No," I said.

"Would you like to talk to an attorney?"

I'd thought that through on my own. "I can't afford a divorce," I said.

Brenda's brow furrowed. "What do you mean? It should be straightforward. You don't have kids or own a home, and you won't have any significant assets."

"Graham signed my name to personal guarantees on the lease of the building and the bank loan."

"Why would he do that?"

"Because he was mad that I wouldn't let him use my parents' trust. We're filing for bankruptcy. I'm really worried I'll lose it and have nothing."

"How much is it?"

"The principal is half a million dollars," I said.

Brenda's eyes widened. "And Graham can't touch it?"

"Not while I'm still alive," I said and laughed lightly. "And that just makes him angry. What I'm concerned about are the creditors coming after it, saying I signed the guarantees."

"Did you have an attorney look at the bank papers?"

"No. Graham handled it. He said there was no need to pay a lawyer since he was one. I don't know how I would support myself."

She waved it off. "Don't worry about that, you can always work for me."

"Thanks, Brenda. I hate to bother you with all this."

She reached across the table and again took my hand. "It's going to be okay," she said. "I'm going to find you an attorney."

CHAPTER 17

When Tracy called to set up the interview, Brenda Berg explained that she wouldn't be at the office, that she had an infant, a baby girl, and worked from home a couple days a week. Still, Berg never hesitated when Tracy said she and Kins would like to talk to her about Andrea Strickland. She said she'd been following the story of Andrea's brief reappearance and subsequent murder.

Tracy reconnected with Berg as she and Kins left Phil Montgomery's office. Berg was about to take her daughter out in the jogging stroller to get her to sleep but said that if they didn't mind talking and walking at the same time, Berg would meet them near two monuments at Waterfront Park just below the Steel Bridge in downtown Portland.

"I'll be in workout clothes and pushing a running stroller."

Tracy and Kins arrived at the monuments before Berg. The Willamette River was teeming with runners, men and women walking in business attire, and a few baby strollers.

"I hope she's not one of those athletic types who walks faster than I run," Kins said, slipping on a pair of sunglasses. "My hip is burning from all the time we've spent in the car."

"Come on, it's a beautiful day. Maybe a walk will help loosen it up."

"I'd like it better if it came with air-conditioning."

Tracy spotted an athletic-looking woman in a white tank top, dolphin shorts, and running shoes jogging toward them while pushing a blue stroller with one hand. She slowed as she approached.

"Hi, are you Detective Crosswhite?" She didn't look or sound the least bit out of breath.

Tracy introduced Kins.

Berg looked like a runner—with bony shoulders; lean, sinewy muscles; and a runner's tan. Tracy had been expecting someone younger, given that Berg said she had a newborn, but the crow's-feet at the corners of Berg's eyes indicated she was more likely late thirties to early forties—Tracy's age.

"Sorry to do this to you," Berg said, leaning down to peek into the stroller, "but she's off on her sleep cycles and this seems to be the only way to get her to nap in the afternoon."

"Not a problem," Tracy said. Tracy looked beneath the canopy that provided the baby shade. The little girl lay wrapped in a pink blanket and wore a light-blue beanie. "How old is she?"

"Five months yesterday," Berg said.

"She's beautiful."

"Thanks. We named her Jessica. She's my angel."

Tracy smiled at the tiny face beneath the beanie and it stirred her own memories. She'd always imagined she'd have children. She'd imagined that she'd live next door to Sarah and they'd raise their kids together. "Do you have other children?" she asked.

"No," Berg said, still smiling at her daughter. "I was more into building my insurance practice and making a living. I met my husband a couple years ago. It took a while before we decided to pull the trigger. Now, I don't know what my life would be like without her. Do you have kids?"

"No," Tracy said.

"Wedded to your job, I'd imagine."

"Something like that," Tracy said. She'd been wedded to finding out who had killed Sarah and it had come at a cost. She'd lost a husband, left a career teaching in Cedar Grove to join the Seattle Police Department, and rarely dated. For years she'd spent most nights going over manuscripts and pieces of evidence related to her sister's disappearance, until she'd hit a dead end, and reluctantly boxed up her work. By then she was in her midthirties and her dating prospects seemed to be cops or prosecutors, and she wasn't interested in bringing her work home any more than she already did.

"I know that feeling," Berg said. As if on cue, Jessica made a noise and Berg added, "We better get moving. Seems to be the only thing that puts her to sleep."

They walked the pavement, Tracy at Berg's side, Kins following a step behind.

"I'm still in shock," Berg said. "This was horrible the first time; I mean when we thought Andrea died two months ago. Now, finding out she was alive? I don't know what to think." She looked to Tracy. "So, she's dead? She *really* is the woman found in that crab pot?"

"That appears to be the case," Tracy said, stepping to the side as two runners approached and passed.

Berg shook her head. "My emotions are all screwed up."

"I take it from your response that you hadn't heard from Andrea," Tracy said.

"No. Not a word."

"How long did she work as your assistant?"

"About two, two and a half years. She left for about seven months, when she and her husband opened their business. When it failed, she came back."

"Was it strictly a professional relationship?" Tracy asked.

Berg nodded. "Andrea was quite a bit younger, and there was that natural demarcation between employer and employee, but we'd occasionally go out to lunch, that sort of thing. I kind of decided that she needed someone. You know she lost her parents at a very young age."

"We know," Tracy said.

"It was tragic. She didn't talk about it, but it came out in her interview and I looked it up. Her parents died in a car accident on Christmas Eve. A drunk driver hit them. From what I understand, Andrea was trapped in the car. I tried to be there for her when she needed me."

"What kind of person was she?" Tracy asked.

"Andrea was quiet, but not necessarily shy. People thought she was shy because she read a lot. That was my first impression too."

"What did she read?" Tracy asked.

"Novels," Berg said. "She had paperbacks stacked all over her desk, novels on her phone and her Kindle. She read all the time, but when you got to know her you realized she wasn't shy. She just preferred not to be the center of attention. She liked to stay on the periphery. Does that make sense?"

"Can you give me an example?" Tracy said.

Berg gave the question some thought. "We had a function at the company—a birthday party for someone. I caught Andrea sitting back and taking everything in, you know? If you didn't know her, you might get the impression she was disinterested, but if you watched her closely, you'd see these little grins, or frowns, maybe a subtle eye roll. It was never blatant or disrespectful, just enough that I knew she was paying attention."

"Was she intelligent?" Tracy asked.

"Very," Berg said, nodding.

"You sound certain of that."

"For someone without *any* college education she was *extremely quick* to pick things up. She wasn't a normal assistant. I'd give her some fairly complex tasks and she'd get the work done in no time flat. I think she was just one of those people who was inherently very smart, very gifted.

Maybe from all the reading she did. You never had to instruct her twice. I was encouraging her to go to college or to get her insurance license."

They approached a second drawbridge. Out on the water, speed-boats zipped by with young men and women in bathing suits.

"Did you know her husband, Graham?" Kins asked.

Berg looked back over her shoulder. "A little. I was inadvertently to blame for that."

"How so?" Kins said.

"Like I said, Andrea was an introvert. She really just preferred to go home and read after work. It became my mission to find her a social life. We had a function downtown and I sort of forced Andrea to attend. That's where she met Graham. Anyway, next thing I knew she's getting married."

"How long after they met?" Tracy asked.

Berg blew out a breath. "It was fast, I'll tell you that. Maybe a month or two. I'm not really sure."

"Did Andrea seem happy?"

"Hard to tell with Andrea—she kept everything so close to the vest, but I thought so."

"We understand she grew up in Southern California. Do you know if she still has family down there?" Kins asked.

"An aunt, I believe, though I don't think they're close."

"Did you subsequently get to know Graham?" Kins asked.

"Not real well," Berg said. "For the most part Andrea kept her work life and personal life separate."

Tracy deduced from the tone of Berg's response that she had not been a fan of Graham Strickland, but was being diplomatic. "But you had occasion to meet him?"

"Just a couple of times. He came to a few functions and every so often he'd come in and pick up Andrea from work."

"What was he like?" Kins said.

Berg smiled but it looked like more of a wince, as if she were in pain. She looked like someone who had an opinion but didn't want to offer it.

"We understand you didn't know him well," Tracy said. "We're just looking for your general impression of him."

"Honestly? I didn't care for him." She again hesitated. "He was just one of those guys who tried too hard. Do you know what I mean?"

"Tried too hard to be liked?" Kins said.

Berg again looked back over her shoulder but this time she paused midstep and stopped. "Yes. That's a very good way to put it."

"What did he do?" Kins asked.

"It was just everything—the way he dressed, his hair, the beard. It was all . . . affected, like he was trying to display a certain image. And the Porsche." She smiled and shook her head at the thought of it. "A red Carrera Porsche. It was all just sort of obnoxious. And I don't think he was any rocket scientist."

"Why not?" Tracy asked.

"Just little things Andrea said—like the marijuana dispensary. Andrea tried to tell him she didn't think it was a good business idea, but she said Graham had done all the research and told her it was going to be a gold mine."

Tracy wiped a bead of perspiration trickling down the side of her face. She could feel sweat between her shoulder blades from the sun, which was at their backs. "Did Andrea ever say she and Graham were having marital troubles?"

Berg became contemplative. "Andrea and I went to lunch after she came back to work for me, after the business failed. She said Graham was cheating on her."

"Did she say with who?" Tracy asked.

"She didn't know, but apparently it wasn't the first time. He'd cheated with someone he used to work with."

"How'd she find out? Did she say?" Tracy asked.

"When the business started to fail, she paid closer attention to the expenses and found credit card charges for hotels and restaurants in

Seattle. He'd said they were related to work, but she called the businesses. They weren't."

"So she was resourceful," Kins said.

"When she had to be," Berg said.

"What else did she tell you at that lunch?" Tracy asked.

Berg shook her head. "In hindsight, I wish I had done something more."

"About what?"

"Andrea said that despite the marital problems, Graham wanted to climb Mount Rainier."

"*He* wanted to climb it?" Kins asked.

"That's what she said. She told me that Graham said it would help if they had a hobby, something they could do together. Then she said he also mentioned taking out a life insurance policy, but only on her."

"Only her?" Tracy asked, giving Kins a sidelong glance.

"I know. I thought it sounded odd at the time, but Andrea said they couldn't afford the premiums on both, and Graham reasoned that if anything happened to him she could live off her trust. You know about her trust, right?"

"We do," Tracy said.

"It struck me as odd at the time, you know, but you don't think about these types of things."

"So what was your first thought when you heard Andrea had disappeared from Mount Rainier?" Kins asked.

Berg hesitated. The baby fussed and she took a moment to soothe her daughter, inserting a pacifier in the baby's mouth. When they started walking again she said, "I guess I was skeptical."

"Skeptical that it was an accident?" Kins asked.

She nodded. "Let me put it this way: I wasn't surprised Graham was a suspect, and I wouldn't have been shocked if they'd concluded he killed Andrea. I told the other detective the same thing."

"Stan Fields?" Tracy asked.

"I don't remember his name. He had a gray ponytail. I told him it all just seemed too convenient. Then there was something Andrea told me about her parents' trust—she said Graham wanted to use the money to help set up the dispensary rather than take out a business loan, but Andrea wouldn't let him and there were restrictions on the trust that prevented it."

"Did she say it was causing strain in their marriage?" Tracy asked.

"It was pretty clear that was the case."

"Did she tell you that?"

"Yes."

"She told you she didn't want to give him the money?" Kins asked, sounding out of breath.

Berg nodded. "She said Graham got upset about it and that he had forged her name on personal guarantees. She feared he'd put the trust at risk. But what really should have set off my radar was something Andrea said when I asked whether Graham had access to the trust."

"What did she say?" Tracy asked.

"She said, 'Not while I'm still alive.'" Berg shook her head at the memory. "She laughed, but it had a sad quality to it, you know? I felt sad for her, sad that she would say such a thing."

They crossed beneath another bridge. "When was the last time you saw or spoke to Andrea?" Tracy said.

"It was that week she left to climb."

"What was her mood like?"

Berg said, "It wasn't always easy to tell with Andrea. I mean, she was pretty even-keeled. I think she'd experienced a lot of sorrow in her life at a young age and it had made her, I don't know, maybe more measured about life, like maybe she didn't expect much."

"Jaded," Kins said.

"That's as good a word as any," Berg said, glancing back at him. "Even when she married Graham I didn't get a sense she was elated about it, just more sort of like, this was how it was."

"Did Andrea have any girlfriends—people she hung out with, maybe went out with after work?"

"The only person I can really think of is Devin Chambers. She worked in the office for one of my partners, and she and Andrea seemed close. Other than that, not really."

"Does Devin Chambers still work at your company?"

"No, she left right about the time Andrea died—or when we all thought Andrea had died—the first time."

"Did she leave because of that?"

"I don't know. She didn't talk to me about it. She told my partner she was moving back east somewhere. I think she had family."

Tracy looked to Kins, who shook his head to indicate he had no further questions.

"Thank you again for your time," Tracy said. "We'll let you and your daughter finish your run." She handed Berg a business card. "If you think of anything else, don't hesitate to call."

As Tracy and Kins walked along the waterfront, back in the direction of the sculptures, Tracy said, "Does it strike you as odd that a woman who believed her husband was cheating on her for at least the second time in a year would agree to climb Mount Rainier with him?"

"Even more so if she was talking to a divorce attorney," Kins said. "Sounds to me like she was planning on walking off and starting over."

Tracy stopped. "Maybe it's like Berg said. Maybe there was more to Andrea Strickland than initial impressions."

"Sounds like it," Kins said, "though I'm not certain what that means, yet."

"What if this wasn't just about disappearing and starting over?"

"You think it was her way of getting even? She set him up to make it look like he wanted to kill her?" Kins said.

"Berg said Andrea believed he was cheating on her and it wasn't the first time."

"So our theory is what? The husband realizes she'd set him up, hunts her down, and kills her to get even."

"Not just to get even. To get what he was after in the first place."

"The money," Kins said.

"She's already dead," Tracy said. "He figures that if he finds her, he finds the money. Since she's already dead, no one is the wiser. He just needs a way to dispose of the body so she'll never be found."

"Okay, but how do we prove it?" Kins said.

"I think we need to find Devin Chambers. If Andrea was going to confide in anyone, it sounds like it would have been her."

"You think that's why Chambers left town, that maybe she was the person who helped her?"

"Ranger Hicks is convinced Andrea Strickland didn't get off the mountain alone," Tracy said.

"Then I'd also like to talk to the aunt," Kins said. "Being dead has to get lonely, and it sounds like she was her only family."

Tracy called Stan Fields on the drive back to Police Headquarters to discuss Devin Chambers. She put him on speakerphone.

"Did you know she's left town?" Tracy asked.

"No, but no crime in that. Why, you think they could have been dykes or something?"

Tracy rolled her eyes while Kins stifled a laugh. "No, but it's possible if Andrea confided in her that they remained in touch."

"She told me she didn't know much of anything."

"Did you ever come across any evidence the husband was having another affair?"

"The employer mentioned that. She said the wife was convinced he was cheating on her, but she didn't have any details. I spoke to the associate at the law firm he'd been hammering and it wasn't her; she said the first time had been a mistake, that she didn't know he'd gotten married, and she was married and had moved on. Hadn't seen or talked to him in months."

"Okay, so you haven't followed up with Devin Chambers?"

"Like I said, I had no reason to. She had receipts indicating she was out of town when they climbed. You have something different?"

"I don't know," Tracy said.

"It's your rodeo, Detective. Have at her if you think there's something there."

Tracy hung up. "I really don't like that guy."

"He's a cowboy," Kins said, smiling.

"He's a jackass." Tracy let a few miles pass, thinking again of Brenda Berg and her baby. Kins had three boys. "You glad you had kids, Kins?"

Kins looked over at her. "It got to you, didn't it? I figured it did."

"What?" she said, sounding defensive.

"Berg and you are about the same age and have a lot of similarities."

"We don't have that many similarities."

"Oh no?"

"So are you glad?" she asked.

Kins gave it some thought. "Not when they crash the car, or tell me the night before that they have a report due." He smiled. "But the other ninety-nine percent of the time? Yeah. I'm glad. Does Dan want to have kids?"

"I'm forty-three," she said, wondering if she'd waited beyond her window.

"I know a woman who was forty-two when she had her first. She has two now."

"They're healthy?"

"From what I know. Have you talked to Dan about it?"

"Yeah, a little bit. But a part of me wonders if his willingness is just because I'm asking. Neither of us is young."

Kins frowned. "People make a big deal about having kids when they're young. Let me tell you, that's not always a good thing. I have a lot more patience now than I did when I was twenty-five, and patience is a big part of being a parent."

"I used to think I'd have kids in my twenties. Now I look back and think I was still a kid in my twenties. At least until my sister died. Things changed after that. It wouldn't have been fair to have kids then. I was too busy trying to find out what had happened to her." She looked at Kins, who, other than Dan, was her closest friend. "So you don't think I'd be too old, huh? You don't think I'd show up at grammar school and have people thinking I was the grandma?"

"So what if they did?"

"I'd be over sixty before he or she turned twenty."

"Yeah, well, I'm not looking forward to having an empty nest in my midforties either. I don't know what the hell Shanna and I are going to do. My kids are the best part of my life."

"I hope you didn't tell Shanna that."

"Hey, I'm old. I'm not stupid. Okay, here's what I think—call it Kins 101. When we didn't have kids, we adapted, right? When we had kids, we adapted. When the kids are grown and out of the house, we'll adapt again. Age doesn't play into any of that. If you love Dan, and you want kids, I say go for it. You'd be better parents than ninety-nine percent of the knuckleheads out there."

Tracy smiled.

"Grandma," Kins said.

"You're such an ass," Tracy said, laughing.

———

Tracy watched Faz spike his fork in the Tupperware bowl on his desk and struggle out of his desk chair as soon as he spotted her and Kins returning. Ordinarily, Faz was like a dog with a bone when it came to Vera's leftovers. He did not forsake them without good reason. It meant he had something of interest to tell them.

"You speak to the bank?" she said over the sound of indeterminable voices from the other three bull pens. She set her purse on her chair, smelling the garlic from Vera's cooking, knowing the smell would linger all day.

"Lynn Hoff told the branch manager she worked for an outdoor apparel company and would be making regular cash deposits," Faz said. "She also opened a personal account and deposited over $500,000. Said it was an injury settlement. For the next several weeks she made daily deposits into and withdrawals out of the business account that correspond with the withdrawals from her personal account."

Kins smiled at Tracy. "Looks like we found her trust funds."

"She was washing them," Faz said. "Probably moving the money out of the country."

"I assume the hubby knew about the trust?" Del said from his cubicle. "Makes for a hell of a motive if he did."

"No doubt," Kins said.

"But that's not the news," Faz said, looking and sounding like a man with a secret. "The news is someone emptied the accounts first thing Monday morning—after Schill pulled her body up in the pot."

Kins glanced at Tracy before turning back to Faz. "How could someone even do that?"

"You have to be physically present to open an account," Faz explained. "Not to close it. Whoever did it, they did it online. But that means they had to know the bank, the names on the accounts, and the passwords."

Tracy looked to Kins. Everything was coming together, and it was all pointing to Graham Strickland. "The husband?"

"Devin Chambers?" Kins said.

"Who's Devin Chambers?" Faz asked.

"Andrea Strickland's friend," Tracy said. "We're going to need to run her down."

"Can we find the money, where it went?" Kins asked.

"I got the fraud unit looking into it," Faz said, "but I'm betting the person immediately routed the money out of the country to a quaint little bank that doesn't ask a lot of information."

"If the person knew what they were doing," Tracy said, wondering how they could prove that person was Graham Strickland. Computer records? Phone records?

"Based on what I've seen so far, they did," Faz said. "At least she did when she was still alive. If it hadn't been for the timing of the withdrawals, I would have said it was her, that she'd thought this whole thing through."

"Except the part about her getting killed," Del said.

"Yeah, well," Faz said.

Johnny Nolasco walked into their bull pen. His appearance had the same effect as a parent walking into a room full of teenagers. Everyone stopped talking. He looked to Tracy. "I didn't get a statement for the brass or the PIO," he said.

"We had interviews early this morning down in Portland."

"I could have saved you the drive," Nolasco said. "Pierce County Prosecutor is reasserting jurisdiction."

"What?" Tracy said, thinking they were just making progress and now Pierce County was going to pull the case back?

"Call came in about an hour ago."

"Who made that decision?" Tracy asked.

"Someone higher up the food chain than me."

"What was their rationale?" Kins asked.

"They have an open investigation and they're farther down the path."

"They *had* a missing persons case," Tracy said. "This is a homicide—in our jurisdiction."

"That's not how they see it. The way they see it, the husband was the prime suspect and remains the prime suspect."

"And they did virtually nothing to prove it. The body was found in our jurisdiction," Tracy said. "Why the hell should we give it back to them?"

"The body was found with a bullet in the back of her head, which means it could have been a body dump," Nolasco said, referring to cases in which the person is killed in one jurisdiction but the body dumped and found in another.

Tracy seethed, suspecting that SPD—Nolasco—had not fought for jurisdiction. The police department in the jurisdiction where a body was dumped was often more than happy to give it up, especially if it appeared that the case would be difficult to solve and would go on the department's books as an unsolved homicide. "Who cares? It was dumped in our jurisdiction. We have it and we're working it."

"At the very least it should be a joint investigation," Kins said.

"Come on, Sparrow," Nolasco said. "She was a resident of Portland and she disappeared in Pierce County. Whatever information exists on the victim is going to most likely be in their jurisdiction."

"This is such bullshit," Tracy said. "She didn't disappear in Pierce County. She was pulled up in a crab pot in King County."

"You want to tell the brass that?"

"Why don't you tell the brass that?" she said, no longer trying to hide her anger. "That's *your* job."

Nolasco's eyes narrowed and his nostrils flared. "I'd suggest you stop making every case about every young woman personal. It clouds your judgment."

"My judgment is fine. What I want is jurisdiction."

"Whoa," Kins said. "Let's all take a second here. I think what Tracy is trying to say, Captain, is that we've made progress, and we hate to give that up."

"Write it up and send it down to Pierce County, Sparrow. This is not our headache anymore. Wrap up what you have going on and send everything down." Nolasco paused and looked around the cubicle. "Have I made myself clear?"

"Yeah," Kins said.

Nolasco looked to Del and Faz, who reluctantly nodded. Then he looked to Tracy. "Do you understand?"

"No, I don't understand, but I heard what you said."

"Then finish up what you're working on and leave this case alone."

—

Tracy spent the rest of the afternoon fuming. She left the office as soon as her shift ended, her anger building as she drove across the West Seattle Bridge. Dan was out in front of her house, dressed in running shorts, T-shirt, and running shoes. He held two leashes, Rex and Sherlock prancing and playing. Tracy was glad to see him. Dan had a way of making her forget work when she came home.

Tracy lowered her window as she turned into the driveway. "You coming or going?"

"Are you kidding? I'd never look this fresh if I were coming." Dan approached the driver's side and they kissed. "I didn't expect you home this early."

"Yeah, neither did I."

He stepped back. "Uh-oh, what happened?"

"Give me five minutes to change and I'll tell you on the run. I need to burn off some anger."

Tracy quickly went inside and left all her clothes on the bed. She changed into her running gear and bolted out the door. Dan, stretching, had the leashes tied to the wrought-iron fence.

"I'm ready," she said.

"You want time to stretch?" he asked.

She took Sherlock's leash and walked down the block.

"I guess not," Dan said, chasing after her.

They walked down the hill to Harbor Way; running downhill was hard on the dogs and on their knees. Then they ran north, along the beach, past the restaurants and storefronts in the direction of Alki Point.

It was a glorious afternoon, the temperature having cooled to the mid-eighties, and many people had come out to enjoy the weather. The beaches and restaurants were crowded and white sails filled Elliott Bay.

"You weren't kidding about the pace," Dan said, huffing and puffing. "We might kill Rex and Sherlock."

Tracy checked her watch. She'd been running at a six-minute, fifteen-second-per-mile clip. She rarely ran seven-minute miles since turning forty. "Sorry," she said, easing off. "Do you want to stop?"

"No, I'm good now," Dan said, after they slowed the pace. "Let's catch our breath at the lighthouse."

Just before the Alki Point Lighthouse, they stopped and took in a view Tracy still found as spectacular as any she'd ever seen—Elliott Bay a rich blue, the Seattle skyline sparkling in the glint of the sun, ferries crossing. The view, and the run, had helped ease her displeasure with Nolasco. At least she no longer wanted to rip his face off.

Dan wiped perspiration from his face with his shirt and continued to catch his breath. "You didn't say why you're home early, but I'm guessing you're not happy about it."

"We lost the woman-in-the-crab-pot case."

"Lost it?"

"Pierce County reasserted jurisdiction and we gave it back to them."

"I'm sorry," he said.

"What really irritates me is I'm sure Nolasco didn't go to bat for us, didn't even fight to keep it."

Dan gave her time to vent. Then he said, "Well, look, it's not often we get to enjoy an early evening like this. Why don't we focus on that?"

"Yeah, I guess," she said.

Dan eyed her. "You're not going to be okay with this, are you?"

"Not for a while."

"Tracy, I know what happened to Sarah makes these cases difficult—"

"Dan, please. That's not it, okay?"

"It's not?"

"No." She paced, frustrated and angry. "Okay, maybe it's a part of it, but . . . the victim was thirteen when her parents died. Then she marries a guy who treats her like a doormat, maybe even shoots her in the head and dumps her into the Sound like bait. We make progress, and when we do, Pierce County, which from what I can tell did nothing when they had the case, jumps in and takes it back—and we let them. It's just not right."

"No, it's not," he said, "but sometimes you've got to let things go, Tracy. It's like my dad used to say. If you take this shit to heart, you die with a heart full of shit."

"That's a beautiful thought, Dan. Very poetic." She stopped pacing and stared across the water to the skyscrapers.

Dan smiled. "Simple man, simple words, but you can't argue with the logic."

A thought had come to Tracy on her drive home, and it returned now as she stared out at the view. Nolasco had said to finish up what they were working on before sending down the file. "Are you still going to Los Angeles tomorrow morning?"

"Bright and early."

"I'm thinking of putting in for a personal day and going with you. We could make a weekend out of it."

"I'm definitely in favor of that," Dan said. "I'll be tied up most of tomorrow in court though."

"Don't worry about me," Tracy said. "I'll find things to do."

"You see, you're already making lemonade out of lemons."

"You sound like a character from *Annie*. Please don't start singing 'The sun will come out tomorrow.'"

Dan laughed and sang, "The sun'll come out . . ."

"God help us," Tracy said, sprinting in the opposite direction.

At home, they filled large bowls of water for Rex and Sherlock and gave them each soup bones from the butcher to keep them occupied. Then they jumped in the shower, followed by a short nap.

When Dan awoke, he rolled toward her. She had not slept.

"You want to go out to dinner?" he asked.

Tracy's mind continued to churn through her conversation with Brenda Berg. Berg said that she'd invested in her career but now she couldn't imagine her life without her daughter. Kins had been right. It had struck a chord. Of course it had. After Sarah's disappearance and Tracy's divorce from Benny, she had invested in becoming a homicide cop, and in trying to resolve her sister's investigation. Before she knew it, the years had rolled by, and she was forty-three, well past the optimal age for giving birth.

She rolled on her side, her back to Dan, looking out the sliding glass doors. "Are you ever disappointed you didn't have kids?"

Dan cleared his throat. "Where's that coming from?"

"I interviewed a woman today who just had her first child at forty. She said she'd been focused on her career. Then she met the right guy and now she said she couldn't imagine her life without her daughter."

Dan propped his chin on Tracy's shoulder and draped an arm across her body. "I don't know. I always thought I'd have kids, so I guess not having any wasn't exactly how I envisioned my life. Why? Do you wish you had?"

"Sometimes. Yeah, sometimes I do."

"Where are you going with this, Ms. Crosswhite?"

She rolled onto her back, looking up at him. "I don't know. Just thinking if I was going to have a child, it's getting close to now or never."

"The proverbial ticking clock."

"I guess."

"What about your job?" he said.

"I could take a maternity leave. And I've done it long enough I don't have to do it full time anymore. Maybe work a split schedule."

"Could you still work homicide?"

"Probably not. But I could work cold cases. Seems like I'm working cold cases anyway."

"Is this because of what happened today, the case getting pulled?"

"No. No, I was thinking about it on the drive home from Portland."

"Because of this woman you met?" Dan said.

"In part."

They lay silent for a moment. Then Dan said, "Have you given any thought to who you would want to be the father?"

Tracy sat up and hit him with a pillow. "I am now."

Dan grabbed the pillow. He wore a shit-eating grin. "I did have a vasectomy, you know. Remember, first marriage, wife didn't want children but didn't like the way condoms felt. I may have mentioned that."

Though hesitant, she said, "I've read vasectomies can be reversed."

"I've read it hurts almost as much as when you get snipped. It's not like rubber bands down there."

"I know. I'm sorry."

For a minute, neither spoke. Then Dan said, "But I would consider it, if that's what you wanted."

"You would?" she said.

He nodded. "I would, but I think we're skipping a step, aren't we? I mean Rex and Sherlock are already confused enough. Is their last name O'Leary, Crosswhite, O'Leary-Crosswhite?"

"It's O'Leary," she said. "I'm an old-fashioned girl."

"Are you proposing to me, Tracy Crosswhite?"

"Not on your life. I may be a badass cop, but beneath this hardened exterior is a girl who wants to be swept off her feet when she's proposed to."

"Really? Good to know. I guess I better not disappoint."

She snuggled closer to him, feeling the heat generated by their bodies and Dan becoming aroused. "You, Mr. O'Leary, have never disappointed."

CHAPTER 18

As big as he was, it was easy to assume nothing scared Delmo Castigliano, but Vic Fazzio knew Superman's kryptonite. Del was afraid of the water. Several years back, they'd had a murder investigation in which the killer broke down and told them he'd dumped his girlfriend's body in Lake Washington. Del had been uncharacteristically quiet on the drive to the Harbor Patrol's offices that morning, and Faz had later noticed him hanging back as they approached one of the police boats. Del had made it on board, but he'd broken out in a cold sweat and spent the day clinging to the rail.

The recollection came to Faz as they approached a narrow ramp leading to a dock that served as the sidewalk for some of the floating homes on Lake Union, including the home of the skip tracer they were going to visit that morning. Del stopped cold and went pale, and his complexion had nothing to do with continuing an investigation they'd been told to leave alone. As Tracy had pointed out, Nolasco had told them to wrap up what they were working on, and Faz had already set his mind on the interview.

"You all right?" Faz asked.

"I thought you said we were going to this guy's home."

"We are," Faz said.

"This isn't a home. It's a lake. I thought when you said he had a home on Lake Union you meant he had a view."

"Del, be honest with me, are you afraid of the water?"

Del swallowed hard and kept his gaze fixed on the catwalk. It was only ten feet long and spanned just a few feet between the dock and land, but he was staring as if it were a rickety rope bridge spanning a gorge over the Colorado River.

"I can't swim," he said, voice soft.

"What d'you mean, you can't swim?"

"I mean I sink," Del said, now sounding both agitated and embarrassed. "I mean like a stone. I go straight to the bottom."

"You never took lessons as a kid?" Faz asked.

"My parents tried, but I couldn't get near the water."

"You afraid of sharks or something?"

"No, just the water surrounding the sharks."

Faz had no phobias, but his mother had been deathly afraid of even the thought of snakes. "You want to wait in the car?"

Del shifted his gaze from the catwalk to Faz. He looked to be seriously considering the offer, but Faz knew Del wouldn't let him do an unauthorized interview alone.

Del took a deep breath. "Just tell me the inside is more like a house than a boat."

"Absolutely," Faz said. "Floors and walls and everything. You don't have to go anywhere near the water."

"Except to cross that bridge and floating sidewalk," Del said, his gaze again fixed on the catwalk.

"I'll go first, okay? You just take your time." Faz stepped onto the metal grate and proceeded across. He looked back at Del as if to demonstrate there was nothing to it. Del shuffled his feet like a man testing ice on a frozen pond, uncertain it would bear his weight. He paused when he reached the short step down to the floating dock. Faz thought it a strong possibility Del was going to turn back, but his partner mustered the courage to lower one leg, then the other.

Thankfully, the dark-stained cedar-shake home was anchored two slips from the end of the pier. Faz suspected he would have needed a towline to get Del any farther.

Outside the front door, a dozen potted plants seemed to have wilted beyond saving in the unseasonably warm weather. The houses on Lake Union were not like what most people thought of when they heard the term "houseboat." Built on massive logs anchored to piers, the homes were not large in terms of square footage but had every luxury of a home, some exquisite. Their real value, however, came from spectacular views of Seattle. Some sold for as much as a couple million dollars.

"You want to have some fun?" Faz asked.

"Not really, no." Del sounded hoarse and swayed like a drunkard fighting to keep his balance.

Faz banged hard on the front door. "Open up. Police!" He banged hard again. "Police. Open the door!"

Faz heard pounding footsteps and muffled voices from inside the house. He stepped to his right and looked between the house and its floating neighbor. A man stepped out onto the upper-story deck at the back of the house and flung the contents of a bucket—likely several prepaid phones and credit cards—into the lake. Inside, Faz could imagine Ian Nikolic's wife getting ready to destroy their laptop computer. He hurried back to the door, banged again, and yelled, "April Fool's!"

Seconds later the door ripped open and Nikolic looked at them with a bewildered and angry expression. Barefoot, he remained as Faz remembered him, though older now. Reed thin, he wore shorts and a ripped T-shirt. He looked like he'd been struck by lightning, his gray hair frazzled as if electrified.

"Damn it, Fazio! What the hell is wrong with you?"

"How much time you got?" Faz laughed. "You weren't doing anything illegal, were you, Nik?"

Nikolic eyed Del with suspicion. "I just threw three perfectly good phones into the lake, and Marta was about to destroy my laptop."

"You can afford it."

Nikolic had once told Faz the police came banging on his door on a tip he'd helped a fugitive slip away. Anyone who knew Nikolic knew it to be a ruse. Nikolic refused to work with fugitives, members of organized crime, or people he suspected of stalking. Many of his clients were well known, and the information he possessed, sensitive. He made a healthy six-figure income, and the first number was not a one.

"I can afford a Ferrari too, but that doesn't mean I want to drive it into the lake. What the hell do you want?"

"Need to talk to you about the woman we pulled from Puget Sound in a crab pot."

"She wasn't mine, if that's what you want to know."

"That's where I was going to start. You heard anything about it?"

"Come on in. You got me out of bed; I haven't even had my coffee yet and I can't think without caffeine." Nikolic looked again to Del. "Is this your bodyguard?"

"Partner. Del, meet Nik."

Del offered a tentative hand, as if any movement would throw him off balance. Nikolic took it, then stepped back, leaving the door open.

"What's wrong with him?" Nikolic asked.

"He's not much of a water person," Faz said.

The bottom floor of the house was Nikolic's office, the upper floor his personal residence. At the end of a narrow, wood-paneled hallway, they entered a room with three desks, multiple computer terminals, printers, and assorted clutter. Filing cabinets lined the back wall. Above them hung a colored print of a man standing in the doorway of a lighthouse built on a rock that looked to be in the middle of an angry ocean, a massive wave bearing down on him. Below the lighthouse it said, "Want to get away?"

A light breeze blew through an open sliding-glass door, bringing the faint odor of diesel fuel and the sound of a boat engine and seagulls cawing. The paddles of a ceiling fan slowly rotated above a barefoot woman standing near the door, sucking on a cigarette and holding a mug of coffee with the word "Gotcha!" on it.

"Sorry to get you up so early, Marta," Faz said.

Marta wore a tank top and shorts. "Good to see you're still an asshole, Fazio," Marta said.

"Some things never change," Faz said.

"Where are your manners, Faz?" Marta nodded to Del like he was the special on the menu. "I assume this is your partner now that you're a big homicide dick."

"Del, meet Marta Nikolic. The Nikolics are two of Seattle's most upstanding citizens."

"How do you work with this guy?" she asked Del.

"It ain't easy sometimes," Del said.

"So what do a couple of big-shot homicide detectives want with a couple of law-abiding citizens such as us?" Marta asked.

Ian Nikolic poured himself a mug of coffee from the stained pot and filched a Camel from his wife's pack. "Let's sit on the deck."

Del looked like he'd just been asked to jump out of an airplane without a parachute.

"Too hot to sit outside," Faz said. "You know me. I don't tan. I cook."

Nikolic and Marta had begun their careers as skip tracers. Clients paid them thousands of dollars to find people who didn't want to be found or to locate money others had wrongfully taken. They were so adept at finding people, even the police department had, on occasion, used their services, which was how Faz got to know them. In fact, they'd become so good at finding people they'd branched out to hiding people—women in abusive relationships, corporate whistleblowers who feared for their safety, and stool pigeons not interested in entering the Federal Witness Protection Program and spending the rest of their lives living in a Midwest suburb as some everyday Joe. For the most part, they kept their noses clean, but getting information often required ingenuity that bordered on illegal.

Nik spoke to Marta. "He wants to know if we've heard anything about the woman who died on Mount Rainier and showed up in a crab pot in Puget Sound."

"Wondering if anyone was looking for her," Faz said.

"Someone looking for a dead woman," Nikolic said, nodding his head. "Not a bad place to start." Nik and Marta blew smoke out of the corners of their mouths toward the open door. "If someone around here helped her, they're keeping it quiet and I don't blame them," Nik said.

"Why's that?" Del asked.

"It's bad for business when your client gets found, worse if she gets killed," Nikolic said. "Not only is your reputation ruined, you got the police and everybody else knocking down your door."

"What about a husband looking to find his wife?" Faz turned to Del. "What was his name?"

"Graham," Del said. "Graham Strickland."

"You heard his name or rumors of a husband searching for his missing wife?" Faz asked.

"I haven't, but I can ask around."

"I'd appreciate it."

"Enough to actually pay me?"

Faz smiled. "Unlike you, I can't afford a Ferrari. I'm making payments on a 2010 Subaru."

Nik shook his head.

"The wife was using an alias: Lynn Cora Hoff," Del said.

Nikolic found a pen amid the clutter and wrote it on a piece of paper. "What was the first name you said?"

"Andrea. Andrea Strickland." Del spelled the last name. "Her maiden name was Moreland."

"And while you're at it, ask around about a Devin Chambers," Faz said.

"Hang on, hang on," Nikolic said. "Give me the last name you said."

"Chambers. Devin Chambers," Faz repeated.

"Another alias?" Nikolic blew smoke toward the sliding-glass door.

"A friend who might have helped the wife disappear." Faz opened up his briefcase. "I was hoping you could take a look at some documents, give me your learned opinion." Faz was playing to Nikolic's large ego. He set his file on one of the desks and pulled out photocopies of Lynn Hoff's birth certificate and the driver's license they'd obtained from the DOL. He handed the photocopies to Nikolic.

Nikolic studied each while sipping his coffee and sucking on the cigarette. Marta extinguished her cigarette butt in an ashtray, blew a stream of blue smoke, and picked up the photocopies as Nik discarded them.

Nik held up the certified copy of the birth certificate. "Looks legit."

"It appears to be," Faz said.

"Likely a real person then. It's easier than using a dead person since they check the death records now." Nikolic continued to study the copy of the birth certificate. "The typeset is intaglio printing, which is appropriate for an official document. And the seal looks good. Can't tell you about the paper from photocopies." He put down his mug and walked to one of the desks, which had a combination light and magnifying glass on the end of a retractable arm. He turned on the light and examined the paper.

"Likely it was quality safety paper, though. If someone had erased or altered anything on the original, you would have seen it on these photocopies."

"You're saying it was a legitimate birth certificate?"

"I'm saying it looks like it, yeah."

"We didn't find a record that a Lynn Cora Hoff is deceased."

"She might not be, or she might be dead but nobody ever reported it," Nikolic said, confirming Faz's suspicion.

"So is the birth certificate stolen?" Del asked.

"Stolen, purchased, or given in exchange for some favor," Nikolic said.

"What kind of favor?" Del asked.

"The privilege of keeping your finger," Nikolic said. "Organized crime does it all the time. They get somebody under their thumb who owes them money and take their paperwork in exchange for not cutting off a finger. Then they sell the ID to pay off the debt."

"Why would they use a California birth certificate?" Del asked.

"Bigger state, more people," Nik said. "If the person who obtains the fake ID doesn't do anything illegal, the real Lynn Cora Hoff would never know someone was using her ID." Nikolic set down the documents and flicked his cigarette butt, still burning, out the door. "I can ask around, but if I find anything, you didn't hear it from me."

"We don't even know who you are," Faz said.

"You don't know how much I wish that were true," Nikolic said.

"You'd miss me," Faz said.

"Like a bad case of the flu. I'll ask around though. This one is getting some notoriety. Someone is liable to start bragging about it."

CHAPTER 19

Tracy pulled to the curb of the Metropolitan Courthouse in downtown Los Angeles.

"So what are you up to today?" Dan asked in a tone that made clear to Tracy that he had figured out she wasn't going to be spending the day at some museum.

"An interview," she said.

"Do I want to ask who the interview is with?"

"The aunt of the woman in the crab pot," Tracy said.

"You mean the case in which you no longer have jurisdiction."

"That would be the one."

"So how are you going to justify it?"

"Thorough police work," Tracy said. Dan gave her a look like he wasn't buying it. "Nolasco said to wrap up what we were working on. I was working on an interview with the aunt. I'll talk to her, write it up, and ship it down to Tacoma."

"And how far do you think that will get you if he finds out about it?"

"Let's hope I don't have to make that argument," she said. "Seriously, though, I can say I was in Los Angeles on pleasure, and didn't talk with Patricia Orr in an official capacity as a Seattle police officer."

"Let's hope you never have to make that argument either," Dan said.

She smiled. "I'll plan on being back around four."

Dan kissed her. "Wish me luck."

"I'm the one driving in Los Angeles. You should be wishing me luck."

She jumped on the I-10 east and settled into a steady stream of traffic. Ten years ago, she would have been dismayed at the sheer number of cars, but with Seattle the fastest-growing city in the nation, traffic had also become a way of life in the Northwest. So had a drought, all along the West Coast, and it had hit Southern California hard, especially with the recent heat wave. The hills had turned a dirt-brown and the sky a rust-colored haze. It reminded Tracy of the grainy images the Mars rover had transmitted back to Earth, and it looked like the slightest spark would cause everything to burst into flames.

Just under an hour into her drive, she merged onto I-215 north into San Bernardino, one of Southern California's sprawling cities, which had become infamous in 2012 as the largest city in the United States to declare bankruptcy, and then again in 2015 when two radicalized Islamic losers killed fourteen innocent people.

She exited onto East Orange Show Road and turned right onto South Waterman Avenue. Her GPS directed her onto Third Street, and she slowed when the voice informed her that her destination, a beige stucco apartment complex, was on her right. She turned into the parking lot and pulled into a spot abutting a wrought-iron fence enclosing an amoeba-shaped swimming pool. Two palm trees towered over the pool but offered little shade.

She slipped on sunglasses and exited the car. As she ascended an outdoor staircase to the second story and made her way down the landing, she heard traditional Mexican music filtering out an open apartment window. When she came to the second door from the end, she knocked. Inside, she heard someone turn off the television and footsteps approach the door, followed by the distinct sound of a chain sliding from a lock and a deadbolt disengaging.

A woman answered.

"Mrs. Orr?" Tracy said.

"You must be the detective from Seattle. Call me Penny," she said.

Tracy introduced herself. She estimated Orr to be early fifties. Though she was in good shape, trim, with defined arms, she had a heaviness to her that Tracy usually associated with someone who'd lived a hard life and felt the weight of it. Orr had "dark Irish" coloring— freckled, pale skin with dark hair that showed just a few strands of gray.

"Come in, please. You made good time," Patricia Orr said. "Traffic must have not been too bad."

"Not too bad," Tracy said. She'd called the night before and spoken to Orr, letting her know the purpose of her visit.

She stepped into a modestly furnished but impeccably clean apartment with cream-colored leather furniture, a few bronze sculptures, and large framed prints. In one print, three Elvis Presleys dressed in cowboy garb aimed six-shooters into the living room. In another, multiple colorful images of a forever-young Marilyn Monroe winked seductively from behind the leaves of a potted fern.

"Andy Warhol," Tracy said. "That Elvis is one of my favorite prints."

"Are you a fan?" Patricia Orr asked.

"I'm a shooter," Tracy said. "My sister and I competed in shooting tournaments all over the Pacific Northwest."

"Do you and your sister still compete?"

"I still get out every so often," Tracy said. "My sister passed away many years ago."

"I'm sorry," Orr said. "Please, sit." She motioned to the L-shaped couch facing a large flat screen. To the right, a sliding-glass door offered a view to the simmering foothills. Orr reached for a pitcher on the coffee table. "Can I pour you some iced tea?"

"That would be great, thank you."

They made small talk, then settled in. "I'm very sorry about your niece," Tracy said.

"I didn't know what to feel when you called," Orr said. "I'd already grieved Andrea's death once. Then to find out she'd been alive . . ." She shook her head, as if confused. "And now she's dead again. It just pains me to think that someone would be so cruel. I hope she didn't suffer."

"It doesn't appear to be the case," Tracy said, not really knowing, but knowing what Orr wanted to hear. The autopsy did not reveal any telltale signs of torture or abuse, and the bullet to the back of the head would have killed Andrea Strickland instantly.

"Do you know what happened?" Orr asked.

"We're in the process of trying to find out," Tracy said. "Obviously, Andrea did not die on the mountain. Somehow, she managed to walk off. What happened after that is not yet known."

"Why would she do that?" Orr asked.

"There's evidence she and her husband were having problems. He'd gotten them into some financial trouble and there are indications of infidelity."

"He didn't abuse her, did he?"

"We're not aware of any physical abuse," Tracy said, though Brenda Berg had indicated that Andrea Strickland hinted at it.

"The other detective said the husband was a suspect; is he still a suspect?"

"When was that?" Tracy asked.

"When he called . . . It was a while ago now, maybe a month. It was when they still thought Andrea had died on Mount Rainier."

"You haven't spoken to that detective since?"

"No."

The lack of contact confirmed for Tracy that Fields had not been working the file. "We're exploring several different scenarios," she said. "I was hoping to get a little background about your niece. I understand she came to live with you when she was thirteen?"

Orr set her iced tea down on a coaster. "It was just before she'd turned fourteen."

"Your sister and brother-in-law died in a car accident."

"Yes," Orr said. "Christmas Eve. It was horrific."

"And Andrea was also in the car?"

Orr nodded. "The accident was late at night on a road not well traveled. Andrea was in the backseat and barely injured, but my sister and her husband died on impact. The highway patrolman said it was one of the most gruesome accident scenes he'd witnessed in twenty years."

"I'm sorry," Tracy said. "How long was Andrea trapped in the car?"

"Close to two hours," Orr said softly. "I can't imagine what that was like."

"How was she, emotionally, when she came to live with you?"

Orr gave the question a bit of thought. "Quiet. Reserved. She had frequent nightmares."

"And you lived here, in San Bernardino?"

"Not here in this apartment; a home out near the foothills, until the divorce." She picked up her iced tea and took a sip, avoiding eye contact.

"Did Andrea have counseling?"

Orr sat back, glass in hand. Her demeanor appeared to have changed, more reticent and closed off. "Yes."

"A doctor here in town?"

"Just a few miles from here."

"What was that doctor's name?"

"Townsend. Alan Townsend."

"Do you know if he's still in practice?"

"I believe he is. I don't know for certain."

"Did the counseling help?"

Orr shifted her gaze to the floor and shut her eyes, but a tear rolled slowly down her cheek. Tracy gave her a moment.

"I'm sorry if this is upsetting, Penny."

Orr nodded, but the tears continued. Then her chest shuddered. "Andrea had been through so much," she said. "I thought the nightmares were from the accident. I didn't know."

Tracy put it together—the divorce, the reluctance to talk about Andrea's counseling. "Your husband?" Tracy asked, the scenario unfortunately all too familiar.

"He was abusing Andrea," Orr said. "It came out in her counseling. He denied it, said she'd made it up, that she lived in a fantasy world."

"What did the counselor say?"

"It was his opinion Andrea was telling the truth. The allegation required that he contact Child Protective Services. They removed Andrea from our home. I moved out because it was quicker than waiting for the divorce to become final, and found a place on my own, a small townhome. Andrea had been sent to another home until, eventually, she came back to live with me."

"Did you determine the truth?" Tracy asked.

"Andrea was telling the truth."

"I'm sorry. Did you become Andrea's legal guardian?"

"Yes. My sister and brother-in-law had it in their will and the probate court had a hearing and the judge appointed me."

"So you could authorize the release of Andrea's counseling records?"

"I could," Orr said. "But why would you need them?"

"We're exploring every potential reason why Andrea walked off that mountain, trying to understand what happened. The records might help. How was she, psychologically, when she came back to live with you?"

"Worse," Orr said. "She became very withdrawn, very nervous. She'd pick at her skin and compulsively bite her fingernails, sometimes until they bled. She also read constantly, everything she could get her hands on."

"Novels?" Tracy asked. "Any specific genre?"

"No, just everything and anything. Westerns, romance, sci-fi, fantasy, mysteries, detective novels. Everything. I would take boxes of paperbacks to the used bookstore every month and trade them in for another stack."

"What did her counselor have to say about Andrea reading so much?"

"He said Andrea had withdrawn from the real world because the real world was too painful. He said books offered her comfort."

"Did she make much progress?"

"In counseling? Some, but she left San Bernardino when she turned eighteen. I came home from work one day and she was gone. She left a note thanking me and saying she needed a change of scenery."

"She didn't tell you she was leaving?"

Orr shook her head. "I understood," she said softly. "Andrea needed to make a life for herself, whatever that was going to be. She needed to get away from here, away from the memories. I understood that."

"Did she tell you where she was going?"

"She said she wanted to live in Portland or Seattle because it rained all the time and she could read. She said she would contact me when she'd settled."

"Did you speak to her after she left?"

"Yes. She kept her word, said she'd settled in Portland, and assured me she was fine. She called a couple of times after that, but not too much." Orr paused. "I really tried to do what was right for Andrea, and for my sister."

"I'm sure you did."

"When I found out my husband had been abusing her, I felt like I'd failed them both. I guess Andrea was just too emotionally scarred, and living here reminded her of those scars. I was part of those bad memories. I just think she needed to get away."

"I'm sure you did your best," Tracy said.

"I tried," Orr said.

"Did Andrea gain control of her trust fund when she turned eighteen?"

"No. At twenty-one she got say over the use of the interest. My sister and brother-in-law originally set it up to pay for Andrea's college. When they died, the rest of their estate rolled into that trust, but it had restrictions. It could only be used for Andrea's well-being."

"Were you the trustee?"

"No, there was a professional trustee. It was very complicated. When she lived with me, I had the trustee roll the interest back into the trust. I never touched a dime. I wanted that to be hers, something good that came out of such a tragedy. Do you know what happened to it?"

"That's one of the things we're trying to find out. It appears Andrea was in the process of hiding it."

"From who?"

"We think her husband. We think that was one source of tension in their marriage. Apparently, he wanted to use the trust to pay off his business debts and Andrea had refused."

"The trust wouldn't allow that," Orr said.

"I think that was the reason for the tension."

"So you think he might have killed her to try to get control of the money?"

"We don't know," Tracy said. She changed the subject. "Penny, have you ever heard the name Lynn Hoff?"

Orr's face scrunched in thought. "I don't think so. Who is she?"

"It appears to be the alias Andrea was using when she was in hiding. Sometimes people will use a name familiar to them, maybe a childhood friend who died, or a relative."

"No," Orr said. "It isn't familiar. Maybe a character from a book?"

"Maybe. Did Andrea have any close friends when she lived here—high school friends?"

Orr shook her head. "Not really." She shrugged. "At least no one that I'm aware of. She didn't like school. Andrea wasn't dumb. Don't misinterpret what I'm saying. She had her father's intellect, and she was curious about things. I think that's why she liked to read all the time. She retained everything she read on a subject. At the parent-teacher conferences, the teachers would all say the same thing. Andrea was extremely bright, off the charts in some areas, but she didn't apply herself." Orr shrugged again. "What was I supposed to do, punish her?" She wiped her tears and made a face as if the thought were ridiculous. "She'd been punished enough."

Tracy gave Orr a moment to regain her composure. Then she asked, "I take it she didn't have any boyfriends?"

"No."

"And no enemies."

"Not that she ever spoke of. She just mostly kept to herself."

"You didn't know she'd gotten married."

Orr frowned. "No."

"You never met her husband?"

"No. But he doesn't sound like a very good man."

"Did Andrea ever mention the name Devin Chambers?"

"Devin Chambers? No. Who is he?"

"She, actually. She appears to have been a friend of Andrea's in Portland."

Orr smiled but it had a sad quality to it. "I'm glad she had someone. She had so much sadness in her life, so much pain."

Tracy thought of Sarah often, of her being subjected to the demented mind of a psychopath the last days of her life. The thought still caused a visceral reaction, and brought a dark cloud of bitterness and anger, but she realized something else, something that had never happened before on any of her other cases. She was starting to realize this case wasn't personal because of the victim's similarities to Sarah. It was personal because of Andrea Strickland's similarities to Tracy. Tracy had also had a wonderful life shattered by tragedy. She, too, had been the daughter of a doctor, living in a beautiful house with a mother and sister she loved. Just as suddenly, her sister had been abducted, and her father soon thereafter shot himself. Her husband left, and everything she had thought would be her life changed forever. For years she had medicated her depression by working out and shooting often, but every once in a while she sat in her apartment, depressed, and wondered why the world had crapped on her.

"Did your ex-husband know about Andrea's trust?"

"Yes," Orr said, "but he's dead, Detective. He died three years ago of colon cancer."

"What about her trustee? What kind of man is he?"

"He's a wonderful man. If he had wanted to cheat Andrea he could have done it easily."

"Can you think of anyone else who knew about the trust?"

Orr gave it a moment of thought. "Not unless Andrea told someone about it."

The comment made Tracy think of Brenda Berg, Devin Chambers, and Andrea's counselor.

"I'd like to get Andrea's counseling records," she said. "I'd need a signed letter authorizing their release. Would you do that?"

"I will," Orr said, "with one caveat."

"Sure."

"I see no reason why any of this has to be made public. Andrea was hurt enough in life. I don't see any reason to hurt her after death."

Tracy agreed.

Orr called Alan Townsend's office, got his call service, and left a message. Toward the end of Tracy and Orr's conversation, Townsend called back and said he could meet Tracy at his office. They set a time and Orr signed a letter authorizing the release of Andrea's counseling records.

Tracy thanked Orr for her time, and handed her a business card as she walked Tracy to the door.

"Do you know who I would contact about her body?" Orr said. "I'd like to have Andrea buried alongside her parents."

Tracy wrote the King County Medical Examiner's phone number on the back of her business card. "They should be ready to release the body," she said.

—

When Tracy opened her car door in the apartment complex parking lot, a blast of searing heat escaped. She waited a moment, then reached in and started the engine but did not get in. She wanted to give the air-conditioning time to do its job. While she waited for the oven to become a car, she thought again of Andrea Strickland, and of her uncle. What kind of a person would take in a young girl whose parents had died in a horrific car accident, and see it as an opportunity for his own sick and twisted sexual desires? It was another reminder that the psychopaths of the world were not always the stereotypical monsters who tortured cats in their youths and lived in solitude.

When the car had cooled, Tracy slid behind the wheel. She left the parking lot and turned on North Waterman Avenue, a four-lane street pocked with palm trees located just around the corner from the St. Bernardine Medical Center. As Tracy had found with most of Southern California, the street consisted of an odd mix of single-family homes, apartment buildings, strip malls, and commercial buildings, as if the city planners had given no consideration to zoning.

She parked on the street and approached a two-story, sand-colored stucco building. Alan Townsend's counseling practice was located on the second floor off an outdoor staircase. The inside looked like a small two-bedroom apartment converted to an office, with the front room the waiting area. The furnishings were dated—shag carpeting, cloth-and-laminate furniture, and nondescript prints. Behind a vacant reception counter were two closed doors with nameplates. The plate on the right was empty. The plate on the left read "A. Townsend."

Tracy slapped a bell on the counter, which emitted an obnoxious ting. Seconds later, the door on the left opened and a middle-aged man with a head of silver hair emerged wearing cargo shorts, a T-shirt, and flip-flops. With a skin complexion more orange than bronze, he looked just like the actor George Hamilton. Welcome to LA.

"Dr. Townsend?" Tracy said.

Townsend extended a hand and flashed a smile so bright it almost caused Tracy to put her sunglasses back on. "You must be the detective from Seattle. Come on in." He turned his back and went into his office. "I don't usually work Fridays so I'm operating without a receptionist. You'll have to excuse me if I look a little disorganized."

"I'm sorry to bother you on your day off."

"Not a bother," he said. "I understand the circumstances. Besides, I've already had a full day. Friday mornings I surf and do a little meditating. I thought I'd get some work done in an air-conditioned office while waiting out the heat. I play tennis in the evenings."

"Surfing around here?"

"The ocean is an hour and a half. That's why I only do it once a week and I go early. It's exhilarating."

"Sounds like a good day."

"Every day we're alive is a good day," he said.

This guy made actors on *Sesame Street* seem depressed.

The back wall was a window facing east toward the San Bernardino hills. The wall to Tracy's left was the ego wall, with framed diplomas and citations, some partially obscured by the leaves of a collection of potted ferns, cacti, palms, and a peace lily. Townsend had a modest desk beneath the diplomas. He took a seat in a leather chair, leaving

Tracy to sit on a two-seat couch. On the wall beside the window was a framed quote.

WHO LOOKS OUTSIDE, DREAMS;

WHO LOOKS INSIDE, AWAKES.

CARL JUNG

The room smelled of incense.

Tracy handed Townsend the signed authorization from Patricia Orr for the release of Andrea's records, which was valid because Andrea had been a minor when she received counseling.

"I was hoping to get your impressions."

"Well, first off I can tell you I was not surprised to hear Andrea had died in an accident on Mount Rainier."

Apparently, Townsend did not know Andrea had not died on Rainier. Tracy decided to explore his thinking. "No? Why not."

"Because I was not convinced it was an 'accident.'"

"You thought the husband killed her?"

"No. I would maintain that Andrea took her own life."

"Why would you come to that conclusion?"

"Because of three years of therapy. This would be the kind of grandiose gesture I'd expect Andrea would choose to leave the world—something to let the world know she'd been here."

"Grandiose? I understood from Mrs. Orr that Andrea was an introvert who hid from the world."

"That was her coping mechanism," Townsend said. "That was how Andrea chose to hide from her problems, to shut them away in a closet, so to speak. But that wasn't who she really was."

Tracy knew that trick very well. She'd become obsessed with finding Sarah's killer, so much so that when she'd finally had to walk away, she'd had to literally shut Sarah's files in her bedroom closet so that she could function. "How would you describe her?"

"Before the car accident that took her parents' lives, and before the abuse at the hands of her uncle, she was described by her schoolteachers and counselors as a bright, well-adjusted, mischievous young woman."

"Mischievous?"

"She liked to play pranks on her classmates and friends."

"What kind of pranks?"

"Oh, she'd hide someone's lunch, short-sheet their beds at slumber parties, put pin holes in the milk cartons so when classmates drank, the milk would dribble down their chins."

Tracy's sister had been similarly mischievous. Sarah had liked to hide and jump out at Tracy and her unsuspecting friends. "Harmless pranks," she said.

"For the most part."

"Were there occasions when the pranks were not harmless?"

Townsend nodded. "A few, apparently."

"Such as?"

"She cut the stem of a bike tire on a classmate who she believed had been mean to a friend of hers."

Tracy considered this. "Could her pranks have increased in their vindictiveness?"

"Yes," Townsend said, "I believe they could have."

"What was your diagnosis for Andrea?"

"Well, Andrea left when she was eighteen, so I can't say for certain."

"You don't know."

"I believe Andrea was susceptible to a dissociative disorder brought on by the trauma and abuse."

"What do you mean by a dissociative disorder?"

"It can be a number of different things. In Andrea's case it could have manifested in an involuntary and unhealthy escape from reality."

"Her excessive reading?"

"Certainly. It's a mechanism used to keep traumatic memories at bay. The person either has memory loss—you can't recall what you did or who certain people are in your life—or she can take on alternate identities."

"Split personalities?"

"In a sense. The person switches to an alternate identity. Someone suffering from a dissociative identity disorder will say they feel the presence of people talking or living inside their head, and they can't control what those people are doing or saying."

"You said 'susceptible.' You don't know if Andrea had a dissociative disorder?"

"Not with certainty. The typical onset is early twenties. She'd left counseling by then."

"How would it have manifested, if she'd had it?"

"A number of different ways. For one, the person can be prone to mood swings and impulsive acts."

"Would an impulsive act be getting married after just a few weeks?"

"It could be."

"Are these people capable of committing harmful acts?"

"Suicide attempts are not uncommon."

"I meant harmful acts against others?"

"Certainly."

"What can trigger it?"

"Again, it can be several things. Another traumatic event—abuse or a perceived abandonment, a betrayal, or just a feeling of desperation."

Tracy didn't need Townsend to explain that, in those categories, Andrea Strickland had been a perfect four for four.

"Were you aware that Andrea had a trust, Doctor?"

"Andrea mentioned it," he said and then looked doubtful. "Or it could have been her aunt said something in passing." He paused. Then he said, "I believe it was the aunt. She said she was grateful Andrea would, at least, always be financially taken care of. Frankly, I was uncertain whether that was a good thing."

"Why is that?"

"Given Andrea's uncertain future mental state, the trust would have made it easy for her to not work, and potentially to engage in an unhealthy lifestyle."

"Drugs?" Tracy said, thinking of the pot store, Genesis.

"Potentially."

"And the trust could have also made her susceptible to persons hoping to take advantage of her, could it not?"

"Yes," he said. "It could have. If they knew of it, of course."

"Of course."

CHAPTER 20

*O*n a Friday night, Devin persuaded me to go out after work. I'd made the mistake of telling her Graham had gone to a bachelor party in Las Vegas for the weekend, which meant I couldn't use him as an excuse to get home. With Graham unemployed, he was around the loft almost all day and most nights. Having my job back felt like a reprieve from having to spend time with him. I left for work early and didn't come home until late. Often I would take the current novel I was reading, and my laptop, to a coffeehouse with wireless Internet access. If I stayed out late enough, I could return home to find Graham passed out, avoid the perfunctory conversations, and sneak off to bed, letting him sleep on the couch.

I was counting the days until our Rainier trip.

With Graham in Las Vegas, I'd have the loft to myself the entire weekend. What I really wanted was to go home and continue planning without having to sneak behind Graham's back, but I decided that I owed it to Devin to spend a few hours with her. I'd dumped a lot of my personal problems on her, and she'd always been there to listen. Besides, she was the only real friend I had in Portland, and soon I would be gone.

She chose a sports-themed bar close to the office that included multiple television screens. Sports paraphernalia hung on the walls and drooped from *the ceiling. I guessed the bar was popular, because the tables filled quickly. We found a couple abandoning an elevated table with two tall chairs a safe distance from the televisions and quickly grabbed it. The waitress, dressed in a black-and-white referee shirt and cheek-hugging black shorts, quickly descended on us for drink orders. She set down cocktail napkins and advised that it was happy hour. Appetizers were just a few dollars. Devin ordered hummus and flatbread and an olive plate. Just the thought of food made my queasy stomach churn.*

"Two Lemon Drops," Devin said to the waitress, raising her voice over the din of the crowd.

"I'm good," I said, shaking my head. "Just water."

"Come on, we're celebrating." Devin snatched the drink menu and handed it to the waitress, who departed.

"What exactly are we celebrating?"

"Your return to work."

"I'm back because we had to file bankruptcy."

"I know, but I'm still glad to have you back. It wasn't the same without you. I don't know how I survived the boredom."

"Listen," I said. "Thanks for being there for me, for letting me unload all my problems on you."

Devin waved it off. "It's no big deal."

"It is. It meant a lot to me. I'm sorry I lost touch when I left. You're my only real friend here."

"That's not true," she said.

"It is. You're the only person I've ever been able to count on."

"Well, I missed not having you around," she said.

I smiled at that. "You mean the girl who goes home every night and sticks her nose in a book."

She laughed. "Okay, so tell me. Have you heard from the attorneys about your trust? Are the creditors going to be able to get at it?"

I don't know what compelled me. Maybe it was just the need to tell someone because keeping it a secret had consumed me. "I'm not waiting for the attorneys," I said.

"What?"

"I can't risk losing my trust, Devin."

"What do you mean?"

"I've hidden it."

"How?"

"I opened bank accounts in a different name."

"How did you do that?"

"I can't say how. I'm sorry, I just can't."

"That's okay. Wow. So you think it's safe?"

"It should be. I'm still in the process of doing a couple of things."

"Where did you learn how to do it?"

I gave a small laugh. "Where else? A book."

"So you just made up a name?"

"Not exactly, no."

"So you, like, have an alias?"

"I guess so."

"Do you have a driver's license?" Devin asked, animated.

"I needed one to open the account."

Devin leaned forward, wide-eyed. "Did you use a famous person's name?"

"No. I used a pretty lame name, actually."

Two young men in business suits, ties lowered and top shirt buttons undone, approached our table and Devin sat back. They were cute. One had sandy blond hair and a shy grin. The other sported one of those trendy two-day-growth beards and a lot of attitude—like Graham when I first met him. With summer nearing, a lot of the businesses hired college interns. These two didn't look much older.

"My friend and I were hoping you could settle a bet," Mr. Two-Day Growth said, which caused Devin to give me a sidelong glance and a roll of her eyes.

"What's that?" she said, playing along.

"I'm betting you're in town for the Nike CrossFit games." He jabbed a thumb at the Brad Pitt look-alike. "He says you're locals out for a drink."

"What happens if you're both right?" Devin said.

"We both buy you a drink," he said, smiling.

The blond looked at me with a sheepish grin. "Are you the CrossFit competitor?"

"Me?" I said, hoping I wasn't blushing. "God, no."

"Well, you look like you could be." He flashed a boyish grin that ran straight through me.

The waitress returned with our two Lemon Drops. Devin said, "Seems we already have drinks, and we haven't seen each other in a while. We're trying to catch up. But thanks."

I was surprised Devin blew them off, which wasn't like her. Unlike me, she relished attention, and she wasn't married. I almost sensed Devin was peeved that I'd been the one mistaken for the CrossFit athlete. I was in great shape, the best shape of my life. I'd need to be.

"You ladies have a nice night," Mr. Two-Day Growth said. They turned to leave, but not before the blond glanced back and gave me another grin.

Devin laughed but it sounded stilted. "Look at you, getting all the attention."

"I think they were more interested in you," I said, trying to be diplomatic.

"Bullshit," Devin said. "He liked what he saw. And you do look great, Andrea." She sort of threw the last compliment away.

"Well, working out five days a week and being under constant stress will do that."

"So the Rainier trip is still on?"

"Yeah," I said, and felt a pang of guilt.

She raised her glass. "To having younger men hit on us in a bar."

I raised my glass and met hers, then pretended to take a drink but only tasted the sugar around the rim.

She set down her drink. "So, you and Graham are staying together?"

"I don't know," I said.

"Can I speak frankly?"

"Sure," I said. I'd never known Devin not to speak frankly.

She turned and glanced at the two men who'd tried to hit on us. "That's pretty much what's out there. Guys too young, looking to get laid, or divorced guys too old, looking to get laid. I know you and Graham have had your problems, but if he's willing to give your marriage a go, you might want to consider it. At the very least go on the trip and see what comes of it. If it doesn't go well, then you can decide what to do."

I didn't get much of a chance to consider her advice. The waitress returned with our appetizers and another round of Lemon Drops. "We didn't order a second round," Devin said.

The waitress nodded at the table shared by our two admirers. "They sent them over."

The blond and his friend raised their beer glasses and smiled.

Devin said, "What do you think? Should we invite them over?"

"Sure, why not?" I said, sensing she wanted to flirt with them.

They turned out to be interns at an investment firm. Both were in graduate school, one at Tulane and the other at Dartmouth. Devin called them smarty-pants. The blond had definitely chosen me, and I talked with him long enough to keep his friend interested, for Devin's sake. At some point Devin noticed that I hadn't drunk my first drink, and she finished it. She also drank my second drink. Four Lemon Drops.

Around 11:00 p.m., the guy hitting on Devin suggested they leave and she agreed. I told his friend I was going to be heading home, and he didn't push it. He'd noticed the wedding ring. He said it was nice talking to me and went back to the table with his other friends.

Devin told her date she'd find him and he too went back to his table. She looked at me and smiled. "You'll be okay getting home?" I could tell from her slurred speech that she was pretty wasted.

"Of course," I said. "You sure you're all right?"

"I'm fine. The buzz will make the sex better."

"Be careful."

"Careful? I'm getting laid. But, first I have to pee." She grabbed her purse, which she'd hung by the strap over the back of her chair, and set it on the table along with her cell phone. "Watch my stuff?"

"Sure."

"Right back." She slid from her chair, stumbled when she hit the floor, but managed to remain upright. "Whoa. Maybe I shouldn't have had that third Lemon Drop."

Four, I thought, but didn't say. "You sure you're okay?" I asked again.

She winked and weaved her way through the tables and the crowd, leaving me alone. I almost pulled out the paperback I carried in my purse, but knew how lame that would look. I surveyed the crowd, my gaze passing over the tables of couples to the group of men standing at the upright table drinking their beers and laughing. Mr. Two-Day Growth watched Devin cross the bar, looking anxious or excited. I couldn't tell. My eyes paused on Brad Pitt. In my fantasy, he looked over at me and I didn't look away. In my fantasy, I stuck my finger in my glass, swirling the drink, then brought my finger seductively to my lips and nibbled on the tip.

Devin's cell phone buzzed.

When I looked down, the phone on the table was neither lit up nor vibrating. It took a second before I realized the noise was coming from inside her purse, which was unzipped. Confused, I looked inside and saw a second phone, the face lit up a pale blue-green. Caller ID did not provide a name, but I didn't need a name.

I recognized the number.

A rush of anxiety hit me so violently the legs of my chair rattled. Nauseated, like I'd been punched in the gut, I fought the urge to throw up.

I looked again.

Graham.

What the hell?

What possible reason could there be for Graham to be calling Devin? To my knowledge, they hardly knew each another. And why would she have a second phone? I fought to control my breathing, to regain some semblance of composure, and to think through what I was witnessing, the gravity and believability of it all. I thought of the credit card charges to the hotels and restaurants in Seattle when Graham said he'd been away on business. Could that have been Devin? Was she the woman he was having an affair with?

The credit card bills included the dates Graham had been gone. His cell phone bill would show his calls and the dates he made them, but I didn't know the number of the phone in Devin's purse.

Still, it wouldn't be too difficult to figure it out.

I looked over my shoulder, saw no sign of Devin, reached inside her purse, and grabbed the phone. The screen indicated she'd received multiple text messages from the same number. Graham's cell phone. Only partial messages appeared on the screen.

Hey, hoping to get . . .

Just got to . . .

Did you talk to . . .

I couldn't unlock Devin's phone without the password to read the full messages. I also couldn't determine the phone number, but I didn't need to.

I looked over my shoulder to the hallway on the other side of the bar and watched Devin emerge, walking toward the table. I dropped the phone back inside the purse, slid from my bar stool, and put on my jacket.

"You all set?" Devin asked, grabbing her purse and her jacket.

"Yeah," I said. "I'm tired."

She paused when she went to zip closed her purse, no doubt seeing the last registered call on the phone. Maintaining a poker face, she calmly dropped her regular phone inside her purse and zipped it closed. She reached out and gave me a warm hug. My entire body tensed. "So, let me guess, you're heading home to stick your nose in a book."

"You know me," I said.

"Like a book," Devin said, laughing. Then she turned and walked toward the table where the guy awaited her.

"Except you're reading the wrong book," I said to her back. I was no longer going home. I was going to the office, to stick my nose in Devin Chambers's computer.

CHAPTER 21

At first, Vic Fazio thought he was having one of those anxiety dreams in which everything feels stilted and magnified. An annoying insect circled his head, buzzing loudly. He couldn't swat it or otherwise make it stop. Then his subconscious gave way to instincts he had honed over decades, a cop conditioned to being awakened at odd hours. He realized the insect was his cell phone. He turned the ringer off at night so as not to disturb Vera, who was a light sleeper, but that didn't keep the phone from buzzing and shaking on his bedside nightstand.

Faz didn't need to open his eyes to know it was still the middle of the night. His inner clock, honed as a parent of two boys, told him. He felt Vera roll away from him, onto her side, well acclimated to life as the spouse of a homicide detective. Except, just then, something else became clear. Faz and Del were not the homicide team on call. They had been working the Andrea Strickland murder, but that case got pulled last Thursday.

Faz reached blindly, missing the phone the first time before finding it. He brought it up in front of his face, the numbers blurry without his glasses, but he could make out only the local 206 Seattle area code. He hit the green button.

"Hello?" His voice sounded like he was speaking through a drainpipe clogged with pea gravel and water. He cleared his throat. "Hello?"

"Hey, Faz. How's it going?"

"What?" he said, confused.

"How's it going?"

"Who the hell is this?"

"Who is it?" Vera asked, rolling toward him and sitting up. "Did something happen to one of the kids?"

"It's Nik," the caller said. "Your favorite skip tracer."

Faz struggled to sit up. Vera turned on the light on her side of the bed. The two of them squinted at the brightness. "Nik?" Faz asked, looking at the nightstand clock radio.

"Who's Nik?" Vera asked.

"What the hell time is it?" Faz said.

"It's three thirty-two."

"In the morning?"

Nik laughed. "Hey, April Fool's, Fazio!"

"Son of a bitch," Faz said under his breath. "What is wrong with you? My wife is worried sick something happened to one of the kids."

"Yeah, and my wife is still pissed at me for throwing her cell phones in the damn lake. So maybe now we have a truce?"

Faz blew out a heavy breath, looked at Vera, and said, "I'm sorry, it's a business call."

"At this hour?"

Faz knew he deserved it. He spoke into the phone. "Is this the only reason you called, to even the score?"

"Come on, Faz, I'm an asshole but I'm not that big an asshole. I got some information for you on that job you asked me to look into . . . for free."

"Strickland?"

"Yeah."

"Okay," Faz said, reaching for his reading glasses and the pen and pad of paper he also kept on the nightstand. "Go ahead."

"Shit, Fazio, it's three thirty in the morning. Call me later and we'll set a time and place to talk."

"Wait, are you telling me you called just to wake me up?"

"That would be vindictive, Faz." He paused. Then he said, "I'm a night owl—in case you think of being funny again." Nik hung up.

"Who was that?" Vera asked, still looking worried.

"You know how you're always telling me I'm not as funny as I think I am?"

"Yeah."

"You're right."

—

When Faz called later that morning, Ian Nikolic told him to meet for lunch at Duke's Chowder House. Duke's was located at the end of a pier on Lake Union.

"Does this guy do anything that doesn't involve the water?" Del said as the waitress led them through the restaurant to the wood deck out back.

Nik sat beneath the shade of white umbrellas shielding the tables, talking on his cell phone. The other tables were full, diners dressed in light shirts and summer dresses enjoying a breeze off the lake that made the temperature tolerable, though Faz could already feel trickles of sweat beneath his shirt.

"I'm going to have to call you back," Nikolic said, holding the phone to his ear, half standing and reaching out a hand to Faz. "My lunch guests just arrived. Yeah, yeah. Today. I told you, I'll get to it today." He disconnected and shook Faz's hand. "Hey, Fazio, you're looking a little tired. Didn't you get a good night's sleep?"

Del laughed and removed his sport coat.

"Yeah, all right, you got me. Now we're even. Vera nearly kicked me out of bed she was so mad."

They settled into seats. Three chairs had a view of the dazzling blue water teeming with boats and yachts leaving and returning to the marina, but Del draped his jacket over the back of the chair facing away from the water.

"You got something against natural beauty?" Nik said.

"That's what the doctor said to his mother when he was born," Faz said.

"I'm good right where I am," Del said.

The waiter appeared, handing them menus. Faz ordered an iced tea. "Make mine an Arnold Palmer," Del said.

"Get the chowder," Nik said, not bothering to open his menu. "You can't go wrong."

Faz and Nik ordered the chowder. "And a loaf of bread," Faz said. "I'm a big dipper."

"Scallop ravioli," Del said, considering the menu. "Look at that, Faz, they got seafood for Italians." He looked up at the waiter. "Is it good?"

The waiter assured him it was.

After the waiter departed, Faz sipped his water. "So what do you got for me, Nik?"

"Someone was looking for that name you came asking about."

"Andrea Strickland?"

"No, Lynn Hoff."

"Yeah?" Faz glanced at Del. Only someone who knew Andrea Strickland had created an alias would have known to ask about Lynn Hoff. "Do we know who?"

"No, and the guy I got the information from is jumpy as all hell, given what happened to her. He said he'd tell me everything so long as I leave his name out of it."

"That's gonna depend on what he told you, Nik. You know I can't make that promise," Faz said.

"I know, but he doesn't. I told him the same thing, but I also said I'd do my best to keep him out of it, act as a go-between. This is one of those instances when the information is more valuable than the source. Am I right?"

"So what did he have to say?" Del asked.

"Someone used a guerilla e-mail account to make contact. Ordinarily, he won't agree to work under those conditions."

"What's a guerilla e-mail?" Del asked.

"It's a disposable e-mail address," Faz said. "It's like a burner phone for e-mail. People use it when they don't want to use their real name or e-mail address. A random address is generated each time the person logs in, and the e-mail is automatically deleted an hour after it's generated." He turned to Nikolic. "What did they want your guy to do?"

Nik shrugged. "Asked him to find someone named Lynn Hoff. Said he was a relative."

"So we don't know if this person doing the asking was a man or a woman," Del said.

Nikolic shook his head. "No way to know."

"So how does the person on your end get information back to an e-mail address that gets deleted after an hour?" Del asked.

"They set up a time to communicate. The client told my guy he'd send another e-mail in seventy-two hours, and if my guy had any information he could e-mail him back. Personally, I like to know who I'm dealing with and won't work that way, but not everyone has my same high degree of integrity." Nik smiled.

"So what did your guy find?" Faz asked.

"He ran the name through the usual channels and came up with the same Washington State driver's license you found. He also ran a credit report and found the name associated with an apartment complex in Oklahoma, along with utility records and a request for installation of a phone in that name for that address."

"I'm assuming that was a false trail," Faz said.

"Turned out it was."

"So the person knew what they were doing?" Del asked.

"Hell, you can read it in books now or watch YouTube," Nikolic said. "Internet is going to put us all out of business eventually. Computers will take over the world. But yeah, the person had clearly done some research or knew what they were doing."

"The skip tracer gave the client this information?" Faz asked.

"He did. The client then said the person might be using a second alias," Nikolic said. He glanced down at his notes in a spiral notebook. "Devin Chambers. He told my guy he might want to start in Portland, Oregon."

"Devin Chambers?" Del said.

"That's the name the client gave him."

"Isn't she Strickland's friend?" Del said to Faz.

"What did he find?" Faz asked Nik.

"He ran the name through the system and came up with a driver's license and an apartment in Portland. My guy takes a drive down to Portland and talks to the neighbors. She'd lived there, but the tenants said they hadn't seen her in a few weeks. Two said she told them she was taking an extended trip out of the country."

"Did she keep the lease?" Faz asked.

"It was month to month. When she didn't pay, the landlord went through the channels and evicted her."

"What did the landlord do with all her possessions?"

"Put everything in storage. She never came back for it."

"So she didn't care about it?" Faz said.

"Doesn't appear she did."

Faz gave that some thought. He asked, "Did Chambers tell any of the tenants where she was going?"

"One thought she said Europe, a long-overdue backpacking trip. She asked one of her neighbors to collect her mail while she was gone. Neighbor still had a big stack of it."

"She didn't ask the neighbor to forward it?" Faz said.

"Nope."

He looked to Del. "Sounds like she didn't intend to come back, but she didn't want it to look that way."

"Definitely," Del said.

Nikolic checked his notebook again. "The skip tracer tracked down a relative in New Jersey, a married sister—Allison McCabe." He spelled the last name. "He called her, said he was the building manager, and told her he had Devin Chambers's furniture, personal belongings, and a stack of mail but didn't know where to forward it."

"What did the sister tell him?"

Nikolic smiled. "She said she hadn't had any contact with her sister in several years and didn't know what to tell him. The sister didn't want anything to do with her. He pressed her a bit and learned Devin Chambers has a fondness for prescription drugs and a related money-management problem. She'd apparently borrowed money from the sister in the past and never repaid it. The sister got tired of it and cut her off. According to my guy, a lot of the mail collected was from creditors and collection agencies, past due."

"Disappearing takes money," Faz said.

Del looked to Faz. "The trust fund."

"I'm thinking the same thing," Faz said. "Just wondering if the skip tracer knew. If Chambers and Andrea were pals, maybe Andrea was helping her out."

Del shook his head. "Then why wouldn't she just give her the money to pay her bills? That seems a lot simpler solution than both of them running."

"Except Andrea needed to get away," Faz said. "Needed people to think she died."

"Sounds like Chambers had reason to disappear also," Del said.

"Maybe they worked out a deal." Faz looked to Nikolic. "Your guy find anything else?"

"He had a woman in his office call up Chambers's last employer and ask for the person who did the payroll. She pretended to be Chambers and said she hadn't received her final check and just wanted to confirm the forwarding address they had for her."

"Did they have one?" Faz asked.

Nikolic nodded. "A drop box inside a Bartell's drugstore in Renton, Washington, but the name on the box wasn't Devin Chambers." Another big smile. "It was Lynn Hoff."

"No shit," Faz said.

"No shit. So the skip tracer has the same woman call the pharmacy, pretend to be Lynn Hoff, and asks if they have her insurance information on her profile. The pharmacy technician rattles off the same PO box. The woman asks if her doctor had called in her most recent prescription and the tech says they have nothing since they filled a prescription for oxycodone a week earlier."

"Confirming Lynn Hoff was still in the area. And your guy passed all this on to the client with the guerilla e-mail account?" Faz asked.

"He did."

"And if a person was so inclined, they could stake out that Bartell's and hope Devin Chambers, or Andrea Strickland, walks in, follow her when she leaves, and find out where she's staying."

Nikolic sat back, sipping his drink. "That's what I would have done," he said.

—

Tracy and Kins were in the car when Del and Faz called. They said they had information but didn't want to share it at the office. Tracy said she and Kins would meet them in the food court in the plaza of the Bank of America building on Fifth Avenue.

Over coffee, Tracy and Kins listened to Faz and Del explain what Nikolic had told them.

"Awfully big coincidence for Devin Chambers to show up in the same city in Washington where Andrea Strickland goes to get her face rearranged and do her banking," Faz said.

"Too big," Tracy said.

"They were friends," Kins said. "So Devin Chambers had to be the person who helped her off the mountain, and maybe the person who looked after Strickland after the surgery."

"And Strickland would have needed prescription drugs for the pain," Faz said.

"Or Chambers was after the trust money," Tracy said.

They all looked at her.

She said, "According to the sister, Devin Chambers had a prescription drug problem and a money problem, right?"

"That's what he said," Faz said.

"So she could have been after both," Tracy said. "And if Devin Chambers was helping Andrea Strickland, she'd have known Andrea Strickland's alias as well as the bank, and probably the accounts and the passwords."

"You think she could have killed her?" Kins asked. "Then moved the money?"

Tracy shrugged. "Strickland was already dead. Chambers would have known that too. It was the perfect crime, so long as nobody ever found the body."

"So maybe we should be looking for Devin Chambers," Faz said.

"Not our case anymore," Kins said, finishing the last of his coffee.

Tracy had not told any of them about San Bernardino, and what she'd learned from Penny Orr, or from the counselor, Alan Townsend. If the shit hit the fan about Tracy continuing the investigation, she wanted them to be able to say they had no knowledge of any of her actions.

"I'll call Stan Fields," she said. "I'll tell him it was something we had going on when the investigation was pulled, that we just now got the information and we're passing it on."

"Nik won't give up his source," Faz said.

"That's not our problem," Kins said. "Let Fields deal with it, if he decides to push it."

Tracy wondered how much Fields would push it.

CHAPTER 22

Tracy called Stan Fields that afternoon and told him he was going to want to meet her. She suggested Wednesday, July 5, her day off. When Fields pressed her for a reason for the meeting she remained vague, but said it would be worth the drive north to Seattle. She suggested they meet at Cactus, a restaurant on Alki Beach. If ever questioned about the meeting, it would be easier for her to explain a lunch on her day off at a restaurant near her home, rather than try to explain why she would drive all the way to Tacoma for an investigation she was no longer supposed to be working.

Wednesday, at just minutes after noon, Tracy sat waiting beneath the green-and-red awnings on the Cactus patio munching chips and salsa and sipping iced tea. Across the street, people packed the beach and the Alki Beach boardwalk, so much so that runners had to venture into the street to avoid the crowd. Judging from the heavy car traffic, still more were coming to enjoy the beach, or to have lunch in one of the restaurants with the billion-dollar view. Tourists clustered around the concrete obelisk commemorating what was supposedly the birthplace of Seattle, or at least the location where the Denny Party settlers landed in the fall of 1851 to establish the first settlement. Native

Americans already living in the area likely would dispute that the area needed finding.

Tracy watched Fields approach the patio from along Sixty-Third Avenue, which ran perpendicular to Alki Avenue. He sucked on a cigarette. The seventies motif continued. Fields wore a gray pinstriped suit, open-collared shirt displaying a gold chain, and aviator sunglasses. Tracy had dressed casually in shorts, a blue tank top, and white shirt.

Fields took a final pull on the cigarette before dropping it and grinding it with his shoe. Inside the restaurant he greeted her. "Traffic is a bitch around here. Good call on the parking."

Living close by, Tracy knew the secret parking locations, like the underground garage directly adjacent to the building.

"Don't these people freaking work?" Fields said, eyeing the mass of bodies walking the boardwalk across the street.

"It's lunchtime," Tracy said. "People in the Northwest know to get out when the sun's shining. The fall and winter can be very long."

Fields removed his jacket and pulled out his chair, sitting. He smelled of cigarette smoke. "In Arizona, you stay indoors in the summer and venture out in the fall and winter."

He removed his aviator sunglasses, folded them, and put them in his shirt pocket. When the waitress approached, he said, "Bring me a Corona with a lime, darling." Tracy fought to keep her tongue in check. Fields directed his attention to Tracy. "So, why all the intrigue?"

"No intrigue. I have some information for you on the Andrea Strickland case, a few things we were working when they pulled jurisdiction."

"No intrigue?" Fields gave Tracy a shit-eating grin. The mustache ends lifted. "Judging from your appearance, you're not working today. You have information for me not in the file you shipped down, but you didn't want to discuss it over the phone, and you asked me to come to you. I've been doing this job a while also."

"Yeah, I know. It's not your first rodeo," Tracy said. "So you got the file?"

Fields nodded. "And I had another chat with Graham Strickland, or, I should say, I tried."

"He's lawyered up?"

The mustache twitched. "Everything has to go through the attorney. I told the attorney we'd charge him and his client with obstruction."

Tracy could only imagine how far that tactic had gotten Fields.

"He told me to put up or shut up," he continued. "We compromised. He's going to make Strickland available for questioning." Fields sat back, watching two young women in shorts walk past the patio before redirecting his attention to Tracy. "Not sure how much good it's going to do since we can't get an exact time on the murder, and there are no forensics to speak of with the salt water doing a number on the crab pot and body. Even if we found the gun, which is less than doubtful, we don't have a bullet. We're working to get Strickland's credit card and phone records to see if maybe he rented a crabbing boat for the day. Not likely." Fields took a chip, dipped it in the salsa, and popped it in his mouth. "In other words, it remains circumstantial, and the little prick knows it."

The waitress returned with Fields's beer, a lime slice sticking out the neck.

"Are you ready to order?" she asked.

"Just bring me that steak dish you have," Fields said. "What's it called, *carne asada*, am I right?"

The woman smiled. "How do you like it cooked?"

"Bloodred. You tell the chef I want it to 'moo' when I stick it with my fork. And throw a couple of them big green peppers on the grill for me also."

Tracy ordered a tostada. "No sour cream or guacamole," she said.

Fields shoved the lime slice into the bottle. "Watching your figure?" He took a sip of his beer. "So what do you have for me?"

Tracy dipped a chip, munching. "I spoke to Andrea Strickland's aunt in San Bernardino."

"Yeah?" Fields said, sounding surprised and irritated. "What? You just happen to be down there, like you just happened to want to spend your day off working a case no longer yours? Don't they keep you busy up here in Seattle?" Fields's eyebrows drew together.

"I also spoke to her counselor," Tracy said, ignoring him.

"Strickland's or the aunt's?"

"Strickland's. The aunt took Andrea to see him after the car accident that killed her parents. She continued when she realized her husband was molesting Andrea."

"No shit?" Fields said loud enough for heads to turn at the other tables.

Tracy sipped her iced tea. "The kid loses her parents in a car accident then has to endure crap like that."

"Not everyone grew up in the *Brady Bunch*," Fields said, taking another sip of his beer.

"Yeah, far from it," Tracy said.

"So she was all screwed up," Fields said.

"Counselor called Protective Services and she was removed from the home until the aunt moved to a new place."

"Charges pressed?"

"I haven't looked."

"What happened to her?"

"Counselor isn't certain but said it is entirely plausible Andrea could have developed what he called a dissociative disorder—multiple personalities she might take on to avoid the real world."

"Sort of like that *Sybil* movie?"

"I wouldn't know."

"Did he name any of these other personalities?"

"You mean like Lynn Hoff? No. But he said Andrea was an obsessive reader and could have taken on the role of the characters in the books she read."

"Let's hope she didn't read *Carrie*," Fields said. "Sounds like she was a train wreck waiting to happen."

"Maybe. He also said she could have been prone to violent acts."

"He ever witness that?"

Tracy shook her head. "Andrea left when she turned eighteen. He said the symptoms likely would manifest, if they were going to manifest, in her early twenties."

"So she could have been a time bomb waiting to go off; did he say what could set her off?"

"He speculated on a number of things—another trauma, abuse, abandonment, or if she felt desperate."

The waitress returned with Tracy's tostada and Fields's carne asada. He stuck it with his fork. "I don't hear no 'mooing,'" he said. The waitress looked concerned. "Don't you worry about it, darling. I'm just playing with you. Bring me another Corona, will you?"

The waitress took the empty bottle from the table.

Fields grabbed his knife and cut at the meat, putting a hunk in his mouth and talking as he chewed. "You said abandoned, like if her husband was cheating on her, or planning on killing her, and she found out?"

"Possibly."

"Okay. So where does this get me?"

Tracy spooned some salsa onto her tostada. "Well, it could explain how a seemingly introverted young woman walked off that mountain in the first place, and went to such extremes to set her husband up to look like he'd murdered her."

Fields lowered his knife and fork. "What do you mean, set him up?"

"According to your report, the husband had no knowledge of the insurance policy naming him a beneficiary."

"That's what he said, but we both know that's probably bullshit," Fields said.

"Maybe not," Tracy said. "No confirmation on the 'girlfriend' Andrea was convinced her husband was sleeping with either. What we do know is she walked off the mountain, but not before she left the debris field of clothes and equipment, which means she had to have brought an extra set to get down the mountain. She didn't carry all that up there for the hell of it. And she obtained a fake driver's license, which all points to premeditation."

"So you're saying she got the insurance policy to make it *look like* the husband was trying to kill her?"

"Or maybe he was trying to kill her and she found out," Tracy said. "But, yeah, getting the policy, consulting a divorce attorney, telling her boss she suspected her husband was cheating on her again, all could have been part of a plan to leave a trail of bread crumbs leading right back to her husband."

"She doesn't strike me as that smart, especially if she was as big a nut job as the shrink says."

"Bundy was a nut job." Tracy let that sink in for a moment. "According to Andrea's boss, she was very bright."

Fields put down his knife and fork and wiped the corners of his mouth with his napkin. "Okay, but the question is, who killed her now? And, assuming you're right about all of this—that she somehow did find out the husband's plan to kill her and she set him up—it would all be reason why he might seek her out and kill her. So we're back to the husband."

"Possibly, though I'd still put his desire to get at the trust fund as the more likely motivation—if he did it, which brings me to the next thing I wanted to talk to you about. Someone *was* looking for Lynn Hoff and for Devin Chambers."

"How do you know that?"

"I asked a friend in the business of finding people to ask around and let me know if anyone was looking for Lynn Hoff. Someone was."

"Someone who?"

"He doesn't know. The client used a guerilla e-mail account to ensure they remained anonymous."

"So that's a dead end."

"Not necessarily."

The waitress returned with Fields's second beer and refilled Tracy's glass of iced tea. Tracy waited until she'd departed.

"My contact said the person initially asked the skip tracer to search for a Lynn Hoff, but other than the Washington State driver's license we found, he also came up empty."

Fields squeezed the lime onto his steak, then shoved the rind into the bottle. "Right, so other than now knowing someone was looking for her, it's a dead end."

"It means someone knew Andrea changed her identity to Lynn Hoff," Tracy said, feeling like she was spoon-feeding Fields his investigation, and no longer surprised that the initial investigation had not produced results. "And, when the skip tracer advised that the usual channels were not bringing up anything on a Lynn Hoff, this unknown client threw out the name Devin Chambers."

"He knew the name?"

"Apparently."

"And Devin Chambers disappeared about the same time Andrea Strickland disappeared," Fields said. "That's what the employer said, right?"

Tracy had included that information in her report of the interview of Brenda Berg. "Chambers told her neighbors she was leaving town for Europe. She asked someone at the complex to collect her mail but made no attempt to recover it, or her belongings. Apparently, she has a sister in New Jersey who said Devin had a money management problem likely related to a prescription drug problem."

"You think she was after Andrea's money?"

"The skip tracer found an address for a PO box inside a drugstore in Renton registered to a Lynn Hoff. The pharmacy also had a record of at least one prior prescription under that name. And Renton is where Andrea Strickland used the name Lynn Hoff to have her face reconstructed, and did her banking."

"You think they were working together, Chambers and Strickland?"

"That's one way of looking at it. There might be another. The ranger I spoke with was convinced Strickland had help getting off the mountain and getting away. Also, two days after Kurt Schill pulled the body up in the crab pot, somebody drained Lynn Hoff's bank accounts, which means that person had to know the bank, the account numbers, and the passwords."

"Right, so you're thinking this Devin Chambers helped her off the mountain and either was working with her or conned her and eventually killed her?"

Tracy wasn't going to go that far. She wasn't going to draw conclusions from evidence she wasn't supposed to have on an investigation she was no longer directing. "I think she might be a person of interest you'd want to talk with."

Fields picked up his beer and sat back, sipping it. "So how come none of this is in your reports?"

Tracy shrugged. "Like I said, we didn't have it yet. Just came in."

"There's no mention of an aunt or a shrink in your file. No mention you'd put word out on the street asking if anyone was looking for a Lynn Hoff. There's no mention of it as work in progress."

"We were told to close the file and get it down to you guys, then finish up anything we were working on. What difference does it make? You have it now."

Fields set down his beer and lifted his napkin from his lap, placing it on his plate, though he hadn't finished his carne asada. He clearly wasn't happy Tracy had stepped on his investigation. Tracy didn't care; she didn't give a damn about Fields's feelings. She cared about finding a killer.

Fields spotted the waitress, made eye contact, and motioned for the check. He reengaged Tracy. "Thanks for the information, and the lunch."

Tracy shook her head. "Your rodeo," she said. "Your credit card."

———

When Tracy arrived home after her lunch with Stan Fields, Dan was sitting outside on one of the two chaise longues on the deck. Far from baking beneath the heat of an unrelenting sun, he looked comfortable in the broad shade of a freestanding patio umbrella. As Tracy stepped out onto the deck, Dan set down a legal pleading bleeding red from the pen in his hand. Rex and Sherlock, who looked like they'd died and found heaven in the same shade, saw her approach, but only Sherlock got up to greet her, tail whipping the air. Tracy didn't blame Rex, who gave her a sheepish eyebrow raise.

Dan looked up from behind round, wire-framed glasses that gave him a professorial look but now would forever be associated with Harry Potter. He'd gone into the office early to catch up on paperwork and make sure there were no fires burning so they could spend the afternoon together.

"When did we get that?" Tracy asked. The umbrella was not only big, but a hideous rust color, though she refrained from saying so.

"It's great, isn't it? I bought it on the way home from the office. I figured with the weather this nice, there was no need to spend the day working inside, plus you're supposed to stay out of the sun."

"I'm supposed to wear sunscreen," she said. "Never thought I'd see the day we'd be buying umbrellas in Seattle that had nothing to do with rain."

"Global warming," he said. "Glaciers melting, oceans rising, drought, famine, dogs and cats living together . . ."

"Are we getting our meteorology from Bill Murray now?" she asked, fairly certain the last part of Dan's sentence was a rip-off from a line in one of the comedian's movies.

"Where were you? Did you go for a walk?" Dan asked.

She sipped from his glass of ice water. "No, I had a meeting."

"On your day off?"

She sat on the edge of the adjacent chaise longue, facing him. "I met with the detective from Pierce County who took over the woman-in-the-crab-pot investigation."

"On your day off?" he asked again. "I thought you couldn't stand the guy."

She turned her attention to the view. "There was some information I had to give him, off the record."

"On your day off?" Dan said again.

"Is this going to be a discussion of my being obsessed with solving every murder involving a young woman because of what happened to my sister?"

"No."

"Then why do you keep saying that?" she said, aggravated.

Dan set down the pleading and took a breath. "You told me the world crapped on this young woman, that she went from being the daughter of a doctor, to an orphan being molested by an uncle, to the wife of an abusive husband."

"That's true," she said.

"So I'm wondering if your trip to San Bernardino has anything to do with you feeling some kind of connection to her."

"Why, do you plan to abuse me?"

"I'm afraid of you, you know that." He smiled to lighten the mood. "Look, I'm just saying that we both know life didn't exactly play fair with you either, Tracy. Your dad was a doctor and you lost him and your sister very near to each other."

"I'm not going to wallow in pity, Dan."

"I'm not saying you should."

"I had a vested interest in this case," she said, thinking of Nolasco. "It was my investigation and yeah, you know, sometimes they are personal. Aren't some of your cases more personal than others?"

"Sure, but in what percentage of those investigations that you make personal is the victim a young woman?"

"A lot," she said. "Because a lot of the people abducted and killed are young women. I'm not sure what I'm supposed to do about that."

"When it's your case, I don't think there's anything you need to do about it. I'm sure it motivates you to do a better job. But when it's not your case and you make bad decisions, then I think you have to question your motivation."

"All I did was follow up on some things. How is that a bad decision?"

"Your trip to San Bernardino was unauthorized."

"It wasn't a business trip."

"Really?"

"Look, I talked to her while you were in court and passed the information on to the detective taking back the investigation. It's in his hands now. He gets the credit for good police work. I don't see that as making a bad decision."

"So you're going to let it go?"

"I have to, don't I?"

They sat in silence. Dan stood. "Okay. I have a few errands to run."

She knew she was being defensive and she knew Dan was only looking out for her. She also knew she had trouble letting things go. She got up and hugged him. "I'm sorry. I don't want to fight about this. Yeah, okay, I feel something for this woman and I wanted to see it through. You're right. There's definitely a connection there and I'm pissed we didn't keep it and I'm sorry if I'm taking that out on you."

"Don't worry about it," he said. "I'm a big boy. Listen, I'll be out most of the afternoon finishing a few things, but we could take the dogs out later when the temperature cools."

"Sure," she said. "I'd like that."

He started inside, then turned back. "Oh, and I talked to my doctor about what we discussed the other day on our run."

"The vasectomy?"

"He says it can be reversed."

She knew it was a lot to ask of Dan, not just the procedure, which would be a day or two of pain, but the lifetime commitment to being a parent. She didn't want him to feel pressure simply because of her own sudden anxiety that she might never have a child.

"Take me out of the equation for a moment," she said. "Would you still want to have children?"

"I can't take you out of the equation," he said. "I'm in love with you. I wouldn't do it for any other person. The question is really one you have to answer. I hate to sound like a chauvinist, but since God didn't give me a uterus, or breasts for that matter, the heavy lifting is going to fall on you for at least the first year. Are you sure you've thought this through?"

"I always thought I'd have children," she said.

"I know," he said, "and live in Cedar Grove next door to Sarah and we'd all get together on Sundays for barbecues and our children would go to school together."

She smiled, but a tear escaped the corner of her eye. "You thought about that?"

"We were best friends," he said, embracing her, "and that was our world. They're good memories, Tracy. They don't have to be sad memories. Now we have the chance to make our own memories, together."

"I'm not sure I deserve that chance," she said.

He pulled back, looking down at her. "Why would you say something like that? Because of Sarah?"

She fought back tears. "She's never going to fall in love, Dan, never going to get married or raise children."

He hugged her. "It wasn't your fault, what happened to her, Tracy. You know that."

Yes, she knew it, but that didn't make her feel better about it. Sarah was always in the back of her mind. "I still think about her—that I never should have let her drive home alone."

"What do you think Sarah would want for you?"

Tracy wiped her tears; more quickly followed. "I know she'd want me to be happy," Tracy said.

"Of course she would."

She wept, head on Dan's chest. When she'd regained her composure she pulled back and said, "I think it's like you said the other day, that we shouldn't take the second step until we've taken the first step."

Dan released her hand. "There's that proposal again." He made a goofy face. "I know I'm a stud and all, but really, you're going to have to sweep me off my feet."

Tracy laughed and playfully hit his chest.

"Okay," he said. "We'll take it one step at a time." He checked the clock on the inside wall. "I have a few more hours of work and some errands, and when I get back we can take Rex and Sherlock down to the beach?"

Tracy smiled. "I'd like that."

Just after seven, with the temperature pleasant and a light breeze blowing from the north, Dan loaded Rex and Sherlock into the back of his SUV.

"We're not going to walk?" Tracy asked.

"I think they're still hurting a bit from their run the other day. I'm still hurting from the run the other day."

"They don't look like they're hurting."

Sherlock and Rex pranced with excitement, whining, tongues hanging out. "They would run until they dropped," Dan said. "We can drive down and get a walk on the beach. I want to go out to the lighthouse."

"Okay," Tracy said, sliding into the passenger seat.

Dan drove down the hill and around the bend. Normally, with parking difficult in the summer, they pulled into a designated lane in the middle of the road, but today Dan drove past the storefronts and restaurants, out toward the lighthouse.

"Are we going to walk the dogs or drive them?" Tracy asked.

Dan turned right into a parking lot just past the V-shaped apartment complex that led to the Alki Point Lighthouse. A cyclone gate on wheels blocked the entrance, and a large sign warned that the area was restricted and trespassers would be prosecuted.

"It's closed," she said, not sure what Dan was expecting at that hour.

"Huh," Dan said. "Let's see if there's a way down to the water."

"Are we looking to get arrested to spice up the day?" Tracy asked. Smaller signs posted in the parking lot indicated the parking was reserved for apartment tenants, and violators would be towed.

"I've never been out here," Dan said. "I just want to take a look. The worst they'll do is ask us to leave." He stepped from the car and opened the tailgate. Rex and Sherlock bounded out and followed him to the cyclone fence. Dan pulled on the gate and the fence rolled to the left.

"It's open," he said.

"No, it's closed," she said, still anchored in her seat. "*You* opened it."

"Come on, let's just take a look. They would have locked it if they didn't want anyone to come in."

"You won't be satisfied until we're arrested, will you?"

"Don't be a namby pants."

"Wasn't I just getting a lecture about doing things that might get me in trouble?"

"That was different; you could lose your job. What are they going to do to us for looking?"

"Arrest us. Accuse us of being terrorists. Send us to Guantanamo Bay. Waterboards."

"Come on," Dan said. He walked away, down the street.

"Okay," Tracy said, opening her door and stepping out. "I guess we're doing this."

She closed the gate behind her and hurried to catch up. The paved road continued past two homes, white with red roofs and porches. The homes reminded her of something out of a 1950s movie. The *Seattle Times* had recently run an article commemorating the lighthouse's one-hundredth anniversary and noted that the two beachfront homes now housed senior Coast Guard officers. Farther down the road, Tracy and Dan came to maintenance buildings, also white with red roofs. A white gravel path led to the lighthouse, which marked the tip of the southern entrance, and the transition from Puget Sound into Elliott Bay.

Tracy followed Dan along the gravel path, half expecting armed guards to appear at any moment and order them to the ground. The door to the lighthouse remained open. Dan stepped inside. Tracy followed. The room at floor level consisted of a museum with photographs and equipment depicting the lighthouse's history. Dan didn't linger, climbing a narrow, winding staircase. Tracy followed him to the second level, figuring if they'd come this far they might as well go all the way. A metal ladder ascended to the actual room that housed the light. They'd need a crane to get Rex and Sherlock up the ladder.

"Stay," Dan said.

Dan climbed the rungs. Tracy followed. Below, Rex whined. "Hush," Dan said.

As Tracy climbed, she couldn't see above her. Dan blocked the entrance. When he reached the top and cleared the ladder, however, she noticed a flickering golden glow. She reached the top rung and Dan extended a hand to help her into the cramped octagon-shaped room, the light beacon in the middle. The glow, however, did not emanate from the beacon. It came from a dozen flickering candles casting shadows over red roses. Out the windows, streams of light from the fading sun glistened on the surface of the water like hundreds of diamonds.

Tracy felt her eyes water and her knees weaken. Dan never released her hand. He dropped to a knee while reaching into one of the pockets of his cargo shorts, producing a small black box.

"Oh my God," Tracy said, feeling herself becoming overwhelmed, tears streaming down her cheeks.

"Tracy Anne Crosswhite," Dan said, opening the box to display a large diamond.

Her chest heaved and her breath caught in her throat. She covered her mouth with her hand.

"Will you marry me?" Dan asked.

—

They sat at a table in their favorite Italian restaurant just south of the point on Beach Drive. Out the window, the sunlight faded behind the islands and the distant Olympic Mountains. The red roses, now arranged in a vase, stood on the table, but Tracy couldn't take her eyes off the ring adorning her left hand, or the man who'd placed it there. "It's so beautiful," she said. "Everything was so beautiful. How did you get this all done?"

"Well, at the risk of not starting this relationship off with complete honesty, I didn't go into the office this morning."

"I figured that. How did you get them to let you use the lighthouse?"

"I have a friend who works with the Coast Guard and is tight with the commander. He had one of the guards leave the gate unlocked and came after closing to arrange the flowers. I called and gave him the cue to light the candles for me. I owe a few people some really good bottles of wine. So, did I do good?"

He'd blown her away. She'd thought they'd get married, but she thought it would be a decision they made together, and then they'd drive down to the courthouse. She never expected Dan to propose, to go to so much effort to surprise . . . and amaze her. She couldn't stop smiling. She couldn't recall the last time her face hurt from smiling so much.

"You did good," she said.

She twisted her ring in the fading light coming through the window, watching the diamonds surrounding the large center diamond sparkle and flicker. Out the window, gentle waves rippled on Puget Sound, and sailboats tacked into and against the wind. It was perfect. The entire night was perfect, until she realized the view was almost directly in line with the honey hole where Kurt Schill had pulled up the crab pot containing Andrea Strickland's body.

CHAPTER 23

Thursday morning, Tracy arrived at the office tired from a fitful night's sleep. After dinner, she and Dan had returned home and made love. Getting to sleep had not been a problem, but she had awakened at just after three, out of breath, her nightshirt soaked with sweat, the way it used to get when she'd been dreaming of Sarah. This time, the nightmare had nothing to do with her sister. This time, in the nightmare, Tracy had been sitting in Kurt Schill's boat on Puget Sound, struggling to raise the crab pot, arms straining to pull the line through the block at the end of the davit pole. It seemed she'd pulled forever, yard after yard of rope winding in a neat circle around her feet until, finally, the crab pot breached the surface. She tied off the rope and carefully slid across the seat, feeling the boat tip off balance. Carefully, she stretched out her arm. The boat inched closer to the water's surface. She strained to reach the cage, fingers twitching, just inches from the metal.

A hand shot out from between the bars, the polished blue fingernails gripping her arm, yanking her overboard, into the dark waters.

Tracy had lain in bed, unable to get back to sleep. Her mind churned over the evidence in the Andrea Strickland case, something about the dream bothering her, though what exactly she couldn't be sure. She read on her Kindle until six o'clock, then got up and made Dan breakfast in bed—which seemed a poor trade for all the effort he'd gone to the day before. After they'd eaten, she made her way into the office.

Tracy stepped off the elevator, in no hurry now that Pierce County had taken back her only open murder. The A Team was back to working their regular schedule. Two months on day shifts, then they'd work a month on nights. She'd do the legwork on her other violent crime cases, and get those that didn't plead prepared for trial. As she walked the hallway, her section came alive. She smelled the bittersweet aroma of coffee and heard the voices of her colleagues and of the morning newscasters from the flat screen. Mentally, she was settling into the thought of a relaxing morning when she entered her bull pen and saw the yellow sticky note on her computer monitor summoning her.

See me in conference room immediately when you get in!

Knowing Nolasco, with the Strickland case no longer filling Tracy's plate, he'd give her some administrative crap—a tedious project like digging through boxes of old files he'd been avoiding but would now say he needed ASAP.

The blinds on the windows had been drawn, preventing her from seeing into the conference room. She reached the open door, about to knock, but caught herself when she saw others seated at the table. She momentarily thought she'd walked in on a meeting. Nolasco sat on the far side of the table beside Stephen Martinez, the assistant chief of criminal investigations—Nolasco's immediate superior. On the other side of the table, the side closest to the door, sat Stan Fields and an officer Tracy could venture a good guess was Fields's captain—a pale, pudgy, officious-looking man bearing an expression like his shorts were too tight and riding up on him.

She also had a good guess why they'd all gathered. Stan Fields had ratted her out.

"Come in, Detective Crosswhite," Martinez said, voice grim. He gestured to the chair at the head of the table. Apparently, she didn't get to choose sides. Nolasco and Martinez sat on her right, Fields and his captain on her left. Faz had once described Martinez as a pit bull because of his short legs and stout body. His salt-and-pepper crew cut accentuated a prominent jaw and he had intense, light-blue eyes. Martinez chose to wear a uniform at all times, and it added to his image as a no-nonsense cop.

Tracy could feel the tension in the room—as if a gas leak could cause an explosion with just the faintest spark.

Fields had only briefly glanced up when Tracy entered, but she'd looked hard at him. He wore a collared gray dress shirt beneath a brown suede jacket. This guy had really missed his decade for fashion.

When Tracy sat, Martinez nodded to Nolasco, who adjusted in his chair, the leather creaking. "Detective Crosswhite, I'm going to cut to the chase here. We've received a complaint from Captain Jessup of the Pierce County Major Crimes Unit that you interfered with their investigation of the Andrea Strickland matter. Do you know anything about that?"

Tracy struggled to keep her temper from being the spark that ignited the room. A part of her was pissed at Nolasco, who could have handled this matter internally, but chose instead to put on a show, likely for Martinez. She shifted her gaze to Stan Fields, not about to let him hide behind his captain. Fields's facial expression remained largely disguised by the thick gray mustache, but his eyes held the bemused glint of a schoolboy who knew he'd screwed up, and had found a way to shift blame. Tracy's initial judgment of Fields had been only partially correct. Yes, he was a sexist, lazy ass, but he was also an insecure, vindictive prick too stupid or arrogant to realize she'd handed him information that could help his investigation, and she'd been content to let him take all the credit—whatever might have come from it. Instead, he'd directed the spotlight back on Tracy, apparently failing to realize it only illuminated his own incompetence. So be it. If Fields wanted to drag her before her captain, she was more than happy to let *his* captain know his detective couldn't find his ass with both hands.

"Do I know anything about it?" she said. "I know that I had lunch with Detective Fields yesterday and provided him with additional information relevant to the investigation."

"What information, exactly?" Nolasco asked.

Nolasco already had the answer to that question because Fields had run to his captain the minute he got back to Tacoma and told him, and Jessup had clearly called SPD. "I provided him with the details of an interview I conducted with Andrea Strickland's aunt as well as her counselor. I also provided him with information we received from a skip tracer I'd asked to determine if anyone in his world had been asking about a Lynn Hoff." Tracy turned to Jessup, speaking to him as if he were a little slow. "If you'd like me to explain who these people are— since you won't find them in your detective's file—I'd be happy to."

Jessup's cheeks flushed red, and the bemused glint in Fields's eyes sharpened.

"When did you conduct the interviews of the aunt and the counselor?" Nolasco asked.

"Last Friday," she said, turning back to him.

"After Pierce County had reasserted jurisdiction," Jessup said to Nolasco, in case anyone in the room was too stupid to figure that out on his own.

"Yes," Tracy said.

"So you flew to Los Angeles on official SPD business after this department no longer had jurisdiction of the case?" Nolasco said.

"No, I flew to Los Angeles on personal business. I spoke to the aunt on my personal day. I didn't know about the counselor until I spoke with the aunt. She arranged for me to speak to him and to obtain Andrea Strickland's file. That's how good police work is conducted," she said, looking again to Jessup and Fields. "I provided that information to Detective Fields."

Jessup said, "Personal business?" not trying to hide his skepticism.

"That's right. I flew to Los Angeles for a long weekend with my boyfriend. I paid for the flight and the hotel, and all meals." She looked to Nolasco. "I used the time to follow through with the conversation I'd set up with the aunt, as you'd instructed."

Nolasco's eyes narrowed in concern. "As I instructed?"

"Yes, Captain. You told us to wrap up anything we had working and to provide written reports to Pierce County so their file would be complete and they could hit the ground running. I had already arranged a telephone meeting with the aunt. Since I was traveling to LA I thought it better to do the interview in person."

Martinez cleared his throat. "Be that as it may," he said, his voice as deep and gravelly as a comic-book villain's. "Your discussion with the aunt was related to the victim's disappearance, was it not?"

"No, it was related to the victim's murder," Tracy said, keeping her tone flat and professional. "Pierce County handled the disappearance. Our jurisdiction was her murder."

Martinez said, "And that discussion took place after SPD had relinquished jurisdiction."

"My discussion with the aunt? Technically, yes."

"So it's really semantics, isn't it, to say you were not on official SPD business?"

"I could see how someone could look at it that way, but I wasn't."

"How would you look at it, Detective?" Jessup asked, clearly struggling to keep his composure.

Tracy had already decided she liked Jessup about as much as she liked Fields. Since he wasn't her captain, she didn't feel compelled to answer him, but she did so because it gave her the chance to take a dig at Fields. "I'd look at it as a dedicated police detective taking steps to complete her file, as instructed by her captain, so that all relevant information could be provided to the agency taking over jurisdiction, with the common goal of capturing the murderer, sir."

Jessup gave her a sardonic smile. "So you think we should say, 'Thank you.'"

"You're welcome."

Jessup flushed again and looked across the table to Nolasco and Martinez, who looked to be suppressing a smile.

"Why not just give Pierce County the information and let them follow up?" Nolasco asked.

"Because I'd already made the contact with the aunt and I thought to blow her off would be unprofessional." Tracy shifted her gaze to Fields. "And because Pierce County had the investigation for six weeks and had yet to talk with the aunt."

"That was a different investigation," Fields said. "It was a missing person case."

"Except you said you thought all along the husband killed her," Tracy said.

"There was no certainty Andrea Strickland had been murdered," Fields said, voice rising.

"Yet you immediately operated under that premise, narrowing your investigation so much that you never spoke to Strickland's best friend or her aunt, and you didn't even know about Andrea Strickland's counselor, or that her friend had also disappeared about the same time Strickland walked off Mount Rainier. Had you done your job, you would have obtained evidence that pointed your investigation in another direction, namely that Andrea Strickland had not been killed, but walked off the mountain and was still alive, possibly preventing the situation—"

Fields slapped the table with the palm of his hand and rose out of his chair. "Yeah, you're great with twenty-twenty hindsight, Crosswhite."

"Hindsight has nothing to do with it," Tracy said, rising from her chair and speaking loud enough to be heard over the others who had jumped in. "Had you done your job, the next logical step would have been to look for Lynn Hoff."

"That's your opinion!" Fields shouted back.

"No, that's good detective work."

"It was no longer your call to determine how another organization conducts its investigation," Jessup said, also standing, his face a red beacon. "Nor is it up to you to critique my department or to step in when you deem it appropriate. You never should have spoken to the aunt."

"Exactly how did it interfere with *your* investigation?" Tracy asked.

Jessup froze for an instant. Without an answer, he resorted to the schoolyard equivalent of "It's mine."

"Because it was no longer your investigation."

Tracy looked to Martinez. "I didn't hide the fact that I spoke to anyone. In fact, I called Detective Fields on my day off and invited him to meet with me so I could immediately provide him with the information. I didn't tell him what to do with it."

Fields said, "I had every intention of speaking to the aunt and to the friend."

"You didn't even know the friend's name. Your file made no mention of the friend or the aunt."

"Enough," Martinez said, quiet but deliberate. "Everyone sit down." After a brief pause to allow everyone to catch their breath, he said, "Have you written up the reports of your conversations with the aunt and the counselor?"

"Yes. I was going to transmit them this morning."

"We also want the information from the skip tracer," Fields said.

Martinez looked to Tracy. "I can provide the information that person uncovered," she said. "I can't provide a name."

"Can't or won't?" Jessup said.

Tracy was in a tough spot. If she said "can't," it could lead them to determine that Faz had actually spoken to the skip tracer. "The information was provided in confidence. It's irrelevant who provided it. It's the substance that matters."

"We'll decide what's relevant," Jessup said. He looked to Martinez. "We want the name."

Tracy continued her appeal to Martinez, who had a reputation for having been a good cop and protecting those that worked for him. "I don't want to burn a source for an investigation that is no longer ours."

"We'll talk more about it," Martinez said. "Is there anything else?" No one in the room spoke. Martinez rose. "Then you'll excuse us, gentlemen."

Jessup and Fields pushed back their chairs. They shook hands across the table with Nolasco and Martinez. Tracy got glares from both men as they departed. Nolasco and Martinez retook their seats.

"I want both reports on Captain Nolasco's desk by noon," Martinez said. "And I want the report on the skip tracer to include a name. We'll decide whether to provide it or not, take you out of it."

"I'll give them everything I have, but I can't give them the name, sir."

"That's not a request, Detective, that's an order. I also want you to verbally provide Captain Nolasco with a full report of your actions, including dates, times, and names with respect to everything you did after Pierce County reasserted jurisdiction."

"Do I need to get the union lawyer involved?" Tracy said.

Martinez shrugged. "That's up to you." He pushed back his chair and stood. "Personally, I think you did good police work, and I never have a problem with that." He again showed the hint of a smile before it quickly faded and he left the room.

Nolasco didn't get up. "You just can't help stepping in the shit, can you?"

"All due respect, Captain, sometimes doing the right thing means stepping in the shit."

Nolasco smirked. "Well, you sure have a knack for it." He put on a pair of cheaters and lowered his gaze to a notepad on the table, pen in hand. "Who else knew about you continuing the investigation?"

Tracy shook her head. "No one."

"No one?" he asked over the top of his cheaters.

"I did this all on a personal day. I don't share what I do on my personal days with people in the office. Frankly, it's no one's business what I do."

"I guess OPA will decide that," Nolasco said. "What about the skip tracer?"

"What about him?"

"That sounds like something Faz would be more inclined to know about than you."

She shrugged. "Not this time. My investigation. My call."

"I'm going to need his name."

"I'm not going to provide it without some assurance Pierce County isn't going to broadcast it and burn a perfectly good source because of their incompetence."

"That's not your call." Nolasco set down his pen and leaned away from the table. "Can I ask you a question, off the record?"

Tracy shrugged.

"Why do it?"

Tracy thought of Penny Orr's statement. "Because Andrea Strickland mattered, and just because the world crapped on her while she was living doesn't mean she should be crapped on in death. Someone killed her and stuffed her body in a crab pot, and the two buffoons who just walked out of here will never figure it out."

"You want my opinion?"

"Not really, no."

Nolasco smiled. "Then I'll give you my professional advice as your captain, because I'm going to put it in the report to OPA." He paused a second. "This job is hard enough to do without making it personal. You make it personal, and it will impact not only you but those around you. Why do you think I'm divorced twice?"

The better question Tracy always wondered was why anyone had married him.

"Why do you think so many of us in this profession are divorced? You don't think I had occasion in my career when a case became personal, when I got too close and paid the price with my marriages and my relationships with my kids? You're not the only one who cares. You think you are, but you're not. The rest of us have just found a way to shut it off. If you don't learn how to do that, eventually you'll hurt yourself and those around you."

Tracy didn't immediately respond because, for once, Nolasco made sense. For once, she couldn't dispute what he was saying. She thought of Dan, and the ring on her finger. She thought of a baby, in a stroller, maybe a little girl.

She spoke softly. "When it's my case, it *is* my responsibility."

"But this wasn't your case," Nolasco said, his voice also measured. "Not anymore."

"It was my case. It should have remained *our* case. The body was found in our county, in our jurisdiction. We never should have given it up."

"I know you don't think I went to bat for you, and I'm not going to waste my time trying to convince you otherwise. That is not your—or my—decision to make. Sometimes we just have to bite our tongues and follow orders."

"Why do you think Pierce County fought so hard to get this case back?" she asked.

Nolasco looked confused by the question. "They had it originally; they had time and manpower invested in it."

"Or maybe they realize this case is going to continue to generate a lot of interest, and it could bring their entire department some much-needed positive publicity."

From the blank expression on Nolasco's face, he clearly hadn't considered this and now wished he had.

"But that doesn't matter anymore," she said. "It's Pierce County's opportunity now."

Tracy provided Nolasco with the additional information Martinez had requested. By the time she got back to her cubicle, it was clear word had spread around the section fishbowl that something was up. Tracy said the meeting was to ensure a smooth transition of the investigation to Pierce County. No one was buying her explanation, though most took the hint she wasn't going to say anything more.

As for Kins, Faz, and Del, she suggested they step outside. Tracy led them around the corner of the building to a patio partially shaded by an overhang. A fountain trickled water over marble levels, like a river. Tracy filled them in on the meeting in the conference room.

"I don't want you taking the blame for something I did," Faz said.

"Something we did," Del said.

"I asked you guys to do it."

"Bullshit," Faz said. "Nobody tells me to do nothing I don't want to do."

"We're big boys," Del said. "And we've been at this longer than you. They can't suspend us all."

"Look, I appreciate the support, but I made the decision to go and talk to the aunt and I understood the potential consequences."

"What the hell is Fields's problem?" Kins asked.

"I told you I didn't like that guy," Tracy said.

"I'm going to call Nik and tell him the situation. He'll get the name of the skip tracer he spoke with," Faz said. "You don't want to get in trouble for refusing an order from a superior officer. They'll charge you with insubordination, and they take that shit seriously. The other stuff is all bullshit. OPA will slap you on the wrist and it'll blow over—if they go to OPA at all. I doubt they will."

"I appreciate that, Faz," Tracy said.

"What the hell?" Kins said. He took a step closer. "Is that a ring on your finger?" He reached for her hand. "That's a diamond."

Tracy held up her hand. "Dan proposed last night."

"It's about freaking time," Del said.

"And you had to deal with this crap this morning?" Kins said.

"It is what it is," she said, feeling surprisingly calm about the situation, even about Fields. Maybe it was just the afterglow of the best night of her life, or the thought that she and Dan were getting married. Or maybe it was something said by the most unlikely person she would have ever expected to impart wisdom. Maybe Nolasco was right, for once. Maybe she needed a way to shut out the job. Maybe she was being selfish. It was no longer just about her. Her decisions could now impact Dan and, someday, possibly their children.

—

Tracy worked her assault-and-battery and other felony cases until the end of her shift, shut off her computer, and pushed back her chair.

"You heading home?" Kins said.

"Yeah, I thought I'd make Dan dinner for a change."

"I talked to Shannah," Kins said. "She wants to have you and Dan over for a little celebration."

"I got a better idea," Faz said, standing up from his chair and slipping on his sport coat. "An evening meal hosted by yours truly and cooked by the greatest Italian chef who ever lived, my wife."

"I'm in," Del said without hesitation. "Vera's cooking? Don't get in my way, Fazio."

"Sounds wonderful," Tracy said. "Maybe you should talk to her."

"Are you kidding? The only thing Vera loves better than cooking is sharing the food with friends. How about tomorrow night?"

"I'm off tomorrow, but let me talk to Dan," Tracy said.

"I can do tomorrow," Kins said.

"I can do any night of the week Vera's cooking," Del said.

"All right, then. Let's do it tomorrow night," Faz said. "I'll check with Vera and you check with Dan."

On her drive home, Tracy took a circuitous route. She wanted to take pictures of the Alki Point Lighthouse and the restaurant, something to commemorate the evening. She'd left her phone at home last evening, when Dan had proposed, thinking they were going for a walk with the dogs.

She stopped at the restaurant, taking pictures of its exterior from the sidewalk. As she turned to get back in the cab of her truck, she spotted an aluminum boat skipping across the water, and it made her think again of Kurt Schill. The young man had gotten the scare of a lifetime when he pulled up the crab pot and saw a human hand.

That thought made her recall her dream.

And what had been bothering her hit her like a dart between the eyes.

CHAPTER 24

The A Team gathered the following evening at Faz's home in Green Lake, a middle-class neighborhood north of downtown Seattle that derived its name from a centrally located, natural lake. Faz had once told Tracy he and Vera borrowed $30,000 from Vera's parents in the 1970s for a down payment to buy their two-story, 2,000-square-foot Craftsman home, and that the high interest rates of the 1980s had nearly bankrupted them. Now, with housing prices again soaring in Seattle, Faz was counting on the equity in the house to fund their retirement.

In addition to cooking, Vera's other passion was gardening. She'd cultivated an English country garden in the front and back yards with stone paths, rambling rosebushes, climbing plants, and dozens of perennials that would have impressed the queen of England. Tracy had never seen it, but Faz had mentioned it, saying, "I like it because I don't have to mow a lawn."

Vera had ceded to Del's request and cooked her famous lasagna. The seven of them—Del was divorced—sat around a simple dining room table beneath the muted lighting of a candelabra chandelier hanging from a box-beam ceiling. Tracy had worried Dan might feel out of place with a bunch of cops and their spouses, but the conversation had rarely strayed to work. Chianti and Merlot flowed liberally, and they ate in a dining room of dark wood walls and burgundy drapes that made Tracy feel as though she'd been transported to a home in a small Italian village. She had expected Vera to be exhausted waiting on them, and was surprised to find it was Faz who brought out the food and refilled their glasses, all done with a white dish towel over his right shoulder. It was clear he was proud of his wife and his home, and he considered it special to have them all together.

When their plates were filled with thick wedges of lasagna, salad, and garlic bread, Faz remained standing.

"Will you sit down, Fazio? I'm like a dog with a bone that I can't eat here," Del said.

"Hold on. Hold on. Vera and I got something we'd like to do." Faz turned to Tracy and Dan. "When we got married, Vera's father gave us this blessing. Now we pass it on to the two of you."

Vera reached behind her and handed Tracy a basket containing a wrapped loaf of her homemade bread, a glass container of salt, and a bottle of wine. "The bread is so that you may never know hunger," she said. "The salt is so that your marriage will always have flavor. The wine is so you will always have something to celebrate."

Faz raised his glass. His eyes watered. "May you have many years together, and may the Lord bless you with happiness and prosperity. Salute!"

They raised their glasses and drank. Kins too wiped his eyes with his napkin.

"Look at all these big homicide detectives crying," Shannah said, dabbing the corners of her eyes.

Tracy pushed back her chair and stood. "At the risk of killing Del . . . ," she said.

Del smiled. "You go right ahead," he said.

She took a breath, fighting her emotions, which the events of the past two days had put to the test. "You all know that I lost my family at a very young age. I've lived alone a good portion of my life, and at times I felt like I was alone—until I made my way to the seventh floor. You people have been like family to me, treated me like family. I don't know where I'd be if I didn't have you in my life. So I just want to raise a glass to all of you and say, 'Thank you.'"

For a moment no one spoke. Vera raised her glass. "Salute," she said.

"Salute," the others said.

"Can we eat now?" Del said, drawing laughter.

They ate everything Vera and Faz put on the table, and it was quite the meal. By the time they reached dessert, homemade cannoli, Tracy felt full. "I'll just have a bite of Dan's," she said when Faz handed her the plate.

"Get used to that, Dan," Faz said. "She'll tell you she's full, then she'll eat your dessert."

"When have I ever eaten your dessert?" Vera said.

"Are you kidding me? How many times have I heard, 'I'll just take a bite' and next thing I know, my plate is clean. Last week I ordered tiramisu. I got one bite."

"Tiramisu is my favorite," Vera said, giving Dan a wink. "Who wants coffee?"

"I'll help you clear the plates," Shannah said.

"I will too," Tracy said, but Dan stood first. "Talk with your friends. I'll clear."

Vera gave a small hoot. "I like him, Tracy. A man who helps in the kitchen is usually even better in the bedroom."

That comment brought more laughter. When the four of them were alone, Tracy said, "I hate to bring up work, but something has come up."

"You're not leaving, are you?" Kins said.

She looked at him like he was crazy. "No. Why would you think that?"

"I don't know. I know Dan's made a good living and you don't have to put up with the bullshit anymore."

"I'm not going anywhere," she said. "It's about Andrea Strickland."

"What about her?" Faz said.

"I don't think she's the woman in the crab pot."

Faz lowered his glass of port wine. "What do you mean you don't think she's the woman in the pot?"

Tracy shook her head. "I don't think that's her in the crab pot."

The three men looked dumbstruck.

"Why not?" Kins asked. "Who the hell would it be?"

"When I first got there, to the beach, the kid who pulled up the pot—"

"Kurt Schill," Kins said.

"Right. He said he thought the body in the pot was a woman, though he'd only had a glimpse of her hand before towing it back to shore. I asked him how he knew and he said, 'Her fingernails are painted.'"

"Bright blue," Kins said.

"Right. But when I talked to Andrea Strickland's aunt, she told me Andrea compulsively bit her fingernails, so much so that they bled."

"They could be fake," Faz said. "Or she could have stopped."

Tracy shook her head. "I asked Funk. The nails were real. And if you've ever met anyone who compulsively bites their fingernails, you know it's as difficult a habit to stop as smoking."

"Got an aunt that was a nail-biter," Del said. "After so many years it chipped her front tooth."

They all sat back, silent, considering the information. Kins said, "So if it's not Strickland, who do you think it is?"

"I think it could be the friend. I think it could be Devin Chambers. She disappeared the same time as Andrea and they were about the same height and weight, similar hair coloring."

"Shit," Del said. "This is going to complicate things."

"We don't know nothing yet," Faz said. "So then, what? Andrea Strickland is dead somewhere on that mountain?"

"Don't know," Tracy said.

"You think the husband killed Chambers?" Del asked.

"Again, too early to know. What we do know is the woman in the pot was changing her appearance, and likely using the money to do it. If Chambers knew about the money, I could see why she'd want to change her appearance."

"So, what then? She and the husband were working together, and he double-crosses her and kills her?" Del asked.

"Possibility," Tracy said. "If he used the private investigator to find her, it would explain why he gave him the name Devin Chambers and asked him to try to hunt her down, and why she was changing her appearance and clearly on the run."

"She wanted the money," Del said.

"She didn't need to run away to get the money," Tracy said. "If she is the woman in the crab pot, she had to know about the alias, Lynn Hoff. And she had to know the bank accounts were in that name, and the passwords. She had to be running for some other reason."

"She thinks the husband is going to kill her," Faz said. "Got to be."

Tracy nodded. "Maybe. But remember, Andrea Strickland told her boss she thought her husband was having another affair. What if the person he was having the affair with was Devin Chambers?"

"I thought they were friends," Kins said.

"Exactly. What if Andrea Strickland found out her best friend is sleeping with her husband? The counselor I spoke with said Andrea could become vindictive, maybe even violent. What if the victim isn't the victim at all? What if the victim is the killer?"

Again, they all sat pondering the ramifications of what Tracy was telling them.

"We don't have the case no more," Faz finally said.

"And if I go to Fields, especially without something more, he'll just run to his boss and say I stole his toys from the sandbox again," Tracy said.

"So we need to be sure," Kins said.

"Funk took DNA from the corpse and Melton ran it through CODIS," Tracy said, referring to Mike Melton, head of the Washington State Patrol Crime Lab. The prior night, she'd thought through how they could be certain.

"So they have the profile in their system," Faz said.

"And Strickland has an aunt in San Bernardino," Tracy said.

"And Chambers has a sister somewhere in New Jersey," Faz said, sitting up and getting animated. "Shit, we could do this. Would Melton run the DNA?"

"If we can get DNA from the aunt and the sister, we can send it to a private testing lab," Tracy said.

"I got an uncle served on the force back in Trenton for forty-five years," Faz said. "I can ask him for a favor."

"And I have a relationship with the aunt," Tracy said.

"Yeah, but you'd still have to get Mike to release the victim's profile to the private lab," Del said.

Tracy shook her head. "No, I just need Mike to send me the profile. I can send it to the lab."

"But what then?" Kins asked. "Say we get the tests and they prove it's not Strickland and it is Chambers. Then what? Where do we go from there?"

"If we get the test and prove it isn't Strickland and it is Chambers, I go to Martinez and Nolasco and tell them."

"No offense, but that didn't work too well for you last time, Professor," Faz said, using Tracy's nickname.

"If the woman in the pot turns out to not be Andrea Strickland, this case is going to generate even more media attention than it already has. It will become a national story. I don't think the brass is going to risk the publicity they could cultivate from a national story about dedicated police detectives doing their jobs to solve a horrific crime, just to make an example of us," Tracy said.

"Especially if we're right," Kins said. "They'd have a public relations nightmare."

"Besides," Tracy said, not able to fully suppress a smile as she looked at each of them. "If the woman in the pot is not Andrea Strickland, then Pierce County no longer has jurisdiction."

Kins sat back, slowly shaking his head and chuckling. Faz and Del caught on. Soon they were all laughing.

"You're unbelievable, you know that?" Kins said. "When did you figure that out?"

"Last night."

Faz raised his glass of port. "Are we going to do this?"

Del raised his glass. "Hell, yeah, I'm in."

"Me too," Kins said, his glass joining the other two. "If there's positive publicity to be had, yours truly can use it."

Tracy looked at them but did not raise her glass. She did not want them in trouble for something she had done. "Faz, you're close to retirement. Del, you have alimony, and Kins, you have three boys."

"You said we were family," Faz said. "This is what family does. We do dumbass shit, but we do it together."

CHAPTER 25

Securing the DNA samples had not been as simple as Tracy would have otherwise predicted. When Tracy called Penny Orr the following day, Saturday, the woman had responded to Tracy's name with caution.

Tracy had given considerable thought to her approach before calling. You didn't just tell a relative over the phone that the niece she thought had died—not once, but twice—might still be alive. You never gave them that kind of hope until you were certain. Tracy had hoped for twenty years, against all reason and odds, that they'd find Sarah alive someday. Even after she'd become a homicide detective and knew that the chances of Sarah being alive were infinitesimally small, she clung to the thought that her sister would beat the odds—so much so that when they did find Sarah's remains, it had devastated her.

She told Penny Orr they wanted to get a positive identification through a DNA confirmation and explained they could do so through Orr.

To her surprise, Orr expressed reluctance. "What would I have to do?"

"It's completely noninvasive," Tracy said, thinking perhaps Orr was under the impression she'd have to give bone marrow, or blood. "I'll overnight you a DNA kit. The instructions are self-explanatory. I'll also provide you with a return shipping label so you can send it straight back to me." That label would have the personal PO box to which Tracy had all of her mail sent.

Orr sighed, still sounding uncertain, and Tracy couldn't completely understand her reticence. "It's just that, if it isn't her, then it raises doubt again about what happened to her. I'm not sure I can go through that again," Orr said.

"I understand this has been difficult," Tracy said. "But if it isn't Andrea, there's another family out there possibly wondering the same thing—what happened to their daughter. They deserve closure too."

Orr seemed to give that argument some thought. After several long moments she said, "Okay. Go ahead and send it."

Devin Chambers's sister, Alison McCabe, had also been resistant, but she too ultimately relented. Tracy suspected that whatever bad feelings had developed between the two sisters, blood remained blood.

The following week, both women shipped back the tests and, with the DNA samples secured, Tracy drove to the squat concrete building on Airport Way South that housed the Washington State Patrol Crime Lab. The facility, located in an industrial area south of downtown, looked more like a food-processing warehouse than home to the state's high-tech crime lab responsible for analyzing the evidence to convict murderers, rapists, and other miscreants.

Mike Melton sat in his office. Today he was not strumming on his guitar or singing. When Tracy knocked, Melton was taking a bite out of a homemade sandwich that reminded Tracy of the cheese sandwiches her mother used to make her and Sarah—two slices of white bread, mayo, and a slice of Velveeta. An apple, an uncapped bottle of water, and an open brown bag sat on Melton's desk.

"Looks like I caught you at a bad time," Tracy said from the doorway.

Melton waved her in as he chewed and swallowed, washing the sandwich down with a sip from the bottle. "Just eating a late lunch," he said. "I was over at the courthouse working on some last-minute prep work for the Lipinsky trial."

"Kins said it could go out next week," she said.

"That's what they tell us." Melton used a napkin to wipe at the corners of his mouth visible beneath his thick reddish-brown beard. Over the years it had become streaked with gray. Tracy had heard the term "bear of a man" used to describe big men, but in Melton's case the analogy fit, and not just because of his size. In addition to the beard, which seemed to get longer and fuller each time Tracy visited, Melton wore his hair combed back off his forehead, the curls touching the collar of his shirt. He also had the build of a lumberjack, with meaty forearms and hands that looked like they could tear a phonebook in half, yet his fingers were nimble enough to pluck the strings of a guitar. Detectives referred to Melton as Grizzly Adams, because of the uncanny resemblance to that TV show's star, Dan Haggerty.

"Come in and sit." Melton walked to Tracy's side of his desk and moved a leather satchel from one of two chairs. The other was stacked with technical books.

"A little light reading?" Tracy asked.

"Just trying to stay on top of everything."

Tracy settled in. Rather than returning to behind his desk, Melton leaned against the edge. "Heard Pierce County pulled the crab pot case."

Melton was no dummy, nor had he just fallen off the turnip truck. As the crime lab's lead scientist, he possessed multiple degrees, none of which hung on the wall of his office. Instead of diplomas, he kept mementos from prior interesting cases—a hammer, a saw, a baseball bat. He also knew that when detectives showed up unexpectedly at his office door they usually wanted something.

"They did," she said. "And left me with a couple loose ends I'm trying to nail down."

"Such as?" Melton said, moving back to his seat and picking up his cheese sandwich.

"DNA. Given the condition of the body, it's the only means for a positive identification."

"Heard the parents were deceased and no siblings," Melton said, taking another bite.

"Found an aunt in San Bernardino. The mother's sister."

"Ah." Melton put down the sandwich and sipped his water.

Tracy had no way to soften the question. "I was hoping you'd provide me with the victim's profile so I can send it to an outside lab for comparison."

Melton leaned back in his chair. "You don't like the work we do here?"

"It would be better at this point to let an outside lab handle it."

"How are Nolasco and Martinez going to like that?" he said, the corners of his mouth inching into a slight grin.

"You heard about that?"

"I hear everything. You know that."

She smiled softly. "They'll like it probably less than they liked me going to talk to the aunt in the first place."

Melton gave her comment a moment of thought. "Well, we send out the profiles all the time when we get backed up and overwhelmed here. In fact, with the Lipinsky matter taking up so much time, I was just thinking we needed to send that profile out so we could speed things up."

Tracy smiled. "Thanks, Mike."

"Don't thank me. Just doing my job. Would it also be better if I didn't ask why you're using an outside lab?"

"Probably."

Melton nodded. "You don't think it's her, do you? You don't think it's the woman everyone said walked off Rainier."

"Like I said, she has an aunt in Southern California who'd like some closure," Tracy said.

"So . . . easy enough to find out."

"Easy enough," Tracy agreed.

Melton again paused. The man was nothing if not deliberate. "Well," he said again, "that is our job, isn't it? To find out with certainty so the victims' families can find closure?"

"I always thought so."

"So my running a DNA profile would just be a means to ensure certainty."

"It would be, if it was still our case."

"Might not still be yours, but it's still mine. I do run this division," Melton said, meaning he was head of all the crime labs throughout the state, including the one in Tacoma that serviced Pierce County.

"I got into a bit of a pissing contest with Pierce County," Tracy said.

"So I hear," Melton said.

"They're not going to be too happy about me doing anything to help solve their case for them. Probably best if you stay out of the line of fire."

Melton scoffed. "What are they going to do, fire me?" The detectives knew that with his expertise, Melton could get a job in minutes at a much higher salary with one of the private laboratories. He stayed at the crime lab out of a sense of duty to find justice for victims' families.

"I don't want you to have to make that choice for me, Mike."

"Which lab did you choose?"

"ALS," she said.

Melton nodded. "They're a good outfit. I know Tim Lane. He's been recruiting me for years. I'll give him a call and tell him to treat you right, put the pedal to the metal."

Tracy pushed up out of her chair and offered her hand. "Like I said, I appreciate it, Mike."

"I know you do," he said, taking her hand. "That's why I'm willing to do it."

—

For the remainder of the week, each time Tracy entered the bull pen, Kins, Faz, and Del, or some combination of the three, would give her a look like she was an obstetrician and they were expectant fathers in a hospital waiting room. Tracy would shake her head to let them know the lab had not called. That Friday, as she worked a homeless-man stabbing case, her cell phone rang. The screen indicated no caller ID but the prefix was for a Seattle number.

"Detective Crosswhite?" the caller asked, causing a flicker of anticipation in her stomach.

"Speaking."

"Mike Melton says I'm supposed to treat you right, and given the size of him, I don't want him angry at me."

—

ALS had an office in Burien not far from the Seattle Police Academy, about a half-hour drive from Police Headquarters. Tim Lane said he could e-mail Tracy the results so she could avoid the drive, but Tracy didn't want to leave a paper trail on her computer. She told him she needed to talk to a witness down his way and would pick up the results. Strange as it seemed, she also didn't want to hear the news over the phone, and Lane didn't question her further. He might have already sensed something was up when he realized he wasn't calling Police Headquarters but a private cell phone.

Tracy and Kins took his BMW rather than a car out of the pool. They did have a witness they needed to speak with in Des Moines, which was just next door to Burien, just in case anyone accused them of using taxpayer time to run down evidence in a case that was no longer theirs.

ALS was located in a business park that included a brewery, a fitness gym, and, apparently, a basketball club. The number of private laboratory services had exploded with the recent advancements in DNA analysis and the concomitant desire of private citizens to find out their ancestry, genetic makeup, and proclivity to get future life-threatening illnesses.

"You done it, yet?" Kins asked Tracy as he pulled into a parking space labeled in white block lettering as reserved for ALS visitors.

"What? Get my DNA profile? No. You?"

"Nah. What do I want to know that for?" Kins pushed out of the car and Tracy exited the passenger side. "My dad's father had Alzheimer's. I worry enough about that stuff without someone telling me I should be worrying. When they tell me they know how to cure it, that's when I'll want to know."

She met him at the hood and they walked toward the entrance. "What about your ancestry or heritage? Aren't you curious?"

"All my life I've grown up thinking I'm English and believed I had to tolerate tea, bland food, and cold and foggy weather. What am I going to do if I find out I'm Italian and could have been eating like Fazio all these years? Besides, you keep going back far enough and we all came from the same place anyway. Had to start with just two, right?"

"God, that means we're related to Nolasco?" Tracy said, pulling open the glass door.

"I'm pretty sure Nolasco's a reptile."

Tracy told the receptionist they had an appointment to see Tim Lane, and they stepped toward chairs in a waiting room with low ceiling tiles, fluorescent lights, and rich-blue walls lined with posters spelling out the lab's various available services.

"This place looks like the preschool we used to take the boys to," Kins said.

Two couples sat waiting. Tracy had also read that parents were getting their genetic makeup analyzed before having children to determine if their offspring were at risk for genetic disorders such as sickle-cell anemia and Down syndrome. At forty-three, Tracy's odds were greater than younger mothers of passing something on to her child.

A door in the corner of the room pulled open and a blond-haired man, partially balding, stepped out wearing a white lab coat over a pink dress shirt and red tie. "Detectives," he said, giving them a 100-watt smile. "I'm Tim Lane." They shook hands. "Come on back."

Tracy and Kins followed Lane down a carpeted hallway. He led them into a nondescript conference room with a window that looked out over a small area of once-green lawn showing patches of brown. Lane stepped to the far side of the table, on which he'd set two manila folders.

"Mike says you're to get the VIP treatment," Lane said, his voice deep and rich.

"Heard you've been trying to recruit him. The detectives would revolt," Tracy said.

"We worked at the crime lab together, many, many years ago," Lane said. "I only lasted five years."

"How'd you get into the private sector?" Tracy asked.

"I majored in chemistry and went back for my MBA. I've always been entrepreneurial and wanted to run my own business. With the advances in DNA and the backlog of cases at most major metropolitan crime labs, I saw an opportunity I thought I could fill. We were one of the first private labs. Now you Google 'private DNA testing' and you get a couple hundred thousand hits."

"How much of your work is for the general public?" Kins asked.

"It's about sixty percent now. When we first opened we were basically an annex for the crime labs. We did a lot of paternity testing. Over the years, with advances in DNA testing and technology to perform that analysis, the crime labs can get through their cases a lot faster than they could when I was there, and don't have as much of a need for outside labs. Eventually, you won't need us at all. You'll get the bad guy's DNA profile, put it up on a cloud, and it will run through all the major databases and spit out results in minutes."

Lane sat. Tracy and Kins took two chairs across the table from him. "Mike also said you guys don't need any hand-holding, so I'm going to get right to it, if that's okay?"

"That's fine," Tracy said.

Lane opened the first folder. "We used the profile Mike sent us as our baseline for comparison with the two DNA profiles you provided. The first profile, we were asked to determine if the person could be the victim's aunt."

"Correct," Tracy said.

"We can determine with a much higher degree of certainty whether two people are related," Lane said, slipping into his comfort zone. Tracy and Kins had both received educations about DNA testing and analysis through their work on several trials, but Tracy let Lane continue. Her father had once taken her to buy her first six-shooter, and although he had been shooting six-shooters since he could walk, he had patiently listened as the seller went through every aspect of the gun, then thanked him for his thoroughness. When they left the store, Tracy asked her father why he had endured the lecture.

"Interrupting a man when he's discussing his profession is like telling him what he has to say isn't important. Besides, you never learn anything when you're talking."

Lane continued. "But without the DNA from at least one parent, we can't be certain."

"The parents are deceased," Tracy said.

Kins said, "So what did you find in this instance?"

"In this instance we performed a statistical analysis based on the match type typically expected for a known aunt-niece relationship. This provides us with what's called a 'kinship index.' A biologically related aunt and niece typically have a kinship index value greater than 1.0. Conversely, if they are not biologically related, the kinship index value is less than 1.0. The closer to or more distant the kinship index value is to 1.0, the more or less likely the two individuals are related."

"And in this case?" Tracy said.

"In this case the kinship index value was significantly less than 1."

Her adrenaline spiked but Tracy did her best to temper her reaction. "So they're not related."

Lane shook his head. "The statistical probability is they are not."

"You said 'statistical probability,'" Kins said. "What are we talking about here? What are the percentages?"

"Negligible. If you want percentages, I'd say it's 99.95 percent they are not related."

Kins glanced at Tracy but also didn't say anything. She knew him well enough to know the wheels were spinning in his head too.

"And the test to determine siblings?" Tracy asked.

Lane closed the one manila file, slid it across the table to Tracy, and opened the second file. "Again, the recommended method to determine whether individuals are true biological siblings is to test their parents. DNA paternity and maternity testing will always provide conclusive results. That not being an option here, we are again left with probabilities. In this case, based on the type of genetic material inherited by each sibling, we determine what's called a 'sibship index.'"

"What did you find?" Tracy asked.

"The sibship index was well over 1. The statistical probability is that the two women in the genetic profiles you provided are full siblings."

Tracy and Kins stepped outside the lab with Tracy holding the results of the two tests. Kins slid on sunglasses against the bright glare. "I'm not going to lie; a part of me was hoping we'd get the opposite result."

"It would have made things a lot easier," Tracy agreed.

"But not nearly as much fun," Kins said. "And 'easier' is never a word I've associated with you."

Tracy stopped at the car passenger door, raising a hand to deflect the sun's glare. "What's that supposed to mean?"

Kins used the remote, and the doors unlocked with a chirp. "Don't get defensive; I'm just saying it seems like lately if something can go wrong in one of our cases it usually does. It would be nice to get a grounder every once in a while."

They pulled open the car doors and slid inside the BMW. Kins started the engine to get the air-conditioning going, but didn't look to be in a hurry to get moving. "What do you think happened?"

"I think we'll make a mistake if we speculate. I think the question at this point is what does the evidence tell us?"

"At this point I'd settle for just about anything that made sense," Kins said.

"Well, we now know for certain that Andrea Strickland is not the woman in the crab pot," she said. "It's Devin Chambers."

"No doubt about that," Kins said.

"We know Andrea and Graham Strickland were having marital problems and financial problems. The business was a massive failure, and the bank, the landlord, and other creditors were banging on their door with personal guarantees that Strickland couldn't begin to pay off. We also know Andrea was sitting on a pile of money she wouldn't let him touch and that she was afraid he'd somehow put at risk with the creditors."

"All true," Kins said.

"We also know he cheated on her and, if you believe what Andrea told her boss, that he was continuing to cheat on her—maybe with her best friend."

"Was he, or did she just want people to believe he was still cheating on her because it fits the profile of a man who'd have reason to kill his wife? Like the insurance policy he claims he knew nothing about."

"Let's say he was cheating on her," Tracy said. "What if the person he was cheating with was Devin Chambers? It gives him a motivation to kill Chambers."

"It gives Andrea a motivation to kill her also," Kins said. "If Andrea's still alive, and I'm thinking she is—somebody moved that money." He pulled out of the parking space. "Let's get something to eat. Maybe food will help us think through this."

"I know a place," Tracy said. "My academy class used to go there."

She directed him to the Tin Room Bar on Southwest 152nd Street in downtown Burien. A tin shop when the street had been lined with industrial businesses, the building was bought by a local entrepreneur who turned half of it into a movie theater and the other half into an eclectic bar and restaurant. The tools from the tin shop were mounted on the walls and the workbenches cut into tables. The renovation had started a revival on the street, which now included half a dozen other restaurants and bars.

Tracy and Kins took a table beneath an Impressionist painting of Mick Jagger, the Rolling Stones' front man. She ordered the fish tacos and an iced tea. Kins ordered a hamburger and Diet Coke. "Modern Love," one of the late, great David Bowie's best-known songs, filtered down from the overhead speakers, and several men and women sat at the bar watching a Mariners game on the flat-screen televisions.

"We've come full circle, haven't we?" Kins said. "We're looking at three options. Either Strickland did kill his wife and staged it to look like an accident. She died on the mountain and it was an accident. Or, she outsmarted him, walked off the mountain, and tried to frame him for her murder—and is still alive."

"Let's start with the first scenario," Tracy said. She sipped iced tea, set it aside, and used a paper napkin and a pen to diagram her thoughts. "On the brink of financial disaster, he pushes his wife off the mountain thinking he'll recover the insurance money and get access to the trust money she's been keeping from him. But the Pierce County DA names him a person of interest, the insurance company won't pay the life insurance benefits, and the wife's money disappears. In that scenario, the obvious person who took the trust money is Devin Chambers, right?"

"That would appear to be the case. She paid cash to have her face reconstructed and took over Strickland's alias."

"Okay, so in that scenario, the husband hires the skip tracer," Tracy said. "The skip tracer finds Devin Chambers, the husband hunts her down, kills her, and drains the bank account."

"So far, I agree," Kins said.

"Scenario two," Tracy said. "He's intending to kill Andrea, or maybe he isn't, but in any event she somehow dies in an accident."

"My opinion is that's the most unlikely of the three scenarios, but just for argument's sake, everything else would remain the same," Kins said.

"Agreed," Tracy said. "So that leaves scenario three."

"She outsmarted him. She figured out he was going to kill her on the mountain, staged her own death, walked off the mountain, took her trust, and is still alive somewhere," Kins said. "So when does the husband realize he's been set up—when he wakes up the next morning in the tent?" Kins said.

"Maybe, but probably more likely when Fields comes knocking on his door asking about insurance policies he's the supposed beneficiary of but knows nothing about, and telling him his wife was meeting with a divorce attorney and making allegations he was cheating on her again."

The waitress returned with Tracy's tacos and Kins's burger. Tracy slid the napkin to the side to make room. Kins grabbed the bottle of ketchup and doctored his hamburger.

"So now he's got bigger problems," Kins said, pounding the bottom of the bottle. "The investigation prevents the insurance payout, and Andrea's separate trust fund is gone, along with his girlfriend, but the creditors are still knocking on the door and he stands to lose everything."

"And he's wondering if the disappearance of the money and Chambers's disappearance are related," Tracy said, stealing one of Kins's french fries. "So he uses a guerilla e-mail account to track Chambers down."

"The skip tracer said the client initially asked to look for a 'Lynn Hoff,'" Kins said. "How would the husband have known about Lynn Hoff?"

"Maybe Devin Chambers," Tracy said. "*If* she and Graham Strickland were initially working together."

"And if they weren't?"

"Then I don't know. Maybe he found something around the house that tipped him off."

Kins bit into his burger and wiped his hands on the cloth napkin in his lap. "You think Andrea could have confided in Devin Chambers?"

"It's possible. The boss said they were close, maybe Andrea's only friend."

"So when she finds out her best friend is sleeping with her husband, why doesn't she just take off? Why go up the mountain at all?"

"Two reasons I can think of. One, she'd confided in Devin about Lynn Hoff, so Devin would know how to track her and the money."

Kins dipped a french fry in ketchup and ate it. "All right. What's the second reason?"

"The counselor I spoke with said it's possible the years of abuse resulted in a dissociative disorder, and that Andrea could become volatile if she were to suffer some acute trauma, or if she felt abandoned or desperate."

"Like finding out your only friend is sleeping with your husband and is trying to rip off your life savings?" Kins said.

"So simply fleeing was not going to keep someone from pursuing her, nor was it going to allow her to get even with either of them."

"So you're saying, in this scenario, Andrea Strickland had to make it look like the husband killed her on that mountain and that Chambers was in on it," Kins said, taking another bite.

"She takes out the insurance policy, consults the divorce attorney, and drops hints that the husband is cheating on her again," Tracy said. "Then she uses the skip tracer to track down Devin Chambers. Chambers disappears and everyone thinks it's the husband."

"Why was Devin Chambers on the run?"

"Chance to start a new life with half a million in cash," Tracy said.

"Maybe," Kins said. "But don't you think it's more likely the husband killed Chambers, but Andrea Strickland moved the money before he could get to it?"

"I don't know."

"I think she's still alive," Kins said.

"We need to find the skip tracer. Maybe there's some way to determine from where those e-mails originated. Maybe if we can narrow it to a city, we can determine whether it was the husband, or whether it was her."

Kins put down the hamburger and continued munching his french fries. "I thought you said those e-mails were anonymous."

"Nothing is completely anonymous. You remember that Harvard student who got busted for calling in a bomb scare to get out of taking finals?"

"Vaguely."

"I looked it up the other night. He used a guerilla e-mail account and an anonymous server, but the FBI determined that he'd logged on to Harvard's Wi-Fi server. We don't have to link the e-mails to a particular computer. It might be enough if we can show they came from someplace like a Portland Starbucks near Graham Strickland's house, or some other place where she's in hiding." Tracy tapped the two manila folders from ALS. "But the first thing we have to do is take this to Nolasco and Martinez and tell them the body in the pot is not Andrea Strickland. That means Pierce County has no basis to assert jurisdiction because there is no longer a connection between our murder and their—once again—missing person investigation."

CHAPTER 26

Tracy and Kins met with Del and Faz over the weekend to discuss the DNA results, and how best to present the information to Nolasco and Martinez. All agreed that, given the volatility of Tracy's relationship with Nolasco, it would be best if Kins took the lead explaining the DNA results and the potential ramifications. None of them believed for a minute Nolasco or Martinez would not see through the ploy, but they hoped two factors would at least make them look past it. Tracy had hinted at the first factor in her earlier meeting with Nolasco—the case was continuing to generate publicity. Most recently, the national news media had picked up the story, and it was a certainty that media coverage would only intensify when news broke that the woman in the pot was *not* Andrea Strickland, but her friend Devin Chambers. Second, Nolasco and Martinez would not be able to deny Tracy's reasoning that Pierce County no longer had a basis to assert jurisdiction.

The four of them asked for a meeting with Nolasco and Martinez Monday afternoon and walked, en masse, into the conference room. Nolasco and Martinez joined them minutes later, confirming that the two men had met prior to the requested meeting, probably to speculate on its purpose. Nolasco and Martinez continued to the far side of the table and settled into chairs. Rather than the four detectives all sitting together on the same side of the table, like rival gangs drawing a line in the sand, Del sat at the head of the table, Tracy at the far end, and Faz and Kins directly across from their superiors.

Nolasco seemed mildly surprised when Kins, not Tracy, handed each of them a copy of the first report from ALS and explained how that report came to exist. Nolasco slid on cheaters, alternately considering the report and looking over the top of his glasses as Kins spoke. Martinez remained hunched over the report, his meaty forearms pressed to the table.

"During one of our end-of-the-day meetings, Tracy was going over what she'd learned talking with Penny Orr, Andrea Strickland's aunt," Kins said. "The aunt said Andrea was withdrawn and prone to anxiety, that she bit her fingernails until, at times, they bled."

"That made me think about the autopsy photographs," Faz said, just as they'd rehearsed, though it didn't sound that way. "One in particular—the one of the victim's hand—jumped out at me. She was wearing blue nail polish."

"You thought of this?" Nolasco said.

"Yeah," Faz said, sounding slightly indignant and doing a good job of making it seem authentic. "I was thinking maybe if she'd put the polish on recently—it might be evidence she had a date and was concerned about her appearance, that maybe she knew her killer. But when Tracy mentioned what the aunt said, I said 'holy shit' and pulled up the photograph."

"Funk confirmed the nails are real," Kins said. "That got us all thinking that the body in the crab pot might not be Andrea Strickland." He directed his final comment to Martinez, who'd remained silent and maintained a poker face.

"Why wasn't this revelation in the report provided to Pierce County?" Nolasco said.

"For the reasons I'm about to explain." Kins picked up a stapled document from the manila file. "What you have before you is a DNA profile of Penny Orr, Andrea Strickland's aunt. The lab compared that profile with the DNA profile the crime lab developed for the woman in the crab pot. There's a 99.95-percent probability that the two women are *not* related."

Martinez looked up from the report. "It isn't Strickland?"

"It is not," Kins said.

"So you were wrong," Nolasco said, directing his comment to Tracy.

"No," Kins said. "We were right. The woman in the crab pot used the name Lynn Hoff to obtain facial reconstruction surgery. Lynn Hoff is the alias Andrea Strickland used when she went into hiding. It's her picture on the driver's license."

"Then how can it not be her in the pot?" Nolasco asked.

"I'm going to explain that now," Kins said. He handed the second report across the table. "This is the DNA profile of a woman named Alison McCabe."

"Who's she?" Nolasco asked.

"She's the sister of Devin Chambers. Devin Chambers was Andrea Strickland's best friend."

"It's Devin Chambers," Martinez said. He'd flipped to the last page quickly to read the conclusion in the report. "How the hell did she end up in the crab pot?"

"That's what we hope to find out, sir."

"What do you mean *you* hope to find out?" Nolasco said, his gaze shifting between the four of them.

Martinez raised a hand and sat back from the table, looking at them like a bemused grandfather considering his grandchildren. Those in the department knew Martinez to be a cop first and a bureaucrat second. The fact that he insisted on wearing the uniform every day reflected how he perceived and projected himself. Tracy was banking on that perception now, banking on Martinez understanding that every good

cop wanted to clear his or her cases, not to pad personal statistics. They
owed it to the families of the victims.

"What your detectives mean, Captain, is if the woman in the crab
pot is not Andrea Strickland, then Pierce County does not have jurisdiction, because the woman who went missing in their county is not the
woman in the crab pot," Martinez said. "Therefore they have no basis
to assert a continuing investigation. Am I right, Detective Crosswhite?"

"I believe you are, sir," Tracy said.

"Detective Rowe?"

"Makes sense to me."

"Perhaps you can explain how you obtained the DNA profiles
of these two individuals," Nolasco said, holding up both documents,
"when you no longer had jurisdiction."

Martinez again raised his hand. "I'm suspecting your detectives
forwarded DNA kits to the individuals and there was a time lag between
when they were sent and when they were obtained for analysis. Am I
right?"

"You are," Kins said.

"You want this case," Martinez said, now shifting his gaze between
the four of them.

"It's our case," Tracy said.

"You understand the ramifications . . . that this will become an even
higher profile investigation when we advise the media that the body is
not Andrea Strickland."

"We do," Kins said.

"Which is going to mean greater pressure that we get this done."

"Understood," Kins said.

"Good, because when we go to bat for you and get this case back,
I'm going to expect it." Martinez turned to Nolasco. "Captain, your
detectives want this case. Let's make it happen."

Tracy followed the three other members of her team out of the conference room and back to their bull pen. They refrained from high-fives or chest bumps. To the contrary, Faz, Kins, and Del all looked as though they'd just walked through a minefield but somehow managed not to take a wrong step—their good fortune more to do with blind luck than skill.

Now they had to wait. They couldn't work on the investigation until, and if, they officially got the case back from Pierce County, but they all agreed they had a moral obligation to advise Penny Orr that the woman in the crab pot was not her niece, and to tell Alison McCabe the more difficult news, that her sister was dead. The first news could be delivered over the phone. The second could not.

"No one should hear that over the phone," Tracy said, remembering the call from the King County Medical Examiner's Office advising her that two hunters had stumbled across human remains in the hills above her hometown of Cedar Grove.

"I'll get my uncle to make a drive back out there and tell her in person," Faz said. "God knows he's done it enough times before."

Tracy would call Penny Orr. "Let's reconvene in an hour and go over what we're going to need and want going forward."

Penny Orr's reaction to the news that her niece was not the woman in the pot had been subdued. Tracy couldn't blame her. She'd now grieved, potentially unnecessarily, twice, and Tracy could not tell Orr with any conviction that Andrea was or was not still alive. She ended the conversation with a promise that the next time they spoke she would have a better answer for Orr.

That afternoon the A Team reconvened at the table in the center of their bull pen with their list of things to do. They needed to have the skip tracer's computer analyzed. If they could determine the location of the sender of the guerilla e-mails, they might be able to conclude whether it had been Graham Strickland, Andrea Strickland, or possibly, though not likely, an altogether different person. They decided to use the FBI to perform a forensic analysis of the skip tracer's computer and Tracy tasked Faz with bird-dogging it.

Faz and Del would also have to recanvass the buildings and marinas, this time with a photograph of Devin Chambers.

"Run the photograph by Dr. Wu while you're at it, confirm Chambers was his patient," Tracy said to Faz.

Tracy and Kins would work with Pierce County, who, according to Fields, had subpoenaed Graham Strickland's cell phone and credit card records, as well as his bank statements. They'd look for evidence tying him to Devin Chambers. The fraud unit would continue working to track the location of the trust funds.

"We should also get a search warrant for the husband's home," Kins said. "I have a contact at Portland PD, Jonathan Zhu. Good guy. We worked a case up here last year. He can help facilitate getting a search warrant with a local judge. When do you want to talk to the husband? I'll call Zhu and coordinate so we can do both at the same time."

"Let's wait at least until we get his credit card records back from Pierce County," Tracy said. "Unlikely we'll get another shot."

"What do we do about Andrea Strickland?" Faz asked.

Tracy gave his question some thought. They'd already mistakenly sent out her picture to all the news services and local and national law enforcement. At present, she remained dead, and Tracy hoped to talk to Graham Strickland without him knowing otherwise. "Let's leave that alone for now."

Late in the afternoon, Nolasco appeared in their cubicle. He had removed his tie and rolled up the cuffs of his shirtsleeves. "You got jurisdiction," he said. "Pierce County is transferring the file back up here."

"They put up much of a squawk?" Del asked.

"That'd be putting it mildly." Nolasco looked to Faz. "They wanted to know how you got the DNA profiles, and don't think for a minute I believed that crap about you remembering an autopsy photo, Fazio."

"You underestimate me, Captain," Faz said.

"Yeah." Nolasco turned his attention to Tracy. "And I'm not buying that bullshit that you got out the DNA kits before we lost jurisdiction, but I'm being told to leave it be, so I'm going to leave it be. But let me be very clear about this. You screw this up and the hammer is going to fall hard on all four of you. It's like Martinez said—you wanted this case. You got it. So get it done." Nolasco left the bull pen, stopped, and turned back. "One other thing. You're to keep Pierce County fully informed of every development."

"What?" Tracy said, not relishing the thought of sharing any information with Stan Fields. "Why?"

"Because that's the agreement reached," Nolasco said. "You provide them with copies of your reports, witness interviews, and anything that has to do with Andrea Strickland. I'm assuming that's not going to be a problem?"

Nobody spoke.

"Good." Nolasco departed.

"Hey, it's a victory," Faz said. "Let's not let him make it feel hollow."

Bennett Lee called Tracy shortly after Nolasco departed their bull pen. Lee wanted to read her a media statement SPD intended to make at an afternoon news conference. He said he'd keep it simple. He'd state that, after DNA analysis, it had been determined that the woman in the crab pot was not Andrea Strickland, the Portland resident believed to have disappeared on Mount Rainier. Tracy asked him why he had to say anything, and Lee told her the brass could not bury the fact that the victim was not Strickland. Lee agreed not to disclose the identity of the woman in the pot, pending notification of next of kin. That meant Tracy would have to expedite any interview of Graham Strickland. Lee would further advise the media that since the body had been found in Seattle, the Pierce County Sheriff's office had voluntarily agreed to relinquish jurisdiction and return the investigation to the Seattle Police Department, but that both agencies would continue to cooperate with each another.

"'Voluntarily agreed to relinquish jurisdiction'?" Tracy said. "Did you come up with that language?"

"That's how they want to spin it," Lee said. "I have a news conference at five if you're interested."

━

When Tracy walked into her kitchen at the end of the day, Dan greeted her with a kiss. He'd formed hamburger patties and was in the process of making a salad. Rex and Sherlock gave her a perfunctory greeting but quickly returned to Dan's side, noses lifted to the counter and eyes glued to the plate of beef.

"When it comes to raw meat, we're a couple of brussels sprouts," Dan said. "You made good time."

"One of the few advantages of working late. No traffic. We got the crab pot case back."

"Saw it on the news." Dan carried the plate of hamburger patties out to the barbecue on the deck. "Vanpelt didn't pull any punches."

"That's why we all love her."

As word leaked that the woman in the crab pot was not Andrea Strickland, speculation rose in the media about the identity of the woman and what it meant. Was Andrea Strickland alive, dead on the mountain, dead someplace else? It had led to a packed news conference and made Bennett Lee's press conference the lead on the local evening news, which the four detectives had watched together in the B Team's bull pen, along with half a dozen other detectives from their section, and the Burglary Section down the hall.

Dan picked up the plate of patties. "Should I put these on or do you want a chance to unwind?"

"No, let's eat. I'm starving."

"You want a hamburger bun with yours?"

"I better not," she said, following him and the dogs out onto the deck. "If I'm going to fit into anything resembling a wedding dress, I better go easy on the carbs."

"You given that much thought?" Dan placed the burgers on the already-warm grill. They sizzled and sparked a small flame.

"I thought I'd surprise you."

Dan nodded, spatula in hand, but she knew him well enough to know he had something else on his mind. "You don't want to be surprised?" she asked.

"No, it's all good. You want cheese on yours?"

"You know, if we're going to get married we're both going to need to do a better job of being honest with each other."

He gave her a soft smile. "I think you should wear a wedding dress."

It had been the last thing she expected him to say, and she stumbled to respond. "You mean an actual wedding dress with a veil and train and push-up bustier?"

"Definitely the push-up bustier," he said, closing the lid on the grill. Smoke seeped out the back. "And I think you should ask Kins to give you away."

She chuckled softly at the thought of it, then realized Dan was serious. "Are you talking about a traditional wedding, Dan O'Leary?"

"I am."

"You do realize we've both been married already."

"Yes, but you never got your wedding."

Dan turned from the barbecue and looked at her with a serious gaze. Tracy had told him she and Ben became engaged the same night Sarah disappeared, but that she'd never had the opportunity to plan the wedding she'd envisioned. Instead, and more because she was afraid of losing him, Tracy and Ben got married in a civil ceremony at the courthouse, just the two of them. Two court clerks had served as witnesses. The decision had been a mistake. Her thoughts and actions had remained focused on finding out what had happened to Sarah, and when she could not move on, Ben had. The divorce papers had come in the mail.

Astonished and moved that Dan had remembered, she wasn't sure what to say.

"I don't need anything extravagant, Dan."

"It's not about what you need. It's about what you deserve."

She struggled again to find the right words. She wanted a traditional wedding. She'd always envisioned a traditional wedding. She just never thought it possible.

"And you deserve the wedding you envisioned," Dan continued. "I know it was a bad time, and I know you'll never say you were disappointed your engagement and wedding got buried by Sarah's disappearance, but I also know there is a part of you that still thinks about what that day might have been like."

"Things happen," she said softly. "Dreams change." She moved to him and wrapped her arms around his waist. "I'm happy I have the man of my dreams."

"And I'm happy with the woman of my dreams," he said, "but there's no reason you can't have the fairy-tale wedding of your dreams too."

She took a deep breath. "You've really thought about this, haven't you?"

He nodded. "I really have. Look, I don't want to say I feel bad for you because I know how much you love to be pitied, but I do feel bad for you. I feel bad that you had to go through everything you've gone through. I feel bad that it all happened on the night you got engaged, and that you never had the wedding of your dreams."

His comment made her think again of Andrea Strickland and her horrible life, regardless of whether she was alive, or deceased. Tracy knew, as much as anyone, there were no guarantees in life. Tomorrow was not a given.

She kissed him. "Is that the reason for the lighthouse and the restaurant—the fairy tale?"

He shrugged and smiled, close lipped.

"Because you are truly a prince."

"Still masculine, though, right? Not the tights-wearing prince who sings and dances."

She laughed. "Definitely still masculine. Okay," she said, "but if we're going for the full-blown fantasy I do have a request."

"Fire away, Cinderella."

"How much pull do you have with that Coast Guard commander?"

"You want to get married at the lighthouse?"

"Unless you have access to a castle."

"I think it will be perfect," Dan said. "And I just so happen to know that they do allow weddings."

She chuckled. "You looked into it already."

Dan feigned ignorance. "Like I said, you deserve the fairy-tale wedding."

She kissed him warmly, again, and could feel their bodies relaxing into each another. "Dan," she said.

"Yeah."

"Turn off the grill so the hamburgers don't burn."

"I thought you were starving."

"I am, but now I'm starving for something better than hamburger."

CHAPTER 27

The following morning, Tracy and Kins were once again traveling south on the I-5 freeway to Portland. They had worked late
putting together a probable-cause affidavit to search Strickland's Pearl
District loft, where he had lived with Andrea and apparently remained.
Kins had transmitted the affidavit to Detective Jonathan Zhu in
Portland. After talking with Strickland, they would accompany Zhu to
a local judge to get a warrant issued. They had no idea what they might
find in the apartment, if anything, but stranger things had happened,
and it was a stone neither felt comfortable leaving unturned.

Kins had also asked Zhu to run Devin Chambers through Portland's
system. Zhu sent back an e-mail with attachments, and Tracy reviewed
them on the three-hour drive south.

"She had two prior arrests in New Jersey in her early twenties, one
for check fraud, and another for obtaining prescriptions from doctors
under false pretenses. Both were expunged."

"Sounds like her sister had her pegged," Kins said.

Chambers spent thirty days in a "sober-living house" and had been
required to attend AA meetings. Her compliance had expunged her
file. Nothing in her bank statements or on her credit card or cell phone

records indicated she'd recently come into money, or that she was pre-paring to flee the country. In fact, she had no savings and very little in her checking account. It wouldn't come close to paying off her consid-erable credit card debt, all of which was also in accord with what her sister had described.

This time, Tracy and Kins did not call ahead to ask Phil Montgomery's permission to speak to Strickland. Instead, Tracy called the law firm where Strickland now worked, and posed as a potential client hoping to set up a meeting. Strickland's assistant advised that Strickland had interviews in the office all morning, and a lunch meeting out of the office, but said he could meet with her at 3:00 p.m. Tracy said she'd get back to her and hung up.

With cell phones, it was always possible Strickland could still call his lawyer, tell Tracy and Kins to go piss in a pool, and sit mute. Tracy sensed that would not be the case. She had the same feeling about Strickland that Stan Fields had shared. Strickland believed he was smarter than everybody, and he would think he could run circles around them. Tracy was counting on that arrogance.

The law firm where Strickland worked was in a converted one-story house in a mixed residential and commercial neighborhood. Most of the buildings had bars on the windows and metal gates protecting the front doors.

"My how the mighty have fallen," Kins said.

"Maybe not that far." Tracy pointed out Strickland's cherry-red Porsche parked in the home's driveway.

"Why doesn't he just put a 'Steal Me' sign on the windshield and be done with it?" Kins said.

Kins parked across the street in a spot where they could view the car. Though it remained warm, eighty-eight degrees, the sky had begun to cloud over and to darken. A breeze rustled the leaves of the trees along the block.

"You and Dan made any plans for the wedding?" Kins asked as they settled in to wait.

"We were talking about it last night. Dan wants a traditional wedding."

Kins made a face. "You mean like a priest and a church and all that pomp and circumstance?"

"Pretty much, though I've told him I want to get married at the Alki Point Lighthouse."

"Can you do that?"

"Apparently. That's where he proposed."

"Nice," Kins said. "You know that guy is making the rest of us look bad. Don't tell Shannah."

"Too late. Why, how did you propose?"

"My last college game, I walked to the stands where she was waiting, and instead of kissing her, I dropped to a knee."

"Please don't tell me you had the ring in your pants."

"Football pants don't have pockets."

"I know."

Kins laughed. "No. Her sister held it for me."

"So what's wrong with that?"

"I didn't think anything was wrong with it. Shannah thinks I did it because with 60,000 fans watching she couldn't turn me down."

Tracy laughed. "Dan wants me to wear a wedding dress and have someone give me away."

Kins nodded, clearly thinking that statement through. "You given that any thought?"

"A little bit. I have a question to ask you."

"Fire away," Kins said, now smiling.

"Do you think Faz would do it?"

"Fuck you, Crosswhite." He laughed, then suddenly sat up and started the car. "There's our boy."

Strickland bounded down two wood steps in straight-leg jeans and a fashionable long-sleeve shirt with the cuffs rolled up and tail hanging out. He slid into the Porsche, fired up the engine with a roar, and peeled out of the driveway onto the street, as if in a hurry.

"Everything is for show with this guy, isn't it?" Kins said, following at a safe distance.

Strickland drove west, made a couple of turns, and crossed the Ross Island Bridge.

"You think he's heading home?" Tracy asked.

"Don't know. Right direction, though," Kins said. "Receptionist said he had an appointment?"

"That's what she said."

Strickland exited just after crossing the bridge. He took surface streets along the Willamette River then quickly pulled to the curb. Kins slid behind a parked car. They watched Strickland exit the Porsche and walk toward the waterfront.

"I hope he's not another one of those people who likes to walk on their lunch hour," Kins said.

"Not in those shoes," Tracy said.

Strickland disappeared beneath a brown awning and entered a restaurant called Three Degrees.

"You hungry?" Tracy asked.

"I am now," Kins said, pushing out of the car.

They ignored the maître d', telling the young woman they were meeting someone for lunch, and found Strickland seated beneath an umbrella at a table on the patio. He had his head down, fingers moving rapidly across the keypad of his cell phone.

Strickland looked up expectantly when Tracy pulled out the chair to his right. His smile quickly faded to confusion, then concern.

"What are you doing here?" Strickland's gaze flicked between Kins and Tracy. His cheeks flushed.

Tracy sat. "We came to tell you good news, Mr. Strickland. Your wife is not the woman in the crab pot."

"I already know that," Strickland said. "It was all over the news. And my attorney called to let me know."

Kins shrugged at Tracy. "Looks like we drove a long way for nothing."

"I would have thought the news would have made you happy," Tracy said.

"Not really," Strickland said. "She's still missing, isn't she?"

"Yeah, there's that," Kins said.

"I've already talked to you about this," Strickland said, dropping his gaze back to his cell phone.

"We're not here to talk about your wife," Tracy said, keeping her tone informal. "We came to ask you a few questions about Devin Chambers."

At the mention of the name, Strickland's fingers paused on the keypad.

"You do know her, don't you?" Tracy asked.

Thunder rumbled in the distance.

Strickland raised his gaze. "Of course I know her," he said, calm. "She was a friend of Andrea's."

"How close were they?" Tracy asked, deciding to play him for a bit.

Strickland sat back and crossed his legs, leaving his phone on the table. The canvas of the umbrella rippled in the breeze, sounding like a sail catching the wind. "I don't really know. She and Devin worked together."

"How much time did they spend together outside of work?"

"I really couldn't say for certain. Andrea didn't go out much after work. She was an introvert."

"How did she spend her time?"

"Reading. She read all the time."

"What was your relationship to Devin Chambers?" Tracy asked.

"I didn't have one," Strickland said, his demeanor still relaxed.

Lightning crackled, a blue-white fork in the distance. Seconds later came another clap of thunder.

The waitress returned. "Would you rather move inside?"

Strickland shook his head. "This is fine," he said, almost as if he were playing a game of chicken with Tracy and Kins.

The waitress looked to the empty chair. "Are we waiting for one more?"

"Yes," Strickland said.

After the waitress departed, Tracy said, "Did you have a romantic relationship with Devin Chambers?"

"What?" Strickland made a face like it was a ridiculous question. "No, of course not."

"Adultery isn't a crime, Mr. Strickland," Kins said.

"I'm aware of that, Detective."

"Your wife told her boss you were having an affair."

"My wife did and said a lot of crazy things, including faking her own death. She wasn't exactly acting rationally."

It was a good argument, one that Strickland and his attorney would hit hard if they ever had to argue that his wife had set it up to look like Strickland had intended to kill her.

"So you weren't having an affair?" Tracy asked.

"I've already talked about this with the other detective," he said. "And as my attorney advised you the other day, we're not going back over old ground."

Another bolt of lightning sparked in the cloud layer just over the bridge. "When's the last time you saw Devin Chambers?" Tracy asked.

This time the thunder exploded overhead, strong enough to rattle the restaurant windows. Strickland shook his head as if he were completely disinterested. "I don't know, months."

"You haven't seen her since your wife's disappearance?"

"No."

"You didn't seek her out to ask if she knew anything about it?"

"No, because as I've already explained, at the time I believed my wife had died in an accident. So what exactly was I going to ask Devin Chambers?"

"Whether or not she knew about the insurance policy your wife took out naming you a beneficiary? Or why your wife would have consulted a divorce lawyer or told her boss you were cheating on her again?" Kins said.

"It was an incredibly stressful time for me, Detectives. I believed my wife had died. Then I'm suddenly being questioned like I'm a suspect in her death."

"You did have an affair though," Kins said. "You admitted that."

"It was a mistake, okay? I've been over this. I'd been seeing the person before I met Andrea. I should have ended it. I didn't. And as you said, it isn't illegal."

The first drops of rain splattered the concrete patio and the canvas umbrella. Strickland acted like he didn't notice.

"Any idea where we might find Devin Chambers?" Tracy asked.

"I assume you would find her either at work or at her home."

Tracy watched Strickland's face for any sign he knew Chambers had fled, but his expression remained completely placid, and his eyes never shifted from hers.

"Are you aware that Devin Chambers told her boss and some of the tenants in her apartment building that she was moving back home to New Jersey?"

"Obviously not," he said. "Or I would have told you that in response to your last question." He turned his head and looked to the interior of the restaurant, presumably searching for his lunch date.

Water trickled over the sides of the umbrella. Kins had to move his chair closer to the table to keep from getting wet. "She never told you that?" he said.

"I told you, I haven't seen or spoken to Devin Chambers in months. We seem to be going in circles." Strickland uncrossed his legs and looked again to the lobby.

"This is the first you heard of it?" Tracy asked.

"Yes."

"Have you ever heard the name Lynn Hoff?" Kins asked.

"The first time I heard that name was when my attorney called and told me you found Andrea's body, and that she had been using that name."

"You'd never heard that name before?"

"No."

"Any idea how your wife obtained her fake identity?"

"None whatsoever, but then it appears my wife was full of surprises, doesn't it?"

"Did you hire a private investigator to look for Lynn Hoff?" Kins asked.

"Why would I hire a private investigator to look for someone I didn't know?"

"Because you thought someone named Lynn Hoff stole your wife's money," Kins said.

Strickland scoffed. "Why would I have thought that?"

"Because your wife had close to half a million dollars that appears to have just disappeared," Kins said. "Or didn't that concern you?"

"As I said, I had other concerns at the time, Detective."

"So you didn't even try to find the money?" Kins didn't bother to hide his skepticism.

"No, I didn't. Why, have you found it?"

"And you have no idea who might have taken it?" Kins asked.

"None."

An Asian woman approached their table. At least six feet tall, she was all legs in tight-fitting blue jeans, high heels, and a sheer blouse that looked to be buttoned at her navel. She gave them an uncertain smile.

Strickland quickly pushed back his chair, intercepting her. "Would you give us a minute?"

He stepped away from the table, water dripping from the umbrella onto his back as he did, and guided the woman inside the restaurant, though not so far that Tracy could not see them.

"You think he'll bolt?" Kins asked, watching Strickland.

"Could," Tracy said.

"He's lying."

"About something," Tracy agreed. "About what, I don't know yet."

After a minute, the woman departed. Strickland rejoined them, ducking beneath the dripping umbrella. He sat back, sipping a glass of water.

"We don't care who you were sleeping with, Mr. Strickland," Kins said. "That's none of our business."

"What is your business here?"

"Finding Devin Chambers," Tracy said.

"Did something happen to Devin Chambers?" he asked. "I thought you said she left the state."

"That's what she told people," Tracy said. "According to a sister, that's not the case."

"And you think I had something to do with her disappearance?"

"Do you know if Devin Chambers and your wife ever discussed your personal affairs?" Tracy asked.

"I can't imagine what they discussed."

"Do you know if Devin Chambers was aware of your wife's money?"

"I doubt it. I didn't even know about it."

"When did you find out?"

"Andrea mentioned it when we went to obtain a bank loan for the new business."

"Did you ask your wife why she hadn't told you before then?" Tracy asked.

"Of course."

"What did she say?"

"She said her parents left it for her in trust and she'd only recently gained control of the money."

"Did you ask her to use the money?"

"No."

"No?" Kins said.

"No," Strickland said, shaking his head. "She said the money couldn't be used to start a business and I respected that."

"It didn't upset you?" Kins said.

Strickland shrugged. "Maybe a little at first, but we discussed it and I understood where she was coming from."

"And you have no idea what happened to your wife's money?" Kins asked, clearly pushing Strickland.

"I've told you, no. If she's still alive, I presume she has it, wherever she is. If she's not, then someone stole it. May I ask you a question, Detectives?"

"Sure," Tracy said.

"Have you made any progress on identifying the woman in the crab pot?"

"We're working on it," Tracy said.

———

The old adage "When it rains, it pours" proved accurate. The summer storm did not blow through. It brought a steady rain, and a drop in the temperature. With no umbrellas, Tracy and Kins made a mad dash to the car, but were still dripping wet by the time they climbed inside.

"He's a piece of work, isn't he?" Kins started the car and turned on the heater.

Tracy diverted the vents, which were spewing cold air. "If he did kill them, he won't be easy to convict; both murders were well thought out.

We got lucky when Schill got tangled with the crab pot." Tracy checked her watch. "What time are we meeting your Portland detective?"

"Three," Kins said. "Let me call him and see if we're still on schedule or if he can move it up a bit."

"I'll call Faz."

Faz advised Tracy that he'd spoken to the FBI about the status of their forensic examination of the skip tracer's computer. So far, it appeared the skip tracer's client had logged on to a server in a public location, and the FBI was optimistic they'd at least be able to narrow that location. "Del and I are about to go out to the apartments and marinas with Chambers's photograph. We'll also stop by Dr. Wu's."

Kins's conversation with the Portland detective was considerably shorter. When he hung up, he swore. "Is nothing in this case simple?"

"What happened?" Tracy asked, disconnecting her call with Faz.

"They got a shooting over at one of the college campuses. My guy's out the rest of the day."

"Can someone else handle the warrant?"

Kins shook his head. "You know how it is. The earliest he can do it is tomorrow morning."

The strain of long days and interrupted sleep had caught up to Tracy. Her clothing was wet and uncomfortable and she felt frustrated. "Well, no sense driving back to Seattle just to turn around and come back down," she said. "I guess we're going to have to get a hotel."

"I just love wearing day-old underwear," Kins said.

They ate lunch and checked into adjacent rooms in a Marriott Courtyard at the end of the waterfront. Tracy made some phone calls and answered e-mails while watching the storm out her hotel window, the sky now a roiling sea of angry dark clouds and the rain coming in sheets. She checked in with Dan and told him she would not be home, then called into the office. Faz and Del had returned to Police Headquarters after canvassing the marinas and the apartments with a photograph of Devin Chambers.

"Nobody recalls seeing her," Faz said. "Only positive identification was by Dr. Wu, which didn't exactly come as a surprise."

"Did your uncle talk to Chambers's sister?"

"He got to her this afternoon. He said it went okay as far as those things go. Said the sister took it stoically and thanked him."

"Any parents?" Tracy asked.

"Deceased."

"Any other siblings?"

"Apparently not. What did the hubby have to say?" Faz asked.

"He don't know nothing from nothing," she said, using a Faz colloquialism.

"You get the search warrant?"

"No. They got a homicide over at one of the colleges, so Kins's guy is out until tomorrow morning."

Someone knocked on her door. The clock on the nightstand read five thirty. She and Kins had agreed to meet at six. "Somebody's at the door. I'll call you later," she said to Faz and hung up.

Kins stood in the hallway looking frustrated. "We're not going to get our warrant," he said.

CHAPTER 28

The jurisdiction cluster had become a whole lot more entangled. Portland Police were exercising control over Strickland's Pearl District loft, and rightfully so. It was now a crime scene, an apparent homicide.

A large contingent of police and emergency vehicles—fire department response units, blue-and-white patrol cars, unmarked police vehicles, a CSI van, and the Portland Medical Examiner's van cluttered the street in front of the three-story brick building. As was always the case, this much excitement was just too much for the local population to ignore. With the storm having passed and the sun again beaming, a crowd had gathered behind sawhorses that closed street access. Uniformed officers directed traffic to detours. Kins slowed as he approached and lowered his window, showing the officer his badge.

"Seattle?" the officer asked.

"We have an interest in another case up north."

"Wherever you can find a place to park." The officer moved one of the sawhorses so Kins could drive through.

Kins parked behind an unmarked Ford in the middle of the narrow street. Around them stood three- and four-story brick buildings that looked to have been originally built for industrial purposes, then renovated, earthquake proofed, and no doubt inspected ad nauseam for compliance with building codes before being turned into mixed-use structures. The area reminded Tracy of Pioneer Square in Seattle. After an urban renewal in the 1960s, Pioneer Square had become home to art galleries, Internet companies, cafés, sports bars, and nightclubs.

The ground floor of the Pearl District buildings housed retail businesses—cafés, restaurants, and what looked like high-end clothing and home-decorating stores. The upper floors, judging from what Tracy could see in the windows facing the street, were residential. Metal additions protruded from the roofs, likely multimillion-dollar penthouse condominiums.

"Busy area," she said, looking around the street. "A lot of people around."

The responding officers had set up a second perimeter at a wrought-iron gate between two concrete pillars. The walkway led to a side entrance to the building.

"I'm looking for Detective Zhu," Kins said, again flashing his shield and ID.

"Third floor," the officer said.

"What unit?" Kins asked.

"Only one unit per floor. It's a loft."

At the end of the sloped concrete walk, they came to a glass-door entrance beneath a forest-green awning bearing the building's address and a symbol, what looked like an ampersand. Inside the lobby, with its wood-plank floors and leather furniture, they walked across to an old-fashioned cage elevator and wide staircase.

"Let's take the stairs," Kins said. "Those things give me the heebie-jeebies."

"What about your hip?"

"I'd rather be in pain than die if that thing falls."

"God, you're paranoid."

"I like to think of it as pragmatic."

As they approached the staircase, Tracy noted three steps leading down to an exterior door. She took them and pushed on the door, which sprang open and led into a parking lot at the back of the building. She exited the building and let the door close behind her. When she tried the handle she found the door locked and noticed, on the wall beside it, a keyless pad. She considered the light stanchions and corners of the surrounding buildings, but did not see any surveillance cameras. Retrofitted metal decks anchored by extension arms and large bolts protruded from the second and third stories and likely obstructed the tenants' views of the parking lot, and anyone approaching the ground-level door.

Kins opened the door for her from the inside and they made their way up the staircase to the third-floor landing. They encountered the final perimeter, an officer with a clipboard and sign-in log just outside the loft door. Kins signed for both of them and again asked for Zhu.

"Hang on," the officer said. He took a step inside the loft. "Detective Zhu? You got a couple of visitors."

Tracy contemplated the door to the loft. Larger than a standard door, it looked solid, with metal rivets. She again noted a keyless lock pad. Neither the door nor the doorjamb evidenced any sign of a forced entry.

An Asian man with young features stepped into the hall. Kins and Jonathan Zhu shook hands and Kins introduced Tracy.

"Well, this is one way to search an apartment," Zhu said. "What time did you talk to this guy today?"

"Right around noon," Kins said.

"Where'd you meet him?"

"We interrupted him at some place called the Third Degree."

"Three Degrees?" Zhu said. "Down on the water?"

"Yeah, that's the one," Kins said. "He was meeting someone for lunch."

"A woman?"

"Yeah," Kins said.

"Did she show?"

"Briefly," Kins said.

"You get a good look at her?"

"Hard to miss. Tall, Asian, good-looking."

"Come on in." Zhu led them inside the loft.

The interior consisted of an open floor plan interrupted only by thick, hand-hewn wooden beams extending to triangular trusses that supported a twenty-foot ceiling. To the left of the entry, Tracy noticed a bench where people could sit and remove their shoes. Above it hung coats and jackets from metal hooks. One coat looked like the coat worn by the Asian woman at the restaurant. Tracy and Kins followed Zhu into a living area of leather couches, a glass coffee table, and a flat-screen TV. The early-evening sunlight streamed into the room through arched windows. In the far corner was a kitchen. Metal steps led up to the second-story landing. They ascended. Partitions shielded their view as they approached a room where most of the activity was centered. Stepping around the partition, Tracy encountered a team of people from the medical examiner's office hovering over and working around a blood-soaked bed, the white sheets and bedding stained a deep crimson red.

"Is she the woman you saw him with this afternoon?" Zhu asked.

———

They stepped from the loft back into the hall. Streaks of light through one of the arched windows cut slash marks across the floor. The noises of the Pearl District filtered up from the street—cars and the sounds of a city. The scene inside the loft was gruesome—a young woman lay facedown on the bed, sheet lowered to reveal her bare shoulders and back, dark hair and blood forming a halo around her head.

"Who is she?" Tracy asked.

"According to her driver's license she's Megan Chen," Zhu said. "Twenty-four years old, shares an apartment in inner Northeast Portland with two roommates."

"Who found her? Who called it in?" Kins asked.

"Cleaning lady," Zhu said. "She's pretty shaken up. We have one of our female detectives talking with her at the station."

"Any estimate on the time of death?" Tracy asked.

"ME says a couple hours at most."

Sufficient time for Strickland to leave the restaurant and get home, Tracy thought. "They find a weapon?"

Zhu nodded. "9mm."

Likely the same-caliber weapon used to kill Devin Chambers.

Kins shifted his feet, the way he did when he was upset, or frustrated. "Any word on Strickland's whereabouts?"

"We sent a couple of detectives over to the law firm where he works. His assistant said he had a three o'clock appointment this afternoon but didn't show."

"That was with me," Tracy said. "I called yesterday to find out if he was around so we wouldn't make an unnecessary trip."

"The assistant tried his cell but it went straight to voice mail," Zhu said. "Apparently, he doesn't keep a home phone."

"You tracking his cell?" Kins asked.

"Trying," Zhu said. "He's had it shut off. We're also working on getting a warrant to track his credit cards and ATM in real time."

Zhu's cell phone rang. "This could be the judge." He stepped to the side to take the call.

"It doesn't make sense," Tracy said.

"What?" Kins asked.

"Why someone who we think went to such effort to plan the deaths and disappearance of two women would shoot a third and leave her in his own bed."

"Nothing in this case has made sense," Kins said.

Zhu lowered his cell and looked at Tracy. "Graham Strickland's attorney called the station. He said Strickland called him twenty minutes ago sounding distraught about a dead woman in his loft and someone trying to ruin his life. He's willing to turn himself in."

"That's good news," Tracy said.

"Yeah, but he wants to talk to you first."

CHAPTER 29

Zhu wasn't happy about conceding to Graham Strickland's request to speak to Tracy before turning himself in. To Zhu, Strickland was a suspect in a brutal murder, and if Zhu had had his way, he would have stormed Phil Montgomery's office with a SWAT team, slapped handcuffs on Strickland, and hauled his ass downtown to an interrogation room in the Police Bureau.

Tracy didn't feel like placating Strickland either, but she had a different agenda; she wanted to know what Strickland knew about the disappearances of Andrea Strickland and Devin Chambers, and she might not get a better chance to find out. Strickland no longer had any leverage and was likely scared. The combination might just wipe the smug expression from his face and cause him to tell the truth—or at least some of the truth.

"If he wants to talk, let's let him talk," Tracy explained to Zhu. "It might be our only chance to get information out of him. At some point his attorney will convince him to keep his mouth shut. You'll get your chance to arrest him after he talks to me."

"I don't like feeling like I'm being played," Zhu said.

"Welcome to the club," Kins said. "This guy is a piece of work."

"He is," Tracy agreed, shooting Kins a look to let him know he wasn't helping their situation. "But the landscape has changed considerably. He's a suspect in two other deaths, and I'm curious as hell how he's going to explain it."

Zhu and his superior relented and Kins drove Tracy to Phil Montgomery's office. Kins waited in the building lobby with the others as Tracy went up in the elevator. Montgomery met her in the area outside his law-firm door. He looked spent, as if he'd just returned to his office after a full day in trial. He still wore a tie and a dress shirt, but he'd tugged the knot from his neck and rolled up his shirtsleeves. Two half-moon-shaped perspiration stains ringed his armpits.

"He's in bad shape," Montgomery said.

Tracy didn't much care, but she wanted to hear what Strickland had to say, so until she believed he was trying to manipulate her, she'd play nice.

"Do you think he's suicidal?" she asked.

"Maybe. He hasn't said much."

"You made sure he has no weapons?"

Montgomery nodded. "Of course. I think we can both agree that this is tantamount to an interrogation while in custody."

"Agreed," Tracy said. She held up her phone. "So, I'm going to tape this. I'll read him his Miranda rights."

"Then for the record I'm going to advise him against this."

"I understand," she said.

Montgomery opened the door and led her inside the lobby. They moved past the receptionist's desk. "He's in the conference room." Montgomery turned left, continuing past an empty cubicle and a darkened office. He stopped outside a closed door, pausing to look back over his shoulder at Tracy as if to say, *Are you ready?*

Then he pushed open the door.

Graham Strickland looked up from his seat at the far end of the room. His forearms rested on the conference room table, hands wrapped around a mug of some drink. Behind him, the floor-to-ceiling windows offered a view from downtown Portland to the distant green foothills. Though he was wearing the same clothes he'd had on that afternoon, Strickland no longer looked so neat and put together, and he wasn't displaying the same cocksure smile or arrogant demeanor. His shoulders slumped. His eyes appeared sunken and his gaze distant and unfocused. He had the sullen expression of a kid who'd been caught doing something bad and knew the punishment was going to be severe.

Montgomery walked around the table to the chair beside his client and set down his legal pad and ballpoint pen. Tracy made her way down the opposite side of the table. She pulled out a chair directly across from Strickland.

When seated, Montgomery said, "I've told Detective Crosswhite I consider this an interrogation in custody, Graham. As such she's going to read you your Miranda rights."

"And I'm going to record our conversation," Tracy said, putting her phone on the table directly between them and pressing the "Record" button.

Strickland nodded.

"Mr. Strickland, we're present in a conference room in your attorney's office," she said. "I'm going to read you your Miranda rights. You have the right to remain silent. Anything you say can and will be used against you in a court of law. You have the right to an attorney . . ." When she'd finished she said, "Do you understand your rights as I've read them to you?"

Strickland gave a subtle nod.

"You have to answer audibly," Montgomery said. He sat at an angle, facing both Strickland and Tracy, the ballpoint pen in hand.

"Yes, I understand," Strickland replied, voice barely above a whisper.

Tracy said, "I understand that you've asked to speak to me."

Strickland nodded.

"Audibly," Montgomery said.

"Yes."

Strickland sat back and took a deep breath. His chest shuddered. He took a moment to get his emotions under control. Tracy waited. She had interviewed sociopaths before and Strickland had all the markings of one. Often intelligent, they could be master manipulators capable of giving command performances that would make the best Juilliard-trained actors look like amateurs. It was not lost on her that Strickland had asked to speak to her, a woman, and she was on guard in the event his request was to try to manipulate her or the judicial process that would inevitably follow.

"I didn't kill Megan," he said.

Tracy didn't respond.

"I didn't kill Devin Chambers and I didn't kill my wife. I know you think I did, but I didn't."

"What did you say to Megan Chen when you met her for lunch today?" Tracy asked.

"I told her something had come up in one of my cases but that I could meet her at my loft when I'd finished."

"Had going back to your loft been part of your original plan?"

"I'd hoped so," Strickland said.

"How was she going to get in?"

"She knew the code."

"You were dating?"

"We'd gone out a few times."

"Tell me what happened after my partner and I left the restaurant?"

"I stayed for a few minutes to check and answer some e-mails, then I called my office and told them I was going to take a longer lunch but that I would be in for an appointment I had at three o'clock." Strickland took another deep breath and raised the mug to his lips with trembling hands, sipping tea. Lowering the mug, he continued. "I made a few phone calls and drove home."

"Did you call and tell her you were on your way?"

"No."

"Why not?"

"Megan liked to surprise me."

"Surprise you how?"

"Can I finish? I think it will become apparent."

"Go ahead."

"I parked in my space beneath the building. Megan's car was parked in one of the guest spaces."

"What kind of car?" Tracy asked.

"Her car? A blue Camry. I took the elevator from the garage to my landing."

"I notice you need a code to get in the front entrance to the building and to your apartment. Do you need a code to access your landing from the elevator in the garage?"

"Yes," he said.

"Megan knew that code?"

Strickland nodded. "It's the same code as the front door." He took a breath, blew it out. "When I walked in, I called out her name, but she didn't answer. I called a couple more times, and when she didn't answer, I suspected she was either taking a shower upstairs or she was hiding."

"Did you notice anything unusual, anything out of place that caused you any alarm?"

"No."

"Why did you think she'd be hiding—because she liked to surprise you?"

"Yes. She'd jump out, or pop out from under the covers."

"She'd surprised you before?"

"Right."

"So what did you do when you got home?"

"I went up the stairs." Strickland's gaze lacked focus. "The bedroom is blocked by a partition. I couldn't see anything. I said her name as I stepped around the partition. I thought she was going to jump out at me . . . and that's when I saw her, and the blood."

"Where was she?" Tracy asked.

Strickland looked up as if he hadn't heard the question. "What?"

"Where did you find her?"

"The bed. She was on the bed."

"In what position?"

"I don't understand."

"Was she sitting up, laying down?"

"She was on her stomach with her left arm sort of draped over her head." Strickland raised his arm and bent it over his head. "Like she'd been sleeping."

That had been Tracy's thought when she saw the body. There was no indication Megan Chen had tried to run or avoid her killer, which meant either she knew him, or he'd surprised her. Both could apply to Strickland.

"And you say she'd done this before, surprised you like that?"

"Yes."

"What position was she in on that occasion?"

"She'd been hiding under the covers. She just sat up and yelled 'Surprise!'" Strickland said without enthusiasm.

"Do you have any explanation for why she would have been on her stomach?"

Strickland shrugged. "Like I said, she looked like she'd fallen asleep."

"What did you do next?"

Strickland shook his head. "I saw the gun on the side of the bed and I just backed away. I hit the stair railing and that sort of jarred me. I don't know. I just turned and ran. I just wanted to get out of there."

"Did you touch her?"

Strickland emphatically shook his head. "No. There was blood and . . ." He closed his eyes.

"Did you touch the gun?"

"No," he said softly.

"Where did you go after you left the apartment?"

"I didn't know where to go." Strickland blew out a breath, as if about to throw up. If this was an act, he was giving a superb performance. "I didn't know what to do. I drove around and tried to reach Phil, but he was in court. When I finally reached him he told me to come here."

"Why didn't you call the police?"

"And tell them what?" Strickland's voice rose in a challenge, but it was only momentary. He sighed and slumped away from the table. "What was I going to say, that there was a dead woman in my bed? The DA had already called me a suspect in Andrea's disappearance, and I know you think I had something to do with Devin's disappearance. Who was going to believe me?"

"What do you mean by that?"

"It's *my* loft. She was in *my* bed. You saw her with me a couple of hours earlier. I'm an attorney. I know how it looks."

And that's what was bothering Tracy. How it looked. It was easy, too easy. Then again, maybe Strickland had intended it to look that way, so easy that Tracy's first thought would be it could not possibly be him.

"Is it your gun?"

"I don't own a gun."

"Did Megan Chen own a gun?"

"Not that I know of."

"Why did you ask to talk to me, Mr. Strickland?"

His eyes went wide, pupils dilated. Fight or flight they called it. Strickland had fled but now seemed intent on fighting. "Because someone is deliberately trying to ruin my life."

"Why would someone want to ruin your life?"

Strickland rocked in his chair and gazed up to the corner of the ceiling. A tear trickled down his cheek. "Because of Andrea."

"What about Andrea?"

He wiped at his tears before redirecting his attention across the table. After several long moments he said, "Look, I did intend to kill Andrea." He paused again. Phil Montgomery never moved. Tracy waited. "She wanted to climb Rainier. I didn't want to do it. That's the truth. I didn't make it the first time and really didn't want to try a second time. I got altitude sickness and I really didn't want to go to the effort to train again. But then . . ." He swallowed and wiped more tears. ". . . I thought about it."

Tracy looked down at her phone to ensure it was continuing to record. She spoke softly, deliberately. "And you saw it as an opportunity to kill your wife."

"He didn't say that," Montgomery said.

Tracy ignored him.

Strickland closed his eyes, rocking in his chair. "Yes," he said, though it was nearly inaudible.

"Did you say, 'Yes'?" she asked.

"Yes."

"Did you kill her?"

"No."

"I don't understand."

"I was going to push her off the mountain. But I didn't," Strickland added quickly. "I didn't do it. What I told that detective about her getting up to use the bathroom was the truth. I didn't do it."

"Tell me," Tracy said. "What happened to her?"

Strickland took a few additional deep breaths. Montgomery sat with his chin resting in his hand, elbow propped on the table. He hadn't taken a note.

"My business was failing. I'd invested everything we had and I was going to lose it all, everything. I'd forged a letter from one of the partners at the firm saying I was going to be made partner and earn a higher salary, and the bank was intimating that I would be prosecuted if I couldn't find a way to pay back the money. I begged Andrea to let me borrow some of the money from her trust account, but she wouldn't give it to me. So I told her that I'd forged her name on the personal guaranties to the bank and to the landlord, and if she didn't give me some of the money to pay off our creditors she was going to lose it all."

"What was her response?"

"She got angry. We fought."

"Did it become physical?"

"I was angry. I'd been drinking. I grabbed her and she kicked me. I hit her. I'm not proud of it, but I hit her. Then I left."

"Had you been abusive before?"

"No. It was just that one time. It was just the heat of the moment." Tracy doubted it. "I felt like everything was crashing down around me and she wouldn't do anything to help me."

Tracy couldn't muster any sympathy, but she went where Strickland directed the conversation. "Where did you go?"

"A bar. I went to a bar near our loft, and I thought about what to do, about how I could get the money."

"You started thinking of ways you could kill her."

"He didn't say that," Montgomery said, giving Tracy a second, quick glance.

"Were you considering killing Andrea as a way to get the money?"

"No, not then," Strickland said. "I hadn't even thought of Mount Rainier then. Andrea brought it up when I went back to the loft two days later, but that's not what I want to tell you. What I want to tell you is this. When I was in that bar that night someone said my name and when I looked up, I saw Devin Chambers."

"Devin Chambers was in the bar?" Tracy asked, skeptical.

"Yes."

"So you knew her."

"We'd met a couple of times but I can't say I knew her."

"Did you ask her what she was doing there?"

"No."

"Had you been to that bar before?"

"Sure, many times."

"Had you ever seen her there before?"

"No."

"And you didn't ask her what she was doing there?"

"No. It was just 'Graham?' and I turned around."

"Was she alone?"

"No, she was with a few people. They were leaving and she spotted me and came over to say hello. I guess I looked like I was in pretty bad shape because she asked me what was wrong."

"What did you tell her?"

"I told her everything. I told her I'd drunk too much and that I was mad at Andrea, and that we'd had a fight. I wanted to make Andrea look bad, you know, selfish. So I just told Devin everything."

"Did you tell her about Andrea's trust?"

"Yes. I said she had all this money and she wouldn't let me use it to help us."

"How did she react when you told her?"

"She said if she'd had the money, and I was her husband, she'd give it to me."

"She said that?"

He nodded.

"Did you go home with her that night?"

Strickland nodded. "Yes."

"And did you sleep with her?"

"Yes. I was just so angry with Andrea," he said in a rush, as if it justified sleeping with his wife's best friend.

"Did you continue to see her after that night?"

Strickland lowered his head. "Yes."

"Was Devin part of your plan to kill Andrea?"

"Like I said, I wasn't even considering it then. I just wanted to hurt Andrea, you know?"

"And you thought sleeping with her friend would be a way to hurt her."

He nodded, looked at the recorder, and said, "Right."

"Why did you continue to see her then?"

"I don't know."

"Did you ever tell Andrea about you and Devin?"

"No."

"Did Devin tell Andrea?"

"I don't know. I didn't think so. I don't know why she would."

"So did you formulate a plan to kill Andrea on Mount Rainier?"

Montgomery looked as if he was about to say something, then stopped.

"Well, like I said, when I got back to the loft Sunday night I apologized to Andrea," Strickland said. "I brought her a couple of gifts, a book and some flowers, and I said I was sorry."

"Were you? Or were you just saying you were sorry?"

"Probably both. I didn't have anywhere to go. And we talked about the stress of the business and how we'd grown apart and that's when Andrea brought up climbing Mount Rainier."

"Out of the blue?"

"Yes."

Tracy wasn't sure she was buying it.

Strickland continued. "I was surprised because I didn't think she enjoyed climbing it the first time. She said it would be something for us to do together, that it would help our marriage."

"But you didn't want to?"

"Initially, I said I'd think about it, but only because I didn't want to start another fight."

"When did you start to think about the possibility of pushing Andrea off the mountain?"

Again, Montgomery remained silent.

"The route Andrea wanted to take wasn't popular. More people died on that route than any other. I began to think that could work."

"What could work?" She wanted Strickland to say it.

"It was just a thought, you know? Like, what if she fell?"

"When did you start to think about it seriously?"

"When Devin brought it up."

Tracy tried not to pause and give Montgomery time to stop the interview. "Devin brought up the subject of killing Andrea?"

"One night, in bed, she said, 'You do know all your problems would be solved if you could just get access to the trust funds.'"

"When was this?"

"It was some time after, maybe a month?"

"Where were you?"

"In a hotel in Seattle; we'd taken a trip to avoid being seen."

"Tell me what she said, exactly."

"Just what I told you. She said that the bank wouldn't prosecute me if I paid back the loan, that what they really wanted was their money, but I already knew that so I said, 'That's great, but Andrea won't let me use it.'"

"And she said, 'What happens to the money if anything happens to Andrea?'"

"Did you know?" Tracy asked.

"No. I'd never seen the trust documents. But I knew Andrea had no relatives, and Oregon is a community property state."

"So what happened then?"

"I found a copy of the trust documents in the house, and from my reading, if anything happened to Andrea, the money would go to me under community property laws—unless she had a will, which I didn't know but doubted."

"Did you tell Devin what you'd found out?"

"Yes."

"What was her response?"

"She said, 'What if Andrea didn't come off the mountain?'"

"And is that when you formulated a plan to push her?"

Strickland nodded. "I did some research." He paused. "Can I get a glass of water?"

Montgomery obliged him from a pitcher. Strickland took a long drink. Then he said, "I decided I could do it the morning we set out for the summit from Thumb Rock. That's the least likely place they would find her body, and if they did, it would be easy to say she fell."

"What exactly did you intend to do, Mr. Strickland?"

He swallowed hard. "I was going to shove her off the edge as we got close to an area called Willis Wall. It's a thousand-foot drop."

"So what actually happened?"

"Just what I told that other detective. We went to bed that night and I remember being exhausted. I could hardly raise my head. I felt drugged."

Tracy remembered what the ranger had said about people being amped up and unable to sleep the night before they were to summit. "Do you know why?"

He shook his head. "I don't know. It could have been the altitude, but I don't know."

"Did you do anything before you went to bed?"

Strickland shrugged. "Not really. We had a prepackaged dinner and drank some tea."

"Who made the dinner and the tea?"

"Andrea."

"Then what?"

"Then we crawled into our bags and I fell asleep. I have a vague recollection of Andrea getting up and saying she was going to go out to use the bathroom."

"Did you say anything to her?"

Strickland shook his head. "I was really out of it, lethargic. I remember my head felt weighted. I fell back to sleep."

Tracy thought again of the ranger's comments. "You were planning on killing your wife and you fell back to sleep?"

He shook his head. "I know how it sounds, but that's what happened. Maybe I had altitude sickness again. I'm telling you the truth."

"Did you set an alarm?"

"I thought I did."

"Did you check when you woke up?"

"I don't remember. I remember waking up and feeling groggy, like I had a hangover, and then I realized Andrea wasn't in her sleeping bag."

"Did you look for her?"

"Of course. I called out her name. When she didn't answer I got dressed and went out looking for her, looking for signs of her, but it had snowed that morning and I couldn't see any tracks."

"How long did you look for her?"

"I don't recall how long."

"What did you think happened to her?"

"I didn't know for sure. I guess I thought she'd wandered off and maybe that she'd fallen."

"How did you feel about that?"

"I wasn't feeling or thinking anything, really, except getting down off the mountain and what I would say."

"Okay, so what did you do?" Tracy asked. She'd read the reports of the interviews Strickland had given Glenn Hicks and Stan Fields and decided to run him through the questions again looking for inconsistencies in his story.

"I packed up and went down to the ranger station and told him what had happened."

"What did you tell the ranger?"

"Exactly what I told you."

Tracy took a moment. She decided to change subjects. "Did you talk to Devin Chambers when you got back home?"

"Not right away."

"Why not?"

"I don't know. I just . . . didn't. I was really confused. I didn't know what to think. And the police department was keeping me busy, asking questions, searching the loft."

"Were you worried about how it might look if there was an investigation and your cell phone indicated your first calls were to the woman you were having an affair with?"

"Yeah, I'd thought about that."

"Did you ever talk to Devin?"

He shook his head. "No. When I tried, I found out she was gone."

"What do you mean, 'she was gone'?" Tracy asked.

"I called her."

"When?"

"I don't remember when, but she didn't answer her phone. So I went by her apartment and knocked. She didn't answer the door and her car wasn't there. The next day I went to her work and waited outside the building for her, but I never saw her. I finally called the office and asked to speak to her. I was told she no longer worked there."

"Can you think of any reason why she would have left?"

"Well, initially, I wasn't sure, but then, when the detective started to ask me about the insurance policy naming me as a beneficiary, and about how Andrea's employer said I was cheating on her, my first thought was that Devin and Andrea had set me up to make it look like I'd killed Andrea, and they'd taken the money and gone somewhere."

"Did you know about the insurance policy naming you as the beneficiary?"

"I knew about it, but that was Andrea's suggestion. And she said she didn't need a policy because she had the trust."

"Did you know Andrea had consulted a divorce attorney?"

"Not until later."

"When did you realize Andrea's money was also gone?"

"When I realized Devin was gone." Strickland glanced at this attorney. "Phil told me the money was missing."

"Did you suspect Devin took the money?"

"Yes." Strickland shrugged. "But what was I going to do? The other detective was asking me why I didn't try to find the money . . . Who was I going to tell? What was I going to say?"

Who indeed? Tracy thought. "Did you try to find Devin?"

"No," he said, shaking his head emphatically. "By then I'd hired Phil and I knew I was a suspect in Andrea's death. It was in the papers and on the news. Reporters were outside the loft, calling me, following me. The last thing I needed was to be looking for the woman I'd had an affair with who'd stolen Andrea's money."

"You didn't hire a skip tracer to find her?"

"A what? I don't even know what that is."

"A private investigator."

"No."

"What about now, Graham? Do you think Devin and Andrea planned this?"

"I really don't know," Strickland said. "But I didn't kill anyone and that's the truth."

"Who else knew the code to your building and your apartment? Who would have known the elevator code?"

Strickland looked at her, and for the first time during the interview, his eyes appeared to focus. "Just Andrea," he said.

―

When Tracy finished interviewing Graham Strickland, it was close to eight thirty. They'd spoken for nearly three hours. In the lobby, Tracy summoned Zhu and told him he could go up. Zhu handcuffed

Strickland and escorted him out of the building to the back of a police vehicle that would take him to the Multnomah County Detention Center Jail. He would be booked on suspicion of the murder of Megan Chen. In the morning, he would be arraigned, formally charged, and based on what he'd told Tracy, plead not guilty. Then the wheels of justice would spin, though not with any great urgency. Whether the King County Prosecutor charged Strickland with the murder of Devin Chambers remained to be determined, and only after what Tracy anticipated would be many hours of discussion.

They now had a link between Devin Chambers and Graham Strickland, but the evidence that he had killed her remained thin and mostly circumstantial. If a jury convicted Strickland of murdering Chen, the powers that be in Seattle could decide there was no reason to spend taxpayer dollars to try him for Chambers's murder. As for Andrea Strickland, in the absence of a body, she remained a missing persons case, and she had no family members pushing that investigation.

Tracy spent another two hours at the Portland Bureau briefing Zhu and his partner on her conversation with Strickland. An IT specialist transferred the recording of her interrogation from her phone onto their system. At the end of it all, tired and frustrated, Tracy returned with Kins to their hotel. The bar in the lobby restaurant remained open. They took a table in a corner. Neither of them had eaten since lunch.

"Kitchen still open?" Kins asked the waiter.

"Let me check. Probably a limited selection. Any idea what you want?"

"A very large burger," Kins said. "Tracy?"

"Huh?" Her brain felt fried. Her adrenaline had been pumping during her interrogation of Strickland; she'd been focused on any subtleties in Strickland's responses and on his posture, trying to detect whether he was lying.

"Do you want to order something from the kitchen?" Kins repeated.

"What are you getting?"

"Hamburger."

She didn't feel like eating something that heavy. "Caesar salad?" she asked the waiter.

"Let me get those orders in quickly. Anything from the bar?"

"Jack and Coke," Tracy told the waiter.

"Make it two," Kins said.

"I don't want to believe the guy," Tracy said to Kins. "I really don't, but I also don't want to *not believe* him because of my personal feelings about him."

"You don't buy what he's saying though, do you?"

"I have questions."

"It doesn't sound like he gave up anything he hadn't already said or that we hadn't already suspected, Tracy. Think about it. Bottom line, he didn't admit killing anyone."

"He admitted he intended to kill Andrea, and he admitted he had a relationship with Devin Chambers."

"It's circumstantial. He's a lawyer; he knows that," Kins said. "And he has a criminal defense lawyer to consult. They both know he can't be convicted for *thinking* of committing a crime."

"It gets us one step closer to both his wife and to Chambers . . ."

"Which we both know he may never be prosecuted for if they convict him of Chen."

"He wouldn't necessarily know that."

"It doesn't get us anywhere," Kins said, shaking his head. "Without some further evidence linking him to her death—"

"Same-caliber gun," she said.

"But without the bullet that killed Chambers there's no way to tie that gun to her murder or to him for that matter."

"So why does he kill Megan Chen? We can come up with a motive for killing Andrea Strickland and Devin Chambers, but what's his motive for killing Chen?"

"Maybe he admitted something to her, and when we came calling he got worried she'd say something."

"So he kills her in his own bed? How does that make any sense?"

"It's like you said, maybe he makes it seem so obvious we'll conclude he couldn't have done it."

The waiter returned with their Jack and Cokes. "Your dinners should be up soon."

Tracy sipped her drink, which was sweet, though she could still taste the sting of the Jack. She set the glass on the table, not wanting to drink too much on an empty stomach. "That's a hell of a risk to take for a guy who, up until then, had been that careful, Kins."

"So is having a third woman connected to you disappear under mysterious circumstances. Where there's smoke, eventually there's going to be fire." Kins kept his glass in hand and sat back in the booth.

"Did Zhu say whether anybody in the building saw or heard anything?"

Kins shook his head. "Nobody else was home yet."

"What about the businesses on the first floor?"

"Separate entrance. According to Zhu, nobody heard a gunshot. It appears the killer used a pillow to muffle the sound."

"That's fairly sophisticated," she said.

"Not for anyone who watches TV."

"Any security cameras?"

"One in the garage, but not in the elevator or the building lobby. Footage from the camera in the garage shows Megan Chen driving in and exiting her car in the direction of the elevator. Half an hour later, Strickland arrives."

"No other cars?"

"Nope."

"The person had to know the code to get into the building and into the loft."

"Exactly," Kins said. "And Chen didn't try to run or get away, a pretty good indication she knew the killer."

Tracy sat back, pushing her tired mind to focus. "So then why was she on her stomach?"

"Maybe she was hiding under the covers, like you said."

"On her stomach?"

"He could have positioned her that way."

"No way. We would have been able to tell from the blood spatter."

Kins shrugged. "Maybe she fell asleep waiting."

"He says he called out when he walked in."

"Which could be a lie," Kins said. "He could have been trying to sneak up on her. She could have also been drinking before their anticipated romp. Toxicology will answer that."

They sat in silence again, Kins staring up at the flat screen, which was tuned to ESPN. Tracy could tell because of the distinct music— which she only heard in her house when Dan visited. The waiter returned with their food.

Kins grabbed a knife and proceeded to cut his hamburger in half. "Not that I would ever deliberately quote Johnny Nolasco," he said, "but maybe we shouldn't complicate this. Sometimes these things are exactly as they seem."

"That's the problem," Tracy said, stabbing at her salad. "This appears to be a simple murder in what, up to this point, has been anything but simple. It seems too easy, Kins, like someone wanted it to look like it is exactly as it appears."

CHAPTER 30

For the next two weeks, the wheels of justice turned, but Tracy couldn't shake the thought that the death of Megan Chen was just too simple, as would be convicting Graham Strickland for that crime. And as the murder of Chen proceeded, it appeared the murder of Devin Chambers and the disappearance of Andrea Strickland—and her money—would be pushed to the back burner.

Out of sight, out of mind.

Nolasco confirmed Tracy's concern when he entered their bull pen on a Wednesday afternoon to advise that a decision had been made—"by people with a much higher pay grade than me"—to keep the Devin Chambers matter open but only to monitor as the Megan Chen proceedings moved forward. In other words, the King County DA was going to ride Portland's coattails. With evidence mounting that Strickland killed Chen, the Oregon DA had charged Strickland with aggravated murder, meaning he could face the death penalty. In light of that possibility, Strickland might be persuaded to seek a deal, admit to killing Devin Chambers—and maybe even his wife—in exchange for life in prison, thus saving the King County taxpayers millions in costs for a full-blown murder trial. If Strickland didn't admit to killing

Chambers, then the same powers that be would reevaluate whether the anticipated cost justified a separate murder trial. You could only kill a person once—Andrea Strickland being the apparent exception.

Besides, Tracy suspected she already knew that answer. Without some evidence tying Graham Strickland to the private investigator searching for Chambers, evidence linking him to the missing money, or evidence proving that the gun used to kill Chen also killed Chambers, the DA would not opt to go forward.

The forensic examination of the PI's computer was still not complete, and a forensic accounting had only confirmed what they already knew—someone had emptied Lynn Hoff's bank accounts after Devin Chambers had been killed. From what they could determine thus far, the money had been wired out of the country, to a bank in Luxembourg, which fiercely guarded customer privacy. Not that it mattered. It was unlikely the money had stayed there long, or that the person had used a name they would know. Likely they'd used a corporate name and quickly rerouted the funds. Locating where it went would take a lot more time and expense, without any guarantee the result would provide the necessary evidence to convict.

"What about Andrea Strickland?" Tracy asked Nolasco.

Nolasco shrugged, and Tracy knew Andrea Strickland was already becoming an afterthought. "Unless the husband admits he killed her, or the glacier up there gives up her body, she remains a missing person. That's Pierce County's problem. Not ours."

Left unsaid was that neither Andrea Strickland nor Devin Chambers had family who'd push for answers or make a stink that the investigations into their death and disappearance were not receiving the proper attention. In other words, there were no squeaky wheels demanding to be oiled.

"We know who killed them," Nolasco said, as if to justify the decision, but which only sent shivers of irritation up Tracy's spine. "We just might not get the chance to prove it. Sometimes that's the way it is. You all know that. The most important thing is Strickland is going to jail for the rest of his life."

In the interim, Nolasco told Tracy and Kins to provide the Portland Police with whatever support they needed in their investigation and prosecution of Strickland.

Tracy spent her days working her other files, but she remained distracted, and for a reason she never would have anticipated. As much as she tended to tune out what Nolasco said, something he'd said early in the investigation, something that Kins had repeated, kept circling through her thoughts, like a repeating message on a Times Square billboard. She doubted Nolasco had meant it as a pearl of wisdom. To the contrary, he'd likely meant it to disparage Tracy, but still, she couldn't get the thought out of her mind. He'd said, "Sometimes these cases aren't as difficult as you make them. Sometimes the answer is as simple as it seems."

In the case of Megan Chen, that certainly appeared to be the case. Tracy kept thinking about that concept with respect to Devin Chambers and Andrea Strickland. Had she made those investigations too complicated? The facts were complicated, no doubt, but what about the human element—the motivation? She'd concluded that, if Andrea Strickland were still alive, she'd acted out of a desire for revenge. Chambers's actions, it seemed, had been fueled by her addiction and greed.

After the other members of the A Team had left for the day, Tracy spread out the contents of the case file on the worktable in the center of their bull pen. Over her years in Violent Crimes, she'd developed the method as a way to help get her unstuck during an investigation. More visual than analytical, laying out the evidence helped her to see connecting threads between the evidence. Her intent was to do what Nolasco suggested, to break the case down to its simplest questions and see if she could find answers.

The first question she wrote on her notepad was the question Graham Strickland had posed. *Who had elevator and front door access code?*

She wrote *Graham Strickland* in block letters. Beneath his name she wrote *Andrea Strickland, Megan Chen, Cleaning Lady, Landlord, Other?*

Tracy circled Graham Strickland and wrote, *Case Closed.*

But what if it wasn't Strickland who'd entered using the code? What if Graham Strickland was telling the truth? What if he hadn't killed Megan Chen?

She drew a second line, put an arrow on the end, and wrote *Not Strickland.*

She crossed out Megan Chen's name. She also crossed out the cleaning lady. That left Andrea Strickland, the landlord, and Other. Of the two known people, Andrea Strickland was a far more likely suspect than the landlord. Random killings were rare, except in the case of psychopaths. The landlord didn't strike her as a psychopath.

Next, Tracy contemplated her interview of Graham Strickland. She sat in her desk chair, put in her earphones, closed her eyes, and listened to the recording of her interview, allowing herself to hear and contemplate Strickland's answers without the stress of the situation. She'd been cautious during the interview. She knew sociopaths sprinkled lies and half-truths into their stories to try to throw off an interrogation, confuse the issues, or raise a basis to argue reasonable doubt, if their prosecution ever got that far.

What were the lies and half-truths Strickland had sprinkled in with the truth?

Had he only *intended* to kill his wife, or had he actually carried out his intent?

Strickland said he'd been unable to carry through his plan, though it wasn't because of a change of heart. He'd said he physically couldn't function, that he'd felt drugged, lethargic, and could not wake from sleep.

Tracy wrote and circled *drugged?* on her notepad. A thought came to her. Under that word she wrote, *Genesis Inventory?*

If Andrea Strickland did have the idea to climb Rainier, and it had been her intent to frame her husband for her murder, her first problem would have been walking off the mountain without him knowing. This would have been especially difficult given Ranger Hicks's statement about it being next to impossible to sleep the night before an ascent with your body amped on adrenaline and anxiety—not to mention even a sociopath like Strickland had to have some anxiety about what he intended to do. So to get off that mountain without her husband knowing it, if she had indeed done so, Andrea Strickland would have needed to knock her husband out—and she had ready access to the drugs to do it.

Tracy rolled her chair back to her cubicle, brought her computer to life, accessed the Internet, and typed in "Genesis, Portland," and "marijuana." The website for the business remained active. She clicked her way through it to the Menu tab and scrolled through Flowers and Edibles. She stopped when she came to Concentrates. Reading further, she noted how marijuana could be ingested in the form of a tea or other type of drink, and remembered her interview of Strickland, still playing on the earphones.

T. Crosswhite: *Did you do anything before you went to bed?*

G. Strickland: *We had a prepackaged dinner and drank some tea.*

T. Crosswhite: *Who made the dinner and the tea?*

G. Strickland: *Andrea.*

She exited the website and Googled "liquid THC," pulling up thousands of hits. She clicked on several and finally found one that described the physical effects. THC could make a person lethargic and impact their ability to concentrate, their coordination, and their sensory and time perception.

She sat back. Graham Strickland could have been drugged.

If that were true, the next question was how Andrea Strickland got off the mountain. According to Glen Hicks—the man who would know best—it was unlikely Strickland had acted alone. Tracy went back to the worktable and wrote the next question.

Who would have helped?

The obvious answer would have been Devin Chambers—except, according to Graham, Devin Chambers had been the person who planted the seed that Graham could get the trust money if he killed Andrea. And, according to Hicks, Chambers had receipts proving she'd been away that weekend. Maybe that was one of Strickland's lies to help his defense down the road. As Kins had said, Strickland could say he'd been forthcoming, that he'd copped to being an adulterer, but that didn't make him a murderer.

But Tracy didn't think it was a lie, and for the reason she'd already told Kins. Admitting to an affair with Devin Chambers provided a thread between Strickland and Chambers that otherwise did not exist. So lying about something like that didn't make a lot of sense. Alison McCabe had also said her sister was a con artist addicted to prescription drugs, something Devin Chambers's credit card balances appeared to confirm. That evidence supported, to some extent anyway, Graham Strickland's statement that Devin Chambers suggested he could solve his problems if he killed his wife. If that were true, it clearly would not have been in Chambers's interest to help Andrea off the mountain. It would have been cleaner and neater for Chambers to let Graham kill his wife, providing Chambers with unfettered access to the money. Andrea would have been dead, and Graham Strickland couldn't very well run to the police and say, *I think my wife's best friend stole the money I was hoping to steal when I killed her.* In fact, as Graham Strickland said during the interview, he recognized that any attention he directed to Chambers had the very real likelihood of circling around like a boomerang and hitting him in the ass. With all the other circumstantial evidence pointing to him, the last thing he needed was a con artist telling the police she was sleeping with him, and maybe even that he had confided to her that he intended to kill his wife by pushing her over a ledge.

Bye-bye, Graham. Hello, money.

So, the simple answer was Chambers was probably not an ally, and not likely the person who helped Andrea Strickland off the mountain.

Brenda Berg? Possible, but Tracy didn't think so. For one, Berg had a newborn baby to consider. Why would she risk it?

Berg had confirmed Graham Strickland's statement that his wife didn't have any other friends. That left relatives or strangers.

Alan Townsend, the psychologist, knew about the trust fund. Tracy wrote and circled his name.

Both of Andrea Strickland's parents were dead. She had no siblings. She had only an aunt. Tracy wrote, *Penny Orr.*

Orr claimed that she'd been estranged from Andrea since Andrea's move from San Bernardino to Portland; that she didn't even know Andrea had gotten married.

So she'd said.

As far as Tracy knew from the Pierce County file, nobody had followed through to determine if Penny Orr was telling the truth. Nobody had pulled Andrea's phone records or e-mail—primarily because Stan Fields didn't think she was still alive. He thought Graham had killed her. If Andrea was alive, if she'd orchestrated the disappearance of her trust, she'd also likely not used her cell phone or her e-mail account to do it.

Tracy sat back, considering Andrea Strickland and Penny Orr. Both, in a sense, had been abandoned under traumatic circumstances and, as Tracy had deduced between Devin Chambers and her sister, blood created a strong bond difficult to ignore or to break. As crazy as it seemed to even consider Penny Orr, Tracy could not dismiss it. For one, who was left? A random person Andrea had paid? Too risky. The person could run to the media first chance they got, seeking their fifteen minutes of fame. Alan Townsend? Maybe.

During their interview, Orr had told Tracy she felt guilty about what had happened to Andrea while under her roof. Could helping Andrea to start a new life have been Orr's way to cleanse herself of her own perceived sins?

What did Tracy really know about Penny Orr?

Nothing.

She went back to her cubicle, hit the space bar on the keyboard, and brought her monitor to life. She logged on to the Internet, pulled up the website they used to conduct LexisNexis searches, and input information to run Penny Orr through the system. The search provided a history of the person's past employers, former addresses, relatives, and prior criminal history.

The history for Penny Orr was short. She'd moved twice, from the San Bernardino home address to a townhome, to the apartment complex. She'd had one sister, deceased. She had no prior criminal history. She'd had one employer.

Tracy's stomach fluttered.

Penny Orr had spent thirty years working for the San Bernardino County Assessor. Sensing something, Tracy opened another Internet page and searched for the Assessor's website. Pulling it up, she clicked her way through the pages until she came to a page announcing that, effective January 3, 2011, the offices of the County Assessor, County Recorder, and County Clerk had been consolidated. To the left of that announcement was a light-blue drop-down menu for the departments' various services, including a link to obtain certified copies of a birth certificate.

CHAPTER 31

The following morning, Tracy prepared for the pushback she was certain she would receive from Johnny Nolasco. She'd spoken to Kins on the telephone the night before and told him what she'd found. He agreed it was a lead worth pursuing. Unfortunately, he was in the Lipinsky trial, the start of which had been delayed, and he would remain in court for at least the remainder of the week, likely longer.

"Her aunt would have had access to certified copies of birth certificates," Tracy told Nolasco as she made her case in his office. She handed him a birth certificate for Lynn Hoff. Hoff had been born in San Bernardino. Her birth date was the same year as Andrea Strickland. "We know Andrea used a certified copy of Lynn Hoff's birth certificate to obtain her Washington State driver's license, and that allowed her to open the bank accounts. This is how she got it."

"So who's Lynn Hoff?" Nolasco asked.

"I don't know and it doesn't matter. Andrea and her aunt weren't going to steal Lynn Hoff's identity or her finances; they were just borrowing her identity to get the driver's license, hide the money, and ultimately disappear. Lynn Hoff would have never known."

"Is there a record of someone putting in a request for Lynn Hoff's birth certificate?"

"That's my point; the aunt wouldn't have to put in a request; she's one of the people who the request would have ordinarily gone through. She found a certificate of a woman born the same year as Andrea. She certified it. And if she did that, she's also likely the person who helped Andrea off the mountain. She has to have been the person—there is no one else."

"Sounds too easy."

"Exactly. You told me not to complicate things, that sometimes these things aren't as difficult as I make them," she said, stroking his ego. "This is a simple theory, but it makes sense and it answers several questions."

"Assuming you're right, and Andrea Strickland is alive, it's not our case. That's Pierce County's case. Send them the information to pursue it."

"It gives us a link to Devin Chambers, which is our case."

"I don't see how."

Tracy knew this is where the argument would sink or swim. She'd thought about it most of the night. It wasn't perfect, but it was plausible. "The aunt helps her create the identity and go into hiding. We have to assume she also helped her to hide the money. Even if she didn't, we know that Devin Chambers used the money to pay for her surgery and for the motel. She paid cash, though she was broke. She thought Andrea was dead. If Andrea was alive, and monitoring the accounts, she would have seen the transactions and realized Devin Chambers was accessing her money. The problem is, Andrea doesn't know where Devin Chambers is, so she anonymously hires a private investigator to find her."

"So why does she kill her? Why doesn't she just take the money and hide it again?"

"Because if she did, Devin Chambers would have known she was still alive, and Devin Chambers was sleeping with Graham Strickland."

"So you think she killed Devin Chambers?"

"Andrea's counselor said it was possible that Andrea could be prone to violence if she became desperate. Devin Chambers, who she thought to be her friend, was sleeping with her husband, planning her death, and had access to the one thing Andrea Strickland had left—her trust fund. It's a lead worth exploring," Tracy said. "It's worth having a conversation with the aunt about it. If Andrea is alive, the aunt is the person most likely to know where she is hiding. Look, Captain, think of it this way." This was the argument Tracy thought might be most persuasive with Nolasco. After a recent hand slapping by OPA regarding questionable investigative techniques he and his partner, Floyd Hattie, had used during their careers working homicides, Nolasco still remained on thin ice. "Portland isn't interested in these two cases and the DA won't want to spend the money to prosecute Strickland if he's convicted of killing Chen. We both know the brass and the bean counters look at the bottom line. So, we could have two open files on our docket through no fault of our own. This might allow us to solve both at the same time— where is Andrea Strickland and who killed Devin Chambers?"

Nolasco sat in silence, thinking about what she'd said. "How does Megan Chen fit into this scenario?"

"I don't know," Tracy said. "Maybe she does, maybe she doesn't. As you said, that's Portland's problem at the moment."

Nolasco rocked in his chair. After several moments he said, "Let me make a few phone calls. This is something I'm going to have to run up the flagpole."

"One last thing," she said.

"What?"

"The money has been moved. Andrea Strickland won't be far behind it."

Nolasco's answer came late that afternoon in the form of an e-mail. It was the proverbial good news, bad news.

You have authorization to interview Andrea Strickland's aunt regarding her knowledge concerning the certified birth certificate for Lynn Hoff. Pierce County desires to remain fully involved. Contact Stan Fields and coordinate travel and interview.

Tracy groaned. Traveling with Stan Fields was punishment enough.

Still, not even the thought of spending time with Fields could dampen her excitement—the feeling she got when she believed she was getting close to answers on one of her investigations. She immediately went online and booked a direct flight leaving Seattle the following morning at 5:55 a.m. and arriving at the Ontario, California, airport at 8:30 a.m. They'd have to rent a car, but they could be at Penny Orr's apartment before 10:00 a.m.

She called Orr. "We may have a development in Andrea's case," she said, deliberately vague. "Will you be home tomorrow around ten to talk?"

"A development?" Orr had asked. "What is it?"

"I'll know more tomorrow. Will you be available?"

"Yes," Orr had said.

Tracy didn't like being dishonest, but she also didn't want to take a flight all the way to San Bernardino only to find Orr was not at home or had skipped town.

CHAPTER 32

Tracy succeeded in securing two aisle seats, one at the front of the plane and one at the rear, so she wouldn't have to talk to Stan Fields during the flight. The guy made her skin crawl even before their little spat in the conference room over jurisdiction. Luckily, the plane was full, which would make her intent less obvious, though she suspected even Fields wasn't oblivious to such things, nor did she really care.

She had a brief telephone conversation with Fields the prior afternoon to provide him the flight information before she left work for home. Neither of them mentioned the prior confrontation, which meant neither of them had forgotten it, but both were intending to bear a less-than-ideal situation.

Tracy arrived at the flight gate at just after 5:00 a.m. When Fields hadn't arrived by 5:20, and the gate agent began to board the plane, Tracy hoped he might miss the flight, but no such luck. She saw him hurrying down the terminal clutching a McDonald's bag in one hand and dragging a rolling suitcase behind him. He'd dressed casually in a polo shirt, jeans, and tennis shoes and what looked like a Members Only jacket.

"What's with the suitcase?" she said when Fields approached.

"In case you're right," he said, "and it is the aunt and she knows where Strickland is. One of us is likely to have to stay a day or two while we get an arrest warrant."

If they found Andrea Strickland still alive, they would have to ask local police to take her into custody while they obtained an arrest warrant from the court seeking extradition. Tracy didn't say it, but she knew Fields would insist on being the one to escort Strickland back to Washington, if indeed she was still alive, so that Pierce County could take the credit. Frankly, she didn't care about the accolades, and since it was a missing persons case, Fields would have the right.

The gate agent announced the boarding of passengers in Zone One. "That's me," Tracy said, turning for the gate.

"I hope this isn't just some wild-goose chase," Fields said.

Tracy didn't bother to turn around. "We'll both know soon enough," she said over her shoulder.

—

She checked her cell phone for messages while she waited in the terminal for Fields to deplane. Kins had sent a text message asking that she let him know the results of her conversation with Penny Orr. When Fields stepped off the plane they made their way to the shuttle buses that would take them to the rental car counter for what her GPS said would be a thirty-minute drive, traffic always being the unknown in Southern California. Tracy expected Fields to press her for more information, but he remained quiet. The less he knew, she hoped, the less likely he would feel the need to interrupt her questioning of Penny Orr.

At nine thirty, traffic was heavy but moved at a steady pace. They arrived at Penny Orr's apartment complex at just after ten. Tracy led the way to the second story and knocked three times. When Orr opened the door she looked curious, though not shocked, which meant she'd viewed them through the peephole.

"Detective? I thought when you called last night you meant that we would talk on the phone."

"Sorry to come unannounced," Tracy said, turning to introduce Fields. "This is Detective Stan Fields from the Pierce County Sheriff's Office. They had original jurisdiction over Andrea's disappearance."

Fields extended a hand and introduced himself.

Orr looked and sounded flustered. "I'm sorry, I'm just a little out of sorts."

"May we come in for a minute?" Tracy said.

Orr hesitated, then opened the door and stepped back. "I don't have a lot of time. I'm packing for a trip."

Tracy noticed two large suitcases in the front hallway. "We'll try not to keep you long," she said. "Do you have a plane to catch?"

"What?" She paused, then said, "Oh, yes, a little later today."

"Where are you going?" Fields asked.

"Florida," she said. "To visit a friend."

"You're bringing a lot of clothes for Florida," Fields said. "Most people I know live in shorts and tank tops down there."

Orr smiled but otherwise did not respond. The apartment had the lemon-fresh smell of a disinfectant, and it looked as if it had recently undergone an industrial cleaning. The television broadcast the local news. Orr picked up the remote from the coffee table and shut it off.

"Can I offer you something to drink?"

"I think we're fine," Tracy said.

"I had my coffee fill on the plane," Fields said.

They moved to the couches. Orr sat in the same location she had during Tracy's prior visit. Tracy sat on the adjacent couch, Fields to her right.

"You said there might be a development?" Orr said. "It must be important for you to travel all this way."

The most logical reason for a police officer to travel two states to talk to a relative of a presumed victim would be to tell them they had confirmed the person's death. Orr looked anxious, but not as though she was awaiting devastating news.

"We think it could be," Tracy said. She wanted to take a slow approach with Orr, and build up to asking her about the birth certificate after laying certain groundwork that would make Orr less likely to deny her involvement. "We spoke to the Mount Rainier Search and Rescue ranger who conducted the search for Andrea. He's convinced Andrea didn't die on the mountain."

"He is?"

"Yes. He thinks the odds of finding so much of her equipment, but not finding her body, is unlikely."

"Then what does he think happened to her?"

A rhythmic thumping and metallic clang drew Tracy's attention to the sliding-glass door, which was open a crack. Construction equipment worked in the vacant dirt lot next door. With all the construction in downtown Seattle, she recognized the sound of a machine pounding a pier into the ground.

"I'm sorry," Orr said. "They're building another apartment complex."

"That's all right," Tracy said. "As I was saying, the ranger thinks it's much more likely Andrea walked off the mountain early that morning."

Orr didn't immediately respond. Again, Tracy would have expected a relative to have some reaction to the news—elation, hope, greater concern. Orr finally said, "But you don't know what happened to her?"

"What the ranger is having a more difficult time understanding is how Andrea could have gotten off the mountain without any help."

"What does that mean?"

"It means he believes it's certainly possible Andrea descended the mountain on her own, but if she did, she would have needed transportation to get away."

"But this is just speculation, right? He doesn't really know."

"It could be," Tracy said. "But he's pretty certain she walked off the mountain."

"Then, perhaps she rented a car and left it someplace," Orr said.

"Unlikely," Fields said. "Rental car agreements are easy to trace. We did a search for her name and the name Lynn Hoff, but didn't get any hits."

At the mention of the name, which Tracy had not wanted to use this early in the conversation, she thought she noticed a flicker of recognition in Orr's eyes, though it could have been recognition of the name from their earlier conversation. Wanting to retake control of the interview, she jumped back in. "Have you heard that name before?" Tracy asked. "Lynn Hoff?"

"No, I don't believe I have," Orr said. "Who is she?"

"The ranger believes that to get off the mountain, Andrea would have required some assistance, someone with a car."

"And you think it was this Lynn Hoff," Orr said.

"No," Tracy said. "Lynn Hoff was an alias Andrea used."

"An alias? What for?"

"To get a Washington driver's license and to open bank accounts."

"Maybe a friend helped her then," Orr said, hands in her lap but picking at a fingernail.

"We considered that," Tracy said. "But Andrea didn't have many friends. In fact, according to the people I've spoken to, including you, Andrea really only had one friend—a woman by the name of Devin Chambers."

"Have you spoken to her?" Orr asked.

Again, Tracy watched carefully for any sign Orr was familiar with the name, but she did not get an immediate read. "We don't think she would have been inclined to assist Andrea," Tracy said.

Orr seemed to be having difficulty swallowing. "Why not?"

"We've learned some things about Devin Chambers in our investigation; she appears to have been having an affair with Andrea's husband. She also appears to have tried to take the money in Andrea's trust fund."

"That's terrible," Orr said. "She should be arrested. Have you located her?"

"She left Portland around the same time Andrea disappeared," Fields said. "She told her employer she was returning home to the East Coast, but that never happened."

"We traced her to a motel in Renton, Washington," Tracy said. "She'd been using the name Lynn Hoff as an alias."

"I thought you said that was Andrea's alias."

"It was," Tracy said.

"I don't understand," Orr said.

"It means Devin Chambers knew about the alias and about the money," Fields said. "She'd used some of the money to try and change her appearance. We think she was going to steal the money and run."

"Do you have her in custody? What does she have to say about it?" If Orr was acting, she was giving a plausible performance.

"Devin Chambers was the woman found in the crab pot," Tracy said. "The one we initially thought to be Andrea. You might have seen it on the news."

Outside, the rhythmic thumping continued. "No," Orr said. She paused. After a moment she said, "I don't know what to say."

"You told me Andrea never really made any friends when she moved here," Tracy said. "She didn't have any parents, of course, and no siblings. We're trying to determine who might have helped her."

"Maybe someone she knew from Santa Monica," Orr said. "A girl-friend from back then."

"Maybe," Tracy said. "But that's a huge risk for someone to take for a friend she hasn't seen or spoken with in years." She paused, watching Orr. When Orr didn't speak, Tracy continued. "We think it was someone Andrea was close to. Someone who would have understood all the tragedy Andrea had endured in her life. Someone who would have had sympathy for her, who would have wanted to help her, who felt an obligation to help her. We can understand that, Mrs. Orr; we can understand why you would have wanted to help your niece."

"Me?" Orr scoffed and shook her head. She looked at each of them. "You think I did it? That's ridiculous. I told you I don't know where she is . . . or even if she is still alive."

"I know that's what you told me," Tracy said. "And I understand why you told me, but Andrea was able to obtain a Washington State driver's license in the name Lynn Hoff because she had a certified copy of a California birth certificate for a woman named Lynn Hoff, a woman who was born here in San Bernardino," Tracy said. "You've worked at the County Assessor's office in San Bernardino for many years, haven't you?"

Orr maintained her composure though she continued fidgeting with her fingers. "Yes."

"And the County Assessor's Office merged with the County Recorder's Office and the County Clerk's Office to cut expenses. Didn't it?"

"So," Orr said.

"So, you would have had access to birth records," Fields said.

"Everybody in those offices would have had access to those records," Orr said. Her voice shook.

"Yes," Tracy said, "but not everybody was related to a young woman seeking a new life."

"We can get a subpoena," Fields said, "and find out when the certified copy of the birth certificate was obtained from the recorder's office. Identity theft is a crime."

Tracy refrained from looking at Fields. She quickly added, "But we're not interested in doing that, Mrs. Orr. Anyone in your situation would have done the same thing given the circumstances. What happened to Andrea is tragic. If anyone ever deserved the chance at a new life, she certainly did. We just want to find her and talk to her."

Tears trickled down Orr's cheeks. She closed her eyes and dropped her chin to her chest, making no effort to wipe the tears away. Outside, the pile driver clanged a steady, rhythmic beat. Slowly, Orr shook her head. Then she spoke in a shaky voice that barely rose above a whisper.

"Why?" She opened her eyes and looked at Tracy. "Hasn't she been hurt enough? Why can't people just leave her alone? She didn't deserve any of the things that happened to her. Why can't you just let her be?" She said the last words as if making a plea.

"I'm sorry," Tracy said, feeling no elation or even relief. "I wish we could. I'm sorry for Andrea, and I'm sorry for you. No one deserves what happened to her, especially so young. I know you were only trying to protect her, and that you believed in your heart you were doing what was best for Andrea, but there are other families now that also have to be considered."

"She couldn't do it any other way," Orr said, "not after her husband signed bank documents in her name. She was going to lose the only thing she had left, the only thing that she could use to get away. Don't you understand? It was the only thing she had left that connected her to her parents."

"I understand," Tracy said.

"No," Orr said, finding her voice and vehemently shaking her head. "No, you don't understand."

"My sister was murdered when I was twenty-two," Tracy said. In her peripheral vision she saw Fields glance at her. Orr looked stunned. "I lost my father shortly thereafter. He shot himself. The grief was too much for him."

"My God," Orr said. "I'm sorry."

"My husband at the time also left me. I lost an entire town and way of life. So I do understand why you did it. But some things have happened because of Andrea's disappearance. People have died. We have to find out why. That's our job. We have to find out why for the families of those other victims."

"You think Andrea is somehow responsible?" Orr paused, looking to both of them. "That's absurd. Andrea wouldn't hurt anyone. All she wants to do is hike and read."

"We still need to talk to her."

For nearly a minute, Orr didn't say a word. She sat looking out the sliding-glass door. A wisp of black smoke spiraled in the hot air. The machine continued to clang. Fields looked to Tracy, who slowly shook her head. She hoped he had the sense not to speak.

"I want to be there," Orr said finally. "I want to be there when you talk to her."

"Absolutely," Tracy said, feeling a sense of relief but also excitement. "We just need you to take us to her."

CHAPTER 33

Penny Orr had sequestered her niece in a family cabin in a town called Seven Pines. From what Tracy could determine, Seven Pines consisted of half a dozen houses at an elevation of more than six thousand feet in the eastern Sierra Nevada Mountains, a roughly three-and-a-half-hour drive north on US 395. Orr explained that the cabin had been in her mother's family for more than sixty years. The family had used it to escape the city on weekends and for extended vacations. If a person was looking to get lost, this was the place to do it. The closest "city" was Independence, with a population of fewer than one thousand. Orr said the cabin had no television, no Internet, no cell reception, and an outhouse.

Tracy called Faz and told him Andrea Strickland was alive, and Penny Orr was taking them to her. Faz asked if she wanted him to talk to the local police. She told him she didn't think it necessary, but she would call him back if something changed.

They decided to take two cars, in case they needed to talk with the local police or seek an arrest warrant. Tracy drove Penny Orr's personal car with Orr in the passenger seat. Fields followed in the rental. Orr said little during the drive, spending most of the time looking out the passenger-side window, fidgeting with her hands, and wiping away tears. At one point she looked over at Tracy and asked, "What will happen to her?"

"It's really too early to speculate," Tracy said. "Until we talk to her and get a better idea of what happened and why, I can't say. What's her mental state?"

"Her mental state? Fine. Why?"

"Her counselor said it was possible Andrea had a break from reality."

"A break from reality?"

"He said she could be prone to violent acts if she became desperate. Have you witnessed anything like that?"

"No," Orr said. "Andrea's not violent. Is that what you think? Do you think Andrea killed Devin Chambers? Andrea couldn't kill anyone. She doesn't have it in her."

"Does she have access to a car?"

Orr chuckled. "Yes. The family kept a Jeep there but it hasn't been registered in years." Orr seemed to give this some thought. "You don't know."

"Don't know what?" Tracy said.

Orr looked as if she were about to speak, then caught herself. "You'll see," she said. "You'll see why she had to run."

As they continued northeast, the US 395 blacktop with its double yellow line cut a sharp contrast to the brown foothills and smothering pale-blue sky. They drove past dilapidated one-room miner shacks and abandoned towns of cement-block buildings set amid high-desert sage and rabbitbrush, cacti, stands of Joshua trees, and fields of jagged lava rock. As they neared Independence, the scenery again changed, the desolate Onion Valley looming, surrounded by the majestic, jagged peaks of the eastern Sierra Nevada. Mount Whitney, sickly gray and snowcapped, rose as the most prominent.

Near three in the afternoon, they reached Independence. Tracy briefly scanned the town for hotels as they drove through the surface streets, in case they had to spend the night. They turned west on Onion Valley Road, a winding ascent into the foothills that, because of the curves, seemed longer than the posted five miles.

As they approached a stand of trees, Orr said, "Slow down. Turn here." They left the asphalt for a dirt road, continuing through the trees and hugging a teal-blue mountain stream. After a hundred yards, Orr directed Tracy to a small area cleared of trees where an old Jeep Willys sat. "Park here. The cabin is just up the path."

Tracy parked beside the Jeep, amazed from its appearance that the car still ran. Fields, following, parked next to her.

"Does she have any weapons?" Tracy asked.

Orr shrugged. "My father has a shotgun. He used it to kill snakes."

"Where is it located?"

"In the closet in the bedroom. I don't think it's been fired in years."

"Any other weapons? A handgun?"

"No," Orr said. She let out a painful sigh. "Can I talk to her first and try to explain? She's not going to understand."

Not knowing the layout of the cabin, and given that there was at least one weapon inside the building, Tracy couldn't allow that to happen. "I'm sorry, I can't do that. But once we get inside and I secure things, I'll give you time to speak to her."

They pushed out of the car. The air had become muggy and thick. Billowing white clouds gathered in the distance over the many mountain peaks surrounding the valley. An oval-shaped lenticular cloud hovered like a UFO. Tracy's father had taught her to read the weather so she would not get caught unprepared. She knew lenticular clouds formed when hot air rose and collided with cooler air. On a mountain, such as Rainier, the clouds could be harbingers of the kind of storms that could kill.

Orr led Tracy and Fields along a dirt path lined with river stones and railroad ties, the only sound the trickling of the stream and the buzz of unseen insects. Another ten yards and Tracy saw a wooden walk, a bridge over a stream leading to a cabin nestled among the pines. Forest-green with a red door, the cabin sat on a foundation of river stones, with a chimney made of the same rocks protruding above the roof. At first glance, the cabin looked like something out of a fairy tale where a gnome or elf might live. It made Tracy think of the Alki Point Lighthouse, and Dan's desire that Tracy have a fairy-tale wedding. It also made her think the cabin was a perfect place for someone whom the world had crapped on to run and hide.

After crossing the bridge, they stepped down to dirt, then climbed two steps to a small porch. The clunk of their shoes echoed on the wood. Orr knocked on the door. She looked like she'd aged during the drive, like someone about to commit an unspeakable betrayal. Noise inside the cabin indicated someone moving about. Instinctively, Tracy reached across her body and gripped the butt of her gun. Orr didn't wait for the door to open. She pushed it in and called out, "Andrea?"

Andrea Strickland had been smiling when Orr opened the door. That smile fell quickly, and her expression changed from bewilderment to the purest expression of pain and resignation.

"I'm sorry," Penny Orr said.

So was Tracy. She now understood what Orr had been alluding to, why Andrea Strickland had been so desperate to get away.

—

The inside of the small cabin looked like an independent bookstore that had outgrown its space. Stacks of books cluttered the furniture, the kitchen table, and the bench seat beneath leaded-glass windows that distorted the view outside. They filled crates in the corners of the room, and overflowed bookshelves. Tracy saw hardbacks and paperbacks of every genre, novels and nonfiction, autobiographies.

Tracy asked Andrea Strickland and Penny Orr to sit on a two-cushion couch while she went to the bedroom closet to secure an old, 12-gauge, Crack Barrel Shotgun, the kind her father had used in shooting competitions. The gun was not loaded, and it didn't look as though it had been fired anytime recently, though it was kept in good condition. She also took a box of shells from the closet shelf. She handed the shotgun and shells to Fields, who set the shells on the mantel and leaned the barrel against the river-rock fireplace hearth. Tracy moved a stack of books from the window seat and sat directly across from the two women. The two-room cabin consisted of the living room and a kitchen area with a tiny wood-burning stove and a refrigerator. In the back, the bedroom was not much bigger than the queen-size wrought-iron bed. In the living room, two wooden posts extended from beneath the floor to wood ceiling trusses, and the room retained the smell of burned wood from the blackened fireplace.

"Andrea inherited her love of reading from my mother," Orr said with a sad smile. She gripped Andrea's hand. "Grandma would come here and read three books in a day. She wore out the library in Independence, but she didn't like having to return the books, so she bought crates at used bookstores and brought them up here."

Andrea Strickland did not raise her gaze from the bearskin rug on the wood-plank floor.

"It looks like a wide variety," Tracy said. "Do you have a favorite genre?"

Strickland glanced at Tracy, then back at the floor. "No," she said softly.

"How far along are you?" Tracy asked. She'd noticed the telltale bump beneath Andrea's stretch pants.

Andrea lifted her head again. "Just a little more than six months now."

"And your husband doesn't know."

Andrea shook her head. "No."

Andrea Strickland was not crazy or vindictive. She had, however, been desperate to get away from an abusive husband intent on killing her, and, unknowingly, her unborn child.

"Andrea, your aunt didn't want to tell us where you were. I found the birth certificate for Lynn Hoff. I figured it out," Tracy said.

Strickland nodded. Orr squeezed her niece's hand.

"I think you can imagine we have some questions, Andrea, about what happened. Will you speak to me?"

"Does she need a lawyer?" Orr asked.

That was always the $64,000 question for the witness and the police officer. Strickland was not in police custody so her right to an attorney under the Fifth Amendment had not been triggered. She had also not been charged with a crime, which meant her Sixth Amendment right had also not been triggered. Given the location of the cabin and the condition of the Jeep, Tracy now had serious doubts Strickland could have killed Devin Chambers or Megan Chen. She'd faked her own death, but to do so was neither a federal nor a state crime. She had not illegally recovered any insurance proceeds, nor was she seeking to avoid paying state or federal taxes. She'd used a fake identification to open bank accounts, but not to commit forgery or fraud, since the money belonged to her. As for defaulting on the bank loans and the lease, her husband had admitted to forging her name on the personal guarantees. Whether her separate property was susceptible to those creditors remained a civil, not a criminal, issue.

In other words, Tracy had no basis to arrest her.

The ugly issue of jurisdiction had also resurfaced again. Tracy and Fields had crossed state lines to speak to a witness, who had led them to another witness. Without a court order, they did not have authority to arrest Andrea Strickland or to extradite her back to either Oregon or Washington, even if they decided they had a basis to do so.

Andrea Strickland had run because she was pregnant, her husband had planned to kill her, and she'd decided she could not risk him killing her baby, or raising a child with such a man. Inside, Tracy was applauding her decision.

"At the moment we just want to talk," Tracy said. "If you prefer to have an attorney present, I'll honor that request. It's up to you."

Orr looked to her niece, who glanced up but gave no indication of her desire. Orr reconsidered Tracy. "Can we have a minute?"

"Sure," Tracy said.

Tracy nodded to Fields and the two of them stepped outside. Fields immediately reached for his pack of cigarettes and lighter, lighting up and blowing smoke into the air. In such a pristine location, it seemed a fundamental violation of the beauty of nature.

"What do you think?" Fields asked. "Personally, I think she's nuts. The aunt might be too."

Tracy bit her tongue. Fields was so predictable. "I think she's a young woman who the world shit on who didn't want the same thing for her child."

"You're a bleeding heart, Crosswhite." He took a drag and blew smoke into the sky. "What do we do if she won't talk? If we leave, she could run again. She's got all that money hidden someplace, and the aunt had her bags packed and ready to go. I'm not buying the trip-to-Florida story."

"We don't have any basis to arrest her."

"What are you talking about? At a minimum, she's a suspect in Devin Chambers's death. She had a clear motive, two actually—the money, and the fact that Chambers was sleeping with her husband."

Tracy almost laughed. "Motive maybe, but not opportunity—not if she's been living out here the whole time."

"Who knows whether that's true or not? She could have driven up to Washington, killed Chambers, and driven back."

"Driven in what? That Jeep isn't licensed and doesn't look like it would make fifty miles."

"She could've rented a car. She could have driven the aunt's car."

"How did she find Chambers?"

"She hired the PI. She drives down into Independence, sets up a guerilla account, gets on public Wi-Fi, and makes inquiries. You said there was a lag time in between her e-mails to the PI and the investigator's responses. This could be why. She was living out here, off the grid. She had to go into town to get Wi-Fi."

"Does she look to you like she wants to run anywhere?" Tracy said. "This is heaven for her. No one bothers her. She doesn't have to deal with a world that has treated her like a doormat. She has her books to read. Mountains to hike. Why would she want to go anyplace else?"

"Because she's got a kid on the way," Fields said. "What, is she going to give birth in a cabin?"

It wasn't a bad point.

"I'm sure Independence has a hospital," Tracy said. "We don't have enough to arrest her."

Fields blew more smoke out the side of his mouth. "Yeah, well, if Strickland decides she's not talking to us, I'm going to arrest her."

"For what?" Tracy said, becoming irritated. "You have a missing persons case. Far as I can tell, you found her. There's no crime in anything that we know that she's done. Your case is closed. Devin Chambers is my case, and I can't arrest Andrea Strickland without an arrest warrant, even if I believed I had sufficient cause."

Footsteps sounded, someone approaching the door. Penny Orr stepped out onto the porch. "Andrea said she has something to tell you."

Tracy stepped past Fields and followed Orr inside.

Andrea remained seated on the couch, but she no longer looked sullen. She looked shocked and saddened. Before Tracy could say a word, Andrea said, "I killed Devin."

Tracy's heart felt like it had leapt into her throat. She glanced quickly at Fields, uncertain what to say, or even if she could get the words out.

"So you killed her?" Fields said.

Tracy snapped back to reality. "Don't answer that. Don't say another word."

"I didn't mean to," Strickland said. "I just wanted to punish them for what they did to me."

"What did I say?" Fields said to Tracy. He removed handcuffs from the back of his belt.

"Andrea, I'm cautioning you not to say another word." She turned to Fields and raised a hand. Fields stopped. Tracy nodded for him to step back outside.

On the porch, Fields wore a shit-eating I-told-you-so grin. "You see, Crosswhite, you just never know with people."

"Nothing she says is admissible."

"The hell it ain't."

"We haven't read her her Miranda rights."

"So I'll read them and ask again."

"Just hang on a second, okay? I'm going to drive down into Independence where I can get cell phone reception and make some calls to get some advice. I'll find the local sheriff and ask him to take her into custody until I can get an arrest warrant that includes extradition back to Washington State. You don't need to handcuff her. Where is she going to run? Just read her her Miranda rights and make sure she acknowledges them, but do not interview her. This is my case. Are we good?"

"Yeah, we're good," Fields said, smiling. "Like I've been saying, this ain't my first rodeo."

"Keys," she said.

Fields tossed her the car keys. Tracy left quickly, crossing the wooden bridge and heading down the dirt path to the rental. She backed the car out and punched the accelerator, leaving a cloud of dirt and dust. She turned onto the paved road and drove down the hill with her cell phone in hand, alternately checking for reception and trying to keep the car on the road. Halfway down the mountain her phone had two bars. She'd missed three phone calls in five minutes, all from SPD. She also had one text message, from Faz.

Alternately shifting her gaze from the winding road to her phone, she read the text.

Call me ASAP. Development in Strickland. Important.

She pulled onto the shoulder and dialed the number. It seemed to take forever for the call to connect.

Faz spoke before she could say hello. "Professor, where the . . . you been? I've been . . . hold of you."

"I'm out of cell range. You're breaking up."

"Professor?"

"Faz?" The phone beeped. The call had failed. "Damn."

She gave a fleeting thought to hitting redial, then decided to get farther down the mountain. She pulled back onto the pavement and navigated the turns. Her phone rang in her hand. She hit the "Speaker" button. "Faz?"

"Yeah. Can you hear me?"

"You're still breaking up."

"We got . . . back."

"Say that again," she said.

"We got the computer . . . back."

"You got the computer forensics back? Faz? What did it say?"

"Professor?"

"Faz, can you hear me?"

"You're really hard to . . . trace the guerilla e-mail account and . . . Wi-Fi address. The e-mail . . . generated from a public address . . . a restaurant . . ."

"I missed it, Faz. Say it again."

"A public address . . . Tacoma . . . Viola."

The car drifted to the right, onto the dirt shoulder. Tracy hit the brakes, spraying dust and gravel, corrected, crossed the centerline, corrected a second time, and pulled to the shoulder and stopped. She sat stunned.

Fields.

Fields had been looking for Devin Chambers. *My God.*

"Professor?"

The phone. "Faz? Faz?"

He didn't answer. "Faz? Faz, I don't know if you can hear me. I'm in a small town in the Sierra Nevada Mountains called Seven Pines. Seven Pines. The closest town is Independence. Faz? Shit. Faz, call the sheriff. Tell him I'm in need of immediate assistance. Faz?" She had no way of knowing if the call was still transmitting, but at least it had not yet died. "Tell him it's the green cabin with the red door. First right turn off the paved road. Tell him to . . ."

The line went dead.

CHAPTER 34

Tracy debated driving down the hill, into Independence, where there was reception, but that would take time and she'd left Fields alone with Strickland and Orr. Her stomach churning, she turned the car around and headed back up the mountain. It made sense now, at least some of it. Fields had presumed Andrea Strickland was dead. He would have known about the money from his investigation and believed Graham Strickland killed his wife for that money. When the money disappeared, Fields would have gone looking for Strickland and for Andrea Strickland's only friend and learned that Devin Chambers had left Portland the same time Strickland disappeared, along with the money. Maybe Fields had withheld other evidence, evidence that convinced him Devin Chambers had taken the money, that she and Graham Strickland had had an affair. Tracy didn't know for sure. What she did know was that to a bad cop, this was like the drug money Fields had spent a decade chasing in Arizona. It was free money. Strickland was presumed dead. Her husband was going to jail. If he could find Devin Chambers, he could find the money, half a million in cash for the taking.

Fields couldn't use police resources to find Chambers, but he didn't have to. He'd spent a decade pursuing drug dealers, living off the grid in the Arizona desert, and finding their well-hidden money. He knew how they laundered money and he knew how to get it. The money was right there. All he had to do was kill Devin Chambers and tell everyone she had absconded with it, and disappeared to points unknown. That's why he'd stuffed her body in a crab pot, seemingly never to be found. Tracy thought again of her conversation with Kins while sitting in the processing room at the Medical Examiner's office waiting for the autopsy. Kins had said a body in a crab pot was a first for King County, but it wasn't a first. Pierce County had prosecuted a prior crab pot case, just two years earlier.

Fields.

If she was right, he was more than just a bad cop. He was a killer. He'd killed Chambers, and he would have gotten away with it, a seemingly perfect plan, until Kurt Schill's one-in-a-million snag pulled up the wrong pot. That brought in another police agency, an agency that was going to dig into the matter. That's why Fields had fought so hard to keep jurisdiction. He didn't want anyone else poking around in his weeds. Once Schill found the pot, Fields needed to make Graham Strickland look like a cold-blooded killer, or at least direct the attention back to him. As the investigating detective into Andrea Strickland's disappearance, Fields had been to the Pearl Street loft, even searched it. He would have known the details on the security at the building, including the keypad in the elevator and on the front door.

It also explained Penny Orr's reluctance to provide her DNA. She didn't want Tracy to find out it was not Andrea Strickland in the pot. It was easier for Orr and for Andrea if Andrea was presumed dead.

Tracy slowed at the turn for the dirt road. Fields had likely gone looking for Graham Strickland at his apartment and instead found Megan Chen asleep in Strickland's bed. He'd killed her too. Tracy had no doubt he'd kill Andrea Strickland and Penny Orr, and she'd just given him that chance. Then he'd kill her. Except right now he didn't know Tracy knew he'd been the one to hire the PI to find Devin Chambers. For the moment, at least, Tracy had the element of surprise.

She hoped that was all she needed.

She drove slowly back to the small parking area, killing the engine the final few feet. She checked her Glock, chambering a round, and quietly exited the car. Slowly, she made her way up the path, gun held low and at her side. She stopped behind a pine tree at the wooden bridge, watching the cabin, hearing the trickle of the creek and the buzz of insects but not seeing anyone. She crossed the bridge to the two wooden steps leading to the porch, eyes scanning the area. Glock in hand, she leaned to look in the leaded windows. Strickland and Orr remained seated on the couch. She did not see Fields.

"Don't move."

The voice came from behind her, slow and deliberate. She heard Fields step around the corner of the house and instantly calculated whether she was fast enough to spin and get off a shot.

"Let the gun drop from your hand, Crosswhite," Fields said. "Let it drop, or I'll drop you where you stand. I said, drop the gun."

Tracy dropped the gun. It hit the wood porch with a dull thud. Inside the house, Orr and Andrea Strickland looked toward the window.

"Turn around."

Tracy raised her hands—a subtle signal to the women inside the house—and turned to face Fields. Fields took another step from around the edge of the house, gun raised and pointed at her. Tracy knew she'd made the right decision. Fields would have shot her before she'd turned.

"You're back awfully soon," he said, kicking the gun away. "Much too quick to have located the local sheriff and made your phone calls. I'm guessing that when you got partway down the mountain you got cell reception about the same location I noticed that I'd lost it. And I'm betting you got an interesting piece of information concerning a certain guerilla e-mail account. Am I right?"

"Why, Fields?" Tracy asked, the words bitter in her mouth.

Fields smiled. "Why not?"

"When did you turn?"

"Turn? Interesting choice of words. Let's just say I picked up a few bad habits working undercover. You see, I realized that with every bust there was all that money unaccounted for, untraceable, not to mention all that product. I'd spent all my time learning how they distributed it so as not to get caught. A fortune. I decided I was playing on the wrong side."

"What about your wife? What about what she died for?"

Fields smiled but it was dark. "Well, let's just say we didn't see eye to eye on things when she found out."

"*You* killed her." Tracy nearly spat the words.

"Depends on your point of view. Drug bust gone wrong," he said, still smiling. "It happens all the time. Agent gets in deep and someone blows her cover. Mine got blown right after they found out about her. No choice but to leave the area."

Tracy had been so fixated on disliking Fields, she wondered whether she'd missed the signs—she could now vividly see all the evidence pointing directly at him. "So when you thought Andrea Strickland was dead, and that her husband had killed her, you saw a chance to get her money."

"You met him. He certainly didn't deserve it."

"But you didn't count on someone having the same thought, and beating you to it."

"It was almost comical when you think about it, the way Devin Chambers played him. Beautiful, really. Poetic justice. She actually offered to split the money with me. I had to give her credit for ingenuity, but I couldn't go through life worrying about her coming back or doing or saying something stupid."

"And the Pierce County crab pot case, was that yours?"

"No, but I did admire that guy's creativity. It's even better than leaving a body in the desert for the animals to feed on. In that instance, you still got bones. Drop a crab pot in the water and there's nothing left of the person, unless some kid hits a one-in-a-million snag and pulls up the pot." He shook his head. "What are the odds, huh?"

"Yeah," Tracy said. "What are the odds? But it doesn't matter now, Fields. Look around you. Where are you going to go?"

His smile broadened. "Are you kidding? Anywhere in the world. I got everything in that bag I brought with me. Fake passports. Disguises. This gun—who knows where it came from? I used to pick these things up half a dozen at a time. It's untraceable. So by the time anyone finds what's left of the three of you out there, if they find you, I'll be long gone. Hell, they might even think my body is out there somewhere too, dragged off by the wildlife. I take Orr's car, or maybe the Jeep, and I drive out of here. I told you, Crosswhite, the desert used to be my home. Now it can be yours."

CHAPTER 35

Fields directed Tracy back inside the house, where they both got a surprise. Penny Orr and Andrea Strickland no longer sat on the couch, and the shotgun no longer leaned against the river-rock fireplace.

"Shit," Fields said, keeping the gun on Tracy as he moved to the back of the cabin and glanced into the room. Tracy felt a breeze from the bedroom and couldn't help but smile.

Fields swore and removed the handcuffs from his belt. "Hug the post, Crosswhite." He motioned to one of the two floor posts bracing the ceiling.

Tracy didn't immediately move. "You know you're not going to get away with this, Fields." She wanted to give Andrea Strickland and Penny Orr as much time as possible to get away. Orr had said Strickland liked to read and to hike, that she had hiked these mountains growing up. Hopefully, Strickland knew the area well, knew its hiding places. Tracy doubted Fields would kill her and risk leaving blood in the cabin so she decided to push the situation.

"I've already called my office, Fields. My guys have people on the way. They know you were the guy who hired the skip tracer. Viola, seriously?" She laughed. "What the hell were you thinking?"

Fields stepped forward, the muzzle of the gun just a foot from her forehead. "I was thinking no one was going to find the body. Now, hug the damn post or I'll drag your body into the mountains, shoot you, and let the animals eat your intestines. I don't really give a shit."

Tracy stepped forward and put her arms around the post. Fields snapped on the handcuffs, started off, then stopped. "I never did like you," he said, and swung the butt of the gun, striking her at the temple.

—

I sensed something wrong as soon as Detective Crosswhite left the room to drive back into town. The other detective, Fields, stepped outside and watched her leave. He returned smoking a cigarette.

"Can you smoke outside?" I asked, thinking of my unborn baby, as well as the large amount of paper in the cabin.

He smiled and flicked ashes onto the floor. "Yeah, a fire out here would be a problem, wouldn't it?"

"I meant the smoke."

"You don't need to worry about that. So, Andrea, where's the money?"

With that one question, I knew Stan Fields had killed Devin Chambers. I'd set her up, just as I'd set up Graham, but it had never been my intent for either of them to die. I only wanted her to be punished for what she and Graham had done, what they'd tried to do to me. But ultimately, I knew what I had done had led to her being killed. I felt like I had killed her.

"I don't know what you're talking about," I said. "Don't you have it?"

Another smile. "You're good. I'll give you that. I don't blame you for setting your husband up, by the way. Having met him, I think he got off easy. You had me fooled. I was dead certain he'd killed you. The question was, Why? These things are never complicated though. It's usually a girl-friend out there, or money—insurance. Sometimes all three. So I did some digging and I found out there's also a big pile of cash unaccounted for. If I can prove he killed you, he's going to jail, and there isn't anybody else out there who knows about the money or cares." He flicked his ashes on the floor again. "Except . . . the girlfriend turns out to be worse than the husband. She'd played him for the money, then went missing the same time you and the money disappeared. So I pull a search warrant for her apartment and for her workstation, grab her computers, and I find a nice trail of evidence that she and hubby were doing the nasty and she had your alias, Lynn Hoff. Tell me, was that part of your plan to set her up?"

"I never wanted her to die," I said. "I just wanted to get away from them and give my baby a better life—the kind of life I had before the car accident. I never thought she'd go after the money."

"You see, your problem was you underestimated her. She was a first-rate con, and to a con, it's all about the money. They don't see things the way you and I see things. They're wired different. They see your money, but to them, it's their money. You just have it temporarily, until they can take it from you."

"So you killed her?"

Fields shrugged. "Had to. But before I could move the money, someone beat me to it. That's when I figured you were still alive. No way Graham knew where the money was, nor would he go after it with me pushing the DA to name him a person of interest in your disappearance. So I'll ask again. Where's the money?"

I didn't answer.

Fields dropped the butt of his cigarette to the floor. It glowed red, smoldering, but he made no effort to crush it with his shoe. He removed his gun and pointed it at my aunt's head.

I was about to speak when Stan Fields turned his head at a sound outside, a car engine. He stepped back to the door and looked out. I knew it was a car. I'd become accustomed to the noises out here.

"Stay here," he said. "Move, and I will kill you both."

Tracy's head ached as if it had split open. As darkness gave way to blurred images, she realized she sat slumped on the floor of Andrea Strickland's cabin, handcuffed to a post. She pulled her body closer to the post to remove the strain on her wrists, wincing at the pain. She lowered her head and touched her fingers to her scalp. When she pulled back, her fingertips were bloody. Slowly, she struggled to one knee. The room spun like a carnival ride and she hugged the post to keep from falling over. When the spinning slowed, she managed to get to her feet, sliding her cuffed wrists up the pole. Nauseated, she fought the urge to throw up and waited for her vision to clear. When it did, she had a bigger problem—getting free. She looked up. The post had been bolted to the ceiling crossbeam with a metal bracket. She looked down. The post went through the floor, likely bolted to a foundation pier. She tugged on the post anyway. It didn't budge. The cabin had been built to last. The post wasn't going anywhere.

Outside the front windows, the sky had darkened, but not from the passage of time. The weather had changed. The distant clouds had rolled in over the mountaintops, everything a rapidly darkening gray. Thunder rumbled in the distance, miles off, and the wind had also picked up. She hoped the dark sky and weather would help to hide Andrea Strickland and Penny Orr.

She looked around the cabin for anything she might be able to use to get out of the cuffs, seeing nothing, growing more frustrated by the minute. She hoped, at least, that Andrea Strickland knew the mountains, knew a place to hide, and would maybe ambush Fields with the shotgun.

She heard what she thought to be another burst of thunder, then realized it was the sound of boots on the wooden bridge.

Someone coming. Fields?

She stepped around the pole so the wood was between her and the door. A uniformed police officer crossed in front of the leaded windows. He wore a khaki-colored shirt and forest-green pants.

"Hey! Hey!" Tracy called out.

The deputy stepped over something on the walk and stepped inside, hand on his gun. "Are you Detective Crosswhite?"

Faz. Her message had gotten through. Faz had not let her down.

"Yeah. Yeah, I am. Did you see anyone else out there?"

"No."

"My badge is on my belt."

The deputy stepped in. He looked midthirties, shaved head, well built. "We got a call from Seattle said there was an officer in need of immediate assistance."

"That would be me. There's a guy around here with a gun, so keep your eyes and ears open. You got a key to the cuffs?"

He holstered his weapon, moving quickly to undo her handcuffs while keeping one eye on the door and window.

Cuffs off, Tracy rubbed circulation back into her wrists. "Tracy Crosswhite," she said. "Seattle PD."

"Rick Pearson," he said. "Inyo County Sheriff's office. What's Seattle PD doing way out here?"

"Came to talk to a witness. How many cars did you see parked out there?"

"Uh . . . two . . . and a Jeep. What the hell is going on?"

Fields was still here.

"Is it just you?"

"Yeah. We're a substation in Independence. There's another deputy working who I can call in. And I can call down to the main office."

"Where's the main office?" She moved to the porch but had to brace herself against the door frame when she became suddenly dizzy.

"That's a nasty cut on the side of your head."

Tracy touched the wound and shook away more cobwebs. "Where's the main office?"

"Bishop."

"How far is that?"

"Forty-five minutes."

"We're going to need as many people as you can get." She stepped onto the porch and retrieved her Glock. "And vehicles equipped for driving out in that terrain."

"Vehicles won't get far out here. Especially not with a storm rolling in."

The storm was a problem Tracy hadn't considered. She moved across the bridge, back toward the parked cars. "There are two women out there and a bad cop who's going to kill them if he finds them. What kind of firepower do you have in the car?"

They approached the deputy's white-and-green SUV.

"Shotgun and a rifle, extra rounds."

"I'm going to need the rifle," she said. "You radio for all the help you can get. When they get here, tell them we're looking for two women, one is midtwenties and the other is midfifties. The guy with the gun is midfifties, gray ponytail, and mustache. He's armed and extremely dangerous. You got a first aid kit?"

"First aid? Yeah, always."

"Radio for help, then I'd appreciate it if you'd quickly bandage my head."

"Where are you going?"

Tracy looked at the scrub and foreboding mountains. "Out there," she said.

"That's some wicked country out there, Detective."

"That's what I'm hoping," she said.

—

When Fields left the cabin, I turned to my aunt. "He's going to kill us. He has to. He's going to kill us all. We need to go."

"Go where?" she said. I could see the fear on her face and hear it in her voice.

"*The mountains. Come on.*" *I quickly grabbed the shotgun and a handful of shells and hurried to the back of the house. My aunt remained on the couch.* "*Come on,*" *I said, more urgently.*

My aunt got up and followed me into the bedroom. I peered out the back window, but did not see Fields. "*Hold this.*" *I handed her the shotgun and slid the window up, but weather and age had warped the sash, making it stick. I lowered the window, put both hands under the rail, and forced it up with all my strength. The window made a screeching noise and raised six inches higher before again becoming stuck. I wasn't sure we could fit, but the window wasn't going any higher.*

I took back the shotgun. "*You go first.*"

My aunt ducked down and wriggled her body headfirst through the window. I grabbed the back of her legs to keep her from falling. She dropped the last foot onto the ground. I handed her the shotgun and slid through the opening, out onto a bed of rocks and pine needles. I got up, quickly brushed off my hands, and took back the shotgun.

I heard Fields say, "*Don't move.*" *For a moment, I thought he was speaking to us; then I realized he was standing around the corner of the house, talking to someone else. We needed to move, fast. My grandfather had cleared the trees around the cabin, a firebreak. The tree line and cover were about ten yards away. Overhead the sky continued to cloud over, what was sure to be an afternoon thunderstorm, which was not infrequent in the mountains. It got hot in the valley, and the hot air rose and met the cold air over the mountains. Day would become night in minutes; thunder would shake the house, and rain would become a torrent, turning the creek into a river. Hopefully, it would be enough to hide our escape. It was our one chance.*

I grabbed my aunt's hand and pulled her behind me, climbing the incline into the trees and hurrying along the footpath that I'd walked as a child, and daily since my disappearance on Mount Rainier.

Tracy slung the rifle over her shoulder and made her way to the house, going around the back, seeing the open window. "Good girl," she said. She was really starting to like Andrea Strickland. The young woman was resourceful. She was a survivor.

She moved quickly to the tree line, saw what appeared to be a foot-path, and followed it in a slow jog that made her head ache.

The dry and barren terrain was nothing like the North Cascades, which were green and damp. This terrain reminded her of lower Rainier, high rock formations, jagged peaks, and stones, but also a few pine trees, flowers, and scrub.

The altitude burned in her lungs. Lactic acid made the muscles of her legs ache, and the wound on the side of her head throbbed, mak-ing her even more light-headed and nauseated. After several hundred yards, she had to stop to catch her breath. The dark clouds over the sickly gray peaks had deepened in color, roiling like a frothing ocean about to unleash its fury. A burst of lightning lit up the clouds and a blue-white fork descended, crackling as it dropped to the ground. Almost immediately, an explosion shook the ground, followed by a low rumble, as if someone were beating a bass drum. If Fields didn't kill her, the lightning might.

Tracy pressed along a rocky ridgeline, but soon realized she was just running. Andrea Strickland had likely left the designated path, taken a different direction, maybe found a safe hiding place. Tracy did not have the skills to track her, but knew Fields, who'd spent a decade in the desert, could likely read the two women's tracks. What she needed was to get to higher ground, to someplace where she'd have a vantage point on the surrounding area, and, hopefully, see them.

She left the path, her ears fine-tuned to the sound of a shotgun or a handgun firing. She moved up the hillside, toward a rock outcropping beneath one of the jagged peaks. The ground beneath her feet became more and more unstable as the hillside steepened. Her boots slid in the rocks with each step, forcing her to bend over, like a bear, pawing her way up the mountain, breathing heavily, perspiring. Another burst of lightning caused the ground around her to crackle. Instinctively, she dropped to her belly, feeling the hair on her arms twitch and stand on end. She covered her ears as the burst of thunder clapped directly over her. Then she felt the first drops of rain, large pellets of water, hit her in the back and splash against the surrounding rocks.

She got up quickly, continuing to climb, the rifle slung over her shoulder and hanging down her back. She had to be deliberate with her movements to keep from sliding down the hill. She reached the edge of the rock outcropping and estimated the rock formation to be thirty feet high. If she could climb it, she'd have a 360-degree view of the entire valley.

The intensity of the rain increased, soaking her clothing. She pressed on, shaking the water from her eyes, climbing carefully.

When she finally scaled the top, she could see the valley, but had to drop to her belly when another bolt of lightning crackled. This time the thunder was a deep, rolling rumble followed by a thunderous explosion that seemed to shake the mountains. When the noise had passed, Tracy scurried back to her feet, removed the rifle, and fit the lens of the scope to her eye, searching the valley for Andrea Strickland and Penny Orr, for any sign of movement.

Not seeing any.

———

My aunt, not acclimated to the altitude or to the physical exertion, was exhausted and having trouble catching her breath. I grabbed her hand and pulled her up the mountain, feeling her falter. Breathing heavily, she wheezed, the rush of adrenaline and anxiety no doubt making it more difficult to catch her breath. I had worked hard to climb Rainier, and I had spent every day since hiking these mountains. I needed to get us out of the valley and into the cover of the rocks, where we could hide, and where

I might have a chance to use the shotgun. I hadn't fired it since I was a teenager, but my grandfather had taught me well. He always said I didn't have to be perfect. I just had to be in the vicinity of whatever I aimed at.

My aunt slipped and gave a muffled scream, but I managed to keep a grip on her hand and stop her from sliding down the hillside.

"You go on," she said, sitting. "I'm just slowing you down."

"I'm not going on without you," I said. "Get up."

"I can't," she said.

I looked down the mountain and saw Fields hugging the ridgeline. I wasn't certain he'd seen us, but he was following our path and he was closing ground. "Get up, Aunt Penny. Get up now!"

She stumbled to her feet. I looked past her, back down the mountain. Fields had turned, looking directly at us. He lowered his head and started to climb the incline.

"Come on," I said to my aunt, "come on." I yanked my aunt's arm, pulling her. The rocks I hoped to reach were another thirty yards, but it was a sharp ascent. My aunt was never going to make it.

Fields kept coming, legs churning, closing ground.

My aunt slipped again and her hand ripped from my grasp. She slid down the loose rock, rolling onto her side, tumbling. She came to a stop halfway between me and where Fields had halted his progress. He looked up at me and smiled, knowing I couldn't get down the mountain fast enough to reach my aunt before he would get to her.

I dropped to a knee, took aim, and fired.

—

Tracy used the scope on the rifle to scan the valley floor section by section. The clouds and the rain had created a gray shroud, making it difficult to see. Several times, she stopped her progress, focusing on what she thought might be people before realizing it was just an odd rock formation, or a plant of some kind. She lowered the scope and wiped the water from her forehead.

She heard what sounded like another clap of thunder, followed by an echo, then realized there had been no lightning strike. The sound had not come from overhead, but down in the valley, somewhere behind her. She turned and repositioned herself on the rocks, raised the scope to her eye, and looked down the mountain. She saw Fields first. He'd dropped to his belly on the side of the hill. Perhaps fifteen yards farther up the hill lay someone else, Penny Orr. Tracy quickly scanned the area. Still farther up the hill she saw Andrea Strickland, the shotgun in both hands, its butt pressed underneath her arm and against her side.

She watched the barrel kick up and heard the reverberation of the second shot. When she put the scope back to her eye, she saw Fields getting back to his feet. Strickland had missed. She'd have to reload.

She'd never have enough time.

Tracy slid to the edge and rested the barrel of the rifle on a rock. She lowered her body to a prone position and slid forward, pressing her eye to the scope, fighting to focus. The gun was too low.

Fields was on the move again, up the hillside. She could only guess Andrea Strickland was frantically trying to reload.

She grabbed a couple of flat rocks, stacking them, throwing others away, and repositioned the rifle. She pressed her eye tight to the scope. Fields closed ground on Penny Orr, who lay on her side, not moving. Tracy's vision blurred from the rain rolling down her forehead into her eyes. She pulled her eye from the scope and blinked away the water, then fit the eyepiece tightly to her socket. She struggled to align the crosshairs on Fields, who continued to move. She'd never hit his head. A center mass shot to the chest was her only real chance. She hoped the deputy had recently calibrated his weapon. She would either be dead-on, or, at that distance, she could miss by two feet.

Fields reached Orr, pistol in hand. He stood over her, alternately looking down at her and raising his gaze, presumably in the direction of Andrea Strickland. Then he smiled, a smug *you've lost* smile, raised his arm, and took aim.

Tracy pressed the trigger halfway, released a low whistle of air, and pulled the trigger.

———

I shot a second time. Fields fell quickly. For a moment I thought I'd hit him. Then, slowly, he rose to his feet. I'd missed. The shotgun was made for close range and only held two shells. Fields smiled. Then he raised his pistol and fired at me, causing me to drop to the ground. When I looked up, he was on his feet, moving up the mountain, toward my aunt. I sat up, groping in my pockets for the extra shells, but my hands had become cold and stiff from the rain and the drop in temperature. I was having trouble getting the shells out of my pocket. When I did, I realized I hadn't cracked open the barrel of the shotgun.

I looked up. Fields was within yards of my aunt. Close enough to kill her.

I dropped a shell and watched it roll down the hill and out of reach. Shaking, I cracked the barrel, blew into my cupped hand to warm my fingers, and fumbled for the second shell in my pocket, but I was distracted, looking at Fields. He was nearly on top of my aunt. I couldn't insert the second shell, fingers cold and fumbling. Fields looked up at me and smiled. I slipped the shell into the barrel. Fields took aim with the handgun, my aunt still lying prone on the ground. I wouldn't be in time. I snapped closed the barrel and shouted.

"No!"

———

Tracy saw the burst of red, an explosion of blood.

Fields's upper body twitched, a spasm, as if he'd been struck by a jolt of electricity. The arm holding the gun swung wildly. She kept aim through the scope, prepared to fire again, but Fields pitched backward, rolling down the mountain, tumbling head over heels, then sliding and not coming to a stop until he was nearly at the trail.

Tracy kept the scope trained on him, watching for movement. Seeing none.

She moved the scope back up the hill. Andrea Strickland slid and sidestepped down the mountain to her aunt. When she reached her, she dropped to her knees, and they embraced. They stayed that way for a moment, then Andrea looked up to the ridgeline, to where she'd likely heard the shot, to where Tracy crouched.

Tracy pulled the scope from her eye, watching the two women without the aid of magnification. She knew how they felt. Tracy's mother had been her only relative after her father's suicide, but they'd had too short a period of time together. Her mother died of cancer just two years after Sarah disappeared, leaving Tracy alone. She hoped Penny Orr lived a long time. She hoped the two women, both damaged, could be the support each other needed.

She sat back against the rocks and tilted her head to the sky, feeling the rain on her face, hearing it splatter around her on the rocks. She thought of Penny Orr and Andrea Strickland. She thought of the sister she'd never grow old with. She thought of her mother and father and the life she'd once had, and the life she'd once lived.

She wished she had one relative still alive, somebody to hug.

Then she thought of Dan and the thought made her cry.

She was glad Andrea Strickland would have a baby, a child of her own to adore, to spoil, to love. And in that moment, she realized it was never too late to bring a child into the world, not one you intended to love with every ounce of your being.

In the distance, lightning crackled, a burst of blue-white light that lit up the clouds. Seconds later, thunder rolled, the storm drifting farther and farther away.

CHAPTER 36

The storm passed and the cabin was bathed in sunshine, though the porch remained damp and drops of water dripped from the metal roof to puddles on the ground. Water rushed down the swollen creek, flowing beneath the wooden bridge and making its way downhill. On the porch, Tracy talked with the deputy, Rick Pearson, and to the sheriff of Inyo County, Mark Davis. Davis had the build of a college lineman, but a youthful face, and a gentle, soft-spoken way about him. Tracy had told Davis where they'd find Stan Fields's body, and Davis had sent a search and rescue team out to retrieve it.

"She's the woman who's been in the news?" Davis asked. He looked through the front window at Strickland and Orr sitting inside. "The one they thought walked off the mountain?"

"She's the one," Tracy said.

Davis shook his head. "What's she doing way out here?"

"Trying to start over," Tracy said.

Davis looked from the window to the valley and the surrounding peaks. "And the body still out there—explain that to me again?"

"Stan Fields," Tracy said. "He's a Pierce County detective in Washington. He had the case originally, realized there was a pot of money nobody might ever find, and came after it."

"And you're investigating the death of the woman whose body was found in a crab pot?"

"That's right."

"And Fields killed her and put her in the pot."

"Yes."

"And Andrea Strickland was just a possible witness."

"She and the woman were friends."

Davis's brow furrowed. He gave Tracy an inquisitive, not-completely-believing look. "What the hell kind of cases do you people get up in Washington?"

"Tell me about it," Tracy said, giving them a tired smile.

"So are you going to need me to swear out a warrant to take her back to Washington?"

Tracy turned and looked again through the window at Andrea Strickland and at her aunt seated on the couch. She knew what taking Andrea back to Seattle meant—an unrelenting media that would hound her incessantly. They would report and speculate and speculate some more. She knew Graham would also come out of the woodwork, claim his allegiance to Andrea, despite everything . . . and to his baby. Andrea would have to fight him, fight for a divorce. Fight for her child. Fight for her trust.

"I'll let you know," Tracy said.

Davis blew out a breath and turned to Pearson. "Okay," he said. "We're going to go see what progress they're making on the body retrieval."

Tracy stepped inside the cabin as Davis and Pearson walked off, crossing the wooden bridge and moving to the rear of the house. When she stepped inside, Andrea Strickland looked up. Penny Orr appeared to be in a daze.

"What happens now?" Andrea asked. "Am I under arrest?"

Tracy sat on the love seat. "You suggested the trip up Mount Rainier?"

Strickland looked surprised by the question and paused to get her bearings. "Yes."

"And your intent was to fake your own death and have your husband be a suspect."

Strickland nodded. "When I found out I was pregnant, I knew I had to go. I couldn't raise a child with a man like that, someone abusive. I didn't want that for my baby. I knew he'd be a suspect, but I also knew he'd never be convicted, not without a body. There'd be no way for anyone to be certain. I wanted it that way. I wanted him to know that I knew what he'd intended to do, and that I was still alive."

"How did you find out about him and Devin Chambers?"

"Devin and I were out together one night. Graham had left for the weekend—at least that's what he told me. I don't know why, but I told her that I was using an alias to move the money. She got up to use the bathroom and left her purse on the table. Graham called her cell phone, or a cell phone. She had two. He had no reason to be calling her."

"How did she know about Lynn Hoff, and about the bank accounts?"

"I went into her work computer that night and embedded all the information. My plan was to tell my boss I suspected Graham was having an affair and to implicate Devin. I figured when they pursued it, they'd search her computers and find the information, suspect her and Graham of plotting to kill me. She must have found the information on the computer. That's likely the reason she took off. I didn't know she was stealing the money until I saw the withdrawals from the bank account. I knew it had to be her and I figured she was going to run."

"So you moved the money."

"My aunt and I moved it overseas," Andrea said. "I don't have a lot of Internet access up here. We went into Independence. I thought that would be the end of it. My aunt told me they suspected Graham but couldn't really prove anything. I didn't know Devin had been killed, but I figured it out when my aunt told me they'd found a crab pot with a woman's body in it and people were saying it was me." She shook her head and wiped away tears. "I didn't mean for anyone to die. I feel like I'm responsible for her death. I feel like I killed her."

"You're not," Tracy said. "Fields is responsible." She thought about that. "And so is your husband, and Devin Chambers, to some degree."

"You reap what you sow," Penny Orr said, lifting her head.

"Something like that," Tracy said.

"How can I raise a child with a man who was going to kill me?" Andrea Strickland said, shaking her head. "And even if I divorce him, how can I let that man anywhere near my child?"

"That's not a legal question. That's a moral question." Tracy smiled.

Andrea gave her an inquisitive look. "I don't understand."

"It's out of my jurisdiction."

Strickland continued to stare at her, disbelieving. Then she asked, "So what do I do now?"

Tracy stood. "You live your life, Andrea. You just live your life. And love your child. And if you're fortunate enough to meet someone down the road, someone who loves you unconditionally, who makes you laugh and smile and forget the bad parts of your past, you grab on to him, and hold on to him with both hands."

"My aunt told me you've been through this," Andrea said. "She said you lost your family."

"I did," Tracy said.

"How did you get through it?"

Tracy gave the question some thought. "One day at a time," she said. "You focus on the good days. You focus on that child of yours."

"Do you have children?"

Tracy shook her head. "No."

"But you found someone, someone who loves you?"

"I did," she said.

Andrea Strickland smiled. "Maybe you'll have kids."

Tracy returned the smile. "Maybe," she said, and she stepped toward the porch.

"Detective," Andrea said.

Tracy turned back. The young woman came close and embraced her. "Thank you," she said. "And I'm sorry about your family, that you had to go through this."

Moments like these, Tracy realized what it meant to be without her family. "I'm sorry you had to go through it, too."

CHAPTER 37

When Tracy returned to work, Johnny Nolasco summoned her into his office. He sat behind his desk, cheaters on the end of his nose, reading her draft report. Nolasco set down the report and removed the cheaters, holding them.

"Am I to understand that you just let this woman go?"

"Yes," she said.

"Are you kidding me?" When Tracy didn't answer, Nolasco said, "She's led two police departments on a wild-goose chase for more than two months that resulted in the wrongful prosecution of her husband and two deaths, and you just let her walk? You want to explain that?"

"Devin Chambers was killed by Stan Fields," Tracy said calmly. "He admitted it to me. That was my case. That was my investigation."

"And Chen?"

"He killed her also. That was Portland's case."

"So what about Strickland? You just let her walk?"

"Well, Captain, as you advised me early and often, that's a missing persons case, and that's out of my jurisdiction. That's Pierce County's problem."

EPILOGUE

September

The morning weather dawned iffy, which was not uncommon in the Pacific Northwest, especially near Puget Sound. On a woman's wedding day, however, it was one more thing to cause worry. Growing up in the Pacific Northwest, Tracy knew you did not plan an outdoor wedding before the Fourth of July. She knew that until that magic date the weather remained too unpredictable. You risked your guests standing in a sudden rain. She'd thought they'd be safe mid-September, but when she awoke, alone—Dan had spent the week at the farm in Redmond, old-fashioned about not wanting to see the bride before the wedding—and looked out the sliding-glass doors of her bedroom, she saw an overcast and drizzly sky.

She fretted for about an hour, then decided to adopt what had been her father's mantra when she and Sarah traveled with him to compete in single-action shooting competitions all over the Northwest. "You control what you can control. You give the rest to God."

By noon, the gray haze had burned off, and the temperatures had topped out at a comfortable seventy-eight degrees.

Tracy had spent the day a bit of an emotional wreck, thinking about how much her father would have loved to have walked his daughters down the aisle on their wedding days, about how much Sarah would have loved to have been her maid of honor, and how her mother would have fussed over her dress and her hair.

Tracy wore a white tea-length bridal gown with lace and an asymmetrical hem. Tucked inside her gown, near her heart, was one of her favorite pictures, a family portrait taken at one of her parents' renowned Christmas Eve parties. They would all be with her today, in spirit, if not in body.

Her hair had been professionally styled, pulled back and tied with white lace. She didn't care if it accentuated her crow's-feet. She wasn't twenty-three anymore, and she wasn't trying to be either. She was happy with her age, and for the first time in a long time, she was happy with her life.

"You ready to do this?" Kins said. He'd worn his blue pin-striped suit that he normally reserved for trial appearances.

"Ready to do this?" she said. "We're not running out of the tunnel for a game."

He laughed.

They stood at the end of a white runner leading to a white awning just beneath the Alki Point Lighthouse. Her castle. Beneath that white awning waited a justice of the peace and, next to him, Dan, as much a prince as any man she'd ever met. At his side sat Rex and Sherlock, wearing white bow ties, her two knights—not always chivalrous, but always there. Forty guests had risen from their white lawn chairs and turned to face her and Kins. The invitation had said to dress casually, in anticipation of warm weather, but Del and Faz, creatures of habit, wore suits and ties anyway.

In addition to her family, Tracy had thought of Andrea Strickland that morning. She wondered where the young woman had gone, and how she was doing. She wondered if she'd had her baby yet, and if so, whether it was a boy or a girl. She wondered if Andrea saw that child as a new beginning, a new life. A chance to start over.

The media frenzy had been intense in the days after the standoff at the cabin, rife with speculation, innuendo, and rumors. When the pack of reporters finally determined the location of Andrea Strickland's hideaway in the mountains, they descended upon Seven Pines, but found the tiny cabin just across the wooden bridge deserted, though filled with hundreds and hundreds of books. One of the reporters filed a story noting that a book rested on the coffee table, fanned open, as if the person who'd set it down intended to someday return and continue reading. The book was *The Diary of Anne Frank*.

"The reader," the reporter wrote, "left the book open to a page with a single sentence underlined."

In spite of everything, I still believe that people are really good at heart.

Tracy wondered if Andrea Strickland had meant it as a message to her.

She looked at Kins and smiled. "I'm ready."

Kins cued the violinist and cellist. A moment later, the man and woman began to play. Tracy walked forward, her arm wrapped through Kins's, holding a bouquet of roses.

"You look beautiful," Kins said.

Tracy smiled. "I feel beautiful," she said.

Today would be one of the good days, one of the days to remember and, she hoped, her own new start to a new life.

ACKNOWLEDGMENTS

So, one of the hot topics at writers' conferences is often whether you outline your novel or whether you're a "pantser." I'd never heard the latter term, short for "seat of the pants." I'm not really an outliner or a "pantser," though I'm definitely more of an organic writer. I take an idea, play with it, and explore where it goes. Sometimes the book unfolds for me, as was the case with *Her Final Breath* and *In the Clearing*. In a weird way, the chapters almost write themselves. I just try to keep up. It's not that simple, but I think you get my point.

Other times, however, it's a struggle, as was the case with *My Sister's Grave*, and with this novel. Usually, I get myself in trouble because I think I have a set idea—in this case, a book that takes place on Mount Rainier. I'd traveled to Rainier with my family and thought it would be a cool place to set a story. Problem was, each time I spoke with an expert in this area, they would ask, "Why does your homicide detective go up the mountain?" I never did have a good answer for that. I suppose there could be a reason, but after several months of interviews and thinking, without success, I decided instead to take a different path. That's not to diminish their help or expertise. Indeed, they each helped me to map out a course on the mountain and explain how someone could climb it and disappear. They also pointed out that what so many people take for granted—getting to the summit—is anything but a given, and at times can turn deadly.

So, my thanks to Wes Giesbrecht for his patient guidance, to Dr. Dave Bishop, who shared with me the time he spent a week hunkered down in a storm on the mountain, fighting to stay alive. Thanks to Sunny Remington, who powered up the Liberty Ridge route in two days, showing me that it could be done—wow! Thanks to Fred Newman, who provided wonderful details. Thank you for all your time and expertise on the mammoth mountain that stands guard over the Pacific Northwest and beckons so many to climb its slopes, including my wife, father-in-law, and my brothers Bill and Tom. I won't be one of them. God didn't give me the body or the blood to climb in altitudes, so I'll stay at the bottom and watch and admire from afar.

Turns out, disappearing is as difficult as climbing Rainier. With all the social media, going off the grid is tough, and people like skip tracers, private investigators, and nefarious individuals have any number of ways to track a person. I read several books on the subject, and I also want to thank private investigator Gina Brent for her insight, and Chief DJ Nesel, Maple Valley Police Department, who, in another life, used to track individuals and stolen money.

Thank you to Detective Jennifer Southworth, Seattle Police Department, Violent Crimes Section, and to Scott Tompkins, King County Sheriff's Office, Major Crimes Unit. Scott began my journey one afternoon when he asked if I ever thought of starting a book with a body found in a crab pot. That's all it took. I was hooked. We sat down and I said, "Walk me through it." They both did just that. Jurisdiction was a big issue in this novel, and Jennifer and Scott patiently guided me through it. I hope I got it right. All characters in the book are fictional, and where I took any liberties, I did so on my own. Any mistakes or errors are also mine and mine alone. I'm indebted to them for their time and expertise.

Thanks to Ms. Meg Ruley and her team at the Jane Rotrosen Agency, foremost among them, Rebecca Scherer. Meg and I have been together now for just about fifteen years and she has managed my career flawlessly. Yes, there is a business relationship, but you'd never know it when we get together. We talk about families and kids and just about everything truly important. She's helped to keep me grounded, and this past year, in particular, I've needed that bit of perspective. Thanks, Meg. Rebecca is a guru at numbers and computers. At any time she can provide an answer to just about any question I ask. Where she gets all that knowledge is beyond me, but I'm grateful to have her on my team. Thanks also to Danielle Sickles and Julianne Tinari, International Rights Director and Contracts Manager, respectively. They get my books overseas and translated so they can be read by so many. And thanks to Jane Rotrosen, who greeted me fifteen years ago with open arms, a big smile, and said, "We're going to sell a lot of books together, kid." They've all believed in me, stood by me, and worked tirelessly to make it happen. A truly great team.

Thanks to Thomas & Mercer. This is book four in the Tracy Crosswhite series and my fifth novel with the team. I still feel like a newbie. They treat each project like it's my very first novel, and always provide me with tremendous respect and kindness. I bounce ideas off them for upcoming novels, work with them when I'm plotting, and seek their advice on promotion. They always have time for my calls, to meet, and to talk. As of this writing, we've hit number one in five countries, with more still to come. Can't beat that.

Special thanks to Charlotte Herscher, developmental editor. This is book five together and she has made me an infinitely better writer. At times I can hear Charlotte in my head saying, "More character development," and I try my best to heed that call because her advice is spot-on. Thanks to Scott Calamar, copyeditor. When you recognize a weakness it is a wonderful thing—because then you can ask for help. Grammar and punctuation were never my strengths, and it's nice to know I have the best looking out for me.

Thanks to Sarah Shaw, the author-relations perfectionist who always has a gift for our accolades, the team dinners, and so much more. My writing wall is getting awfully full with framed book covers. Thanks to Sean Baker, head of production, and to Jessica Tribble, production manager. I love the covers and titles of each of my books, and I have them to thank for a superb job. Thanks to Justin O'Kelly, the head of PR, and to Dennelle Catlett, Thomas & Mercer's PR manager, for all their work promoting me and my novels. Thanks to editor Jacque Ben-Zekry, who is always a joy to be around. Thanks to publisher Mikyla Bruder, associate publisher Hai-Yen Mura, and Jeff Belle, vice president of Amazon Publishing.

Special thanks to Thomas & Mercer's editorial director, Gracie Doyle. Gracie does so many things well, I'm not sure where to start. Thanks for your direction on the story. Thanks for your editorial suggestions. Thanks for your friendship. I'm truly glad to have you leading my team.

Thanks to Tami Taylor, who runs my website, creates my newsletters, and creates some of my foreign-language book covers. I ask Tami for help and she gets things done quickly and efficiently. Thanks to Pam Binder and the Pacific Northwest Writers Association for their support of my work. Thanks to Seattle 7 Writers, a nonprofit collective of Pacific Northwest authors who foster and support the written word. I'm proud to be a member of both organizations. Thanks to Jennifer McCord, a good friend and publisher who many years ago got me on the right path.

One of the cool things I get to do is sell characters to raise money for school auctions. In this instance, I sold two characters to raise money for my daughter's school. Really, however, the thanks go to those with the checkbook. Special thanks to Tim and Brenda Berg. We met through basketball and became fast friends. They are both a kick, and when they started bidding I was blown away. Brenda, I didn't get you the profession you sought in my novel, but I hope I did you justice! Thanks also to Ying Li and to Chong Zhu, who purchased a character for their son, Jonathan, an aspiring writer. I hope one day to be reading his books.

Thanks to all of you, the readers, for finding my novels and for your incredible support of my work. Thanks for posting your reviews and for e-mailing me to let me know you've enjoyed my novels—always a writer's highlight.

Thanks to my mom, who had a rough 2016, but is back and better than ever; to my son, a sophomore in college at the time of this publication; and to my daughter, already a junior in high school. Life is great when I spend it with you. Thanks to my wife, Cristina, who listens patiently when I lament how I'll never get a book finished or write another page, then celebrates with me when I leave my computer and say, "I'm done!"

Ah, the life of a writer's spouse.

ABOUT THE AUTHOR

Photo © 2015 Catherine Dugoni

Robert Dugoni is the Amazon #1 and *Wall Street Journal* bestselling author of the Tracy Crosswhite series, including *In the Clearing*, *Her Final Breath*, and *My Sister's Grave*. He's been a finalist for the 2015 Harper Lee Prize for Legal Fiction, a finalist for the International Thriller Award, and winner of the Nancy Pearl Book Award for Fiction. He is also the author of the *New York Times* bestselling David Sloane series, including *The Jury Master*, *Wrongful Death*, *Bodily Harm*, *Murder One*, and *The Conviction*. *Murder One* was also a finalist for the Harper Lee Prize. In addition to the stand-alone novel *Damage Control*, Dugoni penned the nonfiction exposé *The Cyanide Canary*, which was a *Washington Post* Best Book of the Year selection. His books have been likened to Scott Turow and Nelson DeMille, and he has been hailed as "the undisputed king of the legal thriller" by the *Providence Journal*.

Visit his website at www.robertdugoni.com and follow him on Twitter @robertdugoni and on Facebook at www.facebook.com/AuthorRobertDugoni.